Dear Reader,

They say that people are the same all over. Whether it's a small village on the sea, a mining town nestled in the mountains, or a whistle-stop along the Western plains, we all share the same hopes and dreams. We work, we play, we laugh, we cry—and, of course, we fall in love . . .

It is this universal experience that we at Jove Books have tried to capture in a heartwarming series of novels. We've asked our most gifted authors to write their own story of American romance, set in a town as distinct and vivid as the people who live there. Each writer chose a special time and place close to their hearts. They filled the towns with charming, unforgettable characters—then added that spark of romance. We think you'll find the combination absolutely delightful.

You might even recognize *your* town. Because true love lives in *every* town . . .

Welcome to *Our Town*.

Sincerely,

Leslie Gelbman
Editor-in-Chief

Titles in the Our Town series

OUR · TOWN

COUNTRY COMFORTS

VIRGINIA LEE

JOVE BOOKS, NEW YORK

COUNTRY COMFORTS

A Jove Book / published by arrangement with
the author

PRINTING HISTORY
Jove edition / April 1997

For Gary,
who encouraged me along the way
and is always there when I need him.

And to my editor
Cindy Hwang
who took a chance on me.

COUNTRY COMFORTS

❖ 1 ❖

Gallatin City, Montana Territory, 1874

Josie Douglass knelt by a display of elixirs in the mercantile and fingered an interesting bottle claiming to abolish sore hooves on horses. She picked it up and unscrewed the lid. Taking a deep whiff, she jerked the bottle away from her nose. Pure camphor.

She moved to replace the bottle on the shelf, when a gloved hand tapped her on the shoulder. Josie looked up and saw three well-dressed women in a semicircle staring down at her, their bustled calico skirts blocking the aisle. Not just any women, but the three most self-righteous women in town, headed by the reverend's wife, Portia Potter. Her close friends, Mrs. Samuels and Mrs. Garvey, flanked her.

"Miss Josephine," Mrs. Potter said, raising her lorgnette to the tip of her nose and peering downward at Josie. "We have a problem."

"A problem? What kind?" Josie scrambled to her feet. She preferred to be closer to the woman's eye level and not crouched on the ground like a scared rabbit.

Mrs. Potter sniffed and exchanged glances with her cohorts. "The problem is you. Or, more precisely, that unorthodox household you and your vagabond father are raising my niece in." She pushed her lorgnette farther down her nose and raised her chin a notch higher. "I won't have it. Charlotte is at too vulnerable of an age for anything other than the best influence."

Josie's fingers tightened around the bottle. Her breathing stopped for a moment. "Surely I didn't hear you correctly."

Mrs. Potter crossed her arms over her ample bosom and narrowed her pale eyes. "You are the wrong kind of influence for my niece. Just because Charlotte is your half sister does not give you the right to flaunt your un-ladylike behaviors in front of her impressionable mind. Imagine, riding a racehorse."

Before she could think, Josie opened her mouth. "What I do is not your concern. Lottie means the world to me. I do everything I can to make sure she's well provided for. I'll kindly thank you to keep your opinions to yourself."

Mrs. Samuels and Mrs. Garvey gasped and fluttered their feather fans. Mrs. Potter turned apoplectic, but did not cease. "Heavens, this is precisely the type of behavior I'll not have Charlotte learning. You would do well to heed the advice of your elders, Miss Josephine."

Most of her life Josie had been lucky; she hadn't had the self-righteous Trio's wrath directed at her. Now her luck had changed and she knew she'd made it worse with her rash remarks. However, she couldn't let this insult pass unnoticed.

"Don't worry about my sister, she'll be fine," Josie said, setting the camphor bottle back on the shelf lest she leave the mercantile with it clutched in her palm.

Mrs. Potter stepped closer, almost suffocatingly close.

"Soon I won't have to worry about my poor, deceased sister's daughter, Charlotte."

Something in Mrs. Potter's words stopped Josie. A chill ran down her spine. "What do you mean?"

"I mean, the ladies and I have decided I should take custody of Charlotte. I will be her new mother. I'll be the person to guide Charlotte to womanhood, just as I should have been from the start."

The revelation rocked Josie. Her world spun. She reached out to a wooden barrel to steady her legs. "What did you say?"

The determined gleam in Mrs. Potter's eyes was unmistakable. "I mean to bring Charlotte under my roof. She'll be raised as one of my children."

"No. I won't let you do that. She's my sister." Josie struggled for breath. It felt as if bands of steel had tightened around her lungs.

"I hardly think an unorthodox spinster such as yourself, and a vagabond for a father, will have much say. Even if you were a respectable married woman, I doubt that would change my mind much. . . ." Mrs. Potter let her words trail off as she and her cronies strolled away, promptly dismissing Josie.

No, Josie's mind screamed as she sagged back against the cracker barrel. They couldn't take Lottie away, could they?

Ever since Lottie's mother had died unexpectedly six years before, Josie had put her dreams of having her own family on hold. She hadn't let those years of her life pass by for nothing. Squeezing her eyes shut, she forced back the tears and calmed her racing heart. No one would threaten her family. No one, not even the reverend's formidable wife.

With unsteady legs Josie pushed away from the barrel and burst out of the store, away from the ugly words that had passed there.

Wanting to run but keeping herself to a walk, Josie crossed dusty Main Street, dodging horses and wagons, and headed to the outskirts of town. To home. To the one place where she did not have to think of Mrs. Potter.

A rock lay on the side of the beaten path. Josie drew back her foot and kicked the rock, sending it flying.

There had to be a way to discredit Mrs. Potter's threats. Maybe that's all they were, mere threats. No, Josie thought, Mrs. Potter meant what she'd said.

Josie stopped so fast the hem of her skirt billowed out in front of her. Marriage.

Mrs. Potter had said if she were a married woman, things might be different. Although Lottie was the reason Josie hadn't married by then. She'd been so busy raising her and running the ranch while their father disappeared to hunt for sapphires that she hadn't had the time to consider marrying.

Well, she could fix that easier than she could change her personality. She would find a husband. She would stop Mrs. Potter before the woman even started her crusade. There was only one problem with Josie's idea: Gallatin City had a decided lack of choice men.

Josie turned and looked down the single street of her town, at the few bachelors in her line of vision. The first man her gaze landed on was Slim, the livery owner. Although a good family friend, he was her father's age—too old.

Next she spied the four Barlow brothers all clustered around the small herd of cattle they were driving through town. None of them would do—all they cared about were their horses and cattle. They didn't care if they smelled like week-old straw.

Outside the town's only hotel, in the shade of an aspen grove, Natty the desk clerk sat eating his noontime meal with Bertram from the flour mill. Although much younger than Slim, Natty was too skinny and looked like the proverbial beanpole. Besides, she'd heard that Natty was already sweet on someone else. Bertram had no interest in a wife, he preferred consorting with loose women—*not* the kind of husband Mrs. Potter would approve of.

Josie sighed. Back to square one. As she started toward home again, someone else caught her eye.

A stranger.

Josie couldn't believe her luck. She'd just been lamenting the lack of interesting men in Gallatin City, when in rode a good-looking stranger. This couldn't be coincidence: It had to be a sign. Curiosity immediately propelled her forward.

She tried hard not to stare too boldly. His sun-browned, handsome face captivated her. She'd never seen such a well-defined jawline, complete with a tiny cleft in the chin. His wide lips slid easily into a beguiling smile as he looked around the town.

He glanced her way, touching the brim of his hat with a gloved hand. Thick, glossy brown hair curled ever so slightly from under his hat.

The single tiny gesture made Josie's insides feel all funny, like butterflies were tickling her belly. Never before had one look from a man had such an effect on her.

Who was this man? What was he doing in town? And why?

Josie followed a discreet distance behind him. She had to talk to him. She couldn't let this golden opportunity slip by, especially since he was all alone.

His destination took her to the hotel. Trying to look natural, she sat down on one of the benches lined up outside the entrance. She hoped she just looked like some friendly person wanting to rest her feet.

Jack St. Augustine swung his leg over the back of his horse and dropped to the ground. A cloud of dust rose up around him. He was well aware of the woman who'd been following him since he'd entered the town proper after disembarking from the ferry. What she wanted, he couldn't guess, but he didn't mind pretty females following him.

He had to stifle a smile when she sat down, trying so hard to look casual. Trying too hard. That's what gave her away.

He wrapped one rein of his saddle horse to the hitching

rail and untied the stallion tethered to his saddle. He then secured the stallion next to the gelding. All the while he felt her eyes on him, watching, as he removed his saddle-bags and slung them over his shoulder. He started toward the hotel entrance, and as soon as he set foot on the first step, the woman spoke.

"Welcome to Gallatin City," she said, looking too cheerful for a chance encounter.

"Thanks."

Jack leaned against an awning post and regarded her. A thick black braid hung down her back. Sparkling green eyes gazed at him. Her wide smile warmed him like a summer's day—make that a hot summer day. Her smile sent a jolt of excitement through his body.

His glance lingered on her red lips. They reminded him of ripe cherries. Instantly, he wondered what they would taste like if he were to kiss them.

Chagrined, he tore his gaze away and stared back at her eyes. He'd been spending way too much time in the company of his horses.

"We don't get many new people here, and well, I—I just wanted to welcome you. Since I happened to be the one who saw you." She reddened and glanced away.

"How nice." What did she want? he wondered. It was mighty unusual for a woman to speak so freely in front of a stranger. But then again, ever since he'd left Kansas City he'd discovered the western frontier a place of surprises.

"Will your family be joining you soon?"

"Pardon?"

"Your family. Are they coming too?" She leaned forward, as if eager for his reply. Her fat braid had fallen over her shoulder and now pooled in her lap.

"You mean my folks? No, they aren't coming. Just me." He leaned forward and peered closely at her. "Why?"

She gave a strangled laugh and jumped up. "No reason. Well, it was nice meeting you. I've got to run." With that, she marched away from him.

Jack watched her leave and then lowered his eyes to her swaying rear. Her blue skirt rippled out to the side, reminding him of waves. He smiled. He was surprised at how much he'd enjoyed talking to the woman; in fact, he hated to see her leave. She had an easy demeanor that instantly attracted him.

But, still, she seemed a bit forward for him.

He shook his head, clearing away his muddled thoughts. He'd been smitten with her only because she was the first attractive female he'd seen in a long time.

Back at home the reality of everyday life hit Josie. A heaping basket of laundry waited by the door. Mending filled another basket. Vegetable seeds needed to be planted.

She couldn't waste her time daydreaming about a stranger. There was work to be done.

She'd start in the garden. She much preferred that to indoor chores any day. Josie changed into her linsey-woolsey work dress, wrapped a thick muslin apron around her waist, and lifted the packets of seeds.

Josie knelt in the freshly turned black soil and watched the earthworms wriggle as her hand trowel disturbed their slumber. Moisture from the ground soaked through her skirts, cooling her knees. Taking a palmful of seeds, she scattered them in the prepared rows. She tried her hardest to keep her mind on work, but it kept returning to the handsome stranger.

Was he passing through, or would he be in town awhile? He'd said he was alone, so in Josie's mind that classified him as potential husband material.

Husband material. That brought Josie back to the problem of Mrs. Potter's threats and Josie's decision to find a husband.

She knew scant little about the stranger, not nearly enough to make an informed decision, especially for something as important as marriage. She would have to get to know him, that was all.

He'd seemed nice enough. His soothing, deep voice

captivated her. She could've spent all morning just listening to him. And his eyes. They were such a deep shade of blue, they almost took her breath away. But it was more than just his looks, something inside of him drew her.

Sighing, she patted the soil over the seeds. She reached for more but stopped as she heard her name.

"Josie! Yoo-hoo! Got time to visit for a spell?" Grace Moreland, Josie's best friend, called as she eased her willowy frame down from her wagon. "I saw you race out of the store and I wanted to know why."

Josie smiled and set down the trowel. "Meet me on the porch. I'll be right there."

The second Josie stepped on the porch, Grace shook her head and clucked her tongue. "You should hire help. Look at you. You're making yourself look much older— why, I can even see a hint of sunburn on your nose! Where's your bonnet?"

"Bonnet? I took it off a long time ago. It kept slipping down over my eyes. Besides, I thought my face could use a little color." At Grace's groan, Josie grinned. "I know. I know. Women are supposed to have milky-white complexions. Wait here while I get us some lemonade."

She returned a few minutes later and handed Grace a glass.

"Now, Josie, why did you rush out of the mercantile earlier?"

"Did I rush?" Mrs. Potter's words reverberated in her head. Josie gripped her glass and willed them away. After all, she'd already found a solution to the problem, she hoped. "Maybe it's time I found a husband."

Grace sat bolt upright in her rocker. "What did I hear you say?"

Josie shot her a sideways glance. "You heard me. There's—there's just so much to do around here. A husband could help."

"Josie, I think you're fibbing to me." Grace leveled her chocolate-brown eyes at Josie.

Perhaps she would feel better if she told Grace about

the encounter with Mrs. Potter. "You're right. See"—Josie took a drink, wishing it was whiskey instead of lemonade—"I—I was told by a certain group of women that they think Lottie should not grow up here. They think Father and I are an evil influence."

"Who said that? I can't believe anyone would call you evil." Grace drew her blond brows together. "Josie, was it Mrs. Samuels?"

"No, well, she was there. Mrs. Potter is the one who wants Lottie. Seems she believes since I'm only Lottie's half sister that she has more right to her than we do. As if an aunt has more right than a father and sister." Her voice became more agitated with each word. Josie set her glass down by her feet, afraid she might shatter it.

"Oh, dear. This is a pickle. Let me think." Grace clapped her hands together. "I know, Robert is influential in the community because he owns the mercantile, and as his wife I have some sway also. We can help you."

"No, thanks. I'm going to handle this myself."

Josie squinted and looked across the wide expanse of porch. Her glance fell between the split-rail fence and she stared at the herd of cattle. Black steers with white faces chewed the sweet new shoots of spring grass that rose around their hooves.

Not far from the cattle, horses dozed in the sunshine, tails blowing in the slight breeze. Flies buzzed around the animals' heads.

She, her father, and Lottie had built this ranch. They'd done it as a family, and if she could manage it, her family would stay on this land. Together.

"I already have a plan. I intend to get married," Josie said, resolve ringing in her words.

"Excuse me? Have you been out in the sun too long? See what happens when you don't wear a bonnet? Your brain becomes addled."

"My brain is not addled. I'm serious. If I were married, there wouldn't be a threat to Lottie. It's really very simple." The plan was beautiful because of its simplicity, at least in Josie's mind.

"What does your father say about your marrying?"
Grace asked.

Josie fingered the blue stone that hung around her
neck. "He's up somewhere along the Missouri River,
searching for his fortune in sapphires. It seems he over-
heard some miners in the Hay Bale Saloon telling of
riches beyond measure. So he packed up and left last
week."

"Oh, I'm sorry, how insensitive of me." Grace laid
her hand on Josie's arm.

"It's all right. You think I'd be used to his trips by
now." But she wasn't. It still galled Josie every time her
father left her and her younger sister. And now his sapphire searching had affected the stability of their family.

"Getting back to my idea—" Josie broke off and
smoothed the worn fabric of her skirt.

She glanced from Grace's spotless, fashionable, green
muslin day dress complete with contrasting cream buttons and waistband to her own dirt-smudged dress, and
grimaced. Even Grace's blond hair was swept neatly into
a twist, not a strand out of place. Josie wished she had
some of Grace's fashion sense.

"I'm almost afraid to ask, but go on, tell me about
your idea," Grace said.

"I've thought about this husband thing and believe it
would work well." Josie recalled the dark-haired stranger
and his captivating smile, and knew she wouldn't have
any problem looking at him every day of her life.

"Josie . . . Josie." Grace shook her out of her musings.
"I think you'd better wait and talk to your father."

Josie dismissed Grace's advice and went on with her
thoughts. "I've already decided what qualities my future
husband should have." She ticked them off on her fingers. "One, he shouldn't mind living here, of course,
because I couldn't leave my home. Two, he shouldn't
mind young ladies, because of Lottie. And he should
also—"

"Stop this! It's madness to talk like this. You can't
just pick a husband like you're selecting a racehorse.

For once in your life, I beg you, don't let your impulsive nature rule you.'' Grace had risen and now stood, arms akimbo, frowning down at Josie. ''I'm married and I *know* that marriage is serious business. There's engagements, dowries to select, and plans to be made.''

Craning her neck backward, Josie stared up at Grace and burst out laughing. ''Why, I don't think I've ever seen you in such a state.'' Her normally placid friend now hovered like an angry mother hen.

''I—I—'' Grace stammered, grasped the sides of her dress, and sat back down. ''Sometimes you just throw me for a loop.''

''Grace, please, I'm serious. Would you give me some pointers? Something to help make my campaign successful?''

Grace knit her brows. ''I don't know if I should, it's all so . . . so odd.''

Josie took a deep breath. ''Grace, I'm going through with my plan, whether you help me or not.''

Minutes passed.

Finally, Grace sighed. ''All right, I'll show you how to get a husband.'' She wiggled her ring finger in front of Josie's face. Light reflected off the facets of her diamond solitaire. ''I'll tell you what men want, since I have a husband.''

''So tell me, what do they want?'' Josie hoped she might learn something useful.

''First of all, men don't like bold women. For some reason it intimidates them. So rule number one, act demure.''

''Demure?'' That was about as far from Josie's nature as a fish was from flying. ''That one might be tough.''

Grace leveled her gaze at Josie. ''It's one you'll have to master. Although, with a plan like this, I don't know how you'll manage that.'' She rolled her eyes heavenward. ''Two, men like ladylike and feminine women. They want someone who'll make them proud at gatherings.''

"Ladylike? What do you mean? Like sipping tea daintily?"

"Yes, just be a lady, be gracious and kind. It's easy. Now, rule number three, men like it when you act a little bashful around them. They like to see an occasional blush."

Josie's forehead wrinkled. "Are you sure this applies to all men?"

"Positive. Now, the last thing is that men like weak women. They like to be the strong partner. I guess it has something to do with their male pride. Now, I know you're used to doing lots of work, but for heaven's sake"—Grace punctuated each word with a shake of her index finger—"do *not* let on that you may be strong. It would scare away a potential suitor."

"All right, all right. I think that's plenty for me to remember." Actually, Josie's head reeled from Grace's list. She was sure her eyes were bugging out of their sockets. Surely Grace had gone overboard in her instructions. Men couldn't be *that* picky.

"Good, because I had to give you all my information at once. Goodness only knows what you might've done if I hadn't been here to help. I just hope you heed my advice and don't do anything rash." Grace rose. "I have to go back to the mercantile. Come with me and we can look at the new bolts of fabric we received for the store."

"Fabric. Hmmm."

"Oh, men also love pretty dresses." Grace twirled around, modeling her new dress for Josie.

Josie could use a new dress. She had to look nice if she meant to attract the stranger's attention and discover if he'd make decent husband material. "I'll go."

Josie was eager to see the stranger again. The sooner she could arrange a real introduction, the sooner she could activate her plan. Time wasn't on her side. She didn't know how long Mrs. Potter would wait.

❖ 2 ❖

HOURS LATER, AFTER the sun had sunk behind the Rockies, Jack sat on a wooden barstool in the Hay Bale Saloon with a stiff shot of rye.

The white-aproned bartender with the waxed red handlebar mustache put down his dish towel and regarded Jack. "Yer new in town, I woulda ree-membered seein' the likes o' you before."

"Yes, I just arrived today," Jack said.

"Well, then, lemme introduce myself. I'm Alfred E. Nebblestick. But folks here just call me Red." He gestured to his flaming red hair and mustache.

Jack looked at Red. "Nice to meet you. I'm Jack St. Augustine. Can you tell me how the prospects for a bachelor in this town are?"

"Well, son, depends on what yer lookin' for. If yer lookin' for the easy wimmen, well, we don't got many of them."

Jack took a swig of the rye and shook his head. "No,

that's not what I had in mind. What about the ladies?''

"Well, son, the respectable wimmen, the free ones, there ain't but a few of them. Let's see.'' Red frowned and pulled on his mustache. "There's the preacher's daughter, but she's only a child. We got little Lottie, nah, she's a young-un also.''

"Are there any a bit older?''

Red raised one finger and opened his gray eyes wide. "I got one. Nah.'' He shook his head. "You wouldn't be in'trested in her, why, Miz Douglass is pee-ractically a spinster.''

A vision of a wrinkled, bespectacled, hunchbacked crone filled Jack's mind. "When I came into town today I met a pretty little lady. Had jet-black hair. Freckles. Green eyes.''

"Why, she's the one. She's Miz Douglass.'' He shook his head. "I dunno why a young man like yerself would be in'trested in the likes of Miz Douglass. Why, she's twenty-three. She's gettin' old.''

Jack smiled down into his drink. That would make him old too, at twenty-six, according to the bartender. "She seemed like a real nice person.''

"Oh, to be sure, she is. It's just that she ain't married yet''—Red leaned across the bar and whispered—"kinda makes a man wonder about her, if you know what I mean.''

"I know what you mean.'' Jack imagined a woman desperate to get a husband. A woman who would be so happy for an offer of marriage that she'd be more than willing to do her husband's bidding. That type he could handle.

He remembered the jolt that had hit him when she smiled. The way her eyes had crinkled ever so slightly. Her red lips. Her lustrous hair.

At first he'd thought her overly bold in approaching him, but then he knew from experience that people in the West weren't as conservative as his family. Miss Douglass had just been acting like any other good-natured westerner. Yes, that had to be it.

"So, what brings ya here?" Red asked as he polished shot glasses, then lined them up like soldiers on the shelf.

"Ranching. Specifically, horses. I plan to start a breeding ranch for racehorses." Jack had read about the lush Montana grasses, fertile soil, and wild open country. It sounded like the perfect place for his spread. Even from Kansas City he'd heard the call of this new frontier singing in his blood.

"Ranchin's hard work. Ya got yer land picked out?"

"No, not yet. Do you have any ideas?"

"Me, ifn I was t' start a ranch, I'd look farther east in the valley, more tee-ward Bozeman. Lots o' folk goin' that way."

"I'll consider that."

The idea of his own breeding operation sent a tickle of anticipation down Jack's spine. He was ready to live his own life, and heading west had been the start of his independence. Following in the footsteps of his lawyer father was not for him. He'd given it his best shot for the past five years. Nor did he care for the increased efforts by his mother to wed him to the women she kept selecting for him.

He loved his parents, but he was much too independent to have remained in the same city as them any longer. Tensions had rippled each time he saw them, especially between him and his mother. She had a hard time accepting that her son was not as malleable as her daughters were. Although she would probably go to her grave trying her best to influence him.

Red spoke again. "You plannin' on gettin' hitched? That why you asked about the wimmen? You'll need a woman t' give you strong sons t' help on yer ranch."

Jack stared at the amber drops of rye on his glass. "Yes, if I can find the right woman, I'll take a wife." He remembered the scene with his parents before he'd left. They'd insisted he marry Gloria, their handpicked choice for him. Jack, as usual, had rebelled. He would choose his own wife, in his own time. This was one area where he wouldn't compromise.

Jack felt so strongly about his decision to go west and carve a life of his own, away from the influence of his family, that he'd left home knowing he could very well incur their wrath. He'd arrived in Montana Territory. There was no going back now.

"Top it off, please." After Red refilled his glass, Jack hoisted it into the air. "A toast, to Montana Territory." Then he downed the contents in one swallow.

As darkness settled over her ranch, Josie shut the barn door and headed up to the house. Crickets sang from their hiding places underneath the front steps. The wood creaked with each footfall. "Time to get Lottie to bed," she murmured to herself as she opened the door to their house.

The bright light from several oil lamps almost blinded Josie as she entered. Surrounded by the pool of light sat Lottie. Her hands flew over the sampler she stitched.

"Lottie, why did you light all these lamps? You know how low we're getting on oil."

Her younger sister looked up, an innocent expression on her face. "I thought you always said it was important to see well. If I lit only one lamp, how could I see my stitches?"

"You can sew in the daytime."

Lottie set her sewing in the basket by her feet and sighed. "But this is for the fair. And I wanna win this year. Mary Jane won last year, and I want the blue ribbon this year."

The blue eyes framed by long, dark lashes were almost Josie's undoing. She'd been beguiled by her twelve-year-old half sister's charm many times in the past, but not tonight.

"Joooosiee." Lottie slowly blinked her eyes and let the corners of her mouth droop downward.

"Put all of those lamps out but one. You need to get to bed."

"Oh, all right. But I already have my nightgown on." Lottie held up her arms. Only her head and hands stuck out of the white cotton gown. Tiny pink bows kept the sleeves snug around her wrists. As usual, Lottie's skilled workmanship showed.

After she'd tucked her in, Josie knelt by the bed. "Are you sure you finished all of your lessons for school?"

Lottie's eyes twinkled in the flicker of the lamplight. "Uh-huh."

"Good. Now, go to sleep." Josie brushed back Lottie's blond bangs and gave her a light kiss. "Sweet dreams."

Josie looked down at her sister and her heart constricted. If it was in her power, she'd see that Lottie never had to leave this house.

◆ 3 ◆

"YOU SAY YOU'VE got only one stall to rent?" Jack looked at Slim, the livery owner, and frowned. He had two horses, one of them his prized racehorse, Zeus.

" 'Fraid so. I got lots of my pack mules standin' idle. So I don't have the space." Slim spit a thin, dark stream of chew onto the dirt. His crooked smile consisted of tobacco-stained teeth, or, rather, what was left of his teeth.

"Is there any other place you can recommend?"

"Nope, I'm the only livery this side of Helena."

"There has to be someplace I can keep my racehorse." Jack tried to keep the frustration from his voice. He hadn't come this far only to be turned away.

Another stream of tobacco flew. "There's the Douglasses' place. I know Hunter Bill has taken in stock before. He's a right friendly man, ol' Hunter is."

Douglass. The name rang a bell. Could that be any relation to the dark-haired Miss Douglass who'd greeted him yesterday? "Can you tell me where I can find this Hunter Bill?" The sooner Jack got the matter of his horses settled, the sooner he could scout out land for his ranch and, more important, become acquainted with Miss Douglass.

"I can do ya one better. I'll take ya there."

Several minutes later Jack found himself in front of a modest-sized ranch at the very south edge of town. Mountain flowers bloomed in a profusion of color around the tidy-looking log house and barn. White buttercups, golden asters, and pinkish-purple bitterroots all battled for space.

He grinned. He liked the place. It looked welcoming, not austere and forbidding like his parents' three-story monstrosity back in Kansas City.

"I'll just go see if I can find Hunter Bill." Slim dismounted.

Jack followed him. "I think I hear sounds in the barn."

"Me too. Let's go talk to Hunter." Slim led the way down a worn path and stopped in front of the gaping doors of the barn.

"Hunter? You in there?" the livery man hollered.

"No," a feminine voice answered back.

"Is he in the house?" Slim yelled.

Jack's eardrums rattled. "You could just go inside the barn instead of yelling."

"Oh, reckon I could."

Jack entered the barn and immediately lunged to the side as a fat bale of hay plummeted from the loft.

"Josie? You up there?" Slim asked.

"Yes. What do you need, Slim?" Her muffled voice carried down from the loft, but she herself didn't appear.

"I got a deal to talk to Hunter about. Is he around?"

"No, he's not. You can talk to me."

Would she never come down? Jack thought. He was dying to know if this was the same woman he'd spoken with the day before. She had to be. The names matched. He craned his neck upward and tried hard to peer through the wooden slats of the loft floor. All he got for his efforts was an eye full of hay dust.

Slim talked on as if it didn't bother him not to see the person he conversed with. "You got room to keep a horse?"

"For how long?"

"I dunno. I—"

"Hold on. Let me come down there. It's too hard talking from up here."

Footsteps sounded on the floor above. Tiny bits of hay drifted to the barn floor like yellow snow.

Was the man ever going to get around to introducing him? Jack wondered. He felt like an outsider listening in on a private conversation.

Josie descended the ladder and Jack's glance immediately went up. He knew he shouldn't stare, but he couldn't help it. Her hem had hooked on a splinter of wood, revealing her legs.

He watched as a shapely ankle bared itself, and then part of her calf came into view. So far Jack liked what he saw. Soft, gliding curves and just a hint of muscle.

Ashamed at where he looked and even more ashamed at how he would have liked to see more of her leg, he began studying the ends of the hay bales.

"Slim, I—" Josie broke off her sentence as soon as she turned to face Slim. Her heart skipped a beat. The handsome stranger stood in her barn.

That morning, when she'd rehearsed different introductions to him, she'd pictured herself wearing her best dress, with her hair done up perfectly and her best ladylike behavior on display.

In less than three seconds her wonderful first impression had evaporated like steam out of the kettle.

Her hand went to her hair and smoothed back the top. She hoped she didn't have too much hay stuck in it. She glanced down at her clothes and breathed a sigh of relief. She'd put on her favorite sprigged calico skirt, so she couldn't look too much of a fright.

But he'd just caught her tossing down hay bales, and

Josie knew that wasn't in the least feminine. So far she'd managed to break one of Grace's rules for attracting a man. She cleared her throat, yanked off her work gloves, folded her hands, and struggled to act demure.

"Slim, you didn't tell me you had company."

"Oh, never occurred t' me, Josie. But he's the one who wants a stall."

"Let's go outside. It's too dusty in here from all that hay." Josie led the way. Maybe, she hoped in desperation, if she moved away from the site of her unladylike behavior, the stranger would forget he'd just seen her hefting heavy bales.

"Your father's back, ain't he?" Slim trailed behind Josie. "Haven't seen him in a while. I'd like to hear some of his stories."

"So would I. He's still out hunting for sapphires. He should return soon." Her father was the furthest thing from her mind. Her stranger stood smack-dab in front of her, and she hadn't had time to practice what she wanted to say to him.

"Huh, too bad. Well, anyway, I can't stay. I got people comin' by for some horses. You'll be all right?" Slim looked from Josie to Jack.

Josie blushed at the concern in Slim's voice. She could tell he thought he should stay and act the chaperon. But actually, it suited her to be alone with the handsome stranger.

"I'll be fine."

"Well, all righty. Bring your gelding over to the livery anytime, Mr. St. Augustus." Slim climbed up on his rangy roan.

"That's St. Augustine, not Augustus."

"Whatever." Slim kicked his horse and departed.

Josie realized she and the stranger were now alone. Mr. St. Augustine, she corrected herself. She took a deep breath, smiled, and turned to face him. The moment she'd been waiting for had arrived.

She felt the heat of his gaze on her. Josie shifted her weight and brought her eyes up to meet his.

What did one say to a man she thought would make her a good husband?

"Pretty afternoon." Josie shut her eyes and sighed in frustration. That was not how to start things properly. What would Grace have said? She racked her brain, trying to think of something more appropriate.

Jack glanced around. He gazed up at the puffy white clouds drifting across an intense blue sky. He looked at the cattle grazing in the pastures. "Yes, it is."

Clutching the sides of her skirt, she smiled and tried again. "Slim says you need a place to keep your horse?"

"Yes, I do. He's special and I want only the best for him."

Josie's face glowed. No one took better care of horses than she did. She took his comment as a compliment. Slim must have said good things about her. "You won't find better care anywhere. I do a much better job than Slim ever could." She rolled her eyes. That did not sound meek. Boastful was more like it.

The corner of Jack's lip twitched upward. "I'm glad to hear you're a good caretaker."

"Show me your horse." She gritted her teeth and quickly added "please" when she realized how forceful she sounded. Grace's instructions were hard to follow. They sounded much easier when she'd rattled them off.

Josie thought if she stood there one second longer and stared into his riveting cobalt-blue eyes, she might not be able to tear her gaze away. His eyes mesmerized her and drew her toward him.

"Certainly, you can see my horse." Jack grinned and held out his arm for her to precede him.

A tall, lean, muscular horse regarded her with intelligent eyes. Josie swept her assessing gaze over the animal. Light red dapples in the coat reflected in the sunlight. A pristine white blaze ran the length of his face. She noted the long, blemish-free legs and well-sprung ribs, allowing for good lung capacity.

"He's a racehorse, isn't he? I can tell by his build."

Josie moved closer and a smile stretched her lips. "May I touch him?"

"Of course. You'll need to if I decide to let you take care of him."

"What do you mean, if you decide to *let* me take care of him?" The impulsive words snapped out of her mouth before she could stop them. Instantly regretting the outburst, she swallowed and repeated in a lighter tone, one that she prayed seemed demure, "I hope you'll let me take care of him." Maybe he was hard of hearing and had missed her first statement. She doubted that with one look at his face.

Jack's mouth pulled backward, but he didn't comment on her words. He reached out and stroked the shiny chestnut neck. "He's a special boy. I've raised him since he was a colt."

Josie couldn't hold back her excitement. "He's a beauty."

"You've got a good eye. My sisters can't tell one horse from another. They're only beasts for transportation to them." Jack stopped his hand in mid-stroke and a dark shadow marred his face for one minute.

Intrigued, Josie opened her mouth to ask him about his family, but his closed expression warned her off the subject. "He seems sweet."

"Sure is, and mannerly too." He ran his hands down the stallion's neck. "Touch him all you want."

She watched Jack's slow strokes, his long fingers running through the horse's mane, and wondered what it would feel like to have his hands in her hair. Would her scalp tingle at his mere touch?

His glance met hers and held.

Her mouth went dry and she licked her lips. Suppose he could read her thoughts? Then her chances to appear as a meek woman were doomed. Of course, they might already be. Turning her head, she feasted her eyes on his horse.

"We have a racetrack here. Did you know that?"

"I do. That's one of the reasons I picked Gallatin City."

Josie beamed, pride reflected in the depths of her eyes. "Every year at the fair we have the biggest races. People come from all around to watch and also to enter their best horses. There's a big cash prize for the winner."

"Your races have a good reputation."

"I know. I—" She stopped. She'd been about to say she was preparing a horse for the races, that she had high hopes for her mare, but decided not to mention that fact. Commenting that she trained her racehorse just didn't seem very ladylike.

"Would you like to come sit on our porch for refreshments, Mr. St. Augustine?"

It was Jack's turn to look surprised. "Refreshments?"

"Yes. A cool drink. Little cakes." She failed to mention she didn't have any little cakes prepared. Nor did she have the slightest idea of how to make them. But it sounded like the thing to say. She'd read that in her borrowed issue of *Godey's Lady's Book*. Grace would be proud of her.

She could find something suitable for them to eat.

"A drink would be nice."

She was keenly aware of him walking beside her as she led the way to the porch. She'd never before been this conscious of another person. Josie could sense his body next to hers, almost as if they walked in the same rhythm. She fancied she could even feel warmth emanating from him. She glanced upward and blushed when he caught her staring again.

"Aren't you worried about entertaining me all alone? Shouldn't you have a chaperon?"

A chaperon! She hadn't been chaperoned but a few times in her entire life. She'd been too busy raising Lottie and doing the ranch work to bother about chaperons. "My father trusts me."

Boy, was that an understatement.

"Have a seat, please. I'll go get the refreshments." Josie gestured to a rocker that her father had painted a

Wedgwood blue that past winter when the deep snows had kept him indoors.

She watched Jack just long enough to make sure he sat down, and then she dashed into the house. The door slammed behind her. She swatted ineffectively at the flies that followed inside.

Tapping her toe, she looked around the kitchen, trying to figure out what a lady would serve a gentleman. Her glance landed on the tarnished teakettle. She could serve him tea and hope he wouldn't notice the tarnish. But what to eat?

A lady would have lots of little cakes and finger sandwiches prepared. Unfortunately, she had only cheese and some dried-out biscuits. And meat too, if she counted the elk hanging from a tree in the back of the house.

Somehow Josie didn't think a lady would offer a gentleman freshly killed elk. And from that point onward, she wanted to do everything proper-like.

She quickly wiped off two white porcelain teacups, poured hot water into the kettle, and loaded up a tray.

"Here we are," Josie said, using her hip to nudge open the screen door.

"It looks very, uh, good." Jack eyed the teapot with a colorful towel wrapped around it.

Josie noticed the direction of his glance. "It's to keep it hot. The air can have a nip, even in early May." She hoped that sounded more believable to him than it did to her, as she ignored the sweat trickling down her back.

"I'll keep that in mind." Jack leaned back in the chair and crossed one ankle over his knee.

Josie noticed his well-maintained and polished boots. She glanced down at her own scuffed ones. She even had dried mud clumps around the toes. Tucking her feet underneath her skirt, she removed them from sight.

"Help yourself to the biscuits. The cheese is fresh. I just exchanged several eggs for it yesterday. I'll pour the tea."

"You're being very kind to me. Are you always this friendly with new men?"

Josie sloshed tea over the rim of her cup. Obviously her demure façade wasn't working. She'd have to try harder. "What? Oh, no, I'm not this friendly with every new man. Why, it's just that—it's just that you're here and you asked us to take care of your horse."

"What about yesterday by the hotel?" Jack popped another section of orange cheese into his mouth while he waited for her answer. He seemed to be ignoring the hard biscuit he'd picked up.

"Oh, that. It's—it's a . . . custom. Whoever notices a new person first, they're supposed to greet them." Josie held the teacup before her face like a shield, hoping to hide the guilt on her face.

"I see." Jack liked how her flush enhanced her freckles and brought out the deep green of her eyes. He felt comfortable in her presence. It suddenly occurred to him they hadn't been properly introduced. "This may seem a little awkward, but I don't really know your name."

"Josephine Douglass. My family and friends call me Josie, Mr. St. Augustine."

"Now we're even. See, I was at a disadvantage since you seem to know my name. But my friends and family call me Jack. Short for Jackson. Since you've been so friendly to me, I'd like you to call me Jack." He smiled, crinkling the corners of his blue eyes.

"Jack. I like that." Josie returned his smile with a grin of her own that lit up her face.

"And may I call you Josie? Or would you prefer Miss Douglass?" He inclined forward, eager to catch her words and hoping for acceptance to use her given name. Jack was, for once, looking at his future with hope. Things were proceeding nicely since he'd arrived in town.

"Josie would be fine." She briefly met his glance then her gaze flicked away.

"Excellent. May I say I'm looking forward to getting to know you better?"

"You are?" She set her teacup down with a clatter.

"Yes."

She stammered, "M-maybe we should talk about your horse."

He hadn't meant to embarrass her. Perhaps he should slow down. "As I've told you, I'm very attached to him. So I'll be coming out to ride him and take him over to the track to train."

"But who'll ride him in the races?"

"Who? Why, me, of course."

"But you're so tall. Most of the other riders are small men. Won't that handicap your horse?"

"You seem to know quite a bit about racehorses. Does your father race his horses?"

"No, I'm the one who—I mean, I'm the one who watches and is interested. My father goes occasionally."

Jack wondered what she'd been about to say. That she showed an interest in a sport dear to his heart impressed him. "As much as I hate to say this, I must be going. Should I put my horse in the barn or out in one of your fields?"

"Let's put him in the barn. That way he can get used to our home before I turn him outside."

"I'm sure your father and you know what's best for the horses." He watched her rise and admired the graceful way she seemed to float up from her chair. When she stood, the top of her head came up only to his shoulders, much different from his lanky sisters and mother.

After Zeus was safely stowed in a stall, Jack turned to Josie. As he spun around, his arms brushed against the softness of her shoulders. He jerked backward, almost as if he'd been burned with a hot iron. "Excuse me," he managed to say.

"It was my fault for being so close."

"I'll be back tomorrow to see Zeus. Maybe then you can give me some information about the racetrack." That wasn't the only information he wanted, for she intrigued him. He wanted to learn all about her. What she liked. What her favorite pastimes were. What she thought about him.

"I'd like that," she said.

Jack slipped one foot into the stirrup and swung up onto his gelding. "Josie, it was a pleasure meeting you. I look forward to many more such meetings." He tipped his black wide-brimmed hat and smiled.

"Thank you, Mr. St. Augustine." She took a few steps backward so she didn't have to tilt her head so far to see him, and gave a small curtsy.

"Not Mister, Jack."

As his horse's footfalls clopped on the hard earth, Jack thought of Josie. Yes, he decided, he'd made a good decision when he planned to marry in Gallatin City.

So far Miss Josie Douglass appeared to be everything he was looking for in a woman. She met the image he'd formed in his mind of his perfect wife.

She seemed meek. She displayed that by speaking in a soft tone of voice, blushing at his flirtatious winking, and by her desire to see to his comfort. Her few outspoken comments he brushed off as insignificant. They were probably just due to nerves, he reasoned, as any proper lady would be nervous spending time alone with a man.

She also seemed calm and attentive to him. Just like a woman who would be willing to please her husband. A woman who lived for nothing more than to satisfy her husband.

And another thing, she wasn't afraid of work. She proved that by tossing down the hay bales. That was an important trait to him, because starting a ranch would be hard work.

Josie's womanly figure was also something in her favor. She wasn't tall and rail-thin, or concerned about hiding her femininity, like the women his mother always had selected for him.

He remembered rounded breasts thrusting forward underneath the loose cotton of Josie's shirtwaist. The part of her legs that he'd seen hinted at the promise of more seductive curves. He was one man who found the swell of muscle in a woman to be very appealing.

Yes. He smiled, thinking he should pat himself on the

back. He'd found exactly what he was looking for in Josie. He couldn't imagine a woman more ready to take a husband, nor one so eager to please. It looked like he wouldn't need to seek out other prospects after all.

❖ 4 ❖

Low CLOUDS, GRAY and full with rain, lumbered across the sky. A light drizzle fell, making the early morning even darker than normal. In the distance Josie heard roosters crowing. She paid little attention to them or to cries of the mourning doves. Her attention was focused on the deserted oval track in front of her.

Josie reached down and slipped her fingers underneath the girth, checking its tightness. Satisfied her saddle was secure, she gathered up the reins and guided her mare to the starting line at the racetrack.

"Well, Lady, are you ready to have another go at the track?" Josie asked her mare.

The part Thoroughbred flicked her gray ears backward toward the sound of Josie's voice. The red lining of her nostrils flared as the mare pranced, anticipating the run ahead.

"Easy, Lady, we've got to learn to stand still at the starting line, or else we'll get disqualified."

She took a deep breath, let her weight sink into her heels, and pictured the perfect start to the race.

"Three, two, one. Go!" Josie whispered the countdown. On "go" she gave Lady her head and kicked her heels in the mare's sides.

Lady snorted and took off like a bullet. Josie rose slightly out of the saddle, easing her weight off Lady's back. She felt the powerful muscles expand and contract underneath her. One thousand pounds of horseflesh thundered down the track.

The sudden surge of speed sent a tremor of excitement through Josie. The wind whistled past her ears. The mist changed into a full-blown rain that pelted against her cheeks and hair. Pounding hooves beat out an intoxicating rhythm.

She saw the empty grandstands whiz by. Mud flew up, splattering her legs. They rounded the final curve. Josie loosened the reins, urging Lady on faster.

Her efforts were rewarded with a burst of energy. Lady flattened her neck, her forelegs stretched farther forward, increasing her stride. In an explosion of horsepower, Lady rocketed past the red rails that marked the finish line.

Josie let out a whoop of delight and slowed her mare down. Lady's labored breathing seemed amplified in the quiet morning.

"Atta girl, Lady." Josie patted her mare on the neck and continued cantering down the track. "That had to have been our fastest time yet. We just might win this year's race."

Minutes later Josie dismounted, loosened the girth, and tossed the reins over Lady's head. Moving to the rail, she grabbed her jacket and draped it over her shoulders. Since her clothes were already soaked from the rain, the jacket wouldn't do much good now.

She started toward home, leading her mare. At least the fairgrounds were at the edge of town and she didn't need to pass any houses.

Josie walked on, lost in her thoughts of Jack St. Augustine. What would he think of her racing a horse? He probably would not approve. Most men didn't.

She pictured Jack in her mind. A slow smile spread across her face. His dark hair hung over one eye, giving him an alluring look. Josie's cheeks heated up just thinking about what they could do together.

They entered the barn, relieved to be out of the pouring rain. The walk home had cooled Lady, but Josie needed to remove some of the caked mud from both of them.

Josie had just slipped on Lady's halter and bent down to check the mare's legs, when Lady whinnied. "Quiet," Josie admonished. "There's no need to make all this racket."

Lowering the hoof, Josie straightened and flipped her drenched braid back over her shoulder. Her mouth fell open. Standing directly in front of her was the man she'd been thinking about, Jack St. Augustine.

"Good morning, Josie. You're looking, ah, soaked." Jack grinned and swept his gaze up and down her body.

"Wh-what are you doing here?" she squeaked.

She feared she looked a horrible mess. Clots of mud streaked her face and arms. Water dripped off her jacket, creating a puddle at her feet. Even if she stretched the definition of ladylike appearances, it would not encompass her. Surely her chances with Jack diminished with each passing second.

"I told you I'd come by this morning and see my horse."

"But—but it's so early. It can't be eight o'clock." She longed for a mirror. She needed to know just how awful she looked. Valiantly, she brushed the loose wet strands of hair off her forehead and tried a smile. She didn't taste mud, so she assumed none was stuck to her teeth.

"This is my only free time today." He took a towel off a nearby rack and handed it to Josie. "I'll be leaving later."

She took it, shivering when the tips of his fingers brushed hers. She swallowed, trying to dislodge the tightness in her throat. Was he leaving already? "Wh-where are you going?"

"Just around. I've got business to attend to."

He watched her shiver beneath her sodden jacket and noticed the wet clothing molded to her body. Her sleeves clung to her arms like a second skin. The soaked riding skirt was plastered to her legs, clearly showing the outline of her hips and bottom. He stifled a groan.

Jack hoped he didn't appear to be staring, but he couldn't help it. Seeing Josie in shape-hugging, soggy clothing was too much temptation. His whole body became heated. He forced his eyes to her face.

"Don't you think you'd better dry off? You could catch a chill."

"Oh. Yes, you're right." She began toweling her body.

Watching her rub her stomach triggered something in his own belly. His glance rose, devouring her as if he couldn't look enough. Water droplets hung on her lashes, clumping them together. Tiny trickles of water ran down her cheeks. He imagined himself kissing them away. Would she taste like rain?

Jack stood stock-still and tried to rein in the budding desire he felt for Josie. Watching her shiver made him long to take her in his arms and warm her. The idea alarmed him. Never before had he felt so strongly about a woman. Instead of wrapping his arms around her, he crossed them over his chest.

"What were you doing out in this weather?" he accused.

Josie clutched the towel and looked from him to her mare. "I was out riding."

"Do you often ride in the morning? In the rain?" Couldn't she have ridden at a more decent time of the day? he thought.

"It wasn't raining when we left. Besides, I'll be helping Lottie this morning and doing work this afternoon."

Those were soothing words to his ears. She knew the value of time. Work was an important part of her day.

He liked that. However, he didn't relish the idea of her riding alone in the morning darkness. Something could happen to her, and he wouldn't care for that. His last thought caught him off guard.

"You should get in the house, sit by the fire, and warm your body." His concern caused his words to come out gruffer than he'd meant.

"I'll do that. Just let me put Lady in her stall so she can eat her grain." Josie managed a smile, her white teeth contrasting with the red of her lips.

Her hands slid down the length of the mare's neck, and Jack's groin tightened as he imagined her hands caressing his own body. Disgusted with his sensual instincts coming to the surface, he spun around and scowled.

"Have you had a cup of coffee this morning?" Josie's voice came from inside the wooden stall.

"No." He started unraveling a knotted lariat that hung from a nail, hoping to take his mind off Josie.

"Would you like to come inside and have a cup with me? I know my sister would love to meet you."

His heart raced. Her invitation was inappropriate, but tempting.

"Would you like to?" She stepped out, latched the lower half of the Dutch door, and gave him an inquiring look.

"I think I've time for one cup."

In her bedroom Josie tore off her wet clothes and yanked on a lightweight pale green homespun dress. It was one of her plainest dresses, trimmed only around the neckline with a dark green ribbon. But the loose-fitting, front-fastening dress was easy to put on. Josie wanted to hurry so she could spend more time with Jack.

She glanced in the mirror, groaned, then brushed back her damp hair into some semblance of order.

Excitement rippled down her spine. She just knew he cared about her. Hadn't he been the one to suggest she come inside and sit by the fire so she didn't catch a chill? And didn't he insist she dry off from the rain?

Now all she had to do was remember Grace's instructions. She was afraid being caught riding that morning might have further ruined her chances for seeming like the ideal wifely prospect. But Jack had accepted her explanation for riding so early in the morning. She'd just have to make sure everything she did was ladylike from then on. Absolutely.

Placing her hands on her stomach, she took a deep breath, settling her racing heart, and left her room. As she set her foot down in the hall, she heard her sister's voice.

"You mean you have four sisters? I never had even one brother."

Josie lengthened her stride. Lottie was probably trying to practice her flirting skills with Jack. At twelve going on thirteen, Lottie hovered at the door of womanhood. Boys had suddenly become very interesting to her.

It was just as she suspected. Lottie sat on the divan, her head lowered, looking up at Jack from underneath her eyelashes. Or at least trying to anyway. Her small white hands were folded on her lap.

"Lottie, would you please get us the coffee?" Josie stared at her sister until the younger girl stood up.

"Oh, yes. It'd be my pleasure to serve you, Mr. St. Augustine." Lottie dropped a deep curtsy before retreating to the kitchen.

"I'm sorry if she was bothering you." Josie took the seat that Lottie had recently occupied.

"I didn't mind. It was kind of nice for a change to have a female trying to impress me instead of telling me what to do."

"If she's like this at twelve, I hate to see what she'll be like at sixteen."

"She could outgrow it. Interests change, and so do people."

The sudden edge to his voice startled her. She opened her mouth to ask him about it, but the tapping of Lottie's slippers interrupted her.

"Here we are." Lottie set the tray down on the end

table and batted her eyes at Jack. "May I pour for you, Mr. St. Augustine?" She said his name in a breathless whisper.

The rich aroma of coffee filled the air as Lottie poured out three generous cups.

"Your sister was telling me about your mare." Jack raised his cup to his lips and blew on it.

Josie's stomach tightened. How much had Lottie told him? "What about her?"

"Lottie said you hope to make a racehorse of her. From what I've seen of her, it might be possible."

Josie squirmed. She wanted to change the subject before the truth came out and Jack learned she was the mare's trainer.

"Will you be here for a long time?" Lottie asked, batting her eyelashes once again.

"That all depends."

"Depends on what?" Josie asked before catching herself. She cringed and hoped Jack hadn't noticed her slip.

"Circumstances."

"Circumstances?" That was certainly cryptic, Josie thought.

"Yes, I've got a few projects in the works. I need to see how they turn out."

"I'm glad you're here. Sometimes life here can get sooo boring. I mean, I already know all the boys, and they're sooo dull."

"Lottie! Watch your manners." Sometimes her sister could act so surprising.

"I need to be going anyway. I've got a long day ahead of me." Jack set down his empty cup and rose. He turned to Lottie, took her hand, brought it to his cheek, and rested it against his face. "Miss Lottie, it's been a pleasure meeting you."

Lottie giggled and her face turned the same color as her red hair bow.

After he released her hand, he turned to Josie and nodded. "Thanks for the coffee. I'd like to see you when I return. Take care of yourself and don't ride in the freezing rain anymore.''

"I'll take care." She hugged his words to her heart. They warmed her more than any blanket could. He did care about her.

Josie and Lottie stood on the porch and watched Jack leave. As his horse trotted down the lane, a wagon rattled up and stopped.

Lottie pointed at the team of mules. "Look, it's Aunt Portia coming to call on us."

From her spot on the porch Josie clearly heard Mrs. Potter's sharp intake of breath. The reverend's wife's expression did not bode well. Her florid face had paled and her mouth formed an O of disapproval as she stared after Jack's retreating back. Bright spots of indignation colored her cheeks.

"Well, uh, I've gotta go braid my hair." Lottie ducked back inside.

Only the sound of the banging screen door remained. Josie stood rooted to the porch, and watched the red-faced woman approach. Mrs. Potter's arms and skirt swished in agitated syncopation.

❖ 5 ❖

"JOSEPHINE DOUGLASS," MRS. Potter shouted even before she hefted her bulk up the porch steps.

"Aren't you out rather early for your Saturday morning visits?" Josie didn't like the timing of Mrs. Potter's call at all. And from the sour look on her pinched features, it was evident Mrs. Potter found the timing of her visit even more distasteful.

"Matthew, you get my sewing basket. Sarah, you bring the baby and the diapers." Mrs. Potter kept her pale, narrowed eyes on Josie as she issued orders to her children.

Josie clutched the porch railing. From the looks of it, Mrs. Potter planned to stay a long time. Squaring her shoulders, Josie forced a smile to her face and tried her best to look hospitable. "We're always glad to have you come see us."

"Humph. One wouldn't think so. Especially after what I've seen." Mrs. Potter raised a dimpled hand to her reddened brow and sighed. "I'm just sorry I wasn't here sooner. Then maybe I could have prevented such an atrocity. And to think of my poor niece . . ."

"What atrocity?" Josie felt the floorboards vibrate as Mrs. Potter climbed the porch steps.

Mrs. Potter came within inches of Josie's face. She shook her black umbrella as if it were a staff of life and could give her strength. "I saw him. I saw a man leaving here. In the light of morning, no less. And he was smiling as if . . . as if . . . well, never mind."

Astounded, Josie stared at the reverend's wife. Scarlet blotches covered the woman's cheeks. Her lips quivered as if she longed to give Josie a good tongue-lashing she would never forget.

"I think you've jumped to conclusions. I don't like what you're hinting at."

"Don't worry, I'll get to the bottom of this. And the worst thing is, I saw precious young Charlotte witness the whole situation. It's too much. I need to sit down." Mrs. Potter thrust past Josie and opened the front door. Her children followed after her like dutiful little ducks.

Left with no choice, Josie went inside after Mrs. Potter. She tried hard to take deep, calming breaths. She had to think of something fast in order to divert the direction of Mrs. Potter's thinking. Josie couldn't afford to give any more ammunition to the woman's crusade to adopt Lottie.

"A cup of tea or coffee would be nice, Josephine." Mrs. Potter settled herself on the sofa, ensconced between her two oldest children. A basket of sewing sat to her right, and a smaller basket filled with snow-white diapers waited at her left.

"I'll go get the coffeepot." At least that gave Josie something to do and time to think. Once in the kitchen, she stuck her finger inside the kettle to see if the water was still warm. Hot liquid scalded her. She yanked it out, stuck the finger in her mouth to cool it off, and grimaced as she heard her visitors' voices carry from the sitting room.

"Now, children, I want you to listen. The well-being and the spiritual life of all our parishioners rests with your father and myself. Our shoulders have become stooped with the burden we bear. It's our duty to steer any one of our sheep who might have strayed from the fold."

Her children looked up at her with blank expressions. Even the baby girl stopped gnawing on her fist and stared up at her mother.

Josie rolled her eyes and gritted her teeth. Feet practically dragging, she carried the tray into the sitting area and placed it on a cloth-covered, upended bullet crate that served as table.

"Where did my sweet niece disappear to?" Mrs. Potter's gaze scanned the room. "I'm sure she wants to see her aunt; after all, she'll be spending lots of time with me."

Not if Josie could help it. Lottie would never live with her aunt. "I'll go get her." If Mrs. Potter could be convinced that Lottie hadn't seen anything wrong occur between herself and Jack, then perhaps all would be well. It was worth a try, Josie thought.

Josie walked down the narrow hall and tapped on the closed door off to her right. "Lottie, please come out here. Your presence is requested."

"Do I have to?"

"Yes."

The latch clicked and Lottie poked her blond head out. In a whisper she said, "But she's so mean to you and always so friendly to me. I don't see why we have to entertain her."

Josie raised a finger to her lips in warning. "Shh! Your aunt has excellent ears. She might hear you. Besides, she's family. We can't ignore her. It would be rude." Josie jerked her head in the direction of the front room.

"Oh, all right." Lottie stepped out of her room and they returned to their guests.

"Well, now, suppose you tell me exactly who that man is you were entertaining earlier?" Mrs. Potter squinted at Josie, her lips pinching. Her eyes raked over Josie's damp and tousled hair.

"I wasn't entertaining anyone. His name is Ja—I mean Mr. St. Augustine." Josie caught herself. If she'd said his given name, surely Mrs. Potter would have had a fit of the vapors.

"St. Augustine. He didn't look like a saint to me. Saint or not, no man has any business running about this early in the day to a woman's home, especially when her father is not at home to chaperon." Mrs. Potter reached into her sewing basket and plucked out a pair of trousers.

Josie wanted to point out that Mrs. Potter was doing the exact thing, visiting in the early morning. But then, she knew the reverend's wife set out every Saturday morning at eight o'clock for her visiting rounds. Instead, Josie took a sip of coffee and tried to stay calm.

"He's just keepin' his horse here. Slim from the livery sent him here," Lottie piped in.

"Keeping. The word is keeping. There's a G on the end, young lady." Mrs. Potter pointed her recently threaded needle at Lottie. "And why doesn't Slim have this horse?"

"Sorry, Aunt Portia," Lottie muttered, staring down at the hem of her dress. "The livery was full."

"Humph. I'll see about that. But, Josephine, look at yourself. Look at your hair, it's wet and messy. Your dress looks like it's been donned in a hurry, the waistline is crooked. It's enough to make one wonder." Mrs. Potter stabbed the needle in and out of the trousers several times. "And it's also enough to make me realize where Charlotte belongs."

Josie caught Lottie's frightened glance. So, Mrs. Potter did plan to use this information in her crusade. Steely resolve worked its way through every limb of Josie's body. She wouldn't let anything happen to her sister. She had managed to keep her family together for this long, and she would continue.

One glance at Mrs. Potter's children was enough to solidify her resolve. Josie would not allow Lottie to become like the young Potters. Just sitting there, unsmiling, never saying a word and doing only their mother's bidding. Not a very enjoyable life. Josie felt sorry for them.

She set her coffee cup down and folded her hands so tightly that Josie could feel the pads of her fingers press into her knuckles. "If you have something to say, please come out and say it. Let's not play games."

"Josephine, you look a fright. But really, I know you are old enough to have a family of your own. But must you let your . . . your . . . animal instincts rule with your precious sister around?"

"Animal instincts?"

"Oh, yes. I saw the man come out of your house with my very own eyes. And he had an unholy smile on his face, no less."

"That animal instinct you're referring to was common courtesy. I offered him a cup of coffee. Mr. St. Augustine came over to see his horse and was chilled by the rain. Lottie and I served him a hot drink. As proper citizens, we were concerned about his health."

Josie wanted nothing better than to throw Mrs. Potter out on her rear. But tossing out her sister's aunt wouldn't be very nice, nor would it help the situation, for that matter.

"Oh! Poor Charlotte! Did you see anything? Were you embarrassed?" Mrs. Potter looked stricken. Her face had gone ashen. "You must tell me."

Lottie bit her lower lip and tried desperately not to laugh. "Aunt Portia, he only drank a cup of coffee."

"Thank the good Lord above. You're still so young and innocent. The world awaits you. But now, your sister is old and alone. A man just might hold more temptation for someone like her."

"Excuse me, but I'm still here and I have ears," Josie said. "I'll say this once. I don't like what you're accusing me of, even if you didn't come right out and say it. I am an honorable woman. Do not ever think to question my virtue again, especially in my own home." Josie threw her shoulders back, pinned Mrs. Potter with a lethal gaze, and opened her mouth.

"For your information, Mr. St. Augustine asked for my hand this morning."

The other woman gasped and sputtered. The florid jowls around her face jiggled to and fro. "O Lord above, she's being mean to me. And I, the one who is watching out for her soul and for the soul of my niece. I beseech you, Lord, give me patience." She pressed her palms together in prayer and looked upward. Suddenly she stopped. "What did I hear you say?"

Josie squirmed in her seat. She wished she could recall her impulsive words. She hadn't meant to say such an outlandish thing, but Mrs. Potter made her so angry that she just had to say something. Anything. "I said he asked for my hand."

"As in marriage? That most sacred unity offered by the church?" Mrs. Potter's hands lay idle in her lap for once, the mending temporarily cast aside.

"Yes." Shifting her glance upward, Josie half expected to see a jagged bolt of lightning rip through the roof to strike her for her blatant lie.

The only sound that registered was Lottie's gasp.

"Did he really?" Lottie stared at her sister as if seeing her for the first time. "I wish I'd been there to see it. Did he go down on bended knee? Did he pledge his undying love?"

Mrs. Potter squinted at Josie again. "You are saying a man who is new to town decided he wants to make you his wife?"

The underlying astonishment of the woman's words wasn't lost on Josie. It was clear Mrs. Potter didn't think Josie was ideal wife material.

Perhaps her rash response hadn't been the best choice. Slowly exhaling, Josie tried to settle the nervous knot in her stomach before answering. "Yes, I am. I'm sorry you find that so hard to believe. You of all people should know that the Lord works in mysterious ways." There, Josie thought, let her have a taste of her own medicine.

"Of course I know the Lord works in mysterious ways. But if this man asked for your hand, why didn't he stay and announce the news to me? I'd think a decent, upstanding gentleman would want to share his tidings of joy with the reverend's wife."

"He doesn't know who you are." She had an idea that announcing their engagement was putting her on a collision course with disaster. Josie desperately wanted to change the subject. Her gaze landed on Mrs. Potter's infant swaddled in a pink blanket. "So, I see Elizabeth is growing."

"Yes, she is." Mrs. Potter, however, wasn't going to abandon the previous conversation topic. "Getting back to your intended, where is he from? What is his full name? What does your father think of him?"

Holding up her coffee cup, Josie took a long drink, hoping to formulate some intelligent answers. Her heart hammered. She felt trapped in a hole of her own making.

"His name is Jack St. Augustine and he's from . . ." —*Think! Think!*—". . . from Kansas City."

In the amount of time it had taken her to remember where Jack hailed from, Mrs. Potter's eyes gleamed. "Josephine, is there a reason for such a quick engagement? I mean, as the good Lord knows, a courtship should occur first. Is there something you aren't telling me?"

It felt as if ice were sliding down her spine. Dear God, had she made things worse with her fib? Josie never thought Mrs. Potter would accuse her of . . . of . . . being with child! Her heartbeat accelerated. Josie forced a laugh, hoping to diffuse the situation. "Mrs. Potter, have you never heard of love at first sight?"

The older woman looked doubtful. "Love at first sight? Well, I suppose I shall have to consider that."

Lottie jumped into the conversation. "Yes, yes, I know my sister wouldn't marry for any other reason than love."

Josie felt about two feet high. It was bad enough concocting an engagement, but to have her little sister believe the fib so thoroughly pained Josie. "Ah, well, you never know what will happen, do you? More coffee, Mrs. Potter?''

''No, thank you. Josephine, you must bring your intended over to meet my husband. I know Reverend Potter will have questions to ask you. For we must make sure your future husband is a good, law-abiding, churchgoing man, and we must especially make sure he will be the correct influence for my niece.''

''My fiancé and I will come talk to your husband.'' Josie hoped she wouldn't get struck down for furthering her fibs. If hell existed, she was surely headed there right now. ''But if you could, would you please keep my, ah, engagement to yourself for now?''

Mrs. Potter drew herself up to her full height. ''Something like this, involving one of our church's flock, cannot be kept silent. It's my duty to spread the good word around. Now''—she neatly folded the trousers she'd been sewing—''we must be off. I've other parishioners to call on. I'll be looking for you and your intended in church tomorrow.'' She clutched her umbrella and pointed it at Josie.

''We'll be there.'' Josie watched as all the Potters filed out into the morning. As soon as Josie heard the creak of the wagon wheels, she collapsed onto the sofa and cradled her face in her hands. She'd done it this time. She had really done it. *Grace will have a fit when I tell her,* she thought miserably. She couldn't imagine what Jack would say when he found out.

Lottie bounded over, plopped down next to Josie, and snatched up her hands. ''How come you didn't tell me about Jack? This is all sooo romantic.''

Josie looked at the happiness radiating from her sister's face and knew she couldn't confess her lie. She didn't have the heart to shatter her sister's illusion. ''I wanted to keep it a secret for a little while longer.'' Like a whole lot longer, like when and if Jack ever actually proposed to her.

Lottie's cherubic face scrunched up. ''Can you do that? Can you get married without Father's permission?

And then will Aunt Portia leave me alone?''

Josie stroked Lottie's soft golden hair. ''First of all, we didn't get married. We're only engaged to get married, and I'll tell Father as soon as he returns. Who knows''—she attempted a weak laugh—''maybe by then I'll have decided I don't want to marry Jack.''

''Oh, no. You'd never do that. He's too handsome for you to not to want marry, and you have to think of me. I need you. And if I have a happily married sister, Aunt Portia wouldn't have the guts to cart me off to her house. I know it.''

''I guess you're right. I want you to know you can trust me. I'll make sure you'll never have to worry about living with your aunt. Father and I won't allow it. But enough of this chatter. We've got work to do.'' Josie needed a long time to try to figure out how to get herself out of the mess she'd created that morning. Most of all, she needed to find Jack before Mrs. Potter's words found him first.

After finishing the chores in a hurry, Josie burst through the door to the general mercantile. ''Grace? Grace, are you in here?''

''Josie! Shhh. You don't come barging in a store or anywhere, yelling like a banshee,'' Grace said, holding one finger across her lips. ''It's unseemly.''

''Oh.'' *Unseemly* would seem weak when Josie told her the latest news. ''I just needed to see you, that's all.'' Josie wound her way past barrels of crackers, burlap sacks of flour, and a display of dried fruit as she headed to the soft-goods portion of the store where Grace stood laying out fabrics.

Grace laid a new bolt of red floral calico on the shelf and turned to regard Josie. ''What on earth can have you so excited to see me that you forgot all of my instructions?''

''I didn't forget them, I sort of, um, well, I need to tell you something.''

Grace's thick eyebrows rose. She dropped the material

and focused her attention on Josie. "Why do you keep nibbling at your lower lip? I'm getting worried here. I haven't seen you look so distraught since we were girls and you ruined half your father's clothes in that laundry incident."

Josie tried to laugh, but she only managed to make a strangled sound.

"Out with it," Grace ordered. "I can tell by your expression, you've done something rash. Tell me."

"It's really sort of . . . funny, in a way. I mean, if you think about it." Her phony smile faded and Josie hung her head. With her right hand she reached up and massaged her brow. "Oh, God, it's not funny at all. I can't believe I let Mrs. Potter goad me into saying such a thing."

Grace grabbed Josie's arms and gave her a quick shake. "What are you talking about? What did you say?"

Josie groaned and picked up a bolt of deep green, hugging it to her chest for comfort. She shut her eyes. She had no desire to see the expression on Grace's face. "I told her I was engaged."

"Engaged?! To whom and when?" Grace's voice rose an octave with each word she uttered.

"Well, that's just it. He doesn't know he's engaged to me yet." Josie's fingers dug into the material she held. She even pinched herself to see if this was a bad dream. It wasn't.

Grace staggered backward, leaning against the broad cutting table for support. Her eyes were as wide as saucers. "I'm almost afraid to ask, but here goes. How can he not know about his own engagement?"

"See, Jack came over early this morning to check on his stallion, which he's keeping at our barn. Anyway, Mrs. Potter saw him leave our house and ride off with a big smile on his face." Actually, once she thought about it, the situation didn't sound that bad. They'd only talked and had a cup of coffee. There had been no stolen kisses or embraces, much to Josie's disappointment.

"Stop." Grace waved her hands in front of her, signaling Josie to halt. "Who is Jack and what is Mrs. Potter doing in this story?"

"Jack is now my fiancé, but he doesn't know it. Mrs. Potter was carrying on about loose women. She even accused me! I just got so fed up with her and frightened about her wanting to take Lottie away that I . . . that I told her he'd just asked for my hand and that was the reason for his early visit."

"Oh, dear me. You didn't hear one word of what I said the other day, did you? How could you do such a thing? Did you lose your mind last night?" Color stained Grace's high cheekbones.

"No, I didn't lose my mind, and yes, I heard every one of your instructions. I'll have you know every time I've seen Jack I've tried to be the perfect demure, lady-like creature." So she'd just had one whopper of a slipup. Maybe it wouldn't be so hard to fix.

"Who is he? Do I know him?" Grace took Josie's hands and gave them a reassuring squeeze.

"No, you don't know him. He's new in town. I just met him two days ago." Josie stopped and conjured up Jack's image in her mind. Unknowingly, a smile teased the edges of her lips. He certainly would be a handsome man to be married to.

"Josie?" Grace waved her hand in front of Josie's face. "And? Tell me more about him. This is serious business!"

His image snapped from Josie's mind. "Of course it's serious. His whole name is Jack St. Augustine. Doesn't that sound romantic? Don't you like the sound of Josie St. Augustine?"

Grace threw up her hands. "I give up. I don't know if Josie St. Augustine sounds good or not, because I don't know this man. Please tell me more before some customers come in and I have to help them. I've got to figure a way to help you out of this horrible mess you've created."

"As I said, he's new in town. I think he said he's from Missouri. And he's keeping his racehorse at our ranch."

"No wonder you like him. He enjoys racing just like you do. But I still can't picture him. Tell me what he looks like."

Before Josie could open her mouth, the bell over the front door rang. A family of five poured in the entrance. Three little children ran laughing over to the glass jars brimming with hard candies.

"Oh, dear. I'll be right back. Let me go help the Morrisons before their children eat all of our candy." Grace hustled over to the family.

Josie waved to the Morrisons and then turned her attention to the fabrics Grace had been sorting. Reaching out, she ran her fingers along the soft cottons and lightweight wools. Her sister would be excited to hear about the new selection. She would have to bring Lottie over soon.

Josie picked up the bolt she'd held earlier and examined the material. She held up the corner to her arm, checking to see if the deep green color would suit her. She smiled. She rather liked the way it looked. Immediately she wondered if Jack would like the color on her.

At the thought of Jack, her heart fell. Suppose he would have nothing to do with her after he heard about their "engagement"? She shouldn't have let herself get carried away that morning. Now she might have ruined any chance of a relationship with him.

The little bell over the door tinkled again. Josie looked up to see the Morrisons leaving. Grace hurried back over.

"So you were telling me what Jack looks like. Go ahead," Grace urged.

"He has dark brown hair with shiny gold and red highlights. I know because I saw the sun shine on it. He also has beautiful, warm blue eyes. And when he smiles his eyes crinkle up and sparkle. Oh, yes, and he's quite tall. Much taller than I am."

Grace laughed. "That's not saying much. I'm taller than you are. I think I'd rather just meet him. When can I do that?"

Josie's shoulders fell. "I don't know. He had to leave

on business. He didn't say when he'd be back. Anyway, this morning, when he had coffee with us, he said he—''

"He had coffee with you and Lottie? Alone in your house! I *know* your father's not back yet.'' Grace's jaw almost dropped to her chest. Her hand went to her heart. "Are you trying to see if you can kill me in one day?''

"No, I'm just finishing my story. Yes, he was inside our house this morning. It was raining outside. What's so surprising?''

"Josie! You're not supposed to entertain men in your house, especially if your father isn't there. Don't you remember anything of what I taught you? A lady has to remember to act with decorum at all times.''

"He was already *there,* looking after his horse. I didn't see what it would hurt if he just came in for a cup of coffee.'' Josie groaned. That innocent cup of coffee didn't seem so harmless anymore.

"But apparently Mrs. Potter did! I just bet she'll use that as more fuel for her fire to have Lottie come live at her house.'' Grace paced in agitation. She twisted the sash of her dress around her index finger.

"Yes, she did. And she wasn't any too pleased. That's what started this whole mess of my 'engagement.' She accused me of carrying on an affair in front of Lottie. I thought she was going to take Lottie right then and there. So I, uh, well, I've told you.'' She smiled, but it didn't reach her eyes.

"Oh, Josie, this is not good. This is not good. Of all the people to let something like this slip to. You know how she can't keep her mouth shut. Why''—Grace looked at the clock ticking on the back shelf—''I'm sure she's already spoken to several people today. There's no way we can easily undo this.''

"And?'' A feeling of dread inched up Josie's spine.

"And I hate to think of what your father will say when he hears of this, much less what your *intended* will think.''

Josie twisted her hands together. "Do you think they'll

be upset?'' Her father she could handle, but Jack, she didn't know how he would react.

Grace gave a most unladylike snort. ''Upset? That's putting it mildly. Try shocked.''

''Shocked, huh?'' Josie's feeble smile wobbled and then disappeared. ''I'm sure I can think of something to say to smooth things over.'' She had no idea what that would be.

''Jos, I'm begging you, if you really want to set things straight, *please* remember my instructions and follow them. Do not do anything even remotely rash in the future.''

''Maybe we'll be lucky and this incident will have slipped Mrs. Potter's mind.''

''I doubt it, unless she somehow gets knocked unconscious in the next few hours.''

Josie chuckled at the unlikely image. ''Don't worry so, Grace. Everything will be fine.''

That proved to be a false hope even before the words were out of her mouth.

A pair of young women, the Long sisters, each living up to their namesake, sashayed into the store, all smiles and nudges as they looked at Josie. ''Why, Miss Douglass, I believe congratulations are in order for your upcoming nuptials.''

Josie forced a smile. ''Thank you.''

It seemed Mrs. Potter had wasted no time in spreading the word.

In the tiny parlor off the front of Howard's Eatery sat three women. Portia Potter had decreed the sunny room as the official meeting place of Gallatin City's Ladies Auxiliary. The Auxiliary consisted of fifteen women, but only three were present at this unofficial meeting.

Portia sat in an overstuffed wing chair. She sipped her tea, but her foot tapped constantly.

''My dear Portia, whatever is the matter?'' Mrs. Samuels asked. She sat in a well-padded Queen Anne chair directly across from Portia. She was as tiny as Portia was large.

"Yes, Portia, please tell us what is causing you such distress," Mrs. Garvey added.

Portia set down her bone china teacup and sighed. She closed her eyes and slowly shook her head from side to side. "It's Charlotte, or, more precisely, the horrible influence Josephine is upon my dear, sweet Charlotte."

The other women shook their heads knowingly.

"Did something new happen?" Mrs. Garvey asked, her forehead creased with worry.

"Yes, it did. I am almost ashamed to admit what I witnessed. It can not bode well for my Charlotte." She clasped her hands tightly and shuddered.

"My dear Portia, please tell us. You know how we hate to see you suffer so. Please share your burden with us. As you know, my Mary Jane is friends with Charlotte, and if there is anything I need to know, please tell us," Mrs. Samuels said.

"I'll tell you, but please try not to be shocked when I do." Portia unclasped her hands, pressed them against her lap, and met her friends' glances.

Mrs. Samuels and Mrs. Garvey leaned forward in eager anticipation of a juicy morsel of gossip.

"Yesterday when I went over to visit my dear Charlotte, I found her"—Portia stopped, took a fortifying breath of air, and then continued—"I found Charlotte up in a tree."

Mrs. Garvey gasped. "Surely you didn't find the young woman up in a tree like some common tomboy!"

"Did Charlotte see you?" Mrs. Samuels asked.

Portia had paled. "No, I could not announce my presence when I found her up in the tree like a boy. I was too shocked. Imagine my niece climbing trees. That is not the behavior of a young lady."

"Goodness me, no. Where was her sister?" Mrs. Garvey rose and paced the small room. The click of her heels was muffled by the many layers of her skirt.

"Josephine was nowhere to be seen. But I just know it was her bad influence that caused Charlotte to act so

. . . so . . .''—Portia groped for words—"so *unfeminine*."

"I just hope my Mary Jane knows better than to climb trees."

"This is a horrible situation," Mrs. Garvey stated.

"It gets worse," Portia added.

"How so?" Mrs. Samuels had opened her fan and began fluttering herself.

"Her dress had caught on a limb, and I''—Portia swallowed—"I could see her petticoats! They were right there, in broad daylight, for all the world to see. I tell you, I about fainted."

"Goodness gracious!" Mrs. Garvey scurried over to Portia, grasped her hands, and gave a light squeeze. "Oh, Portia. However is Charlotte to become a well-mannered young woman if she does such things?"

"That is one of the main worries of my life. That is why I believe that we must keep our eyes on Josephine. We must keep track of her behavior. We cannot let her unorthodox ways influence my niece. After all, it was my sister's dying wish that I make sure Charlotte grows up into a beautiful, polished young lady." Determination snapped back into Portia's pale blue eyes.

"You are so right, my dear Portia," Mrs. Samuels said. "I will be able to keep an eye on Josephine, as my Mary Jane spends time over at their house with Charlotte."

"I too will keep my ears open. I especially think we must pay attention to Josephine's engagement. It all happened so *quickly*," Mrs. Garvey said disapprovingly as she sat back down.

Portia pursed her lips and nodded sagely. "Yes, I will be most interested to see exactly who this man is who asked for Josephine's hand. We must stay alert. Charlotte's well-being is at stake."

❖ *6* ❖

JACK HAD BEEN riding for several hours, searching for the best place to start his ranch. Finally he thought he'd come upon the perfect area. He rode his gelding up the grassy embankment. Water ran down his horse's legs in rivulets. The Gallatin River, which he'd just forded, was deeper than it had looked. He stopped and frowned at the turbulent, rushing water. Would this area be prone to spring flooding when the winter snow melt started?

Narrowing his eyes, he looked critically at the shafts of grass waving in an endless sea. Bright green, so juicy and fat. The sweet spring grass tempted even his horse. Every so often his horse would try yanking the reins out of Jack's hand so he could grab a mouthful.

Jack calculated he was about twenty-five miles east of Gallatin City, in the vicinity of Bozeman.

He looked around. Towering trees stretched to the heavens. Cottonwoods. Red cedars. Ponderosa pines. Enough trees to provide wood for fences, barns, corrals, and a house. Two golden eagles spread their mighty wings as they swooped above Jack on their way to a high nest.

"I do like the looks of this valley. There's plenty of grass. Lots of trees so I can build. Water nearby."

On either side of him, mountain ranges marched north to south. The lower hills were rolling, undulating, like waves of green and brown. The farther slopes rose higher, some almost fanglike. Several peaks still had snow covering their tops. The bright white glared against the deep blue of the sky.

Settling back in his saddle, he smiled and relaxed. The beauty of the land captivated him. It was such a contrast to flat, wind-blown Kansas City. He doubted he could ever leave Montana Territory. He felt at home and at peace in the wild, open country. Here was a place he could call home and really feel like he belonged.

Montana was everything he'd hoped for. Out here he could raise his family, surrounded by the comforting mountains. Meeting Josie had been the icing on the cake. He'd found the perfect woman for a wife.

He laughed short and sharp, thinking he was done with scheming, headstrong women. His humor died suddenly as an unwanted scene from his past intruded. He could see and hear it as if it unfolded directly in front of him on an outdoor stage.

"Jackson," his mother had said. "Gloria will be eagerly awaiting letters from you. You know we all look forward to the day when you wed her. Don't dally in the uncivilized wilderness you insist on traveling to."

The muscles in Jack's neck had tightened while trying to ignore the implications of his mother's words. "As I told you before, I'm not marrying Gloria," Jack stated evenly.

He looked at Gloria. At the auburn hair pulled back into a bun so tight that the corners of her eyes slanted backward. At the thin, pinkish lips. Her straight, narrow nose. She was the spitting image of his mother and sisters. And he knew that he could never marry her.

"Jackson, don't be a goose. You know how I'm looking forward to uniting our families," Gloria replied, ignoring his words.

"I told her to already start acting like one of the family. Since we all know you *will* marry her. You have a high sense of honor," his mother said, nodding and smiling in approval at Gloria, her handpicked choice for Jack's future wife.

Jack had stood there, listening to his mother ignore his wishes once again, and he knew he had to act. He could no longer remain in Kansas City.

His mother and Gloria had both looked so sure of themselves that they failed to see the defiant fires spark in Jack's eyes.

Suddenly Jack felt wood jamming into his palm. The last traces of the scene with his mother before he'd left for Montana vanished like a wisp of smoke. He shook his head, looked down, and realized he was clutching the saddle horn so hard it had dug into his palm.

The memory cast an unwanted shadow upon his new life. He needed to get rid of it.

"Montana will be my home," he shouted to the endless sky overhead, shaking his fist. "No one can take that away from me."

"Hey, chickies, chickies," Josie called in a singsong voice as she entered the henhouse. The minute she stepped inside, the hens began squawking. Their noisy cacophony filled Josie's ears. She wished she'd strapped on a hat to at least dim the sound.

"Hey, chickies, I hope you have lots of eggs for me. Mrs. Samuels is coming over to pick up a basketful. She's giving us two apple cobblers in exchange."

With her basket hanging from her left arm, Josie moved to the first hen. Josie gave the hen a little push and smiled as she discovered two brown-speckled eggs in the straw nest. She carefully lifted them out and set them in her basket.

"That's a good girl," she said to the hen as its beady

black eyes stared at her. In a ruffle of feathers the hen resumed her roosting, never minding that her eggs were now gone.

Josie proceeded around the tiny, smelly room until her basket hung heavily from her arm. "That should do it, ladies. Keep up the good work." Ducking, Josie slipped out of the low doorway and into the fresh air and sunshine. She took a few gulps of cleansing air.

She pivoted toward the house and slowly started up the flagstone path. As she walked, her engagement rose foremost in her mind. What would Jack's reaction be? Was there any hope of him agreeing to it?

The sound of laughter jerked her thoughts from Jack. Across the yard Lottie chatted and giggled with her best friend, Mary Jane Samuels.

Josie paused, watching her younger sister. It was a terrible shame for a twelve-year-old girl to worry about being removed from the only home she'd ever known.

Smiling at her sister's unbridled enthusiasm, Josie felt less worried about her fib. She had done the right thing. For now, at least, her sister was safe. Mrs. Potter hadn't mentioned any further threats to adopt Lottie. When Jack returned, she could worry about explaining the situation, but until then Josie would push those worries from her mind.

She marched up the walk, opened the house door, and set the egg basket down. Josie had a few minutes before Mrs. Samuels would come for her eggs and Mary Jane. That gave Josie just enough time to read a few pages in the latest issue of *Godey's Lady's Book* that Grace had lent her. If she was lucky, there would be an article on undoing personal disasters.

Later that evening, after Josie had cut slices of the apple cobbler for herself and Lottie, they sat out on the porch enjoying a rare, warm spring evening.

"That sure was good cobbler Mary Jane's mother made," Lottie commented as she licked her fork, trying to get every last bit of the dessert.

"It certainly was. Next time you see Mrs. Samuels, thank her again. I just don't have any talent for baking desserts." Josie could make a decent loaf of bread. Muffins and biscuits that were edible. But every time she tried to bake a pie, she somehow managed to get the ingredients botched up.

"I'll tell her. In fact, I'm gonna ask Mary Jane's mother to teach me how to bake an apple cobbler."

"You are?"

"Yeah. I want to learn." Lottie rocked, frowning down at her empty plate. Her round cheeks gave her face an endearing silhouette.

Even though it shouldn't have, Lottie's desire to learn things, even baking an apple cobbler, from another woman hurt. It only made Mrs. Potter's assertion that she was unfit to raise her sister reverberate in Josie's head. She tried to keep the panic out of her voice. "Why? Don't you like what I can teach you?"

"Josieeee, everyone knows you can't bake a pie. Why, remember last Fourth of July? The blueberry pie you made tasted distinctly like salt. You forgot the sugar."

"Thanks for reminding me." The memory of that day still stung.

"Anyway, I need to learn to bake pies. Then I can win the heart of my beau. Like you did."

"What?"

Lottie glanced quickly at her sister. "My beau. My intended, you know, what Jack is to you. If I can bake pleasing pies for him, he'll wanna marry me. Mary Jane told me so."

"You're twelve. You're too young to start thinking of such things. And besides, I never baked a pie for Jack."

"I'm almost thirteen," Lottie huffed. She counted off the years on her fingertips. "I can get married in about four years."

Josie knew Lottie would be interested in boys one day. But so soon? Josie had no idea of what to tell Lottie about relationships. She herself had never had the time for them.

She snorted. She had one now. She was engaged to a man who still didn't know it yet. No matter how hard she tried, just when Josie thought she'd pushed the debacle to the back of her mind, somehow her impending nuptials seemed to jump to the forefront.

Lottie continued to speak. "I want my husband to fall in love with me right away. Like Jack did with you. Why else would he ask you to marry him so soon if he hadn't been struck by love at first sight?"

Josie groaned. *Poor Jack. He doesn't know he's been afflicted with love at first sight.* "Lottie, why don't you think about your entry for the upcoming fair instead of worrying about a husband, either yours or mine. We can talk about them later, like when Father comes back."

"That's no fun. I want to hear everything he said to you. Did he kiss you? What was it like? Tell me. Tell me, you always tell me."

"Lottie! Really, such questions. It's all pretty personal, but I'll tell you this. He didn't kiss me." As much as Josie would have liked to have felt his lips, she hadn't had that particular opportunity, and now she wondered if she ever would.

"Can't you tell me what he said?"

"No, I can't." And that, at least, was the truth.

Lottie's feet swung back and forth, kicking at the air. She suddenly smiled, deep dimples denting her cheeks. "Know what? When you and Jack marry, he'll be my brother. I've always wanted one."

"A brother, huh? Right now it's time for you to go to bed. Tomorrow is Sunday and church."

Lottie rose and gave Josie a kiss. "Maybe Father will be home tomorrow. I sure miss him."

"Me too, sweetie. Me too."

After Lottie disappeared into the house, Josie sat on her rocker and stared up at the stars. The sound of her breathing echoed in her ears.

Thousands of little lights twinkled. Josie wondered if Jack was looking at the sky and what his thoughts were, if he was thinking of her. Maybe, a tiny corner of her heart suggested, Jack was thinking about asking her to marry him. Perhaps he had indeed fallen immediately in love with her. At least she could hope for that to happen.

Unbidden, a single tear ran down her cheek. Josie closed her eyes and prayed Jack St. Augustine would return her feelings. Prayed he would want her, for her sake and for Lottie's sake. For it would be utter humiliation to have to confess to the town that Jack had never proposed in the first place.

❖ 7 ❖

Horse-drawn wagons clustered under the trees at the side of the freshly painted white church. The church sat in the middle of town, but the founding fathers had allotted a generous grant of land with plenty of shade trees for the worshipers. The lawn was kept neatly manicured and beds of flowers butted against the path leading to the chapel door.

Children and adults clad in their Sunday best filed up the wide steps. On the landing stood Reverend Potter, flanked by his wife, welcoming their flock.

Josie gave Lottie's hand a quick squeeze before glancing down at her outfit. She'd put on her best navy blue dress, complete with corset and a light blue bonnet. She'd stayed up late the night before, polishing her boots until they gleamed.

Since she'd become the center of attention, she thought she'd better appear immaculate. She didn't want to give the citizens anything more to gossip about.

"She's staring at us," Lottie whispered, holding her gloved hand up to shield her lips.

"Who?"

"Aunt Portia."

"Lottie, she looks at everybody as they come to church."

Josie glanced up to the top of the stairs and realized Mrs. Potter did indeed have her eyes glued to her. Josie swallowed, remembering their last encounter. She had promised to bring her fiancé to meet the reverend and his wife today. And here she'd shown up with only her sister.

"Look who's here! If it isn't my dear niece Charlotte and her sister," Mrs. Potter boomed as she held open her arms, looking to all the world like Josie and Lottie were her little lost souls.

Reverend Potter turned his head. "You don't need to shout, Portia. I'm standing next to you." Reverend Potter was a bear of a man, taller than his wife and practically as broad.

"Charlotte, my dear, I'm so glad to see you." Mrs. Potter spun around and peeked inside the open chapel doors. "I see there're a few spots near the front for you and your sister."

"Thank you, Aunt Portia." Lottie dropped a curtsy in front of the woman.

"But where's your intended, Josephine?" Mrs. Potter's gaze scanned the surrounding people. "I don't see an unfamiliar face."

"Funny you should notice." Josie's voice came out light and carefree, a complete contrast to how she felt inside. "He's, um, still out of town on business. He hasn't returned yet."

Mrs. Potter's eyebrows lifted toward her hairline. "Doesn't he know Sunday is for the Lord? What kind of a man is he?"

"I'm sure he's attending church wherever he is." Her gut felt as if it were twisting in knots. It was not good at all to fib in front of the church. She decided it would be best to keep her mouth closed, lest she be struck mute for her multiplying lies.

"Well, you had better go find your seats. The service will start soon." Mrs. Potter turned and ushered the remaining people into the church.

Josie followed the flow of people and sat down next to her sister. Mrs. Potter's comments burned in her mind. What kind of man was Jack St. Augustine? After all, she really didn't know that much about him. Suppose he wasn't at all what he seemed to be?

No, she thought as she gripped her small leather-bound Bible in her right hand. Deep in her heart she knew Jack was an honorable man. She would have sensed if something was amiss. For most of her life she'd been a good judge of character.

"Psst, Josie, the reverend's coming in. Stand up." Lottie poked her in the arm.

Automatically, Josie rose, opening the hymnal to the appropriate song. Her voice joined the others as they sang praises to God. All thoughts of her bungle left her mind as she concentrated on the soothing melody.

Throughout the sermon Josie listened attentively. She kept her eyes focused on the reverend's flowing black robe and gold cross. Out of the corner of her eye, she saw several women stealing surreptitious glances at her. A few even smiled and dipped their heads in approval. Josie wanted to sink lower in the pew. Instead, she held herself erect and ignored the hard wood pressing on her bottom.

At the end of the sermon, when Josie thought it safe to relax, her eyes opened with a start as Reverend Potter closed his Bible, smiled, and looked straight at her. Silence descended in the church.

She froze and stared at the carved cross behind him. Josie didn't have to imagine all eyes focused on her. She knew everyone in the church stared at her, along with the reverend. She could feel their eyes boring into her as if their glances physically touched her.

"And so, my congregation, as we come to the end of

another worship service, I want to take the time for this announcement of glad tidings.'' His beefy face softened and he beamed at Josie.

Lottie jabbed her elbow into her side. The smile on her sister's face couldn't have been any wider. Josie felt one inch tall. Her mouth felt like cotton. She prayed she didn't look like an elk caught in some hunter's sights.

''It has come to my attention that congratulations are in order for our Miss Josephine Douglass. I want to be the first to proclaim my felicitations on your impending nuptials.'' Reverend Potter spread his arms out in a sweeping gesture, looking as if he were trying to wrap the whole congregation in his embrace. ''For those of you who do not know, a wedding is forthcoming. Miss Douglass, the congregation will keep your good fortune in their collective heart.''

Murmurs of assent rippled through the church.

Josie forced a smile on her lips. It took every ounce of strength to hold the smile in place. Her hopes of her ''engagement'' being forgotten as yesterday's news were dashed. With one sentence Reverend Potter not only had endorsed her engagement, but had made sure all knew of the event. Her self-dug hole had just become a bottomless pit.

All chances of undoing her impulsive words were now gone.

Reverend Potter brought his hand down upon the pulpit and switched from discussing weddings to pontificating upon the lack of stewardship and giving on the part of the congregation.

A rush of air escaped her lungs. She was safe for now. Every person in her line of vision had jerked their heads forward and were staring at the Reverend.

''. . . and so my good wife and I will expect to see all of you at the church social and fund-raiser in two weeks. The good Lord's work cannot be done by slackers and empty coffers. Amen.'' Reverend Potter's arms shot up in the air as he drove home his parting words before leading the closing hymn.

She relaxed, enjoying the momentarily lack of attention. Josie sent up a prayer that the reverend's crusade for funds would override the citizens' curiosity about her engagement.

All hopes of that were dashed before Josie exited the church. Women and a few young girls all crowded around Josie, blocking her path, firing questions.

"Where is this fiancé?" Mrs. Kimball, an elderly matron all bedecked in black silk, asked.

"What does he look like?" Mrs. Garvey added.

"Why'd he ask you?" Daisy Fredericks asked, her brown eyes crinkling in avid curiosity.

"How come he's not here with you?"

"What does your father think of your fiancé?" The elegant and rich Mrs. Parker asked, while pointing her hand-embroidered silk fan at Josie.

Josie felt disoriented. Never before had she had such a string of questions aimed at her. She looked at each face, some curious, some doubtful, and some happy, and felt panic as she'd never felt before. She had no idea what to say to these information-hungry women.

Just as she opened her mouth to attempt to answer one question, she saw Grace forcing her tall figure through the throng.

"Excuse me, coming through." When Grace had reached Josie, she put her arm around her shoulders and faced the women. "Josie will answer your questions later. Right now I imagine she's still a little overwhelmed by your kind wishes. I believe fresh air is in order."

"Thanks," Josie whispered as they moved toward the door. Lottie followed behind.

Most of the remaining women stepped aside for Josie and Grace. They whispered to one another as Josie passed.

Grace lowered her voice. "I should have guessed the reverend would make such an announcement. I almost considered telling you to stay home from church today."

"I couldn't do that. I told Mrs. Potter we'd be here."

Josie acknowledged a well-wisher with a smile and nod of her head.

"What do you mean, we'd be here? Do you mean Jack and you? Has he returned?"

"Yes and no."

They burst out into the open and Josie immediately felt better. She no longer felt as if she were being squashed, nor was she being compelled to make up any answers. From now on she wanted to stick to the truth.

Grace stopped on the church lawn, folded her arms, and stared at Josie. "What do you mean yes and no? Jack has either returned or he hasn't."

"He's not back yet, but I have an idea he'll be here soon." Josie shut her eyes and imagined the usual smile on Jack's face being replaced by an angry scowl when he'd heard her news. She didn't want to see his bright blue eyes darkened with scorn.

"Jos? Don't look so sad. I didn't mean to be so harsh. It's just that this situation is snowballing out of control. I'm trying to help." Grace touched Josie's arm and smiled. "You do have to admit it is one heck of a situation."

Grace's support gratified Josie. She knew her friend would stand by her no matter what. A ghost of a smile crossed her face. "I guess I really did it this time."

"True." Grace searched Josie's face, looking for encouragement. "Do you think there's any chance he will actually want to marry you?"

"You make it sound like that would be an awful thing, to be married to me."

"Oh, no. That's not what I meant at all." Grace gave Josie a comforting squeeze on her hand. "I meant, do you think he wants to marry?"

"I don't know. I just don't know what he'll think." Josie suddenly wanted to go home and be gone from all these prying eyes. Moisture beaded in her eyes and she hurriedly wiped it away before the tears could fall.

"As soon as you talk to him, let me know. Then we can plan what you can say to the townsfolk. I need to go find my husband now." Grace embraced Josie before leaving.

"I will. Time to go home, Lottie. And quickly," she added at a much lower volume. Josie wanted to make her getaway before the curious women surrounded her once more.

Her sister skipped up to her and fell in step beside her. "Everyone sure's happy about your marriage."

Josie's eyes flicked downward, noting how clean Lottie's dress had managed to stay when most of the other girls had dirt smudges on their hems. "So it seems. But let's not think about that just now. Let's just walk home and think about the words of the sermon."

Lottie's blond brows drew together, and she looked at her sister as if she'd just sprouted horns. "If you say so, but I can't recall when we last did that."

The words of the sermon were miles from Josie's mind. Jack would return soon to see his horse and her father would also return from his sapphire searching. The two most important people who needed to hear her information would be the hardest to break it to.

She needed to think and plan her words carefully.

"Miz Josie!" a small boy said as he skipped up.

"What is it, little Tom?" Josie looked at the youngest son of the Samuelses and smiled. His once-spanking-white starched shirt was covered with dirt. There were even grass stains on the elbows. She wondered if his mother would make him clean the garment as punishment for soiling it.

"Pa wants you t' bring over the bull first thing t'morrow mornin'."

"So soon?"

Little Tom shook his head so vigorously that his white-blond hair fell in all directions. "Yeah, he needs 'im. Bye." He skipped off as soon as he finished his last sentence.

"Mr. Samuels isn't wasting much time," Josie mumbled to her sister.

"Nope. Sometimes men get so set on one thing that

they can't think about anything else," Lottie said.

Josie stopped in mid-stride. "Where on earth did you hear such a thing?"

Lottie glanced up, her creamy cheeks turning a dull red. "Uh, Mary Jane and I heard her mother talkin'."

"You shouldn't listen in on other people's conversations." Although Josie had to agree with the statement, if her father's obsession with sapphires was any example.

Sometimes it just made Josie want to scream at their father. To shout some sense into him. But she never would. No matter how mad he made her, he was still her father and she loved him with all her heart. Josie hoped he wouldn't be angry when she told him what she'd done.

The next morning Josie strapped on an old gingham sunbonnet and wrapped a fringed shawl around her shoulders. The sunny day was deceiving. There was a bit of a nip in the air.

She hadn't found the appropriate words for her upcoming encounter with Jack. All day yesterday she'd thought and thought but had come up with nothing suitable. If she was lucky, she'd have a few more days to think.

"Lottie, while I'm gone would you please get the eggs from the hens and bring up the jars of seeds from the root cellar?"

"I'd rather sew. The fair is approaching."

Josie shot her a glance that left no room for argument. "Those chores need to be done."

"Oh, all right. But don't make me plant the seeds all by myself."

"I won't. As soon as I get this bull over to the Samuelses, I'll be right back to help you."

"Why doesn't Mr. Samuels come get it himself?" Lottie raised a jam-covered biscuit to her mouth.

"He says he's afraid to handle the bull. He just wants it left out in his pasture to"—Josie broke off, she wasn't sure how to put it—"to make baby bulls."

Lottie squealed. "Jos!"

"Well, it's the truth. Be a good girl. I'll be back soon."

Lottie sat finishing her biscuit and listened to her sister's voice as Josie coaxed the stubborn bull along.

Although Lottie loved her sister, sometimes Josie could be all work and no fun. No wonder Mary Jane had said she was almost a spinster. Work seemed to be the only thing that mattered to Josie.

Except now. Jack's proposal had changed that. Maybe now that her sister was to be married, Josie would become more fun.

Since her sister was to be married, she'd also need to start paying more attention to her looks. Why, Josie still wore her hair in a single braid. Not stylish at all. It would look much prettier in a softer, more feminine style. She'd have to experiment, try different styles on her sister's hair. Josie should look her best for her husband-to-be. Everyone knew husbands liked pretty wives, even she did, and she was only twelve.

"I've got it!" She leapt up from the chair and ran to Josie's room. There, next to her sister's bed, was a treasured copy of *Godey's Lady's Book*.

Reverently, Lottie picked up the magazine and opened it. "Somewhere in here there's got to be a hairstyle that's perfect for Jos." Lottie stretched out on Josie's bed as she perused the pages.

She turned the pages, completely ignoring the passing time. The pictures of beautiful women in stylish clothing enthralled her.

Just as Lottie prepared to flip a page, she heard a horrible wail come from the direction of their back pasture. Heart pounding, she jumped up, ran to the rear of the house, and peered out the kitchen door.

The ragged crying continued.

Lottie scanned the field. Then she saw it. One of their cows that was due to calf stood under a shrub, emitting the horrible sounds.

Picking up the bottom of her dress, Lottie ran over. As she neared, the cow looked at her with pain-hazed eyes.

"Oh, oh, oh." Lottie stood there, wringing her hands, not sure what she should do. Her sister usually handled these problems.

The cow lurched and stumbled to her knees. She cried out as her several-hundred-pound frame hit the earth. Lottie could swear she felt the ground tremble beneath her feet.

"Just stay right there, I'll go get my sister." The cow's cries brought tears to Lottie's eyes. Blindly, she ran to the house.

Before she reached the door, she collided with a solid form of a man.

"Aahh!"

"Easy now, little one. What's the problem?" Jack said awkwardly. The last thing Jack had expected when he came to visit his stallion, and also Josie, was to find an upset young woman.

"Th-the c-cow, B-Belle. She—she's in pain." Lottie wiped her cheeks, brushing the tears away.

"What's wrong? Can you tell me?" Jack bent down, putting him closer to Lottie's eye level. "I've got some experience in dealing with injured animals."

"Y-you do?" Lottie blinked up at him and kept hold of his arms. Her fingernails pressed into his skin.

"Yes. Ever since I was a young man about your age, I've been taking care of animals. You could call it an interest of mine." He straightened and took her hand. "Now show me where this cow is."

"She's in the back." Lottie tugged at his arm, pulling him toward the pasture.

Her hand clutching his so tight was a new sensation for Jack. Her gesture seemed to have so much trust and hope in it. He found he liked it.

He parted his lips to say something, then shut them as a cry of pain reached him. "I can hear her. Let's hurry."

Shortly, they arrived at the cow's side.

Jack dropped to his knees. He felt the swollen belly. His lips pulled into a thin line. "Something's not right."

"C-can you help Belle?" Lottie looked pleadingly at Jack. "We need her baby to live."

In one swift motion Jack rose. "I'll try. Where's your sister?"

"She took a bull to Mr. Samuels. She should be home soon."

"She did what? Never mind. Come on. I need to get some supplies up at the house." A petite young woman should not be walking around with a bull, Jack thought with just a bit of righteousness tinged with concern.

"What are you gonna do?" Lottie ran to keep up with him.

"I'm going to try and pull the calf out."

"Pull it out?"

"Yes. It's the only way to save either of them." Jack had pulled a calf only a few times. He didn't look forward to the job ahead. It would be hard, sweaty, and sticky. But none of that mattered if he could save both animals' lives.

"Please. Please save them," Lottie begged.

Jack looked into her innocent, honest blue eyes and found his heart softening further. "I'll try. I'll try my best."

"Lottie, did you hear that horrible noise?" Josie burst out of the house and stopped in her tracks when she spotted Jack. All color drained from her face.

"Oh," Lottie wailed, "I'm so glad you're home. Belle is in pain and Jack is gonna pull out her calf."

Josie and Jack's eyes met.

"Is that true?" Josie asked.

"Yes." Jack stared at her. He didn't like the sudden pallor to her skin.

"Then I'm going to help you," she announced.

❖ 8 ❖

Josie reached out for the door frame for support. She didn't quite know what to make of Jack's expression. It wavered between disbelief and admiration. But never mind that, Belle needed help.

"Are you sure you want to help me?" Jack asked, shifting his weight and looking uncomfortable with her proclamation.

"Yes. She's our cow. I can't let either her or the baby die." Josie didn't care that she was being anything but docile and ladylike. She'd ruined that chance with only a few words three days earlier.

"I know what I'm doing." Jack refused to break eye contact with her. "I won't let either of them die."

"Good. Now, what do we need?" Josie's anxiety grew. Each second that marched by could mean the difference between life and death for both animals. She couldn't afford another dead calf.

"Rope, water, and soap. And some iodine." Jack turned and strode out the door.

"Lottie, get the iodine out of the medicine bag and I'll grab a rope and the soap and water."

Josie sprang into action. She ran to the barn, grabbed a length of coiled hemp, and sprinted after Jack.

Belle's bawling reached her ears before she even had a chance to slip under the fence. Josie skidded to a stop in alarm. Cattle usually never made noises when they were birthing. The pitiful cries tore at her heart. The expectant mother must be in terrible pain.

Picking up her skirt with one hand, she darted to her cow, trying not to spill the bucket of water.

"Here's the soap and water." Josie set the sloshing bucket down next to Jack. Lowering her shoulder, she let the coil of rope fall to the ground.

"Great. From the looks of things, it appears that the calf is either too big or turned the wrong way. I need to go in and feel." Jack stripped off his shirt and tossed the tan garment to the ground.

"Go in and feel?"

"Yes. I need to stick my hand in her birth canal. I might have to go in all the way up to my shoulder."

Josie's face turned several shades of red as she stood there, digesting Jack's words. She was too shocked to put her hands over Lottie's ears, who'd arrived and stood next to her, gaping.

Jack glanced up, noted the women's expressions, and immediately blushed himself. "I—I mean I need to feel what position the calf is in."

"Oh," Josie managed to say in a tiny voice. She knew they were only talking about her cow, whose life was at stake, but the words Jack used so freely! They shocked her to the core. She wished desperately for a wide-brimmed bonnet to hide her burning face from his. To top it off, he was practically naked in front of her, with only his trousers on!

"The soap. I need the soap." Jack held out his hand, palm up, fingers spread.

"Here, here it is." Josie thrust a square bar of home-made honeysuckle soap in his outstretched hand.

"Is—is she gonna make it?" Lottie asked. She sat on the grass by the cow's head, stroking behind the animal's cream-colored ears.

"I'll do my best," Jack said, working up a thick lather on his left arm. Once he'd gotten it completely white with lather, he knelt down next to the cow.

"Is this going to hurt her?"

"No, it shouldn't. I doubt she'll even feel me." Jack closed his eyes as he inserted his arm. With his free right arm he palpated along the cow's belly, trying to gauge the position of the calf.

"Well?" Josie had to know what he'd found.

Jack didn't answer. He stared in concentration down at the cow. His sharp gasp of breath alarmed her. "What? What's wrong?"

"Contraction. She just wants this baby out. I thought my arm was going to be crushed." Slowly, Jack inched backward and withdrew his arm. He sank down onto his heels. His grim expression reflected the seriousness of his words.

"It's as I thought. The calf's too big to make it out on its own. We're going to have to pull him before he dies. If it's not already too late."

"Too late!" Lottie jumped up and ran around to join the adults. Tears shone in her blue eyes. "It can't be! I thought you said you'd save Belle's baby!"

"Shh, Lottie. We'll make sure both mother and baby will be fine. Now, go back to her head and continue stroking Belle's ears like you were." Josie's words sounded more sure than she felt at the moment. If Belle had been in labor a long time, the chances of having a breathing baby were slim.

Her spirits sank. She'd been hoping to get a winning calf from this cow. Now it looked like they could lose both.

"I need the rope. I'll tie it around the front legs and

then pull.'' Jack moved quickly, securing the rope around the calf's legs.

"Now what?'' Josie asked, intrigued by Jack's skill and knowledge. No one she knew had ever done such a thing before.

"Now I brace both my feet, hope she can still push, and I pull as hard as I can.''

Jack braced his feet, strained backward, and gritted his teeth. He grunted. He pulled. Sweat beads dotted his brow and upper lip. Veins stood out in his neck.

"Calf's—not—budging,'' he ground out between clenched teeth.

"Come on, mama, push, please. We can't lose you now,'' Josie pleaded with the exhausted cow. "Try again, Jack, please.''

"Here goes.'' Putting all his weight onto the rope, Jack pulled and strained.

"I see it coming!'' Josie pointed to the now-visible knees and upper legs. "Pull harder.''

With one final grunt Jack gave a mighty heave and quickly fell onto his rear as the rope slackened.

A wet, sticky calf slid to the ground, landing on Jack's lower legs.

"Oh! He's out. Is he alive?'' Josie stared in wonder at the new calf before her. She dared not get her hopes up too high, in case the calf was dead.

It was a huge bull calf with long, gawky legs. A black broom of a tail curled against his side.

"Rub the afterbirth off and cut the navel cord,'' Jack said between heavy, gasping breaths. "Let's see if we can get him breathing.''

Josie picked up his shirt without thinking and rubbed the newborn vigorously. Nimbly she cut the cord and dabbed the end with iodine to ward off infection.

Seconds later the bull calf emitted a robust cry. His mother raised her head and answered back. Josie felt tears stinging at the corners of her eyes. They'd done it. They had saved his life.

"He's alive! He made it.'' Lottie left her position at

the cow's head and ran around to look at the newest arrival. "He's sure pretty. And big. Can I hug him?"

"Better let him stand up and find the milk first," Jack said, wiping the sweat from his eyes. His chest rose and fell from his exertions.

"Here you go, big guy." Josie lightly grasped the calf's head and guided it toward the milk source. At first the newborn's legs wobbled and almost buckled, then he took a few hesitant steps, bawling for milk.

Then, with a lusty suck he latched on to the nipple and took his first nourishing taste of milk. His mother turned her head and regarded her baby with affection.

A stream of tears streaked Lottie's cheeks. She took the edge of her white apron and dabbed at her face. "Can I hug him now? I don't care if he is all slimy."

"Sure," Jack answered. "Hug him all you want. I was worried that I wouldn't be able to save him. A live, healthy calf is something to be proud of."

Josie, too, thought she might cry, but she didn't want to do so in front of Jack. Instead, she bit down on her lower lip and watched mother and baby.

"We should probably leave them alone. The danger's over." Jack crossed to Josie and touched her wrist with his hand.

The light, innocent gesture took Josie totally off guard. Her breath quickened as her senses focused on the small area of the hand he touched. She wondered if he felt the effect too. She sure hoped so.

"Um, yes, yes, you're right. Come away, Lottie. Let's give the new mother some time alone with her baby. You can come out here later and look at him," Josie said, knowing the time to confess the engagement drew nearer but dreading it just the same. How did one go about informing a man he was now engaged to her? she wondered.

"Your sister's right." Jack moved to rinse his arm off.

"I knew you could do it. I knew not just any man would propose to my sister. You'll make her a neat husband and me a neat brother." Lottie beamed at Jack.

Jack froze. The lather on his arm slid down, momentarily forgotten. Sunshine created rainbows in three large suds on his wrist. In a low, quiet voice he asked, "What did you just say?"

❖ 9 ❖

"Husband. Since you asked my sister to marry you, that's what you'll be. I'm so glad you'll be my new brother."

Above Lottie's head, Jack's gaze trapped Josie. The panic she felt at the church yesterday was nothing compared to how she felt now. Sweat slithered down between her breasts. Her heart pounded like a war drum. Her stomach felt queasy. She hadn't meant him to find out like this.

"I *proposed* to your sister?"

The innuendo of his words was lost on Lottie, but not so with Josie. His blue eyes had darkened to the color of storm clouds and his face set in harsh lines.

"Uh-huh. She told Aunt—"

"Lottie, that's enough for now. You must be over-wrought about the birthing. Why don't you go on up to the house and sew?" She had to get her sister away. She wanted no witnesses to the upcoming scene.

Lottie let go of Jack and backed away. "No, I'm not upset. But I'll leave. I guess you want time alone. Maybe you two wanna smooch." Lottie winked at Josie.

Josie bit the inside of her cheek. Kissing was probably the furthest thing from Jack's mind just then. He stood there, deadly quiet and still, like a tempest ready to burst.

"I'll go now and leave you alone." Lottie ran off toward the house.

That left her alone with Jack, an angry Jack if his rigid posture was any indication. Perhaps she should try to humor him. Laughter helped in these situations. Or did it? What would she know of these situations anyway?

"Um, Jack, I have to tell you something. In a way it's sort of funny." Her attempt to laugh came out a croak instead.

Jack crossed his arms, fists balled, and continued to stare at her stonily. "I think I've an idea of what you're going to say. But go on, I want to hear this in your own words."

Josie knew it was inappropriate, but she couldn't help staring at his naked chest. It was right in front of her, at eye level, and it gave her something to think about instead of the anger in his eyes.

Sweat glistened on his skin, making it slick. Muscles rippled along his back and shoulders as he shifted position and tensed. His darkened nipples stood out in contrast to his winter-pale skin. No doubt his skin would turn golden as he spent more time outdoors.

"Well? Are you going to say anything?" he prompted.

Swallowing, Josie struggled to find the right words. "Ah, sometimes I can be sort of impulsive and say things without thinking. And this was one of those times. That's all."

"That's all?" Jack's words lashed out like a whip. He stalked over and snatched his bloodstained shirt, wiping the dried lather on his arm. He stared at her, as if willing her to deny the words she'd spoken.

She took a step backward. His sudden fury frightened her. Suppose he turned on her? She had to regain control.

"See, it's like this. The reverend's wife saw you leaving the other morning and she accused me of''—Josie dropped her gaze to the ground, she knew her face was reddening, she could tell by the heat in her cheeks—"of being a loose woman and I, well, Lottie told you what I said."

Jack flung his soiled shirt on the ground and spun to stare at her. "Dammit, how could you have said something like that? That I asked you to marry me? I thought you were different."

"I—I didn't mean to." He was angrier than she thought. A part of her heart crumbled, the part that had hoped he would welcome a marriage to her. Now she knew that would probably never happen. Tears threatened to spill down her cheeks. She was damned if she'd let him see her cry.

"Didn't mean to? It doesn't sound impulsive to me, it sounds so—so . . . calculating. It's something a domineering, scheming woman would do. And I've had my share of those types of women." Jack kicked at a clod of dirt and sent it flying.

Josie hung her head, quickly wiping her eyes with the back of her hand. She refused to let him see her cry. She hadn't planned on this being so painful, or that he would flat out reject her.

She forced herself to remain focused on the conversation. Time enough later for misery. "Well, if you hadn't left me that morning, I wouldn't be in this situation, and neither would you."

His head snapped up. "If I hadn't left you? Explain."

Was he so dense that he couldn't figure it out? "You left me standing on the porch when the reverend's wife pulled up for her visit. If you'd just had the courtesy to stay and say hello to the woman. She knew my father wasn't home. So she jumped to conclusions and assumed that we, that we . . ."

"That we what? Had relations? That I compromised you?"

"Yes! See? Now do you understand?"

He spun around, placing his back to her and uttered a guttural sigh. "How in the hell was I supposed to know who the woman was and that she would have such an idea?"

Josie stood her ground. "You still shouldn't have left me in such a predicament."

He turned back around and snorted. "That's water already under the bridge. I thought you were different. I really liked you. You were so different from . . ." He let his voice trail off, and his eyes stared past her, at the distant mountains.

His words gave her pause. She looked up at him and was surprised to see his face had softened, not much, but it had. His jaw was no longer clenched with tension. "I am sorry. I'll understand if you want me to tell everyone the engagement is off," she said.

He didn't meet her eyes. "That should be simple enough if only your sister and the reverend's wife know."

Josie's hands shook. She had to continue. "Actually, a few more people know about it."

"A few more? How many is that?" The iron edge returned to his voice.

In the brief interval before she answered, Josie heard the newborn suckling and the grass crunch under the cows' hooves. All normal, contented sounds. She wished her world were normal too.

"The whole town," she mumbled quickly, hoping he wouldn't catch the words.

He had. His arms dropped to his sides. "Did you say the whole town?" At her nod, he continued. "Jeez, Josie, couldn't you have kept this to yourself until you'd discussed the situation with me?"

"I never meant this to happen. It just did." Josie hated this conversation. She wanted it finished.

Jack slapped his hand to his forehead and paced. "You'll just have to tell them that our plans changed, that's all."

"I will?" The tiny hope she still harbored in her heart

sputtered and died. He'd said no. He was supposed to play the gallant gentleman and agree to the engagement. She had too much to lose.

"Well, hell's bells," Jack said. "I really should go."

A cool breeze kicked up. Jack shivered. He looked down at his dirty, stained shirt on the ground. "Do you think I could borrow one of your father's shirts so I don't catch a chill riding back to the hotel?"

"Sure. Come on up to the house." She spun and walked away. She didn't want him to see the disappointment etched on her face. How could she save her sister now if Jack refused to cooperate and marry her?

"It'll take me a long time to get all the stains out of it," he said, looking at the shirt.

Before she realized what she was doing, Josie opened her mouth. "Leave it here. I'm pretty good about getting stains out. I'll wash your shirt."

"You would? This isn't another type of trick, is it?" Jack stopped and stared at her. The shadows had returned to his eyes.

"No, it's not. Washing your shirt is the least I can do after all the trouble I've caused. I'll understand if you want nothing more to do with me." Josie spoke those words honestly. She'd been the one to make the horrible error and she would be the one to correct it, even if it meant that her dream would never come true.

Jack had done a more important job than he knew when he helped save their calf and cow. "I won't forgot your assistance today. If that bull calf had died, any hope of building up our cattle herds with new blood would be dead also."

"Guess it was a good cause I sacrificed my shirt to. I don't mind that. I hate seeing prize livestock go to waste." He bent over and picked up the shirt that he'd tossed earlier.

His comment gave Josie hope. She would discuss anything as long as it wasn't the ruined so-called engagement. "Do you do this often? Help animals?"

"When I can." Jack finished rinsing his arm off and threw out the dirty water.

Josie clutched the empty bucket as they walked through the pasture up to the house. A tense silence surrounded them. It was as if their joint effort to save cow and calf had somehow brought about an unspoken truce.

They walked on until they arrived at the back door. Jack reached out and held it open for her.

"Why, thank you." All couldn't be lost if Jack was still acting chivalrous toward her. The bud of hope in her heart opened again.

Lottie appeared instantly in the kitchen. "I can't wait to tell my friend Mary Jane what we did this morning." Turning her attention to Jack, she said, "She's my best friend, you know."

"No, I didn't. But I'll remember that."

"You will?" Lottie stared at him. "Really?"

"Yes, really." A slow red stain crept up his neck as Lottie continued to gaze adoringly at him.

"Lottie, please don't stare. It's not polite." Josie knew her little sister was infatuated with Jack, and she could hardly blame her. But she was thankful for Lottie's interruption. She needed more time to think, to see if she could salvage the mess she'd made with Jack.

She tried hard not to let her own curious eyes roam over toward Jack and stare at his uncovered upper body. But she couldn't help notice the chill in the air had caused his nipples to stand erect. Immediately she tore her glance away.

"Here, come and sit down. I'll go get you a drink of water." Lottie moved to fetch a glass and a pitcher of water.

"Thanks. I won't stay long. I've got to leave after I get cleaned up and put on a fresh shirt." Jack followed Josie to the sitting room.

Josie hastily left Jack's tempting body and retreated to her father's room. She hadn't missed his last comment.

Once she slipped through the door, she slumped down onto the bed. She kept picturing Jack's glistening body straining and struggling to bring a new life into the world. Her thoughts, however, dwelled on the glorious muscles rippling, the smooth stomach, and the smattering of chest hair.

She sighed and fell back against the mattress. What would his chest feel like if she were to touch it? Stroke it?

Surely it was sinful to think of such things. She had no right to look at him the way a wife would. Better to busy herself selecting a shirt for him to wear than moon over what was now probably lost to her. Sitting up, she stared at the shirts hanging from pegs.

Josie chose a lightweight red flannel. The deep color should look good on Jack, she thought, and the material would keep him warm.

She scurried back to the sitting room.

"I found a shirt for you," she said, waving the red garment in front of her.

Jack set down his glass of water and stared at Josie. "You look a mess also. Both of you. You two should change." He pointed to the front of Josie's dress and to Lottie's apron.

"I'll get to that soon enough." Actually Josie had been considering leaving her soiled dress on until she finished mucking out the horses' stalls. It wasn't as if she needed to look her best anymore. Jack had made it clear he no longer wanted to be near her. The only reason Jack hadn't stormed off sooner was that he needed a clean shirt, not because he desired her company.

But now she took a good look at herself. A *mess* wasn't quite strong enough a word.

Blood and fluid stained the whole front of the dress, and her once-white sleeves were now a mixture of colors. She looked frightful. She chuckled. "I guess I do look pretty bad. Even you, Lottie, you've got stains on your apron."

"Aw, it was an old one anyway. I had it on for my chores. But I can go put a fresh one on for you, Jack," Lottie said, trying to bat her eyes flirtatiously.

Jack smiled at her, and then all traces of joy vanished when he looked at Josie. "No need to hurry and change on my account. I'm leaving."

"Hand me your dirty shirt so I can wash it." Josie extended her arm.

Jack rose to leave. Just as he turned toward the door, it crashed open and a bearded man barged in. Jack froze in surprise.

The wild-looking man ran right at him, bellowing, with fists swinging. The stranger collided with Jack, knocking him flat on his back. Stunned, Jack saw a work-roughened fist draw back and fly at his jaw. The last thing he heard was Josie's voice before the fist connected with his jaw, sending his head crashing against the wooden floor slats.

"Father! What're you doing?" cried Josie.

❖ *10* ❖

"LOOKS LIKE I made it home in the nick of time," Hunter Douglass said.

"Father! How could you?" Josie clapped her hand to her mouth and stared in shock at the scene in front of her. Her round eyes were glued to Jack's fallen body on the floor. She pressed her fist into her teeth. How could this have happened?

"Josie girl, you're upset, an' I don't blame ya. But can't ya see, honey, I came home just in the nick of time. This brute here, he might have killed you."

Lottie's high-pitched cries penetrated Jack's groaning. "Papa! You hurt Jack! Josie's husband m-might be dead. Y-you could've cracked open his skull. What if his brain is leaking out on the floor?" Lottie wrung her hands, her face contorting in anguish.

Hunter bent down and stared at the unconscious man and back up at his daughters. Disbelief flickered across his craggy face. "Did I hear you say he was Josie's husband, Lottie?"

She nodded. Her blond curls bounced. "Uh-huh. Well, sorta. He's gonna be."

Slowly, Hunter eased to his feet. "Josie, suppose you tell me what this is all about." He looked down at the immobile man, obviously still not convinced he wasn't an intruder intent on evil deeds.

Josie didn't know where to begin. Her situation seemed to be going from bad to worse, all in the space of a day.

These were hardly ideal conditions for her father and Jack to meet for the first time. Even if Jack had refused to acknowledge the engagement, Lottie wasn't aware of that, and Josie needed to spare her sister from the knowledge for at least a little while longer.

"He helped Belle deliver her calf. That's why we all look so, so . . ." She swept her hand down the front of her stained skirt. That about wrapped things up succinctly enough, Josie thought. Except for the minor detail about an engagement gone wrong.

Hunter scratched at his thick black beard peppered with silver. His blue-eyed gaze went from his elder daughter to the man flat out on the floor. Hurt and doubt lingered in his expression. "How long was I gone?"

Josie's mouth opened. Her brow furrowed. "I don't understand."

"How in the hell could I have been gone so long that you would up an' take a husband without my approval?" Hunter grabbed the tin water pitcher and took a long swallow.

"He's not my husband exactly. Lottie has things mixed up. I'm only engaged, that's all. Nothing to worry about." Ha! She couldn't stop her fibs now if she had to. She was even lying to her own father just so she'd spare herself the humiliation of letting Lottie know how Jack had rejected her.

"But what about Jack?" Lottie sat on the floor next

to Jack's prone body. Her hands clasped and unclasped while her lower lip quivered.

"He'll come around soon enough," Hunter said.

Josie's heart constricted when she looked at Jack lying helplessly on the floor. "Father, how could you?"

Sometimes her father's impulsiveness really irritated her. Like right now. What made it even worse was knowing she could be just as impulsive as him.

"Aw, honey, I'm sorry. But look at things from my point. Here I am, comin' home after huntin' for sapphires for weeks. Along the trail I hear horror stories about children being attacked by desperate men. And what do I see when I step into my own house?" He stopped and glanced up at Josie, begging her with his eyes to understand him.

"What did you see?" She knew what he saw. She also wished he'd stop his habit of banging open the door when he returned. No wonder Jack had jumped away from her.

"I saw my two girls covered with blood, and a strange man, without a shirt on, stretching his hand out with what looked like a bloody rag in it. So I did the only thing a decent father would do. I protected my babies. Knocked the varmint out." Hunter nodded his head and folded his arms, certain he'd done the right thing.

"I do wish you'd asked questions first." Josie knelt down beside Jack's head and grimaced as he moaned. With a light touch she pressed her fingers to his head, feeling for stickiness. Her eyes closed and she drew in a steadying breath as her fingers slipped though his silky, soft hair.

"Sometimes a man can't ask questions first. For all I knew, he could have had a gun in his hand. Then what would I've done if he shot one of my babies?"

"He wasn't going to shoot us. He was only reaching out for a shirt to wear. He could have taken a chill." Josie laid the back of her hand on Jack's forehead. "He doesn't feel hot. Lottie, fetch a wet towel and let's try to revive him."

"Sorry about this. But you know I did it only out of

love,'' Hunter said sheepishly at Josie, averting his eyes from the fallen man.

''I know.'' Josie's anger faded as she saw how sorry her father looked. She supposed love could make him act first and question later.

Lottie scampered back from the kitchen brandishing a dripping towel. ''Here's the cloth. I hope he's not hurt too bad. Papa, did I tell you I helped with the calf?''

''No, darlin', you didn't.'' A look of pure, unabashed love wreathed Hunter's weathered face in softness. He reached out and wrapped his big arms around his younger daughter.

Josie held the wet towel and averted her eyes. Her father rarely looked that kind and loving around her anymore. She would like a loving hug too, every once in a while. Sometimes Josie thought her father took her for granted. And it hurt her to the core. She clutched the towel harder, holding back the emotions fighting to rise to the surface.

''I think he's going to be fine. Jack just had the wind knocked out of him,'' Josie said, keeping her attention on the man in front of her. She gently dabbed the blood from his lips.

Jack's ribs rose and fell in a steady rhythm. He stirred and blinked his eyes open. ''What the hell happened?''

Josie was less then ten inches from his face. She felt his warm breath caress her cheeks and smiled. She liked being this close to him, and after today she might not have another chance. ''There was a misunderstanding.''

''Misunderstanding? There seems to be a lot of those around here. Hell, I feel like I've been kicked by a full-grown steer.'' Jack braced his arms behind him and pushed up into a sitting position.

''Father, help him to the sofa. Maybe he should rest.'' Josie didn't like the way Jack's eyes seemed to be having trouble focusing.

''Move aside, honey. I'll help him up.'' Hunter bent down and reached to aid Jack.

The second Hunter's hands landed on his body, Jack recoiled.

"Easy, I'm not gonna hurt you anymore. Now that I know you aren't some stranger bent on hurtin' my daughters. I hear you want to marry my Josie."

"Father? *You* are their father? I'd hate to meet any of your enemies," Jack said, attempting humor, but failing as he groaned instead.

"Indeedy, I am. The one and only Hunter Douglass." Slowly, he maneuvered Jack to the sofa. "What's this about a weddin'? Don't you know it's not right not to ask the father's permission?"

"Father, please. He could be in pain." Again Josie lamented the timing of her father's return. Couldn't he have waited until she and Jack had decided how to tell the town the engagement was off? She prayed Jack wouldn't denounce her in front of her own father.

"Could I put on that shirt you were going to let me borrow?" Jack asked, glancing down at his exposed chest.

"Of course. Father, I was going to lend him one of your shirts until he returned to his room at the hotel. Is that all right?"

"Yep, sure, fine. But how do know so much about him? What makes you think I'll let you marry him?"

Lottie chimed in. "He's keeping a horse here."

"So that's how that animal ended up in our extra stall. I thought for a minute there you girls had gone and purchased a horse without my approval. Like you seem to have gotten yourself engaged without my approval," Hunter said, eyeing Josie.

Practically everything has to be purchased without your approval, Josie thought, though she kept her comments to herself. "Slim recommended us to him. And I knew you would like the additional income. Can't we please talk about my, uh, engagement later?"

"You mean your weddin'. Don't see why we can't put it off indefinitely. Far as I'm concerned, there'll be no weddin'. I can't just let my daughter up and get engaged

without my permission, and so far I don't recall givin'
it. End of discussion." He turned to regard Jack, but
addressed his words to Josie. "Why'd Belle need help?"

"Her calf was too large, it was dying. So Jack happened to be here when Lottie heard Belle's cries and he
helped pull the calf out."

"Pull it out? You mean like pullin' out a splinter?"
Skepticism shone in Hunter's eyes. One side of his mouth
quirked back.

"Father, it was much more than that. He saved their
lives. That's why we all look so filthy. If you had just
asked before acting . . ."

"That's my girl, always watchin' out for our interests." To Jack he added, "You can see why I like to
keep her around."

Josie flushed at his last comment. She didn't like the
sound of her father's words, nor did she like the posses-
sive way he was acting toward her. Her father had practically flat out denied any possibility of an engagement,
not that there ever was an official one. But Josie had
hoped she could remedy that, and now it appeared like
she might never get the chance.

"I can move my horse if he's going to be a problem,"
Jack managed to say. Normal coloring had returned to
his face. He licked his lips and made a wry face as he
tasted the coppery blood.

"No, no. Leave the animal here, I'm not one to squab-
ble over more money. Josie's capable of takin' care of
it. Here now, lemme see that lip. Looks like you're gonna
have one hell of a fat lip. Sorry about that. But when you
become a father, you'll understand why I did it." Hunter
bent down and scrutinized his handiwork. "Not that I
think you should be the father of Josie's children," he
added.

"Actually, I'm feeling much better. If you'll just let
me up, I think I'd like to leave. I can see to my horse
later." Jack tried to rise from the sofa, but Josie stood
directly in his path.

"You're not going anywhere yet. You need to take it

easy.'' Josie stood, hands on hips, looking down at Jack. She knew her demure impression was long gone. Between her and her father, Jack would probably never want to marry her, not in a hundred years. Her only hope was if he'd addled his brain from his fall and couldn't remember all that had gone on previously. She doubted that, but it was worth a hope.

Jack's head throbbed from the bang on the floor. His lower lip ached. His whole body was sore from pulling the calf. All he wanted to do was to get away from these peculiar people. Especially Hunter Douglass. For an older man, he still had one hell of a swing. And Josie, she'd disappointed him. He had thought her nothing like his mother and sisters. But it seemed Josie was not the sweet little thing he'd thought her to be.

''You can't go! What if the new mama needs you?'' Lottie had sidled over to him and peeked at him from around Josie's body.

''The new mama won't need me. She can take care of everything from now on.'' Jack's heart softened, even though he tried not to let it. Lottie's honesty had a way of taking the edge off his anger.

The looks of concern on the sisters' faces were almost his undoing, especially Josie's worried expression. For as long as he could remember, he couldn't recall any time when his sisters had looked so worried about him, even when he'd broken his leg as a child. He could get used to people being concerned about him.

He cursed his soft heart. He should be planning his getaway. He shouldn't remain in the Douglass household one second longer. Hadn't he already discovered Josie wasn't for him? And hadn't he already told her he wouldn't go through with this sham of an engagement?

Then why could he still hear her accusing words ringing in his ears? Had he really been wrong to leave her when he good and well knew that a woman had pulled up the very same moment he was leaving?

Something nagged at the back of his mind. Guilt? Would the proper thing have been to stay and see that all went well? Hell, yes. He *knew* what the proper thing to do was, but he'd failed to do it. He should not have left Josie in such a vulnerable position. Hell's bells, what should he do now?

"Are—are you sure Belle won't need you?" Lottie sounded doubtful. Her eyes were still swollen and puffy from her tears.

"Yes, I'm sure," Jack said, rubbing his temples with his fingertips. "That mama cow will take care of her baby. You'll see."

"Ya know," Hunter interjected, "I think a swig of whiskey would help the poundin' that's probably in yer head. I'll go fetch it. I know I sure could a swig or two." He spun on his heel and disappeared into the kitchen.

Jack looked at Josie. "Does he always greet people that way?"

"Oh, no. But I must say, he does act without thinking sometimes. I'm so sorry he hit you. I hope you're all right." Josie cocked her head sideways, drawing her brows together as she studied him.

Jack squirmed and shifted his gaze. He felt very exposed lying on the sofa with his borrowed shirt hanging open, especially since he now felt guilty about his actions the other morning. He shoved the remaining buttons in their holes.

"I'll be fine. I see where you inherited your impulsiveness. Maybe I should see if Slim can keep my stallion at the livery. I don't want to risk another one of your father's fists."

"No! I mean, please, I'd like you to leave your horse here. Father said he was sorry, and now that he knows who you are"—Josie shrugged—"he wouldn't dare think of touching you again."

Jack groaned and stretched out his aching arm muscles. His swollen lip throbbed with each word he spoke. He really should get as far away from these people as possible. Moving his horse would be for the best. But he couldn't leave yet, not with this horrible feeling of guilt ballooning inside him. "What do you think, Lottie? Should I keep Zeus here?"

Lottie's head bobbed up and down. "Uh-huh. You should. I mean, your horse already likes it here, and you wanna see how Belle and her calf are doing. It wouldn't be nice to move him."

Jack raised his eyebrows. "Is that so?" He fought his urge to chuckle. Lottie certainly didn't mince words. He had to admit, the Douglasses were one of the oddest families he'd ever met. Maybe that was what kept him there.

No, what kept him there now was the desire to right the situation with Josie. He'd acted dishonorably toward her, and one lesson he'd always lived by was never to bring dishonor to a woman.

Heavy boot steps reverberated in dull thumps on the floor, heralding Hunter's return. "Here ya are, my boy. Good whiskey. I bought it on my way home from the riverbeds not too long ago."

Jack grinned. It was quite a change to go from intruding murderer to "my boy" in the space of less than an hour. "Thanks."

"Don't mention it. You wouldn't be in this mess if it wasn't for me. Like I keep sayin', I feel awful. Here." Hunter thrust out a clean shot glass.

"I guess we all did look pretty bad." Jack took the glass and poured himself a hefty drink. He tossed the contents down his throat. With any luck, his headache would soon be gone.

"Well now, since I'm home, why don't you girls update me on what's been happening." Hunter dropped into a chair and looked at his daughters. "Other than gettin' engaged behind my back, but I think I already took care of that bit of nonsense."

The topic of conversation piqued Jack's interest. He was about to leave, but decided he would stay and learn more about Josie. The information might prove helpful, then he could figure out how to do right by her. He leaned back into the sofa cushions.

"I've been working on my entry for the fair. I'm making a morning dress and a sampler. Do you want to see them?'' Lottie sat in the chair next to Hunter. Her hands gripped the armrests and she stared raptly at her father.

''Love to, pumpkin. But not now.'' He reached out and laid a bear-paw-sized hand on Lottie's arm. ''And you, Jos? How's the ranch been?''

Josie swallowed. Her gaze flicked from her father to Jack to the floor. ''I sold the bull you've been wanting me to sell. I got a good price for him. Of course, I had to deliver it. Mr. Samuels didn't want to touch it.''

Hunter laughed and slapped his knees. He threw back his head and filled the room with his full-bodied laughter. ''Samuels always was a mite squeamish. Don't see how he's made it this long out here on the frontier. What about the calves?''

''Well, today we got a big healthy bull calf.''

''And? When I left we had four cows due. What about the rest of them?''

''One of them died. It was born in the middle of the night, in the far corner of the pasture. There was nothing we could do. But the other three are fine.'' Josie glanced at Jack and noted his interest.

''Damn, I hate to lose any animals. But that's what happens every now and then.'' Hunter shook his head and stroked his full beard. ''Well, then. So other than that, I take it all has been fine?''

A short silence preceded Josie's words.

''Yes, Father, other than the lost calf, we've been doing all right.'' Josie folded her hands in her lap and smiled at her father. The perfect picture of feminine innocence.

Jack stared at her in curiosity. He wondered if she would admit to being the one to falsify their engagement. Reluctantly, he found himself admiring her courage. For someone who had managed to get herself in quite a muddle, she was putting up a brave front.

''Good. Good. That's what I like to hear. Now,'' Hunter said as he jumped to his feet and crossed over to his saddlebags, which had been dumped near the door.

"Now I'll show you what I've been doing."

Lottie squealed and leapt from her chair. "Did you bring me a present? Do I get a pretty necklace like Josie has? What did you bring me?"

"Slow down, pumpkin. Lemme look inside here." He unbuckled the pouch and extracted a small package wrapped in newspaper.

"Is it for me?" Lottie asked again, bouncing in excitement.

"Uh, I can leave now if you want me to." Jack wasn't sure if he should stay and watch a private family matter. He knew his family would strongly disapprove of an outsider witnessing a personal moment. Family business was exactly that to them. Family members only.

"No, don't be foolish. *I* love to show off efforts of my labors, and since I know there's nothing between you and my Josie, I know there's nothing to worry about," Hunter said.

The way Hunter said that brought Jack up into a more alert position. Somehow, he felt like he'd just been issued a challenge. This bothered Jack, but he knew it shouldn't. But if anyone was going to deny his intentions toward Josie, it would be him.

"Looky here, my girls." Hunter reached in and slowly opened his hand.

Cradled in his palm were a few blue stones, catching the light and winking it off the rough surfaces. Three sapphire stones, all a strong, brightish blue and about the size of peas, glowed.

Josie sucked in her breath.

"Are those all for me?" Lottie looked like she'd just been handed the pot of gold at the end of the rainbow.

"One of them, pumpkin. One of them. I thought I might have the other two taken to a jeweler in Helena or Bozeman and have them made into cuff links for me." Hunter stared down at the blue treasures in his palm, the representation of weeks of work, and grinned like a schoolboy.

"Did you say cuff links?" Josie made a strangling

sound and her lips flattened into a thin line.

"Sure did. Won't they be pretty?" Hunter picked one up, held it up to his sleeve, and admired his future cuff link.

"Wouldn't it be better to sell one or two?"

Hunter dropped the sapphire back into his palm and pressed his fist against his chest. "Sell 'em? What in tarnation for? These are mine. Found by my hard work. Backbreaking work, I might add."

"But, Father, the money would be nice," Josie argued, having a hard time keeping her disbelief reined in.

"Josephine, we have company. He doesn't want to hear about this. And besides, you just told me you sold a bull. So there's no need for me to sell these precious sapphires."

"Yes, Father." Josie's hand reached up and absently stroked the sapphire pendant her father had made for her.

Jack watched her hand, and for the first time noticed her necklace. She had a good-sized dark blue sapphire encased in a silver setting. The stone looked to be approximately three to four carats. His mother's fascination with gemstones had given him the ability to judge a stone's weight and quality.

"Where did you find them, Father?" Lottie asked, staring at the little stone Hunter had given her to hold.

"Ah, ah, ah." Hunter wagged his finger. "That's *my* secret. I can't let the whereabouts of my hunting grounds be known. I will tell you this though. I found them in a gravel bar in the Missouri River somewhere between here and Great Falls."

Josie snorted. "That's a span of over one hundred miles. You certainly aren't giving anything away with that statement."

"That's my motto. Always safe instead of sorry."

"Those look like nice stones, Mr. Douglass," Jack said.

"It's Hunter, call me Hunter. Say, are you something of a rock hound also? Maybe you'd like me to introduce you to minin'. I tell you, it can get into your blood."

Jack smiled and shook his head. "My mother was the rock hound in our family. But thanks for asking. I need to stick around here and do my work."

"Well, if you change your mind. It can be great fun searchin' and findin' treasures that are yours just for the takin'." A faraway look came into Hunter's eyes, as if he could hear the distant gemstones calling his name.

"I'm glad to finally have met you, Hunter. But right now I need to go back to the hotel. I've got some business to attend to." Jack stood up and willed away the slight pounding that drummed in his head.

"Hey, wait a sec. I'll go into town with you. I wanna see my buddies. Then I can get to know you better. I know Josie has work to do, so I'll leave her to it. Thank God I have her around here."

"Sounds . . . fine." Now Jack could give Hunter the money for his horse's board. That was something he felt awkward about handing over to Josie. He also felt wary. Not too much earlier the man had punched him in front of his daughters. What would happen when they were alone?

Jack looked sideways at Hunter as they rode toward the hotel. The life and vibrancy emanating from the man astounded Jack. It was easy to tell that Josie got her love of life from her father.

Hunter's strength also surprised Jack. As far as Jack knew, his own father had never punched anyone in his life. But then, Hunter lived in the wild frontier of Montana Territory as a sapphire miner; definitely not the genteel life of a Kansas City lawyer.

"Well now, that horse of yours, the one back in our barn, do you mean to run 'im in the races at the fair?" Hunter asked as he settled back into the cantle of his saddle.

"My stallion?"

"That's the one. Have you raced him before?"

"Yes, but only in informal races back home in Kansas City."

"I reckon you know Josie is keen on racing also. Her gray mare, the tall, gangly looking thing, is who she has her hopes on right now." Hunter glanced over at Jack and grinned. Fine lines fanned out from his eyes. "I don't see what she thinks is so wonderful about that horse. Me, I like a horse with meat on its bones and sturdy legs." He gave the gelding he rode a pat on its thick, cresty neck.

"Tell me more about Josie's mare." Learning more about Josie had been Jack's whole objective for this ride to town, and he wasn't going to let it slip by. After all, he and Hunter were in agreement over one thing, that he should not be engaged to Josie. But if he wanted to do right by her, should he consider it? No, that was too drastic. There had to be another way.

Hunter shrugged. "What's to say? I know she's planning on entering the mare in the fair races. But I'm not sure who her rider is yet."

"How long has Josie liked racing?"

Hunter cocked his head and raised one eyebrow. "Mighty curious about my little Josie, aren't you? But then, I guess for somebody who wanted to be engaged to her, it would be only natural to share her interest in racing."

Jack's muscles tightened to the tension of a bowstring. He didn't like the sarcasm in Hunter's words.

"You could say I'm a racing aficionado. But tell me, aren't you worried about Josie and Lottie when you're out searching for sapphires?" Jack had to ask that question, curiosity gnawed at him. He wondered how a father could leave his two daughters to fend for themselves in the wilderness. Well, Gallatin City wasn't exactly a wilderness, but still.

The Douglass ranch was a distance from town. The road leading from the town's main street to the Douglasses was little more than a worn path. Jack glanced on either side of the path. What few houses he saw were spread far apart. Would a distant neighbor hear Josie's or Lottie's cries for help if it ever came to that?

"Worried about Josie? She's been handling things for so long, I know I can trust Lottie to her when I'm gone. My Josie, she's got a level head on her shoulders. All common sense, not the least idealistic like me or Lottie. That's why I keep her around."

"Keep her around?" Jack almost choked getting those words past his throat. They definitely were not the words a man wanted to hear about a woman who might be his future wife.

Future wife? The reins almost fell out of his hands. What *had* gotten into him? He was no more planning on marrying Josie than he was planning on drilling a hole in his head.

"Sure, I need to keep her around. Lottie needs her. What would I do without her? I mean, Slim from the livery stable keeps an eye on my girls when I'm gone. So I know everything is in good hands when I'm not at home."

"But what if Josie were to marry?" Jack couldn't believe he just said that, and to her father no less. *Where* was his brain? He tensed, waiting for Hunter to throw another punch for such a bold question.

Hunter stopped his horse and stared at Jack. "What did you say? Josie marry? Maybe you didn't hear me when I said I hadn't given my permission for her to wed. Besides, I don't think she'd ever want to leave the security of her own home."

I think you're wrong, Jack thought as he struggled to choose his words carefully. "I was just curious, having several sisters of my own. I remember them always talking about men and having men waiting in the parlor to visit them."

"Hmmm. Can't say as if I've had much experience with that type of situation. But I do remember courtin' my first wife, that would be Josie's mother."

"Josie and Lottie have different mothers?"

Hunter nodded. "My first wife died when Josie was nine. A few years later I married the woman who was Lottie's mother, and she died when Lottie was six. So ya see, I don't put too much stock in marriage. It's too full of heartache and death. That's why I like to keep my girls near me. They're all I've got.''

It did not sound like Hunter intended to let either of his girls leave home, especially Josie. And that fact would make marriage very difficult. He shook his head. Had his brain been jarred from the punch? His senses must be muddled. He had to get away from this train of thought.

As soon as they entered the town, Hunter waved to practically every person they passed. The sudden transition from countryside to town never failed to amaze Jack. All of a sudden buildings popped up, as if there were an imaginary line drawn where the town proper could start.

''Well, I enjoyed talking to you. But I'm goin' off to the Hay Bale Saloon to meet some of my friends. Lemme know when you're taking your horse out to run, I'd like to see 'im. It's always good to watch a race, gets the blood flowin'.''

''I'll do that.'' Jack waved and continued on to the hotel. As the town had only one street, all activity occurred there. Jack found he couldn't ride the length of the street toward the hotel without encountering several curious glances. He suspected he was being stared at for one reason: his engagement to Josie.

Regardless of Hunter's words, Jack knew he had to do his best to protect Josie's reputation. Since he'd been the one to run away that morning, he'd have to be the one to take matters into his hands.

His strong sense of honor told him what to do. For now he decided he'd tell Josie they could let the engagement continue for a little while, until they could think of a way to end it and still save her reputation. And his too. Since he was new in town, he didn't want people thinking him callous.

Something else swayed his decision, but he couldn't quite identify it. Maybe it was that look of vulnerability he'd glimpsed in Josie's eyes.

''Hell,'' he muttered, praying he was not making a

huge mistake by continuing the engagement charade with her. If he had a lick of sense, he would run from Gallatin City. But he couldn't. He had a responsibility, and he prayed Josie would not be his downfall.

Jack entered the hotel and went to the desk. The only ornamentation in the lobby was a giant Oriental rug in the middle of the floor. A table and some chairs would have enhanced the lobby, Jack thought.

"Mr. St. Augustine? You all right?" Natty, the young desk clerk, asked hesitantly, eyes glued to Jack's swollen lip.

"I'm fine. It's nothing."

Natty's shock of red hair stuck up directly above his left eye from a severe cowlick. "If you say so." He sounded doubtful. "Anyway, I want to be one of the first to congratulate you on your engagement."

Apparently Josie hadn't lied when she said news of the engagement was all over town. Jack mumbled an incomprehensible reply.

"Oh, also, there's a telegram just delivered for you." Natty handed him a folded piece of white paper.

"Thanks." Jack wondered who would have sent him a telegram.

As his eyes scanned the print, his heart hammered in his chest. The words blurred through a haze of anger.

❖ *11* ❖

Jackson, the telegram read, since we have not heard from you, i can only take that to mean you are busy settling into a house. your father and i have decided your wedding to gloria should take place in montana. telegraph me so i can plan the details. if i don't hear from you, i will take that to mean we come immediately. mother.

Jack's fingers gripped the paper. His breath came fast and furious.

Only a few months had elapsed since he'd left Kansas City, and it looked as if that wasn't time enough to escape the reach of his mother's grasp. He was building his own life, and here was his family, still trying to butt in from one thousand miles away.

Why had his mother sent the telegram? Had he done something before he left to alert them as to his true intentions of staying out West? Did they suspect he wasn't returning to Kansas City?

"Uh, Mr. St. Augustine?" Natty interjected, chewing on his lower lip. "Is—is there something the matter?"

Jack crumpled the telegram in his fist, feeling satisfaction as the words were crushed in his palm. "Yes, but nothing I can't handle."

"Good, good. I hate seeing things go wrong, especially for someone as kind as you. Most guests don't bother givin' me even a simple hello. But you always do." He shook his head, sending his cowlick dancing.

"Well, thanks. Any other messages?" Jack hoped there might be information on the property he'd inquired about.

"No, sorry."

"Let me know if there're any others." Jack waved and strode over to the stairs, taking them two at a time. His insides continued to roil at his mother's presumptuousness.

Jack slipped his key in the lock and shoved the door open. Stepping inside, he crossed to the bed. The wooden frame creaked and groaned as he dropped down on the mattress.

He stared unseeing at the gaudy green vine patterns covering the walls. The ordinary sounds of a city street, wagon wheels rolling, creaking carriages, horses neighing, went unnoticed.

The telegram was still wadded into a ball in his hand. Slowly, he opened his fist and smoothed out the paper. He stared at the black words neatly typed out.

He couldn't believe his parents were still trying to control him. It was as if they hadn't heard one word of what he'd said before coming out West. What would it take to get through to them?

He wouldn't put it past his mother to have already posted a wedding notice in the Kansas City paper. He could just see his father drawing up a marriage agreement between him and Gloria.

The telegram was a solid reminder of how persistent his parents could be, even if mountains and rivers separated them.

Jack jumped up, strode to the window, pushed aside the starched white curtain, and looked out. He saw the mighty mountains rising upward, the verdant green forests of pines, and the wide open, deep blue sky. This would be his home. Here was where he belonged, not in Kansas City.

He needed to take action. Now.

First he needed to discover when his mother had sent that telegram and from where. He needed to stop them from coming out to Montana. There was no reason for them to travel all the way to Gallatin City. There'd be no wedding between him and Gloria. The trip would only be a waste of his parents' precious money and time.

Second. Ah, the second decision. The one where he selected a meek woman to marry. His first choice for that role was turning out to be decidedly unmeek. Josie might not be as strong-willed and opinionated as his mother, but Miss Douglass certainly had a mind of her own. He lowered his rear to the windowsill and ran his fingernail along the thin glass.

Was there the possibility that Josie would turn out to be a biddable woman? He grunted and stilled his hand. A woman who'd announce a false engagement hardly seemed like the ideal candidate. But then, he hadn't come across any other available women, and Josie was appealing to say the least.

His head lolled backward, resting against the window frame. Gingerly he felt the fat lip that Hunter had bestowed upon him and winced at the pain his slight touch created.

If he told Josie that he'd go along with the engagement, then in effect he could be stuck with a shrew. On the other hand, he had a sense of obligation to her. But there was also the issue of her father to consider.

Jack knew Hunter wasn't keen on the idea of his elder daughter marrying. From their short conversation on the way to town, it sounded like Hunter would continue to deny the existence of an engagement, if one ever did exist.

Uncertainty wavered in him. He knew he should do the honorable thing, but if he did, would he become trapped in a snare of his own making?

Jack let the curtain fall, stood, and headed for the door. He'd reached a decision.

Later that same afternoon, as the sun cast long shadows on the ground, Josie threw open the door to the root cellar and peered at the dim, musty-smelling interior.

She descended the few steps carved into the side. The dank, earthy aroma hit her full force as she stepped onto the floor. A chill permeated the air and Josie shivered, rubbing her hands up and down her arms for warmth.

The cool, dark root cellar perfectly matched her mood.

Ever since her father's return, things had been tense around their home. Her father hadn't asked her again about the engagement to Jack, or how it might have happened. In fact, her father's lack of interest in the possibility of her marrying reaffirmed his earlier words, that he wouldn't consider such an event. It angered her that her father so easily dismissed such an occasion for her.

Granted, it wasn't a true engagement, and no one knew that but she and Jack. But she still thought her father should have offered congratulations instead of instantly denying it. How could he think he'd let her marry only when he was good and ready for her to be wed? To top matters off, when she'd told him about Mrs. Potter's crusade to adopt Lottie, he'd denied the possibility of that happening as well. Said the old biddy would never touch his baby girl.

She kicked a rock out of her way. She rolled her eyes, recalling what her father had been eager to talk about.

Cuff links.

Why on earth her father thought he needed new cuff links was beyond her. When did the man think he would wear them?

"Men!" She threw her arms up in the air in frustration.

She glanced around the dimly lit space. She made out

the vague shape of jelly jars, cylindrical cans, and square
wooden crates. To her left stood a barrel filled with salted
meat. Almost all the contents of the root cellar had been
placed there by her own hands. Pride in her hard work
forced a faint smile to her lips.

Seeing the solid proof of her efforts turned her
thoughts to her father's latest remark. That he didn't
know what he'd do without her. Piddle, she knew very
well what he'd have to do. He'd have to stay home and
tend to his ranch, and that was something Hunter Douglass just didn't want to do.

A chill pricked her scalp as his words echoed in her
mind. Did that mean he would refuse to let her marry?
Ever? Did he aim to keep her there just so he could
merrily go about doing whatever he wanted to do, whenever he wanted to do it?

Never! She wouldn't let that happen. She was twenty-
three, old enough to make her own decisions and live her
own life. Her father's needs couldn't keep her there, nor
could her younger sister.

Or could they? After all, she wanted to marry in order
to protect her sister. She was sacrificing for her family.
She was sacrificing so she could keep them together. She
wasn't marrying so she could leave her home. She loved
her home, and all she wanted to do was protect it. That's
all she'd been doing when she'd announced that Jack was
her fiancé.

She wondered what he'd said about the engagement to
the people he'd encountered in town. She imagined her
name was pretty much ruined right about then if he was
going around denying an engagement. Mrs. Potter would
return and snatch Lottie away if Josie couldn't think of
another plan quickly.

Josie knew she had stronger feelings for Jack than she
should. Several times during her chores she'd stop and
think of Jack, wondering what it would be like to work
alongside him. Every time she had looked at him her
body felt all warm, and when he smiled at her her insides
went all mushy.

Of course, since she'd told him of their engagement, he hadn't smiled at her. But he would again, she was sure of it.

"Josie! Are you in there?" Lottie called, and stopped just outside the entranceway, her body blocking the light.

At the sound of her sister's voice, Josie reined in her drifting thoughts. She loved her sister and wanted to protect her. It hadn't seemed like such a bad thing to falsify an engagement at the time. But so far all Josie had managed to do was botch things up.

"Yes, I am. Come on down."

"Can I help you?" Lottie asked.

"Sure, you can help me bring some things up to the house. Here." Josie held out a jar of blackberry preserves.

"Mmm, you mean we get to put preserves on the bread I made for dinner? That'll be good." Lottie hovered in the doorway, hesitating before descending the stairs. She didn't like going down in the root cellar. The small, dark area scared her.

"That's right. I want us to have a nice meal for Father's first full day back. I'm hoping if we can show him all the tasty food he missed while out searching for sapphires, he won't want to leave so quickly."

"That's a good idea. But I wanted to tell you, I got all the seeds planted and the markers up in each row, so we know what's where. Do you think Father will like that?"

"Yes, I do." No matter what Lottie did, their father always seemed to be impressed. She would be showered with compliments while Josie's contributions went unrecognized. Josie hated being a tad jealous of her sister, but sometimes she was. She craved affection as much as Lottie did. She'd enjoy a compliment or two thrown her way.

"Let me just grab the meat I'm going to cook for dinner." Josie picked up a salted section of elk meat in one hand and closed the door with her other. She flipped the latch down and it fell, reverberating in its brackets.

"Do you think Jack will be joinin' us for dinner?" Lottie asked innocently. She fluttered her eyelashes and shook her blond ringlets.

Josie stopped in her tracks. Her sister was acting like a seasoned flirt. Where had she learned that behavior? "Why do you ask that?"

"I dunno. I just thought, well, you know, he's—he's kinda handsome. Sorta how I always picture my husband. I'm so jealous he's gonna be your husband." Lottie pursed her cupid's-bow lips.

"I'll tell you something. I think he's handsome also, but that'll be our secret." That was putting it mildly. Sometimes Josie thought she couldn't keep her eyes off the man. She found him more delicious to look at than all the candy in the mercantile.

Lottie's continued chatter about Jack bothered Josie. She found her fibs deepening. Josie hated to shatter the illusion that her sister held. Every question Lottie asked about Jack, Josie felt she had to answer somehow, even though she knew she was not telling the truth. Why she just didn't come out and tell Lottie that she and Jack were no longer engaged was beyond her.

But Lottie seemed so happy for her. Whenever she spoke of her "new brother" her eyes sparkled and her whole face reflected happiness. Josie loved to see her sister happy and she didn't want to be the one spoiling it. Just this once Josie didn't want to be the damper of reality and ruin her sister's joy.

"Jos? Can I ask you something?"

"Sure, honey, what's up? Why the troubled look?"

"It's—it's just something that's been bothering me."

"What is it? You can tell me."

"Yeah, I know, but it's sorta about you. Well, actually, it's Father. Whenever I bring up you and Jack, he acts real funny and says he wants me to stop talking foolishness. And I'm afraid."

Josie stopped and stared at her. "Afraid? Afraid of what?"

Lottie blushed a fiery red, her cheeks almost matching

the dark red preserves clutched in her hand. "It's just—it's just that I don't think he likes Jack. Why else would Father not want to talk about him? And if Father doesn't like Jack, what's to stop him from not liking the man I wanna marry later?"

A soft breeze blew the loose strands of hair off Josie's face. She smiled. Lottie was getting upset over nothing, fretting about her wedding which might not take place for at least five years. But Josie remembered young ladies had a tendency to worry about the oddest things. At least this took Lottie's mind off her Aunt Portia and the possibility that she'd be forced to go live with her aunt.

"I wouldn't fret about that if I were you. I'm sure Father likes Jack. You know how Father can be, he likes to hear himself talk. I'm sure the news of an—an impending wedding just threw him. If Father didn't like Jack, he would have told him to move his horse."

Lottie bit her lower lip and looked up at her sister. "Are you sure? Because I know you would never lie to me."

Josie suddenly felt very hot in the afternoon sun. Her heart constricted. If only she could tell Lottie the truth, but she'd gotten in over her head and didn't quite know how to remedy that now. She hated to be a disappointment in her sister's eyes.

"Yes, I'm sure."

From now on, she vowed, she'd do her best to be honest with her sister, and with Jack. Because maybe, if she were the perfect lady and bowed to Jack's wishes, he might not find any more fault with her. That might be her only chance to put her plans back on track.

"Good, 'cause I *do* want you to be happy." Lottie's forehead creased as she spoke. It seemed to Josie that her sister was almost trying to convince herself of her own words. She thought it odd, but dismissed the feeling as they reached the house.

Far away, on the muddy waters of the Missouri River, a riverboat steamed upstream. Wispy white smoke plumed out of its tall smokestack. Below the decks, in the plushly outfitted cabin, two women and one man sat sipping cocktails. Along the room's walls were four trunks, including one that held the contents of a wedding trousseau.

"Gloria dearest, I do hope you don't get seasick. It might be a long trip to Gallatin City." Mr. Beauregard St. Augustine tamped tobacco inside the bowl of his pipe as he spoke. "You want to look your best when Jack sees you."

❖ *12* ❖

ONE DAY LATER, as the sun passed over its zenith, Jack tied his gelding to the hitching post outside of the Douglasses' barn. He lifted his face and tilted his hat back, enjoying the sun's warmth. Birds flitted from branch to branch, filling the trees with song.

He headed toward his stallion's pasture, a confident swagger in his stride.

All had gone well at the telegraph office. He'd sent his message. His parents would now know not to make the futile journey out to Montana. Jack felt good knowing he'd averted a potential disaster. And disaster would have been the only result if his parents had brought Gloria out to Gallatin City.

He'd also scouted out a promising-looking area of land. His breeding ranch was coming closer to being a reality. What he needed now was a good mare to mate with his stallion.

Immediately Josie's gray came to mind. Even though

he hadn't seen the mare run, from the looks of her she promised to be a good sprinter.

Now the only question was would Josie sell her mare to him? For Jack would want the mare at his ranch so he could monitor her pregnancy. But he couldn't do that unless he owned the mare. Unless Josie lived with him. This brought him up short.

In order for that to happen, he would actually have to marry Josie. And that was not in his current plans.

He'd made the decision to continue with the engagement Josie had concocted, otherwise the guilt would have been too much. He hated knowing he'd been the one responsible for her rash actions. Guilt, however, wasn't the only thing making him go along with the engagement.

He was new in town and wanted to make a good impression on the citizens. He could hardly do that if he denied Josie. In fact, if he continued with the engagement, he'd be helping both himself and Josie.

If only he could think of another way to help them both, but just then he couldn't think of a darn thing.

Jack stopped at the fence, propped his elbows on the top rail, and regarded his horse. The stallion had his head down, grazing. As Jack looked at the chestnut animal, his heart swelled with pride and hope. That stallion was to be his foundation sire for the line of racehorses he wanted to breed. He recalled the lush grasses of the homesite he'd scouted and knew it would be a good place to raise horses and a family.

He turned his head toward the house and wondered if Josie was home. He needed to tell her about his change of mind regarding the engagement. As soon as he completed the thought, the front door opened and out walked Josie. He smiled. He'd forgotten just how pretty she was.

Sunlight reflected off her loosely bound raven-black hair. The cherry-red lips she'd been born with were the perfect compliment to her pale, freckled skin and dark hair. Again he wondered if they tasted as sweet as they looked. Perhaps he should kiss her and find out.

"Josie! Hello," he said, hurrying his steps, eager to

look at her face, to smell her fresh lemony scent.

He looked at her and his heart began melting. How could he have been so rude to her yesterday? She seemed anxious, her smile a little uncertain. A faint blush stained her cheeks, although he didn't know if that was due to him or whatever she'd been doing inside. He liked to think just looking at him caused her to blush.

Josie finished putting on a pair of gloves. "I thought I heard a horse coming up our path."

"You did. I came out to see my stallion and give him some exercise. Do you want to come along?" He hoped she would agree.

Josie stopped about two feet from him, averting her eyes. "Actually, I think that'd be very nice. Since Father has been home, he's been helping with the work. Right now he's fixing our indoor pump."

He looked at her carefully. She didn't quite seem herself. She seemed, more . . . more proper-like and subdued. He frowned. As much as he hated to admit it, this new personality didn't suit her. "Does he usually help when he's home?"

Briefly, she met his glance and then looked down. "Usually he only does a few of the bigger jobs that I have trouble with. But yesterday he took interest in the cattle and the ranch as a whole. He said it was just nostalgia, but whatever it was, I'm glad he decided to help out."

"My father does his own version of helping out." Like hiring someone whom his mother had selected to do the job, Jack thought. There was no way his father would ever get himself dirty and greasy by working on a pump.

"Will he be coming to Gallatin City?"

Jack grinned, then winced as his fat lip throbbed. He'd taken care of that yesterday. "Nope, he's not coming out here in the near future."

"Too bad. Shall we get our horses ready before my father finds something he needs my help with?" Josie started toward the barn.

Jack followed at her side. He noticed each time the

swish of her skirt brushed against his leg. The material caressed his calf, teasing him. He wondered at his heightened sensations whenever he was near Josie. Whatever the reason, he wouldn't complain. He rather liked it.

He glanced over at her hands, at the exceedingly white gloves she wore. "Do you want to go change your gloves?"

Josie looked down and adjusted the gloves around her fingers. "Um, no. I just put these on. I think they're appropriate for riding, don't you?"

No, he didn't really think they were appropriate at all for riding. Especially with all that frilly lace around the cuffs. But then, Josie would know more about women's riding fashions than he. He did have to admit the gloves looked quite feminine, and he liked that. "If you like them, then they're just fine."

"Good," she murmured, not meeting his gaze.

"I see Zeus is out in a pasture by himself. That's probably a good idea to keep him separated from your mare. You wouldn't want them to accidentally mate." Jack's eyes widened at her sudden look of surprise. He bit his tongue and cursed his careless remark. She might be a ranch girl, but that didn't mean such topics as breeding wouldn't embarrass her.

Josie cleared her throat and looked past him at the barn. "Let's get our horses ready and then head out for a nice ride."

"Shouldn't you ask your father if it's all right for you to go riding with me?"

Josie's head snapped around, and for a second emerald fire glimmered behind her eyes. "No, I don't need to ask his permission. He told me to go riding anyway." At his astonished expression, she continued in a softer tone. "I mean, I'm old enough to make my own decisions."

Her sudden spirit startled him. The vibrancy shining from her eyes ignited some hidden fire buried within him. Oddly, he found her energy sexy. Somehow, when Josie spoke her mind it did not remind him of his mother. His mother didn't crackle with life the way Josie did.

"Ready?" Josie asked after they'd saddled the horses. "I know a real pretty area. On the way there's a nice flat piece of ground. We can let the horses gallop if you'd like." She adjusted her riding skirt around her legs.

Jack watched, half hoping for a glimpse of her fair skin or a shapely calf. Catching himself, he swore and tore his gaze off her. He should know better then to stare, hoping for an eyeful. "I think it might be better if we kept to a nice, slow pace. I don't want anything to happen to you."

Josie bowed her head to keep from betraying her smile. She would have loved nothing more than to feel the wind rush past her face as Lady raced across the grass. But she needed to remember her ladylike appearances if she had any hope of salvaging a relationship with Jack. So to that end she'd decided her best option was to play the lady as well as she could, even if it killed her. Once Jack realized what an excellent fiancée she'd make, then she could gradually let her natural personality emerge.

"Nothing will happen to me. But we'll only canter across the field. Follow me." She clucked to her mare and headed to the back of their property, toward the forested wilderness of pines, firs, and spruces that stretched on in an endless sea of green.

"We just stay along this side of the fence until we cross the little stream. And then we'll head up into the hills if you'd like," Josie said. Did that sound too bossy? She hoped not. She'd forgotten how hard it was to be demure. If only Grace were there, coaching her.

"Do you ride this way often?" Anxiety tinged his words and he flashed her a worried look.

Josie's heart leapt. Jack looked downright concerned about her. If he didn't have any feelings for her, she doubted he would sound so worried. It was the first good sign, since his denial of the engagement, she'd had from him.

"Sometimes. Usually I come this way only when my friend Grace rides with me. She likes to get away and go where there's no people every once in a while. Her husband owns the mercantile, so she deals with people all day long.''

''Well, I'm glad you don't ride off into the wilderness by yourself. What if something were to happen to you?''

Jack's concern warmed her heart. A cozy, snug feeling surrounded her like a soft blanket. He *did* care about her. That was a very encouraging sign. ''I'm grateful for your concern, but so far nothing has happened to me. Believe me, I'll be extra careful from now on.'' She'd do anything to please him, just so they could meet at the altar and exchange those two simple words, *I do.*

''Good, I feel better already.'' Jack gave her a quick smile and held her eyes for a few moments before looking away.

''Me too,'' Josie said so softly that only her mare heard the words. ''Me too.''

''Hey, there's the calf we pulled.'' Jack raised his hand and extended his index finger at the black calf and the spotted cow grazing on the far side of the fence. ''He and his mama look like they're doing fine.''

''They are. Thanks to you. He'll be a big, strong bull one of these days.''

''Will your father sell him or keep him?''

''Keep him. I've already said—I mean, I already suggested he'll make a fine stud.'' She swallowed, a little panicky at her tiny slip. She hadn't meant to sound so authoritative, but it came naturally. ''He'll improve our stock, and Father agrees.''

''I'll be eager to see how he turns out as he grows up.'' Jack continued to watch as the calf nosed under his mother for milk.

''You will? So you'll be around for a while?'' She hoped she didn't sound too eager.

''I plan to be around for a long time.''

Satisfied that he hadn't said he was taking the first stagecoach out of town, Josie let the topic drop there. ''Here comes the creek. I hope your horse doesn't mind crossing water.''

Water gurgled and splashed around boulders in the middle of the stream.

"Are you kidding? He loves to get wet. If I'd let him, he'd lie right down and take a good roll in the stream. Never mind that there's a saddle on his back."

Josie laughed, picturing the sight. Jack's saddle would get soaked, Jack would be soaked also, and the horse wouldn't care one bit.

"What's so funny?" Jack asked as his horse stepped into the water and slapped the surface with his right front hoof. Jets shot upward and out, sprinkling Josie and her horse.

"I was just picturing you all sopping wet. Looks like he wants to roll right now."

"He's not going to." Jack pulled up on the reins, and kicked the horse forward and out of the stream.

"Actually, we use that stream for lots of things." Josie looked down at the clear running water and saw the dark, silvery bodies of fish dart about. "But the best thing we use it for is to make ice cream."

"Ice cream?" Jack jerked his head around and regarded Josie, a quizzical expression on his face.

"Uh-huh, we get a big piece of ice, put it in a bucket, mix the custard, and then keep the whole thing lowered into the water to freeze the mix and keep it cold. It's our favorite treat." Her mouth watered just thinking about the sweet frozen concoction.

"I'd love to have some. Do you think you could make some soon?"

Josie would trudge up the mountain by foot and carry the chunks of ice she found barehandedly for him if she had to. "Sure. You could come and help me find some ice in one of the upper mountain streams. But I'm not sure if there's much ice left."

"I'd love to. Just name the time and place."

She wanted to say right now, but they didn't have a bucket for the ice. Besides, if they went later, it would give her another excuse to be alone with him. And she definitely would enjoy that. "We'll try to go at the end of the week."

"Fine with me, I'll keep a day open."

Josie fingered Lady's reins. If her father stayed home for a while, she would be able to get away to fetch the ice, but if he left again . . . She pushed those thoughts out of her mind.

Today was a beautiful day and she was alone with Jack. For all she knew, it could be the last day she ever spent with him. She planned to make the most of it. There was no time for maudlin thoughts. Maybe she could even get him to kiss her.

"Let's canter a bit," Josie said. Before he could respond, she squeezed her legs around Lady and urged her mare forward. The gentle rocking motion only whetted her appetite for more speed. A good run would be exhilarating now, and she would love to test Lady's speed against Zeus's.

"He wants to run," Jack said as he fought with his horse. His stallion tossed his head and pulled at the bit, straining for release.

"We can, you know." Josie already felt Lady's stride lengthening and her pace increasing.

"No, I don't want anything happening to you." Jack flashed her a grin.

She half wanted to let Lady run, but she didn't want Jack to think she often raced across the land with her horse. She did, usually on the racetrack, but that was a small detail that Jack didn't need to know right then. Some things were best left unsaid.

As the tree line approached, the horses slowed their pace. Josie felt wonderful, riding alone with Jack. It was as if they were the only two people in Montana Territory. She didn't want this day to end.

"I'll lead the way up the path. There's a little clearing that's pretty." Josie positioned her mare in the lead.

"Sounds good."

The ground sloped upward as a narrow dirt path came into view. On either side, wildflowers, pink columbines, purple bitterroots, reached skyward for the sun's nourishing light. Thick clusters of firs and spruces punctuated between hardwoods gave the air a sharp, tangy scent.

Once in the clearing, Josie dismounted and turned to Jack. "Here we are. We can rest for a bit." She wasn't in the least tired, but knowing she and Jack were alone sent a delicious thrill down her spine. She was looking forward to getting to know him without any distractions, and she hoped he felt the same.

Jack looked around. "You're right. It sure is pretty out here." From the clearing on the hillside they had a clear view of the distant mountains. They could also see Gallatin City nestled like a toy town near the juncture of the three rivers. Overhead, a brilliant blue sky stretched over them like a giant canopy.

Taking his eyes off the view, Jack led his horse over to a cottonwood and tied him to the tree. "Here, let me tie Lady up for you."

"Thanks." Josie handed him her reins and spread her skirt out on the grass like a blanket and sat down. She smoothed down the material and then glanced at her gloves. She barely suppressed her groan.

The white gloves she'd pulled on earlier in her attempt to appear feminine now had a brown stain the width of her reins running across the palms. The backs were covered with a light coat of dust. She should have listened to Jack when he suggested she change gloves. Maybe he wouldn't notice the stains.

Jack returned and sat facing her, keeping two feet of grass between them.

Josie hoped she looked appealing to him. She knew he looked wonderful to her. His windblown hair curled around his shirt collar, enticing her fingers to smooth it down. His face glowed with life, and his lips looked so full and red. Kissable, would be one way to describe them.

"Tell me more about yourself," he prompted, putting his hands behind him to support his back.

"Where should I start?" She had to pull her mind off

contemplating him. He sat so close, his broad shoulders blocked the breeze. His presence captivated her attention.

He shrugged and smiled, showing white teeth. "How long have you lived in Gallatin City?"

"Practically since it was a city. We came here in 1860. You should have seen the place then. Only a few make-shift buildings and lots of tents. But Father had heard of sapphires in the Missouri and had a feeling about this little town. Plus, he'd fallen in love with Mrs. Potter's sister, Patricia."

Josie stopped. She knew she was babbling, but she was nervous.

"Do you like it here?"

"Well—" She paused, thinking. Her life had been nothing but hard work since she came here. But she had good friends and neighbors. "Yes, yes, I do."

"Would you ever consider moving away?" Jack leaned forward, narrowing the space separating them, and caught her glance.

"Move? Where to and why?" His question took her by surprise, as did his suddenly closer body.

She'd never thought of moving away. Maybe, in the dark of the night, when no one was around, she might have fantasized about leaving. But she'd never told any-one that secret and she felt guilty just contemplating it. She had her family to think of, especially Lottie.

"Just wondering. Will your father remain at home for a while now?"

"I hope so. It's sure nice when he's around. Lottie and I so enjoy the stories he tells about his expeditions." Josie found it hard to think with Jack so close. All she wanted to do was stare at him, to drink in every detail of his face, but she knew that would be highly improper.

"Lottie must think of you more as a mother than a sister. I think she's very lucky to have you."

Josie reddened at the compliment. "Th-thank you. She depends on me a great deal." She glanced up and found him staring at her.

"You shouldn't be embarrassed by my compliment."

He lifted his hand, placed his fingers gently under her chin, and tilted her head up.

The second his hand landed on her skin, her pulse leapt. His feather-soft touch heated her. She looked into his blue eyes flecked with brown and saw only warmth mirrored there. She had no power to look anywhere else. His gaze drew her in, caressed her, and filled her with longing.

"Josie, I . . ." Jack's voice trailed off. His fingers slid up to cradle her cheek and then slipped backward to the nape of her neck. He leaned forward, mouth parted.

Josie licked her lips as she watched him come nearer. Her stomach felt as if a bird were flying around inside and she actually felt quivery. He was going to kiss her and the anticipation was agonizing.

Only the merest inches separated them. His breath fanned her face. She leaned forward, closing the gap.

His other hand reached up and cupped her cheek. His eyes slid shut as he softly placed his lips on hers, gently, almost reverently. His arms slipped lower, wrapping around her shoulders, pulling her snug against him.

When his soft lips met hers, Josie wanted to cry out. His embrace was so full of tenderness. The gesture said more than words ever could.

He sucked gently at her lower lip, caressing it with his tongue. Josie forgot to breathe, his touch swept her away. Warm, tingly sensations started in her lower belly and spread heated tendrils throughout her limbs. She rocked toward him, parting her mouth.

As soon as her lips opened, Jack pulled away, drawing in gulps of air. His blue eyes had darkened to the color of turbulent water. "Josie, I'm so sorry. I never meant to kiss you so soon. I don't know what happened to me. I hope you'll forgive me."

Josie wanted to tell him to come back. Her lips felt naked without his warm ones covering them. Her shoulders felt cold without his arms around her. Instead, she folded her hands to keep them from shaking. "You're forgiven. I—I didn't mind."

Jack turned his head and looked at her. He let one corner of his mouth pull up into a crooked smile. "It was kind of nice, wasn't it? I guess we'll have many more of them to look forward to if we're to be engaged, at least outwardly engaged."

Josie nodded and opened her mouth to agree, but snapped it shut. Did she hear what she thought she heard? "Excuse me, what did you say?"

"I said, we can have many more of those as an engaged couple. Although we'll be the only ones who know it's not official. Don't look so shocked." Jack reached up and stroked her hair.

"Well, I, um, ah, yes. I thought you wanted nothing to do with me, that you didn't want to be engaged. But what do you mean by outwardly engaged?" She knew her cheeks were turning red and his hand on her hair distracted her. Was her plan really back on track?

His fingers traced her jawline. "Now, how can I refuse such a pretty lady as yourself? After all, as you pointed out, I should not have left you to face the reverend's wife all alone. This is the least I can do, for both of us. If we let the townsfolk go on thinking we're engaged, both our reputations are saved, until we can think of a better alternative."

She shivered at his touch and shook her head in agreement. She did not feel encouraged by his words. He sounded more like he was doing her a favor and that he wasn't agreeing to the engagement due to any feelings he might have for her.

Calling it temporary was not what she had in mind or needed. What she needed was an honest-to-goodness husband.

His acceptance wasn't at all what she'd envisioned either. She'd pictured him confessing his love at first sight. Pledging undying devotion to her.

Oh, well, obviously that was not meant to happen to her. And besides, she'd wanted the wedding so she could protect her sister. She wasn't supposed to have such strong feelings for Jack. Her emotions were throwing her plans off-kilter, and it shouldn't be that way.

If she could just persuade Jack to make the engagement real, then her problems would be solved. Now she felt like she stood in limbo.

"I see I've got you speechless. Maybe we should try another kiss now that I know it doesn't hurt my swollen lip." He moved closer and lowered his lips to hers. Devilment twinkled in his eyes.

Josie's heart raced when his tongue nudged her lips apart. Never in her life had she imagined the pleasure a kiss could bring. His tongue touched hers, teasing, licking, sending waves of bliss all the way down to her toes.

She sighed into him and pressed herself against his solid, hot body. If this is what an unofficial engagement would entail, she was more than ready for it.

Abruptly, Jack pulled back. Heavy-lidded eyes regarded her. "I can see I wasn't wrong about you. There is a fire within you. But we really shouldn't be doing this. Kissing, I mean."

"Why not?" She didn't find a problem to it.

"Because it's inappropriate, that's why. And speaking of inappropriate, we shouldn't be up here alone. Suppose someone saw us? We should leave. I'll go get the horses." Jack rose and strode to the cottonwood where he'd tied the animals.

Josie stood up, feeling abandoned. He didn't need to run off so fast, she thought, she would have liked to just nestle close to him. She didn't think a kiss or two was scandalous. Who would see them out here? The birds? A squirrel or two?

A slow, heated longing started in her stomach at the mere remembrance of their lips becoming one. Perhaps he didn't have the same needs as she? Or, worse, what if he did not like kissing her at all? She knew his kiss had rocked her world, but how did it affect him? He couldn't still want to keep his distance now, could he?

Against her better judgment, she knew her feelings for him were bordering awfully close to love. And it scared her because she didn't know whether or not he would return her love. Had she inadvertently threatened her plans by falling for him?

"Here you go, Josie, your mare." Jack held Lady's reins out to her and sketched a bow.

She should have been happy at his smiling face, at his courtesy, but she wasn't. They seemed forced. He'd never bowed to her before. It looked so formal. So impersonal. She snorted. Of course it was impersonal. Jack had said the engagement was only temporary. Why would he bother to bring their relationship to a more personal level?

"Thank you," she murmured.

"You're welcome. After you." Jack held his arm out in front of him, motioning for her to go first down the mountainside.

After the exciting kiss they'd shared, Jack's suddenly polite and distant demeanor depressed her. If he'd meant what he said about a temporary engagement, then why did he kiss her twice? Josie hoped Jack did indeed feel something for her.

As inappropriate as it was, she liked his embraces and hoped her lack of experience hadn't scared him off. And as inexperienced as she was, she could tell Jack had been affected by the kiss also. She recalled his ragged breath, his hammering heart. Now, how could she convince him to make the engagement real?

❖ *13* ❖

THE RIDE BACK to the ranch was accomplished with few words exchanged between them. The squirrels chattered, birds sang overhead, and the wind whispered through the sparsely dressed trees, but she and Jack did not say much to each other. Josie thought it was an uncomfortable silence.

The awkwardness seemed to have started after their second kiss. Josie almost wished for the kiss never to have happened. That way, maybe she and Jack would still be talking.

She also wondered how he could so easily talk of ending the engagement when an alternative solution had been found. It left a bitter taste in her mouth, knowing Jack was interested only in their reputations, that he felt so little for her.

Either way, it didn't put her in a good position. She was still no closer to securing a husband, and that meant Lottie was also at risk. She should be somewhat happy.

At least Mrs. Potter and the townsfolk could go on believing a wedding was forthcoming between her and Jack. For right now Lottie was safe.

As they neared the ranch house, Josie noticed her father out behind the house. Something hung from a nearby tree limb.

"Let's go see what my father has," Josie said, nudging her mare in that direction.

"All right."

"Josie, my girl. Looky what Slim and I went and got us." Hunter motioned with his skinning knife to the elk hanging suspended from the tree.

Josie stifled a groan. Their meat barrels were filled with elk. They didn't need more. "Did you say Slim helped you?"

"Yup, he's gonna take half. I figgured there'd be plenty of meat left for us. See, aren't you glad I came home?"

Her father would find out soon enough about all the meat in the root cellar. "Yes, we're glad you're home."

Hunter spied Jack. "Hey, Jack, want to learn how to prepare the meat?"

Jack's eyebrows rose. "Yes, I would. I need to learn all I can."

"Good, good. Get down off your horse and hand 'im to Josie. She can take care of the animals."

"If you think she won't mind." Jack hesitated.

"Naw, Josie won't mind one bit. Besides, this here is men's work," Hunter said. "It can get ugly, and I don't want her to have to witness anything like that."

Josie's hands tightened around her reins. She couldn't believe her ears. Why was her father being so protective of her now? How did he think they ate while he was gone?

"But I can help," Josie protested. She was not about to give up without a fight.

"No, Josie. This is no place for a woman. Women would just get in the way and be squeamish." Hunter stared at his daughter, crossing his arms in a wide-legged stance.

"But how do you think—"

"Josephine, take the horses. They're gettin' all nervous standin' here." Her father raised one hand, extended his index finger, and pointed at the barn.

She felt cheated. Deceived. Barely swallowing her anger, she attempted a weak smile. "Fine. I'll be in the barn." With that sentence she took Jack's reins and turned the horses away from the men.

Long afternoon shadows stretched across the grass as she walked Lady into the barn. Quickly, she untacked her and put the mare in her stall.

"You were a good girl today. I'm proud of the way you behaved with a stallion so near. You deserve a treat tonight. I'll see if there are any apples left in the root cellar before I go to bed." Josie placed both hands on either side of Lady's nose and gave her a kiss.

Lady whickered softly and stayed pressed next to Josie for several minutes.

Josie enjoyed the sweet horse scent, but holding Lady close could not compare to being held in Jack's arms. His body had been firm and hot all at once. She gave a little shiver of delight, remembering the tantalizing feel of his tongue in her mouth. Lady butted her with her muzzle, bringing Josie out of her reverie.

"Bye, girl, I've got to take care of Zeus." Pulling away, Josie gave the mare a good-bye kiss before leaving.

As she brought Zeus into the barn, she itched to mount up and take a ride. He was such a beautiful horse. His brown eyes hinted at intelligence and kindness. The glistening chestnut coat gleamed with good health. His body was soft and silky to the touch. She wondered what it would be like to race him. Would he run like the wind?

Obediently, he stood while Josie slipped his saddle and bridle off. Picking up a brush, she curried him where there were traces of sweat. Her hand pausing in midstroke, her thoughts turned to Jack.

He'd been the one to initiate the kiss, so he had to feel something for her. But what? And did he intend to inform her father about the resumption of their "engagement"?

She hoped he wouldn't do it while they were preparing the meat. Her father had an impulsive streak a mile long and he had a sharp knife. Would her father refuse Jack's offer? How she wished she could be there to hear what they were talking about.

She longed to know what Jack thought of her. Did he find her at least a bit attractive? Was she what he'd hoped for in a wife? Obviously not, or else he'd want a real engagement.

If she went in the kitchen and sat by the window thinking about what to serve for supper, she could accidentally overhear the men's conversation and it wouldn't *really* be eavesdropping. That sounded like a good idea to her. She ran out of the barn and toward the house.

Before she reached the porch, her sister intercepted her. "What are you doing, Josie?"

Josie skidded to a stop. "Uh, just going in to start our supper." Her heart pounded, and adrenaline surged in her veins. She felt like she'd been caught red-handed, even though she hadn't done anything wrong.

Lottie frowned. "That sounds boring. Come with me. I wanna try out a new hairstyle on you. I saw this picture in *Godey's Lady's Book* that I think will look good on you."

"Lottie, I—" *I really must go eavesdrop,* she longed to say but didn't. She looked at her sister's hopeful face and knew she couldn't deny Lottie their time together. "I'd love to have you give me a new hairdo."

"Good." Lottie grabbed her sister's hand. "C'mon, I brought the brush and comb outside." Lottie pulled Josie to a bench by the flower garden. At one end of the bench, two flower wreaths sat, one of Lottie's earlier projects.

"Here, you sit down so I can do your hair." Lottie pushed Josie onto the bench. She handed the brush to Josie. "Hold this while I undo your braid."

Josie held the brush and shut her eyes while her sister

raked her fingers through her hair, unraveling the thick braid. "So you think I need a new hairstyle?"

"Uh-huh. You're engaged now. You should look pretty every day. Lots of people are lookin' at you."

Josie knew that only too well.

"Here, give me the brush. I gotta brush your hair first."

Josie let her mind wander while her sister worked on her hair. She kept thinking how much happier she'd be if Jack had agreed to a real engagement. Now Josie had to worry about how soon he'd decide to call it off and also how that news would affect her sister.

This situation was no better than before. In fact, it was worse. While everyone else thought she and Jack were a happily engaged couple, only she would know the truth. She'd have to cope silently with the knowledge that her life could erupt at any moment.

She just had to convince Jack that she was worthy as a wife. Until then she'd do her best to be the perfect fiancée and hope Jack would come to care for her.

Lottie laid the brush down on the bench. She gathered up sections of Josie's hair, working it into an intricate style. "Did Father tell you he might take us all into Bozeman?"

"He said what?" Josie twisted her head, undoing all of Lottie's work, and stared openmouthed at her sister.

"Josieee, you just ruined your hairdo," Lottie cried.

"What did you say Father wants to do?"

Lottie's frowned at her sister's black hair. "He's gonna take us to Bozeman. He heard they have a real good jeweler, where he can get his cuff links and my necklace made. I said we'd like to go with him. Doesn't that sound like fun? Goin' into the big city?" Once more she gathered up Josie's hair, keeping a tight hold on the sections.

Josie's first thoughts were of the ranch. Who would look after it while they were off on some silly chase after cuff links?

Next, and more important, her thoughts turned to Jack.

How could she leave him? She needed to convince him she was the woman for him. How could she do that if she weren't here? Plus, they were supposed to make ice cream together. How could they do that if she was off in some distant city? What little ice remained would be melted.

No, she couldn't leave. She needed to be near Jack. She had to make him realize that a true engagement and a wedding were the best thing for both of them.

"Well, Jos, what do you think about my idea? We can go to the big stores and look at fabrics for the next dress I'm gonna sew. We can see all the pretty, fashionable women, and learn all the latest styles." Lottie sighed and looked dreamily off into the distance, picturing all the finery in her mind.

"I don't know, Lottie. I just don't know. Father hasn't said we're going for sure, has he?"

"Not yet."

"Maybe he'll decide he doesn't want these cuff links after all." Maybe Josie could convince him to sell the sapphires for some needed money. And while she was at it, maybe she could persuade him to stay near his ranch and for him to let her marry Jack. With her father remaining at home and herself happily married, Mrs. Potter wouldn't dream of adopting Lottie because all would be normal in the Douglass household.

Her eyeballs rolled backward. Those were hefty goals she had set for herself.

Lottie pouted. "But what about my necklace? You have one." She stepped sideways, holding Josie's hair in one hand, and touched the stone hanging around her sister's neck with the other. "I want one too."

She'd unwittingly hurt her sister's feelings. "I'm sorry, Lottie. I know how badly you want your own necklace. Perhaps a trip to Bozeman would be nice." She highly doubted it, but wanted to placate Lottie. And though she hated to admit it a corner of her wanted to see the latest fashions, so she could look pretty for Jack.

When the front door opened, both sisters turned their

heads and looked at the approaching men. Lottie accidentally let go of Josie's hair, completely ruining her second attempt at her arrangement. Wishing now that she had never let Lottie do her hair, Josie did her best not to look as self-conscious as she felt. She just hoped Jack wouldn't think her brazen with unbound hair in the middle of the day.

"Lottie, why don't you go on inside and get cleaned up for supper?" Hunter steered her in the direction of the house.

"Oh, all right." Looking disappointed that she wouldn't be able to observe the proceedings, Lottie went to the back door.

Josie looked at Jack, and when she noticed his wide eyes, she blushed. He gaped at her loose waist-length hair.

"Say, Jack," Hunter interjected. "How about you stayin' over here for supper? I made a big batch of my venison stew. I'd call it repayment for helpin' me prepare the elk. What do you say?"

"I wouldn't want to impose."

"No imposition. I insist. We'd love your company. After all, you helped me. How could I refuse you a meal?"

"Well, sure." Jack flicked a quick glance at Josie, trying hard not to stare at her flowing hair. At her encouraging smile, he agreed. "I'd like to."

Josie watched the men's interchange with hope brewing in her heart. It seemed her father and Jack were becoming friends. A good sign. If Jack became closer to her father, it would make it harder for her father to deny the engagement.

She joined in, hoping to make Jack feel more welcome. "There's plenty of space around our table."

Jack looked from one Douglass to the next. He hesitated before speaking. "It'll be my pleasure. But I better go see Zeus first. I feel like I've been neglecting him lately."

"I'll go with you. I need to feed the horses." Actually,

she was dying to ask him what he'd said to her father.

"Oh, Josie. I forgot to tell you. I also invited Slim for dinner. He's gonna come an' pick up his portion of the meat. So you'll need to set another place." Hunter turned and left them alone.

"Sounds like you'll have a full table. If it's too much, I can leave." Jack moved closer to her as they walked down the well-worn path to the barn.

"No, it'll be fine. You should stay." The last thing she wanted was for him to leave her. After all, he had kissed her that very afternoon. She smiled whenever she remembered the feel of his lips on hers. She longed to repeat the experience.

As they strolled to the open barn doors, Josie kept wishing he would at least hold her hand. She felt his body next to hers. She could practically feel the energy radiating off him. When she accidentally swung her arm in a certain way, she brushed against his hand.

Hope surged each time she touched him, but he never took her hand.

She wasn't too disappointed though. They had the whole evening stretching out in front of them. Perhaps they could steal away for a few moments alone and try kissing again, this time underneath the stars. Josie smiled, but then frowned. Suppose Jack hadn't mentioned the engagement to her father? If he were to discover Jack kissing her, would he threaten to throw Jack out of town for good?

❖ *14* ❖

AFTER REMOVING HER dirty work dress and boots, Josie sat down on her bed before donning a clean dress for dinner. She had on only her camisole and petticoats. She shivered as the crisp evening chill inched across her skin. She laid back on the feathered softness and pulled a blanket around her. Pretending it was Jack's arms, she relived his kiss.

His lips had felt so tender, yet so alive and demanding on her own. His hands had held on to her so gently, but she could feel the strength in them. She prayed that he'd enjoyed the kiss as much as she had.

Voices from the sitting room drifted underneath her closed door. She could hear her father's deep voice launch off into another one of his stories. Josie smiled. For all his faults, she couldn't help but love the man. He meant well and was doing the best job of fathering he knew how to.

Suddenly, she was eager to rejoin the group, especially

Jack. She sat up and looked over the few dresses she had hanging. Her lips turned down. She didn't see anything that would look exciting to Jack. All she saw were plain, ordinary dresses. Except one.

She wanted to look ladylike, feminine. Pretty. So she finally decided upon her dove-gray dress which had a soft fullness in the bodice. It even had yellow ribbons securing the cuffs instead of buttons. She remembered she had a length of gray satin ribbon that Grace had given her. She could wrap that around the end of her braid. The wide, shimmery ribbon should look somewhat feminine, she thought as she hurried to dress.

She took a deep breath as she left her room. She smoothed down the front of her dress. What would Jack think of her now? Once she was all cleaned up, did she look more like wife material? she wondered. Would that generate more enthusiasm in him?

"Why, there you are. I was about to send Lottie in and see what happened to you. My stew's ready." Hunter motioned to the kitchen, where the scent of meat, onions, spices, and potatoes wafted in the air.

"I just wanted to get cleaned up." So far, Josie noticed, she hadn't received the reaction she'd hoped for. Nobody had said she looked pretty, or even decent. Her forehead wrinkled.

Jack and Slim rose as she entered the sitting room. "You look very nice," Jack offered.

His eyes traveled from the top of her recently brushed hair to the hem of her skirt. Her cheeks blossomed. Finally, the person she'd wanted to notice her had.

"You look purty, Josie. May I take you to your seat?" Slim walked up to her and held out his arm.

Josie looked from Jack to Slim. She would have preferred her fiancé to escort her, but she didn't want to offend an old family friend. "Sure, that would be nice."

"What do you say, Lottie? Shall I walk you into dinner?" Jack offered his elbow to Lottie.

"Why, thank you." She gave him a curtsy and giggled.

Josie found herself propelled to her seat at the table, and to her dismay, Slim claimed the chair next to her. This was not how things were supposed to work out. Jack was to sit next to her. She managed a halfhearted attempt at a smile when she noticed Slim holding out her chair. Muttering thanks, she sat down.

Looking up, she realized Jack sat across from her. That wasn't so bad, she decided; at least she could look at him during the whole meal.

"Watch out, everyone. Hot pot's comin' your way." Hunter hefted a big iron kettle of stew and set it down in the middle of the table. The dishes vibrated as the pot's weight hit the table. He bent over and sniffed the steam. "Um-mmm, sure smells good, if I do say so myself."

"Hunter, looks like you outdid yourself on this one," Slim said as he shoved a napkin down the front of his checkered shirt.

Jack shifted the direction of his gaze and looked at Slim. He wondered exactly how often Slim took his meals at the Douglasses'. Jack realized he felt irrationally envious of Slim and Josie's family. They all seemed to get along so well; he didn't sense the tension that usually surrounded his parents' dining table.

"Do you eat here often?" Jack asked.

"Occasionally." Slim reached out and ladled stew onto his plate. "When Hunter's gone, I stop by and check in on the girls. Been doin' it for years."

"Puts me at ease when I'm away," Hunter interjected as he scooted his chair in.

"I understand." Jack still struggled to grasp how a father could leave his daughters alone so often. Granted, he had Josie to look after the ranch, she was more than capable, but suppose something happened to her? Jack's muscles tightened at the mere thought of Josie harmed.

Puzzled, he glanced down at his empty plate. He wanted to know when he'd started feeling so strongly about Josie. When did he suddenly decide he couldn't bear to see anything happen to her? Why was he so easily forgetting that it was she who had gotten him into this engagement business in the first place? That she had a tendency to be headstrong, like his mother?

He needed to keep his distance from Josie if he intended to end the engagement once he figured out how to save both their reputations. And kissing her that afternoon had not helped. It only made him want to explore more of her body and soul. In fact, he now wanted to kiss her again and feel her soft body pressed up against his.

His thoughts should most certainly not be headed in that direction. There would be no wedding and therefore no chance to become intimately acquainted with Josie.

"Here, let me serve you." Slim's voice cut into Jack's musings.

He glanced up to see Slim take Josie's plate and heap a good portion of venison stew on it.

Jack watched, his eyes focused on Josie. He should be the one serving her, he thought, once again envious of the evident close friendship with Slim.

"I'd like to be served by a man too," Lottie said, batting her long, dark eyelashes at Jack.

He chuckled. Lottie was going to be a heartbreaker in a few years. Jack felt sorry for all the young men who'd become smitten with her. "Would you? Hand me your plate and I'll fix it up for you."

Just as Jack raised a forkful to his mouth, Hunter interrupted.

"I think we should say a blessing. Bow your heads." Hunter glanced around the table, making sure everyone complied with his request, and grunted his satisfaction. "Thank you, Lord, for this food and family. Amen. All righty, dig in." Hunter began eating like a man long separated from food.

Jack hadn't realized how hungry he'd been until he tasted the savory stew. The corn muffins were excellent, crumbly and tasty. Everyone else must have felt the same, because conversation died as they all enjoyed the dinner.

The meal was quite a contrast to the ones at his parents'

house. Formal plates and silverwear were used every day. Each course was carried in separately by servants, not placed in the center of the table like it was here. Jack could easily help himself to more stew, which he did and noticed everyone else did too.

"Wonderful." Hunter pushed his plate back, tilted his chair onto its rear legs, and patted his stomach. "Can't eat another bite."

"What about the apple cobbler that's warming?" Josie said, smiling at her father.

"Cobbler? I plumb forgot about that. But I suspect there's room in here for a slice." He gave another pat to his belly.

"Everyone stay seated. Lottie and I will clear the table and bring the dessert."

Josie rose, and when she leaned forward to gather her plate, Jack saw just a barest glimpse of cleavage. His heartbeat quickened.

He tore his eyes away. He had no business ogling Josie. If they were to end the engagement, which would be the best thing, he did not need to stare at her. Where were his manners? But curiosity nagged him. He wanted to know what the rest of her looked like, more than he should.

Was her skin creamy and soft? Satiny and smooth? Desire pulsed through his veins. All of a sudden his clothes felt tight, like they were constricting his blood flow. Jack shifted his gaze to Hunter, hoping to God Hunter hadn't seen where his eyes had been staring. "So, uh, is venison stew your specialty?"

"Well, now, that it is. See, I can get it all fixed up in the morning and let it cook over the fire all day. Then, when it's time for the evening meal, I just scoop it out."

"I see. That's a good thing to do." Jack really hadn't wanted a diatribe on the preparation of the stew, he just wanted to make conversation so his thoughts wouldn't run rampant. He was only temporary engaged to Josie, so he definitely should not be thinking of the marriage act while seated at the same table with her father. Besides, there wouldn't be a consummation.

"Jos, how about fillin' up our water glasses?" Hunter asked, holding up his empty cup.

"Sure."

Josie lifted the porcelain pitcher and refilled the glasses. When she stopped by Slim, Jack noticed that Slim's eyes were not on the water. Instead, he looked directly at Josie's bosom as she leaned over to pour.

Jack's eyebrows rose. Men, even if they were family friends, he thought, should not be staring at that area of Josie. Never mind that that was where his eyes had been. His case was different. *He* was engaged to her. He needed to distract the staring man. "So, Slim, is my gelding giving you any trouble?"

"Huh? What did you say?" Slim jerked his eyes off Josie and focused on Jack.

Feeling satisfied that he'd halted Slim's visual violation of Josie, Jack repeated his question.

"Naw, he's a real easy keeper. If you want, I can maybe take both of your horses in a week or two. I got some people buyin' some of my pack mules."

Josie had stopped right next to Jack, and he could feel her body stiffen. Was she worried he was going to leave? "I don't think so. I believe my stallion likes it over here."

Josie relaxed and he felt her barely pressing against him. He glanced up and caught her eye. She looked relieved.

"Here's your water. Lottie and I will bring in the cobbler." Josie poured him a glass and quickly stepped back toward the kitchen counters.

"Here comes dessert," Lottie said as she and Josie set down plates in front of everyone and then sat down.

Jack bit into the warm cobbler. It tasted great. Sweet, sugary apples practically melted in his mouth. A long time had passed since he'd tasted an honest-to-goodness dessert. And he liked a sweet every now and then.

"So, Josie," Hunter said between bites. "Did you hear about Bozeman?"

She lowered the forkful of cobbler back to her plate. "Bozeman? What about it?" Her glance flicked to Lottie, who just smiled, winked, and continued eating her dessert.

"I thought we'd all take a little trip there. You know, see the big city. See the fancy townfolk. Visit the jewelers."

Immediately, Jack's attention was riveted to the conversation topic. Normally he would have excused himself at a pending private talk, but since he'd gotten to know the Douglasses, they didn't seem to mind if he listened. Besides, he had a personal interest in Bozeman. The land he wanted to purchase was closer to that city.

"Visit the jewelers?" Josie sounded disbelieving, like she hoped her ears had deceived her.

"Yep. It's been a long time since we were there."

Josie looked from her father to her sister's face. Each had an expectant expression. Josie's own mouth worked, but no words came out.

"Just think of all the fun we could have. We could go look at material. Look at fashions. Look at the fancy women. And you can pick out your wedding dress or material, and—"

Jack stiffened at the word *wedding*.

"Lottie, that's enough," Hunter said. "There's no reason for any talk about weddin's."

Josie still said nothing, but her lips had flattened.

Jack wondered about the reason for her silence. Could it be possible that she didn't want to go to Bozeman? Had she been there before and found she didn't care for the city?

"Father, it's not that easy to just up and go into Bozeman. For one, we'd have to be gone more than a day. What about the ranch?"

"Now, Josie. You know I can always come over and feed the animals. I've helped out before, haven't I?"

Slim reached into his pocket and withdrew his battered tin of chewing tobacco.

"I guess so," Josie agreed, not sounding too convinced.

"Sure, Jos. Slim would be glad to help out. An' I'm sure he'd want you to have a good time. Get away from all your work. You've been workin' too hard. Learn to enjoy yourself." Hunter nodded, pleased with his speech.

"C'mon, Josie. You wouldn't want me to be all alone in the big city? What if somethin' happened to me? Besides, we've gotta have fun once in a while. Why, we could become fancy city ladies and we could look at wedding things and we could . . ." Lottie continued to add her bit toward persuading her sister.

Jack watched Hunter's face slide into a scowl while Lottie chattered about the wedding. Jack hadn't told him that he was still engaged to Josie, nor had he asked Hunter's permission. He should at least inform the man, even if he didn't ask for his blessing. Maybe he should go to Bozeman with them and spend lots of time with Josie. Then perhaps Hunter would come to accept his presence.

Josie looked from face to face. Finally her eyes settled on Jack. "All right. We can go. But not for very long. We don't want to waste all of our money on a hotel."

Hunter looked affronted. He tugged on his beard. "We don't want to look like country bumpkins either."

That drew a laugh from Lottie.

Even Josie's lips turned up in a half smile.

"Then it's settled. We leave for Bozeman." Hunter slapped his palms on the table and stood up. He looked over to the dying fire in the hearth. "Now we just need to figure out when."

"I hope we go soon. I wanna get ideas for my dress I'm makin' for the fair." Lottie gathered dishes and set them on the counter near the pump.

"Not too soon. I've got lots to do around here before we head to Bozeman." Josie helped her sister with the dishes.

"My good old Josie. Always keeping my interests at

heart. Don't know what I'd do without you." Hunter smiled affectionately at his elder daughter.

Those were words Jack didn't relish. Once more it sounded like Hunter would raise a stink at the prospect of an engagement. Jack wondered what kind of future he and Josie could have if her own father didn't want her to leave. Either way, he found himself looking at the future with uncertainty. Not only had he let his feelings for Josie get out of hand, but her father seemed to be putting up an impenetrable barrier.

Jack brought his thoughts up short. When did he start thinking he and Josie would be having a future together? Could a few stolen kisses have affected him that much? No. He was made of stronger mettle than that. All he'd have to do would be to keep his distance from Josie.

Simple words. Then why did he not believe his own thoughts?

Pressing the chewing tobacco against the side of his cheek, Slim talked around his wad. "Just lemme know when you want me. I'll meet you in the Hay Bale tomorrow night, Hunter, and you can tell me when to come on over."

"Sounds like a good time. Maybe we should go over there tonight."

"Naw, let's stay here and enjoy the company of your purty gals," Slim said, grinning at Hunter's daughters. "Say, I hear the oldest Barlow is plannin' on enterin' his black in the races."

Jack had planned on leaving, but he certainly wasn't going to go now. Horse racing was his life, and he needed to learn as much as possible about the local favorites so he could gauge Zeus's chance for success.

"Slim, do you watch all the races? Are you familiar with the horses?" Jack asked.

Slim spoke up. "Sure do. Matter o' fact, I got a horse I'm gonna run in one of the earlier races. You can't run a livery and not be interested in horses. But you could say I know the skinny on all the horses. It's my business to."

"Josie and I go to each race," Hunter said. "Let's move out to the sitting room while my girls clean up the meal. It'll be quieter." He led the way from the clattering dishes.

The small rectangular room was centered with a cluster of chairs and a sofa arranged in a square in the middle. A thick bear pelt lay on the floor in front of the hearth. Another soft pelt was draped over the back of the sofa, its fur glistening in the crackling firelight.

Jack settled into one of the single chairs by the sofa. He hoped when Josie joined them she would sit on the sofa next to him.

"I ain't never seen this horse of yours run. When do I get to see him practice?" Slim crossed to the front door, opened it, and spat out a stream of his chew.

"Tomorrow afternoon. I heard there's going to be a few men at the track holding a mock race. It should be good practice for Zeus." Jack could hardly wait to let his horse stretch his legs on a real dirt oval. No more makeshift, uneven tracks for him.

"Did I hear you say you're going to ride tomorrow?" Josie and Lottie had finished in the kitchen and had joined the men. She looked around and quickly sat at the end of the sofa nearest Jack.

His chest swelled with satisfaction. "That's right. Late afternoon. Are you going to come watch?" He forgot about the rest of the people in the room and focused only on Josie.

"I'd love to." She looked into his eyes and held them, unblinking. "I've been looking forward to watching him run ever since I first set eyes on the beautiful animal."

He suddenly wanted to hear her telling him he was the one she'd been looking forward to meeting all her life. But that sounded so sentimental, so unlike him, he cringed at the thought. Maybe this temporary engagement business *had* gone to his head. He'd have to get a grip on himself.

"I'll be sure and look for you along the rail." Jack stared into her green eyes. He loved how they contrasted with her dark lashes and brows. Her pale face with a smattering of freckles was the last thing he pictured every night before he fell asleep. He stifled a groan. He could no more stay away from her than he could harness the moon.

"Look for all of us," Slim interjected. "I just know Hunter and Lottie will want to be there. As well as myself."

"Why, Slim, that's real sweet of you, but don't feel you have to. I mean, if you're busy at the livery," Josie said.

"Nope, I'll be there. After all, I have an interest in this horse. He could be my competition in the race. And I like nuthin' better than to watch horseflesh thunder down the track. Will I see a certain gray there tomorrow?"

Josie's eyes widened and her mouth fell open slightly. She stammered. "I—I don't think so. Unless Mr. Samuels is running his dapple gray."

"I guess it's only fair to check out the competition before the big race," Jack said, wondering which animal in the livery was Slim's racehorse. He couldn't recall seeing any that looked particularly promising. And he also wondered about the meaning of Slim and Josie's last comment. Were they referring to her gray mare, Lady?

"Yep, gotta check out the competition. There's a mighty big purse for the fair races, and I aim to see some of it," Slim said.

"I'd love to have you all watch Zeus. He seems to do better if there's a crowd." Jack grinned. Josie and her family wanted to watch him race. His own parents had never come to view any of the races in Kansas City.

It had hurt Jack, but he'd refused to acknowledge it. Here, under the umbrella of Josie's family's eagerness, the past pain reared, visible and real. He wished his parents had taken an interest in his racing passion at least once. His fingers tightened around the wooden armrest. Now it was too late.

"Good! I can come too. I'll bring Mary Jane. She

hasn't met you yet, although I've told her all about you, Jack.'' She looked over at Jack and winked. ''And she thinks you sound sooo handsome.''

Jack shifted his glance away from Lottie. Her words made him uncomfortable. His eyes sought Josie, and she smiled at him. Her captivating smile made the past remembrances about his parents retreat. Josie would be there for him. And suddenly that was important to Jack.

✦ *15* ✦

SHORTLY AFTER THE sun had risen, Josie stood, coffee mug in hand, staring at her father. She hadn't seen him so eager to start his work in many years. She even heard Lottie singing from her room. Josie had an idea why her family was suddenly a bunch of eager-beavers. The upcoming trip to Bozeman.

"Jos, why're you standing around with your teeth in your mouth? There's work to be done." Hunter pulled on his boots, stood up, and stomped his heels down.

"I'm surprised at how eager everyone is to get to work, that's all." She took a gulp of the coffee, nearly scalding her mouth in the process. Her father had sounded cheerful. Usually it took him several cups of coffee to even wake up. If she didn't know better, he was almost acting like he did before leaving to search out sapphires. Her throat closed. He wasn't planning on leaving again so soon?

"Well, there's nothing to be surprised about. Can't a

man look forward to working his own land?''

Josie's brows rose. He was up to something. ''I guess I was just being silly.''

''That's my girl. Now, let's get to work. We've got a race to attend this afternoon and our big trip to Bozeman coming up. It's never too early to plan for a trip, I always say.''

She knew it. It *was* the Bozeman trip. She relaxed. Her father wouldn't disappear to hunt sapphires with this Bozeman trip on the horizon.

''Hey, Jos, tell Lottie I left her some mending in the basket. I'm goin' to work on the fence lines.'' Hunter shrugged into a coat and slipped out the door, coffee tin in his hand.

''You don't have to tell me. I heard Father.'' Lottie swept into the room, her blond curls pulled back away from her face. ''Guess what?'' she said to her sister.

''What?'' Josie looked at her sister, briefly wondering if Jack would desire her more if she had Lottie's pale beauty. Foolish thought, she decided.

''I've already laid out a few things for our trip. It'll be sooo exciting.''

Josie groaned. Both her father and sister were not going to let her forget about Bozeman. ''Go get something to eat. I'm going to start my chores.''

The morning passed by in a blur. Doing laundry for three people kept Josie occupied. Her hands were cold and the skin on the pads of her fingertips had grown all puckery from constant dipping in the water. The clothesline, which stretched from one cottonwood to another, fairly sagged from the weight of the damp clothes. At last, after stopping only briefly for a noon meal, Josie fastened the last pin to the last clean shirt.

After putting away her washing supplies, Josie sat on her bed, readying for the outing at the racetrack. She tucked one foot underneath her and brushed her hair, preparing to rebraid it.

''Jos, you in there?'' her father asked, tapping on the door.

"Yes, you can come in."

Her door swung silently open.

"You look mighty pretty, sitting there with your hair all loose like that. Reminds me of your ma." Hunter stopped just short of the bed, and his face softened.

"Do you really think I look like her?"

"Sure do. The same pretty dark hair, green eyes. The only difference is she was taller. You take after your grandma." His eyes clouded for a second and he looked away, blinking. "There are times when I miss your ma something fierce. Sometimes I feel like it's no fair how hard life is. The price it extracts. Makes me realize how much I love you."

Josie sat there, feeling like she should say something, but she didn't know what. The pain and longing was clearly evident in her father's voice.

As quickly as Hunter's melancholy came, it left. He cleared his throat and jammed his fists into his pockets. "Well, now, um, Josie. Hurry and finish, it's almost time to go to the racetrack."

"Aren't we going to go over with Jack?" She had hoped they could all go together.

"No, he's already left."

"What? When did he come?"

"Oh, I spoke with him before I came to see you. He seems real excited to be racin' his horse. Should be fun to watch. I've got the wagon hitched up. Since Lottie's friend is over visitin', I thought we'd all drive to the track." Hunter spun on his heel and left her room.

Josie's fingers flew down her hair as she finished the braid. How could she have missed Jack? She should have heard him ride up.

A burst of giggles from the next room reminded her why she'd never heard Jack. Lottie and Mary Jane giggled loud enough to pierce one's eardrums.

Standing up, she glanced down at her freshly washed skirt and matching basque. The maize calico two-piece outfit accented her dark hair, while the basque was close-fitting enough to show her feminine curves. She looked neat and clean, even if it wasn't the latest style. Maybe she should pinch her cheeks to make them rosy.

She hoped Jack would appreciate her efforts. She knew he didn't share her feelings, and her feelings had come dangerously close to something she didn't want to acknowledge. She fought against the seed of love in her heart. It could lead to only one thing. Pain. Never could she admit her vulnerability to him.

She left her room and proceeded out the front door. Before her stood the wagon, horses hitched and ready to go.

"C'mon, Josie. We don't wanna be late." Lottie waved her hand.

Josie crossed to the wagon and climbed in.

"Now, girls." Hunter twisted around from his perch on the driver's bench and looked at Lottie and Mary Jane. "There could be lots of people at the racetrack and maybe lots of nervous horses. I want you to stay close." He shook his index finger for emphasis.

"Father, we won't go anywhere. We wanna watch Jack. Mary Jane's never met him." Lottie looked at her friend and grinned mischievously.

Josie didn't miss the exchange, and she poked Lottie's arm.

"Ow, what'd you do that for?" Lottie scowled at Josie and slid closer to Mary Jane.

"Miss Josie, you sure look pretty today," Mary Jane said.

"Thank you." Josie briefly wondered if the other townsfolk would also think she looked nice, then dismissed the thought. In her mind, only one person's opinion mattered. Jack's.

She was nervous. Today would be the first time they were together in public since the "engagement." What was going to happen?

After the church steeple, the grandstands were the tallest structure in town. It was easy to spot them from anywhere in Gallatin City. The only thing the grandstands lacked for the mock race were the American flags.

During real races, the flags flew proudly above the grandstands.

Josie noted the grandstands showed signs of the harsh winter. The once-pristine white boards were now a dull gray in spots. The fence that separated the racetrack from the spectators was also in need of another coat of paint. To her left, Josie watched people climb up into the low bleachers that were scattered along the railing.

Josie couldn't believe the number of people who'd turned out for the mock race. It looked like one-fourth of the town had turned out to see the horses practice. Everywhere she looked she saw children running, groups of women gossiping, and clusters of men smoking.

When their wagon arrived on the grounds, all the people within viewing distance stopped their conversations and stared at them. They nudged one another, whispered, and gaped. Josie wanted to sink down into the bed of the wagon. She felt like a steer on display. Obviously the citizens had not forgotten about her engagement.

Josie scanned the grounds, ignoring the inquisitive glances, and looked for any sign of Jack or Zeus. Her brows drew together at the sight of so many people. How on earth was she supposed to find anybody in this crowd?

"Lots of people here," Hunter said as he steered the team to an empty spot next to the rail.

"Where is he?" Mary Jane demanded as both girls leaned forward, looking past Hunter.

"I dunno, I can't see him. Josie, where's Jack?" Lottie pulled on her sister's sleeve.

"Girls, don't pester Josie. I see some of my buddies. I'm goin' to go talk to them. You two don't stray too far." Hunter climbed out of the wagon and held up his arms to assist the females.

"Don't hurry," Josie said, hoping that when she saw Jack, she'd have more time to talk with him and enjoy his company. For some reason, she felt less comfortable talking to Jack with her father around. She scoffed. The answer to that was simple. Her father didn't know that she and Jack were still engaged, nor would he be pleased.

For some reason, Jack hadn't mentioned it to her father, and now it looked like she would have to be the one to do that. She couldn't have her father denouncing her good news all over town, nor could she let him say anything to Lottie.

"Keep an eye on your sister," Hunter said to Josie. With that he walked away to join a group of men.

"Don't I always?" Josie muttered to no one in particular.

A sudden flurry of movement down on the track caught her attention. A dark horse bucked and reared, whinnying loudly. The rider wrapped his arms tightly around the horse's neck, trying to stay on. The other mounted men moved their horses farther away from the berserk animal.

Josie shook her head. She'd know that black horse anywhere. Clyde Barlow's stallion. The horse had no manners or common sense. How Clyde thought he could win a race with that animal was beyond her. "I see one of the Barlow horses is giving its usual display of temper."

Neither her sister nor Mary Jane commented. They were too busy scouting in the area. No doubt looking for Jack, Josie thought.

"Look!" Lottie bounced up and down. "There he is! I recognize his horse."

"Where? Where?" Mary Jane was shorter than Lottie and had to bounce twice as high.

Josie felt her own heartbeat flutter in response. Just to her right on the track was Jack. He and his beautiful chestnut horse were headed right for them. With the bright spring sunlight shining down on him, he looked positively gorgeous.

Golden highlights glinted in his rich brown hair. His blue eyes were twinkling. And his clothing! His shirt was open at the collar and seemed to cling like it was painted on, not to mention what his tight trousers did to his legs. Josie sighed. What she wouldn't do to make him her husband.

''He's coming to see us! He's coming to see us! Now you can meet him. Remember, his name is Jack St. Augustine.'' Lottie's excitement was not wasted on her friend. Mary Jane couldn't stop giggling or smiling.

Josie took a few steps forward and placed her hands on the rail. She needed something to hold on to when she looked up into his face and noticed his soft expression. Her insides heated up and her legs felt wobbly knowing the smile was for her alone. He *must* feel something for her.

Before she could open up her mouth in a greeting, Lottie burst forth.

''Jack. Hello. I brought my friend Mary Jane with me. You said you wanted to meet her. Here she is.'' Lottie pulled the other girl forward. They both dropped curtsies.

Jack glanced to Josie first, winked, and then turned his attention to the younger girls. ''It's a pleasure to meet you, Miss Mary Jane. Lottie has told me all about you.''

''Did you hear that? He called me Miss Mary Jane.'' Mary Jane collapsed into another fit of giggles.

From her vantage point on the ground, Jack towered above Josie. She had to tilt her head backward to see him. He looked just right on the back on his horse. Two good-looking creatures, both standouts from the crowd.

''I'm glad you made it here. I was beginning to wonder if you were going to come, especially when I went to your ranch to get Zeus.'' Jack had moved his horse forward a few steps, bringing him even with Josie.

''Of course I'd come. I'm sorry I missed you at our house. I was dressing.'' She dropped her glance. She could feel eyes boring into her from all directions. Even though no one had come up to them yet, she could practically feel their curiosity in the very air she breathed. How one engagement could be so fascinating mystified her. Didn't these people have anything better to do? she wondered.

''Well, you look very nice. Makes me glad I came over and said hello before we raced. Such a pretty lady, I'll try and win for you.''

His low, gravelly voice did strange things to her. She alternated between hot and cold. No one had ever wanted to win a race, not even a mock race, for her. Nor did they usually call her pretty. Jack's words made her feel special. She beamed up at him. "I'd like that."

"I'll see what we can do." He took one hand off the reins and stroked Zeus's sleek neck.

Josie watched, entranced, wondering what his touch would feel like on her own heated skin, knowing the embrace on the mountainside had only whetted her appetite for more. She swallowed and quickly looked away. She shouldn't have such thoughts.

"Um, have a good ride. Watch out for the black Barlow horse, he's kind of wild." Now, why did she say that? Couldn't she have thought of something more personal? More romantic?

"Don't worry, I've been staying away from that untrained animal ever since I arrived. They were sort of glaring at me anyway."

"The Barlows do that. Ignore them." Lord knew, she tried her best to ignore them. She remembered them calling her a silly female trying to race a mare. Just let them wait to see what kind of competition Zeus gives them. She drew herself up, thrust her shoulders back, and smiled.

"Thanks for the advice. Do you have any more for me?" He gazed at only her, and ignored the snickers of the younger girls. He also did a good job of ignoring the pointed stares from the interested bystanders.

She gripped the rail harder. She could drown herself in the pools of his blue eyes if she wasn't careful. "Watch the far corner, it's kind of scary over there for the horses."

"Far corner. Right, I'll remember that. After the race I can walk him home next to your wagon if you'd like."

"We'd love it." She meant to say *she'd* love it, but thought it might sound more appropriate if she included her whole family.

With one last lingering look, Jack sighed and spoke.

"It's almost time. I want to warm him up. I'd hate him to cramp up after the race."

"Good luck." Excitement built in Josie. She could hardly wait to see this horse race. She regretted that she couldn't be riding Lady today, but that was hardly the proper thing to do. Especially since she was trying to convince both Jack and Mrs. Potter that she was as feminine and proper as anyone could wish.

But she did regret she hadn't been able to work with Lady as much since she met Jack. Josie only hoped the decreased training schedule wouldn't hurt her mare's chances of putting in a good race.

"We'll be cheering for you, Mr. St. Augustine," Mary Jane said as she and Lottie waved him off.

"Now I've got nothing to fear with all you pretty ladies cheering me on," Jack called over his shoulder.

That latest gallantry sent Lottie and Mary Jane into another fit of giddiness. It was all they could do to restrain from jumping up and down with excitement.

Josie too felt like jumping up and down, but instead, she settled for the quiet knowledge that Jack found her attractive and had sought her advice. Not that there was any reason for her to tell him how she knew about the far side of the track, not yet. The time would come for that. But not now. The horses were warming up. It was almost post time.

Five sleek horses moved into formation at the starting line. All heads turned toward the track. Hands rose to shield eyes from the slanting sunlight.

One man raised a pistol to fire the shot signaling the start of the race. Silence fell over the gathered onlookers.

Bang!

The horses shot forward. The pack surged as one. Josie craned her neck, keeping her eyes on Jack and Zeus. Her blood raced in her veins as if she were the one riding and not just watching.

Jack had his horse on the edge of the pack. When the group passed Josie, he was closest to her. She could see the muscles rippling with each ground-eating stride Zeus took. In a haze of dust they were gone, disappearing around the bend in the track.

"Go, Jack!" Lottie yelled, clapping her hands.

Josie strained her eyes. It was impossible to see who was in the lead. As the group reached the far corner, she noticed the only black horse suddenly dart away from the group. She drew in a quick breath as she noticed the black heading straight for Jack's horse.

The crowd gasped, waiting to see if the inevitable collision would occur. Pipes hung suspended from men's lips. A few women shrieked and turned away.

Soon the pack swept around the corner and were on the straightaway. Jack's horse strode past the unruly black, averting the collision. As one, the crowd let out a sigh of relief. Josie relaxed the fists she hadn't known she'd clenched.

The black had lost all interest in racing and was plunging and twisting the width of the track. Quickly, Josie jerked her eyes from the black.

Jack's horse surged toward the lead. She held her breath, stood on tiptoe, straining to witness the finish.

At the last few furlongs the lead horse's rider whipped his mount, causing the animal to bolt forward and cross the line. Wild cheering broke out from the crowd. Whoops and hollers filled Josie's ears as well as words of sympathy. She ignored them and kept her eyes on her fiancé.

Jack and Zeus had placed second.

"He lost," Lottie wailed as the winning horse ran past.

"No, he didn't. It was only a practice run. I'm sure Jack is saving his horse for when it really matters." She too was disappointed Jack hadn't won, but after all, she rationalized, it *was* only a practice.

Lathered with sweat, Zeus cantered by. Jack grinned and waved.

"See, he just waved. He's not upset at all. I'm sure he knew what he was doing."

"Where's Mr. St. Augustine going?" Mary Jane asked.

"I imagine to cool his horse off. After running a race like that, it's pretty important to let your horse calm down and return to a normal temperature."

Mary Jane and Lottie looked at Josie like she was crazy.

She knew the younger girls didn't share her enthusiasm for horses and their well-being. Josie just shrugged. "I'm going to walk around for a few minutes and say hello to some of the people. Try to stay out of mischief."

"We will. We're gonna wait for Jack. He'll want to talk to us. C'mon, Mary Jane, let's go get a lemonade." Lottie took her friend's hand and they scampered toward the shaded refreshment cart.

Out of the corner of her eye Josie saw women moving toward her, no doubt eager for more fodder for gossip. Taking a deep breath, Josie turned and faced them. She wanted to make the first move.

"Oh, Josie darlin'! We just had to come over and speak to you," Mrs. Adams said as she approached at a brisk walk. The bottom of her skirt was liberally coated with dust, as it was too long, with a impractical train, but that never stopped her from trying to set fashion trends.

Josie squared her shoulders. "Why, here I am. What would you like to talk about?"

Mrs. Adams and the four other ladies who'd accompanied her all fluttered their fans and tittered. "Silly darlin', how can you not know why we're here? We wanted to congratulate you on finding a husband." She leaned forward, confidante-like, and whispered. "Tell me, how did you manage it?"

Josie stared at Mrs. Adams. She hardly knew where to begin. "It's simple. We just fell in love at first sight." She raised her hands, palms up and fingers spread. "That's all there is to it."

"Oh, me, oh, my. Love at first sight. How I envy you. Don't all of us women hope for such good fortune. Do remember, we all want to meet this man." Mrs. Adams closed her fan as she and her cronies glided off to the refreshment wagon.

If that was any indication of the type of conversation she could expect to have, Josie was sorely tempted to just go back to the wagon and sit. But she continued on, vowing not to let the inquisitive people ruin her day.

She exchanged greetings, acknowledging the congratulations on her upcoming nuptials, the condolences on Jack's loss. Being on a first-name basis with the whole town made it hard for her to escape notice. She kept her chin up and tried hard not to let the bold stares and obvious whispers frighten her.

Josie couldn't remember when her presence had caused such a stir. Other women who'd been engaged hadn't received this much attention. Obviously, it was something of a novelty when the town spinster managed to catch the newest single male, and a handsome one at that.

She did wonder how her father was reacting to all the congratulations he was bound to receive. Would he ignore them or deny the existence of an engagement? Suddenly, she wished she'd talked with her father before they'd left their ranch. She didn't know what she'd do if he contradicted her words.

Trying to keep her eyes focused ahead and a smile on her face, Josie did not see Mrs. Potter swooping in from the side.

"Josephine Douglass, I'm still waiting to be introduced to this fiancé of yours. Tell me, when are you going to bring him over to our house so we can meet him properly?" Mrs. Potter stood, hands on hips, her voluminous skirts swaying in the breeze, and waited for an answer.

"Mrs. Potter, how nice to see you." Inwardly, Josie groaned. Of all the people to run into, she had to come across the one she least wanted to see. "I—I didn't think you watched the horse races."

"Of course I do. My dear husband comes, so I follow him. Lord knows, we need to pray for all your souls. Betting on horses. It's the devil's work. But enough of that. When can we expect you? It's hardly proper for a

young woman to be engaged without her fiancé having
been introduced to the reverend.''

She certainly was never short of words, Josie thought,
trying to hold on to her smile. "I'm sorry we haven't
been over. Things have been kind of . . . hectic. I promise
we'll come over next week." Josie glance upward,
checking to see if a lightning bolt was headed toward
her. Next week she would probably be in Bozeman with
her family. That, however, was something she didn't
think Mrs. Potter needed to know.

"We'll be expecting you. After all, an engagement
isn't truly sanctioned until the good reverend, my husband, has given his blessing to both parties." Mrs. Potter's glance followed a trio of men. Her eyes narrowed
as she witnessed them exchanging money.

"Horse races." Mrs. Potter shut her eyes and clucked
her tongue while shaking her head. "Now, that makes
me wonder why the good, God-fearing citizens of this
community fritter away their hard-earned money on
games of chance, such as racing, when they could be
saving it for the good Lord's work."

Ah, the church fund-raiser tomorrow. That had slipped
Josie's mind. Every citizen was expected to attend and
bid on the various items up for auction.

"I must be off. There are other souls for me to save.
Please tell my niece to come and visit me soon. I told
Charlotte I look forward to having her at my house, even
if it is only for a visit."

Josie felt the breeze created by Mrs. Potter's abrupt
departure.

She barely had enough time to collect her thoughts,
when a slender hand landed on her arm. Josie turned and
smiled in relief when she saw Grace.

"There you are. I was afraid that was you Mrs. Potter
had in her clutches." Grace laughed at Josie's expression.
"Each time she comes into the mercantile, she asks about
your fiancé. It's as if she's starved for information."

"Starved? That's putting it mildly. She practically ordered Jack and me over to their house. She said an en-

gagement wasn't official until her husband blessed both of us." Josie was relieved to have found a friendly face. And one that wasn't eyeing her in curiosity. "Say, what are you doing here?"

"I came for the match. That's all Robert talked about all morning. He wanted to watch and see who might be this year's race winner."

"If both of you are here, who's minding the store?" It was unusual for both Grace and her husband to be out of the store during operating hours.

"Mrs. Boggs. She helps out during the week. It keeps her busy ever since her husband passed on."

"Ah. Did you see Jack?"

"I think so, but I don't know what his horse looks like. I assume he's the one who came in second, since I've never seen that horse before."

Josie nodded.

Grace lowered her voice. "All the other women seem to be staring at you. I think they're jealous of your good fortune. If only they knew the whole story." She laughed. "Are things still fine between you and Jack?"

Josie's blush answered for her. "Yes, I think so. He agreed to continue the engagement." She failed to add that Jack considered the engagement only temporary. It would be true humiliation for Josie to admit that, even to her best friend. Besides, Josie would remedy that soon enough.

"Good, good. Are you still trying to be a lady? I mean, after your big blooper of saying you and he were engaged prematurely, I thought Jack might need some real convincing."

"What do you think?"

"Josie, that's not important. You *are* still being lady-like, like I taught you?" Grace inclined forward, brows puckered.

"I'm doing my best."

"What about demure?"

"I'm trying. I can't totally change my personality. He'll have to take me as I am, mostly."

"Hmmm. Oh, look. Robert is signaling me. He's ready to go back to the store. Let me think about this and then we can talk about it later." Grace took Josie's hand and gave it a warm squeeze. "I'll come by and visit soon."

Josie sighed and turned to head back to the wagon. Her spirits rose as she realized who was waiting by it. Jack. She hurried, hoping she wouldn't look too eager.

Portia Potter stood underneath a tree and frowned. She hated seeing so many of the church's congregation wasting time and money on horse races. She snapped her umbrella open, as the tree she stood under didn't provide much shade.

If she had her way, there would be no horse races in her city. But that was out of her control, since her husband enjoyed watching the animals run. Her gaze skimmed the nearby crowd and suddenly lit up. Now, there was something, and someone, she could control.

Charlotte.

Portia's lips curled up as she saw Mary Jane Samuels leave Charlotte. This was her chance. Portia quickly strode over to her niece.

"Charlotte," Portia called, eager to have her niece to herself. "Hello, my dear. I hate to see you at such an occurrence, but I am here for you."

Lottie's eyes grew round as she realized who was addressing her. Some of the lemonade in her cup spilled over the side. "Aunt Portia, I—I didn't expect to see you here."

Portia wrapped her free arm around Charlotte's shoulders and steered her toward the tree she had recently been standing under. "I realize it is shocking, but if you feel you cannot be near the evil influence of gambling, which seems to be sanctioned by your sister, I'll understand and take you home. To my house."

Lottie stopped dead still. Her face was as white as plaster. "Aunt Portia, my sister doesn't gamble. She—she takes care of me."

"Nonsense, you are a young woman, and at such an

impressionable age, I'm afraid.'' Portia pulled Lottie closer, secure in the knowledge that only she could do right by her deceased sister's daughter. ''I know you think you need to live with your father and sister, but the truth is, they cannot make you into the young woman you can be. Only I can.''

Lottie's lower lip quivered. Her gaze darted back and forth, looking for any sign of her sister. She desperately wanted Josie. Lottie had never been so scared in her life. ''A-Aunt Portia, please don't hold me so tight, it hurts.''

Loosening her hold, Portia continued. ''I must tell you, I am disappointed in you. Do you know what I saw the other day?''

Not trusting her voice, Lottie only shook her head. She blinked, trying to clear the tears from her eyes.

''This pains me to say it, but I found you up in a tree. I was too shocked to say anything, but it proved to me that you will never find a decent husband if you continue to live with that unorthodox sister of yours.'' Portia clucked her tongue.

''I—I was only u-up in the tree for a few minutes, reading. It's peaceful up there, and no one saw me, so I don't think I did anything wrong.'' Lottie took a step away from her aunt. She was afraid Aunt Portia, with her large size, could easily drag her away and lock her inside the Potter house.

''Charlotte, I saw you, and if I saw you, who knows who else might have?'' She pivoted so she stood face-to-face with her niece. ''Doesn't this prove to you that your father's house is no place for a young woman? You should be in town, learning to be a lady. What potential suitor would want a tree-climber for a wife?''

Lottie was frozen with fear. She could not tear her gaze off her aunt. Aunt Portia's face was only inches from hers. Lottie watched her aunt's thin lips and generous cheeks move with each word. Did her aunt really think a potential suitor wouldn't want her?

Portia reached out and shook Lottie's shoulder.

"Young lady, did you hear me? You did not answer me. That is another fault of yours I must correct."

"I—I won't climb trees anymore." Lottie's voice shook.

"That's my girl." Portia released Lottie and fussed with Lottie's hair before stepping sideways. "I'm glad we had this little talk. We'll have more of them when you are under my roof. Now, I must go meet with the Auxiliary members. We have a lot to discuss." Portia lifted the bottom of her black skirt and walked off.

Lottie wiped her eyes with the back of her hand and bit her lip. Her heart thudded like she'd just ended a long reel of dancing, only without the joy dancing gave her. What her aunt said couldn't be true. Her sister loved her and would make sure she grew up properly. And she would find a beau—her sister had.

Swallowing the rest of the lemonade that her aunt almost made her spill, Lottie's fears began subsiding. She believed her sister would keep her safe. Right now she wanted to go back to their wagon and wait for her sister. She wanted the feeling of security Josie brought her.

Lottie returned the empty cup back to the lemonade cart, keeping a smile on her face, and searched for Mary Jane. Smiling was harder than she thought. Her tummy felt upset and she was afraid she might burst into tears. But she couldn't. She couldn't let anyone, especially Josie, know how frightened her aunt had made her.

"Where've you been?" Mary Jane asked as she met up with Lottie. "Let's go back to your wagon and wait for Mr. St. Augustine. Maybe he'll call us pretty ladies again." Mary Jane grasped Lottie's hand and pulled her toward the wagon.

"You don't have to pull me, it's not becoming," Lottie warned.

"Look who's gonna walk home next to us," Lottie said, her eyes shining. She pointed at Jack.

"I see." Josie drew in a breath, trying to still her racing pulse. Then she glanced back at her sister. Lottie's eyes had a glassy look, the type of look they usually had after she'd been crying. Josie opened her mouth to ask her sister what had happened, but Jack spoke first.

"What did you think of our performance?"

Jack walked his horse in circles, cooling the animal down.

Josie looked from the sweaty horse to the windblown man. "I thought you ran well. For a while there it looked like you two would pull ahead. But then Mr. White started whipping his horse."

"Me too. Originally I didn't come out here with the intention of winning today. But when I saw your pretty face, I wanted to win for you. I'm sorry I didn't."

"Don't feel too bad. I know how important it is to save your horse's strength for when it really matters." At Jack's odd look, Josie blushed and shifted her gaze. How long could she keep her racing a secret from him? What if he discovered her at the track one morning? She'd have to be careful until the time presented itself to tell him about her hobby.

"At least I know we've got a great chance of winning at the fair." Jack gave an affectionate pat to his horse.

"Did you hear us cheering for you?" Lottie fell in step beside Jack.

He furrowed his brow and pursed his lips. "I think so. But it's hard to tell with all the wind rushing past your ears."

Josie knew that sensation well. It was one she relished. "Hey, Lottie, did Father say if he was coming home with us?"

"Nope, he said to go on home without him. He's gonna be at the Hay Bale." Lottie turned her attention back to Jack. "We can walk next to you, Mary Jane and I."

Jack glanced up and caught Josie's eye, almost pleading with her to rescue him from the overly attentive young ladies.

"Girls, I think you should ride in the wagon. You can talk to Jack back at home." An idea suddenly formed in

Josie's mind. Since she didn't know how long her father would be gone, perhaps she'd ask Jack to stay for dinner. Once her father got to talking, he forgot all notions about time. It'd be a shame to waste perfectly good food, and she could use the time alone with Jack to sway his opinion of her.

As Josie drove the team home, she only half listened to the excited chatter of the girls behind her. Her glance kept slipping over to Jack, who walked next to the wagon.

His horse's breathing seemed to have returned to normal, and Jack no longer looked flushed. As she looked at Jack, her heart swelled and a warm glow infused her whole body. She knew now what that strange feeling she felt for him was. She'd actually fallen in love with him. The question was, would he ever return her love?

"Thanks for your advice back there at the track," Jack said, breaking the silence.

Josie's smile broadened. "You're welcome. Would you like to stay for dinner?"

His eyes widened. "Is it all right with your father?"

She spoke before she thought. "Of course. He might not be there, but he'd hate for the food to go to waste. Besides, you should get nourishment after racing." She rolled her eyes. She hadn't meant to lay it on that thick.

"If you're sure. I don't want to impose."

"No imposition. As long as you don't mind stew again. But it's flavored differently. I made it this time."

"I can hardly turn down a home-cooked meal by my fiancé, now, can I?"

Josie gripped the reins. Her lips curved upward. He seemed eager to taste her cooking, and in her mind she equated that with a reference to their future. Maybe Grace's hints were helping. She'd been doing her best to be a lady, and so far, her actions seemed to please Jack.

Yes, she was on the right track. Soon Jack would want a real engagement with her. Nothing could stop her plans now.

❖ 16 ❖

JACK GROOMED ZEUS longer than necessary in the barn once they'd arrived at Josie's ranch. His thoughts kept turning to Josie and what he should do about her. Oh, he knew what he'd said. He'd said he would go along with an engagement for now. He'd had no choice. He had to restore her honor and his. Well, he'd done that by confirming their engagement with everyone he'd met in town and he should feel better. Instead, he felt more confused than ever.

He hadn't told her father of the engagement. Knowing Hunter's volatile temper, Jack had thought it better not to. It wouldn't do any good to get Hunter all riled up over a future wedding that wouldn't come to pass.

Although, what Hunter must have said to all the well-wishers about the engagement was a puzzlement to Jack.

Jack also felt guilty for the other reason he'd agreed to the engagement. He needed Josie's mare for his breeding operation. Of course he hadn't told her that yet. And that would hardly sound noble of him anyway.

Hell, he should just offer to buy the mare. Since he and Josie wouldn't be marrying, he'd be no further in his quest for a mare than he was before.

He was supposed to be thinking of a plan, of a way to end his commitment and to keep both their honor intact. So far he continued to come up blank on that end.

But what alarmed him most was the state of his affections for Josie. He shouldn't have any for her, and, dammit, he did. He'd realized that when he'd kissed her. Hell, if he was being honest, why not admit he'd been smitten with her from the very start? One look at her impish face had done that. She had a vitality that attracted him. Her zest for life matched his own. Even her love of horses seemed equal to his.

He groaned. He had to end the engagement, didn't he? Josie wasn't at all the meek, demure creature he'd imagined as his life mate. Had he been wrong about his ideal woman?

His hand stilled on his horse's mane. Even though he wasn't sure he wanted Josie as his wife, the thought of her spending her life alone, or, worse, the thought of other man tasting her sweet lips pained him. Leaning over, he rested his head against Zeus' neck. "What am I going to do, boy?"

Jack listened to the steady breathing of the horse, trying to think what he should do. A battle raged within him. His heart wanted to take a chance on Josie, but his mind warned him against her, against her headstrong personality.

Even her invitation for dinner seemed rather forward. The lack of a chaperon didn't seem to bother her in the least. But he rationalized that if she had enough food, she'd rather see it eaten instead of going to waste.

It bothered him slightly that her father wouldn't be there. However, he'd seen enough of Montana to know that the people who lived there went by their own rules. He still needed to change his way of thinking from his conservative upbringing to the more openmindedness of the frontier. Then her invitation wouldn't have come as any surprise to him.

All they would be doing was eating a meal. There would be no kissing. At least not when Lottie was around.

Kissing.

The mere thought brought his head up. Lately, it seemed all he could think about was what they'd shared on the mountain. The embrace had stirred a powerful emotion deep within him. His body wanted Josie, and he was afraid his heart did also. But his mind? His mind rebelled, recalling his domineering mother, and Josie's father, who seemed set against Josie ever marrying and leaving home.

Therein lay the problem.

Suppose Hunter still refused to let Josie marry? Jack had heard Hunter say time and time again how much he depended upon Josie. Even her sister needed her. Trouble was, Jack was starting to think that he might also need Josie. And that scared him. Because it meant his heart was talking louder than his mind, and his whole life Jack had prided himself on his levelheadedness.

He threw his brushes into the tin bucket and put Zeus in his stall. It was time he saw Josie.

After supper Jack and Josie went outside to sit on the rockers on the front porch. Lottie had remained inside, busy sewing. The evening air wasn't as chilly as the previous nights, it even held a hint of warmth. In the distance a lone owl hooted.

Jack settled back into his rocker next to Josie. "That was a good meal. I enjoyed your version of the stew. Thanks."

She glanced over at him and smiled. "Glad you liked the food. I'm just sorry my father wasn't here to enjoy it too."

Jack stretched his legs out and crossed his booted ankles. This was something he could get used to doing.

Josie really was a very comfortable person to be around. "How long do you think he'll be gone?"

Josie sighed. Her chair creaked as it rocked back and forth, quicker now. "Who knows. He could be back in one minute or three hours."

Jack sensed an underlying frustration to her words. "Does that bother you?"

"Not so much anymore. I guess you just get used to it. Although it would be . . ."

"Would be what? Why did you stop?" Curious, he sat up and regarded her. Josie stared off into the darkness. Her jaw jutted forward and she had her lower lip drawn between her teeth.

She started, glanced at him, and looked away. "It's nothing."

"Tell me. If you can't talk to your fiancé, who can you talk to?" Jack surprised himself with those words.

"Do you mean that?" She looked at him and gave a little smile. "It's just that, sometimes I would like to have a normal life. It would be nice to know when my father would be home and to know that Lottie will grow up in a regular household. That she'll be safe and secure."

Jack felt his heart growing. She wanted the same thing he did. A simple life. "I understand. I too like stability."

"Oh, I didn't say I wanted a stable life. I kind of like the unknown. I just want my father to stay at home more often."

Her denial surprised him. The way she said it, she made a stable life sound like the worse thing that could happen. "The unknown. Can't say as I've ever thought about that much. I guess it bothers you when you father goes off on his sapphire-hunting trips."

"Yes, it does. He's our father and the workload is less when he's around to help. And Lottie feels safer when he's home. He shouldn't get so caught up in his gems." With the balls of her feet she stilled her chair.

"I don't go off searching for gems."

"I know. Neither did my father at first." Her voice grew softer.

Jack stared out into the twilight. A multitude of colors streaked the sky. Deep purple, orange, and pink stretched endlessly above, dissipating into the blue of night. "Do you think I'll get gold or sapphire fever too?"

The only sound was Josie's soft exhalation. Jack held himself back from prompting her to answer. She would reply in her own time.

"I hope not."

She sounded so forlorn, so sad, he rose to his feet and went to her. He wanted to comfort her. He kneeled, taking her hand in his. He rubbed his thumb across her knuckles. The back of her hand was much softer than her palms. "Josie, believe me. I came out west with the intention of starting a ranch. My gems will be horseflesh, not a cold mineral."

She looked at him. With her free hand she covered the top of his hand. "I—I want to believe you."

Jack looked up, noticing her full, shining lower lip. He reached up, cupped his hand behind her neck, and pulled her closer to him. When he had her within inches of his face, he paused. His good intentions of not kissing her flew right out the window. He searched her face, noting her liquid-green eyes, the trust inherent in them, and then kissed her.

At first she held herself back, then she relaxed and gave herself to him. She opened her mouth and ran her tongue around the contours of his mouth. She flicked at his teeth, deepening her response.

Jack could hear the blood pounding in his ears. He had never before been this affected by a kiss. He wrapped his arms around her and held her tightly, feeling her curves nestle against his body.

His mind registered a snapping sound in the darkness, but he wasn't interested in the noise. Probably just some raccoon out foraging for a meal. He ignored it.

Jack's hand traced lazy trails up and down her spine. He wished the chair weren't between them. He wanted to feel her hot body next to his.

Her answering moan stirred his blood. He pulled her

closer, reveling in her nearness. It felt right, being this close to her.

Neither heard the porch steps creak, nor did they notice the furious man standing near them.

Jack sensed something amiss. He never got a chance to do anything about it until the voice boomed in his ears.

"What in tarnation is going on out here? On my front porch?"

Josie yelped and yanked herself out of Jack's arms.

Jack scrambled to his feet.

Livid, Hunter stood before him. The older man's eyes blazed, his lips were pulled back, his every muscle tightened as if he were ready to fight.

"I repeat, what in tarnation do you think you're doing to my daughter? I oughta tan your hide for this!" He thrust his face into Jack's. His eyes were narrowed to tiny slits.

Before Jack could say a word, Josie jumped in. "Father! Please, we were only kissing good night."

Those were the wrong words.

Hunter's face turned crimson. His hands closed to fists, planted on his hips. "Kissing! Why you, you're a single woman. You have no business tradin' embraces with him."

"If you'll let me say something, sir—" Jack attempted.

"I'm the one doing the talking here. It seems you've done enough damage for one night."

"Father, please! I'm engaged to Jack. He asked me the other day. It can't hurt for us to share one little kiss."

"It's true, we are . . . engaged, Hunter." Jack stood his ground, refusing to bow to her father's temper. He'd done nothing wrong. Well, maybe they shouldn't have gotten so carried away with the kiss, but still, it was no cause for alarm. And maybe he should have told Hunter about the engagement earlier, whether it was an official one or not. Well, Hunter knew now.

"Wife! Husband! Whatever makes you think I'd let you marry my daughter? You never asked me if you could.'' Hunter's face relaxed somewhat. He shoved his hands in his pants pockets.

''Father, I'm twenty-three years old. I'm of age. I don't need your permission.''

''Did you ever think I might *like* to be asked? A father likes to know he's appreciated, that he still has some sway in your life.''

The emotional exchange was too much for Jack. In his family, such a discussion would be done in the privacy of his father's library and in hushed tones. Never in Jack's life had he had a talk at this decibel and on a front porch for all to hear.

''Look, I'm sorry I kissed Josie. I'll try not to let it happen again.'' There. That should placate her father, even if Jack knew he would have a hard time keeping that promise.

''You'll kiss her over my dead body. Now, I don't want to hear any more about this engagement or marriage business. There isn't one. I thought you understood that the first time I said it.'' Hunter glared at him before pivoting on his heel and stalking into the house.

''Father, you can't order me about as if I were a child!'' Josie said to the vibrating door. Her hands were clenched into fists. ''I can be engaged if I want to be.''

Jack and Josie stood staring at each other, neither making a move.

Jack cleared his throat. ''Uh, look, don't let your father worry you. He's just upset.'' Jack reached out to touch her, but stopped his hand.

''Maybe you're right.'' Josie looked miserable, like she expected Jack to flee into the night and away from the Douglasses'.

''Well, I guess this is good-bye. I might see you tomorrow. I need to come and check up on Zeus. Good night.''

'''Night.'' Josie looked wistfully at him before turning to go inside.

Jack stepped off the porch and into the darkness of the night. As he neared the barn, he paused and looked back at the house. Through the trees it looked warm and cozy. The light from the oil lamps gave off a soft glow. Pale wisps of smoke curled skyward from the chimney top. He glimpsed Hunter moving around and he wished it was he inside with Josie.

Right then he didn't want to go to his lonely hotel room. He no longer wanted to crawl into a chilly bed with only his thoughts for company.

Suddenly, he didn't think he could face the empty room yet. He wanted the company of other humans. He would go to the Hay Bale Saloon.

A half hour later, Jack leaned on the bar and watched the men play games of poker and faro at the scattered tables. He wasn't particularly proficient at either, so it suited him to watch.

He reached for his whiskey just as Red, the bartender, stopped in front of him. Red's black vest and spanking white shirt reflected in the varnished bar top. By his elbows he'd secured red lace garters.

"Word is that yur spendin' time with the Douglass woman. Even got yurself hitched to her." Red held up a shot glass and wiped at the nonexistent spots on the rim while waiting for Jack to speak.

"I'm keeping my stallion at their barn, so yes, I guess I do see Josie a lot. And yes, we are engaged." The remark made Jack a tad uneasy. News spread quickly in such a small community. He was used to a larger city, where his comings and goings weren't easily noticed.

Red shook his head. "I dunno why you'd waste yur time with her. The whole town knows she was spinster bound before you showed up an' offered her yur hand. She's kinda like a charity case, if you ask me."

"Just because she's marrying later than most women doesn't mean there's anything wrong with her. And I don't think of her as a charity case." Jack bristled. He didn't like anyone making derogatory remarks about his fiancée. *His* fiancée?

Red put down the shot glass and leaned closer to Jack. His voice took on a conspiratorial tone. "Mind you, it's not her looks. She's right purty enough. It's just her age. Why, everyone knows if a woman doesn't get herself hitched before a certain age, things ain't the same.''

Jack's eyebrows rose. He had no idea what Red was trying to say, but was curious.

"Do ya know what I'm talkin' about? It's a known fact that certain, uh, wimmenly parts don't work after a certain age. So you might want t' rethink marryin' her. You can't be sure of gettin' children with her.'' He flushed and snatched up another shot glass to polish. "Now, us men, we don't have that problem.''

"Is that a fact?'' Jack tried hard not to laugh. His lips quirked. The man's words were so ludicrous. If Red hadn't clearly believed so fully in his own statement, Jack would have assumed that he was just making a bad joke.

"Sure is. Now, if you want yurself a good, young, functionin' gal, I might suggest you go on over to Bozeman. There's more to choose from than here. Miss Josie got along fine without you.''

"What does that mean, she got along fine without me?''

Red refilled Jack's glass. "It just means, Miss Josie can do fine on her own. She's got her sister to look out for, ya know.''

"I think her father also shares some of that responsibility. Besides, Josie is a grown woman capable of making her own decisions.''

"I know how you outta-towners are. You come to our little city, get our wimmen all riled up, an' then at the first hint of somethin' better down the trail, you up an' leave.'' He replaced the cap on the whiskey bottle with a satisfying twist.

Jack didn't like to be called a liar. His muscles tensed. He leaned forward and stared into Red's eyes. "Are you telling me that I became engaged to Josie only on a whim?'' Truth be known, he'd never asked Josie to marry him in the first place, but the bartender didn't need that bit of information.

"Not sayin' anythang of the sort. I'm only curious why a good-lookin' man like yurself would waste yur time with Miss Josie."

Before answering, Jack took a swig of whiskey. The cool beverage felt good as it slid down his throat. "I'll tell you this. I don't consider Josie an aging woman. She's someone I'd be proud to call my wife."

His statement succeeded in coaxing a crooked smile from Red. "Glad to hear it. I hope you understand, that I'm just doin' my job as bartender. It's my ree-sponsibility to make sure I dispense the facts. And that I do."

"You sure do. I need to head on now." Jack tossed a few coins on the polished wood bar and observed Red eagerly pocket them. He straightened up, nodded to the few men looking his way, and left.

Once again he found himself alone in the dark evening. But this time he didn't feel so lonely. He had his and Josie's future to think about. Tonight he'd discovered that he really wanted her for his wife. He simply couldn't think of anyone else in that role.

He also needed to think about what to do about Hunter. Jack decided he would use the time in Bozeman to convince Hunter he was the right man for his elder daughter. That would be no small task. Once away from all the prying eyes and inquisitive people of this little community, Jack was sure he could win Hunter over.

❖ 17 ❖

THE CHURCH FUND-RAISER could not have been held on a worse day. Dark, threatening clouds lurched across a sunless sky. Mist hung in the air.

The only thing to be thankful for, Josie thought, was that the rain held off. She squinted through the window up at the iron-gray clouds and knew that rain could not be long in coming.

Normally, the fund-raiser was held on the church grounds, with a picnic following. Everyone dressed up, but not quite in their Sunday best. The fund-raiser signaled the first social event of the summer season, one Josie usually looked forward to.

Today, however, she was nervous. The women of the town still hadn't stopped staring at her and asking questions about her upcoming nuptials. It seemed they could not get enough of her.

Because of the weather, Reverend Potter had decreed the fund-raiser move inside. So everyone had gathered up their goods and filed into the church, where they now stood packed together like sardines. This only made Josie even more aware of how interesting everyone found her.

Josie felt suffocated. The press of bodies was almost too much. She would have rather stood in the drizzle than be crammed inside.

"All right. Let's start the bidding." Reverend Potter's loud orator's voice easily cut through the din of the townsfolk's chatter. "We'll start with the baked goods." He held aloft a cherry pie for all to see.

Her mind drifted while she half listened to the various prices shouted out. Last night remained clearly etched in her mind. She recalled the quiet companionship of Jack, their soft conversation, the happiness she felt when he reached out and kissed her. And then her father had barged up the stairs and ruined the perfect moment. She squeezed her eyes shut, wanting to erase that part of the evening.

Her father's anger had been uncalled for. Why should one little kiss have him in such a state? After all, she was a grown woman and could make her own choices. She wondered whether he would change his mind about the engagement if she informed him that she planned that she and Jack live under the same roof with him. Or did her father's animosity stem from something else? Suppose her father really did not care for Jack at all?

Only when the gavel was brought down on the podium did her attention snap back. She realized several people were giving her odd looks. Josie shook off her heavy thoughts and forced a smile to her lips. After all, she was newly engaged. She should be beaming with joy.

The baked goods auction had finished. Reverend Potter had moved on to the jams and jellies. Four jars of her special blackberry preserves were Josie's contribution to the fund-raiser.

"Now, my good congregation. Next we have the special preserves made by our newest engaged woman. Josie Douglass. Who will bid for these?" The reverend's dark eyes scanned the crowd, looking for a certain person.

Silence descended upon the church. Heads turned to look about. Josie felt eyeballs staring at her from every direction. Still no one spoke up.

She knew no one would bid on her preserves. Jack was supposed to be the only bidder. It was an unwritten rule among the citizens. Only Josie had a horrible feeling that Jack didn't know this. She swallowed as she started to hear whispers. Pride kept her smile in place.

"Come now, surely there must someone who wants to bid on these?" the reverend said, rising up on tiptoe so he could better scan the crowd, seeking his targeted bidder.

The silence hung, thick and unbearable. Even the whispering halted. All eyes that were riveted to Josie now switched and stared at Jack.

Sweat slipped down her spine. She felt like a lamb at slaughter. Agonizing embarrassment plagued her. Time seemed to have stopped. Why wasn't Jack speaking up? She knew he was there. She'd caught a glimpse of him in the back corner.

A thin, reedlike woman near Jack cleared her throat and jerked her head toward the front, making sure Jack had seen her movement.

Jack glanced around, slowly turning beet red and opened his mouth. "Umm, I'll bid on those preserves. I'll bid three dollars for all the jars." The assembled crowd fell back, clearing a path for him to walk to the front.

Murmured exclamations rippled through the crowd.

Josie clutched the pew in front of her. Her relief was so great, she thought she might have dropped to the floor. Why hadn't she remembered to tell Jack about the fundraiser tradition? She was lucky he'd been there. She hated to think about how embarrassed she would have been had Jack not shown up.

Reverend Potter brought the gavel down in a swift motion. "Sold! To this young man newly united with our community."

As Jack went up to accept his jars, Josie could hear

the women around her whispering. It did not escape their notice that Jack sought her glance and grinned broadly.

Blushing, Josie looked down at the floor.

Mrs. Samuels sidled up to her. "Josie, that's a high price. Did you do something different this year?"

Panic set in. She felt trapped by the wall of people surrounding her. Mrs. Samuels kept looking at her with an odd expression in her eyes.

"No, I didn't. I used the same recipe I use every year."

"Oh, I see. Well, when we waited for so long for your fiancé to bid on the preserves, naturally we began to wonder if everything was fine between the two of you. You know how concerned our little community can be."

Josie pressed her fingernails into her palm to steady her voice. Since when, she wondered, did Mrs. Samuels start taking Josie's problems to heart? Probably since she'd become Portia Potter's close friend. "He's new in town, and I'm sure he was just confused. As you saw, he eagerly bought all my jars."

"Yes, I did see. It seemed he was a little too eager, almost like he was forced. I just hope this upcoming marriage of yours will work out. I'd hate to see you suffer heartbreak."

What unease Josie had felt at the stilted conversation now turned to anger. How dare Mrs. Samuels suggest her marriage might not work out! It was almost as if Mrs. Samuels were eagerly awaiting for some scandal, just so she would have something to gossip about.

"Thanks for your concern, but it's not necessary. I assure you Jack and I are perfectly content."

Mrs. Samuels patted her on the arm. "We all know how relieved you must be. Finally finding someone willing to marry you. We all know how you've sacrificed your life for your sister. Lord knows, you should have several children of your own by now, like I do."

If Josie hadn't been careful, her jaw would have been hanging wide open. "Is that so?" Josie hoped the words came out nicer than she felt inside. What she really wanted to do was to give Mrs. Samuels a piece of her mind, but Josie knew that would cause more trouble than it was worth.

"Just doing my job as a concerned citizen. Engagements can be fraught with peril. I need to check on my children now." Mrs. Samuels strolled away.

The room had become much too hot. Josie had a hard time getting a decent breath of air. The smell of so many bodies packed together overpowered her. She even thought her clothes were shutting off her circulation. Josie smiled at the people who stared at her and quickly made her exit.

The mist had stopped as she stepped out on the landing. Only a few clusters of people were outside, mostly men, smoking cigars or pipes. Children frolicked, playing games of tag or marbles. They didn't care about the weather.

Descending the stairs, Josie crossed the lawn until she reached a wrought-iron bench under a big box-elder tree.

She breathed deeply, filling her lungs with the clean air. It felt good not to have bodies pressing against her constantly. Just as she shut her eyes, she felt someone sit down beside her.

"I've been trying to find you all afternoon. I went to your house, but no one was there," Jack said.

Josie's heart sped up. Seeing Jack made her smile. "I've been here, inside, all day long. But with the crowd, it's hard to maneuver."

"And with your short stature, that makes it even harder."

"Thanks a lot." She glanced over at him and saw he was only joking. "Thanks for buying my preserves. I'm sorry if you were surprised. I should've told you about the tradition."

He planted his hands behind him and leaned backward. "Yeah, I was surprised. I wondered why all the women near me were giving me the evil eye. I thought maybe I had stepped in manure or something." He stopped and stared into her eyes.

Josie glanced up and couldn't look away. The myriad of emotions she saw in his blue eyes astounded her. He was looking at her as if he really wanted her, as if he might actually care about her feelings. She knew it was silly to believe he might actually love her, so she was content with this. For now.

His mouth parted and his tongue flicked out, wetting his lips. He'd looked that way right before he'd kissed her on the porch last night.

Kissed her!

Quickly she came to her senses. They were sitting in the churchyard. Engaged or not, they couldn't kiss now. All the citizens of Gallatin City were only steps away. Reverend Potter could come outside at any moment. No matter how badly she might want to feel his lips on hers again, now was not the place.

Springing to her feet, she put more distance between them. "Well, maybe we should go back inside."

Jack sat in silence, gazing up at her. What had just happened? Why had she suddenly sprung up as if he were a rabid animal? He felt hurt that she didn't want to sit with him.

"Why? It's so crowded in there. I'd rather sit out here with you. I prefer your company."

Josie paused, pressed her hands against her skirt, and glanced from the door to Jack. She looked torn. "I—I don't know. I should go find my father."

"You won't find him inside. I saw him and a few others sneak out." Why did she want to find her father? The Josie he knew would be glad to spend time alone with him, or so he'd thought. Hunter Douglass was someone he didn't want to encounter right now.

"I guess I should have known my father would leave early." She looked at the jars by his side. "I hope you like my preserves." She'd taken a step closer to him, but her eyes kept straying to the church door.

He held up one heavy, sealed jar. Thousands of tiny, dark seeds were dotted through the mixture. "I'm sure I will. You made it."

She blushed and dropped her gaze. "Thanks."

Jack's brows drew together. He didn't like this Josie. This overly quiet, demure behavior did not sit well on her at all. She seemed so dull and lifeless. "Is something bothering you?"

"No, no. Why do you ask?"

"You keep looking at the door as though you're expecting someone to walk out, and you won't even look at me. Am I so terrible to look at?"

"Of course not!" She seemed to remember herself. Life snapped into her green eyes and her cheeks were tinged with red.

"Good. I was afraid I'd done something. I thought we had a nice time last night on your porch." Had her father given her a tongue-lashing after he'd left? Could that be why she was acting so nervous and shy? Did she no longer want to go on with the engagement?

Just as he finished saying those words, the church door opened. Josie twirled and stared at it.

"There you are. I wondered where you went. I should have known you'd be outside." A tall, slender woman approached them.

"Grace, you startled me," Josie said, laughing a little nervously.

"How on earth could I do that?" Grace picked up the bottom of her dress to avoid the wet grass.

"Oh, um, never mind. Have you met Jack St. Augustine yet?"

Grace stopped, and a wide smile spread across her face. Her eyes twinkled. "We haven't been formally introduced. But I've seen him in the store. Robert's talked to him."

Jack rose and bowed. "Jack St. Augustine. And you must be one of Josie's friends. I'm pleased to meet you." He instantly liked the honest face of this woman. And he could tell she cared for Josie.

"I'm Grace Moreland, a longtime friend of Josie's. She's told me a lot about you. She made you sound fascinating. I was wondering when I was going to get to meet you.''

Josie twisted her hands together at Grace's forthright words.

Suddenly he was feeling better. He hadn't been wrong about her. If Josie had told her friend all about him, then she must have feelings for him even if she was acting oddly today. ''Well, here I am.''

''That was some price you paid for Josie's preserves. It about gave Mrs. Potter a fit of the vapors. But I'm sure the reverend will thank you.'' Grace looked from Josie to Jack and couldn't keep the smile off her lips.

''I do my duty. Would you like to sit down?'' No sooner were the words out of his mouth than the drizzle started up.

''No, thanks. I came to tell Josie that Reverend Potter is beginning to auction some of Lottie's items. I'm going back inside. I don't want the rain ruining my new hairdo. Bye!'' Grace waved and left.

''Did you really tell her all about me?'' Jack wanted to know exactly what the two women had said. What kind of things would Josie tell her friend about him?

Josie stammered. ''Well, I—I, um, told her what I knew. I mean, we are engaged. If you'll excuse me, I want to go back inside and find Lottie. I should be with her when her items are auctioned.'' Wistfully, she glanced at him, looking as if she wanted to say more but shouldn't.

''Go on, find your sister. I'll see you soon enough.'' It pained him to let her walk away with unanswered questions lingering in his mind. He wanted to know why her behavior had changed.

Finding himself alone in the fine rain, he grabbed his jars and started walking to his horse. He'd go back to his hotel room. He saw no reason to stand in the rain, nor did he want to go back into the church.

He hadn't liked some of the stares a few of the women had sent his way. He'd done nothing to warrant their intrusive looks. They reminded him of his mother and sisters. He'd half expected them to march over and begin drilling him with questions.

With his sleeve Jack wiped the dampness from his saddle and mounted. He would much rather have stayed and been alone with Josie, but he couldn't. He'd lingered too long. It was time to see about beginning work on his ranch. His and Josie's ranch, he corrected himself. And to do that, he needed to go to Bozeman. And lucky for him, Josie would be there also.

The mist had moistened the dry road, so his gelding didn't kick up any dust. The streets of Gallatin City were deserted. Not a single horse was tied to a hitching post. The only sign of life he saw were two dogs lying underneath the raised wooden walkways.

He looked at the storefronts facing the street, with their false fronts and neatly lettered signs. Each building had the look of being well taken care of. There wasn't a single sign of neglect. It all spoke of citizens who were proud of their town.

The large, block-lettered sign for the livery rose before him. Stopping before the door, he swung his leg over and dismounted. He heard whistling as he entered the barn.

The horse standing in cross ties in the middle of the barn aisle whinnied at their arrival. Slim was bent over a front hoof, cleaning it out. When he heard Jack, he lowered the foot and straighten up.

"Afternoon, Jack." Slim wiped his hands on his protective leather apron.

"Hello, Slim, am I interrupting something?"

"Nope, I was just finishing trimmin' his hoof. Church fund-raiser over already?"

"No, but I'd seen enough and bought four jars of preserves, so I decided to leave." He stopped his horse just inside the high arched door and uncinched the saddle.

"So you bought Josie's preserves, eh?" Slim walked forward and opened the door to the tack room with his foot for Jack.

"Yes. Little did I know it was expected of me. I stood there wondering why all those people were suddenly staring at me, when it hit me that I should bid on Josie's items. Why aren't you at the fund-raiser?'' Immediately, Jack regretted his words. He'd learned the hard way that western men value their privacy.

Slim's eyebrows drew together, and he let a stream of tobacco fly. ''Well, now, you could say I had other work to do.''

''Oh.'' Jack hoisted the saddle from his horse and placed it on the rack. He took a brush and started grooming the dirt off the gelding.

''You do know that Hunter is takin' his girls to the big city?''

The ''big city'' Slim was referring to must be Bozeman, Jack surmised. ''I heard him talking about going there. But he didn't say when.''

''Well, Hunter was just here and he told me that he's takin' them first thing tomorrow morning. The reason I'm tellin' you this is 'cause of your horse at their place.'' Slim stopped, unhooked the cross ties from the horse, and led it to a stall. ''I'm gonna be the one takin' care of their place.''

Jack's hand paused. It was just the information he needed to know. The Douglasses' departure date. ''Are you? I remember you telling me you often helped out there.''

''Sure do. If you didn't have a horse there, I wouldn't be telling you this. But on account of that, I figured you should at least know.'' With one hand he slid the stall latch firmly into place. The sound of metal on metal grated in the quiet barn aisle.

''So they're leaving tomorrow morning?'' Since Jack had made his decision to leave for Bozeman, the only thing that had bothered him was not knowing when Josie and her family would be there. He hated to miss them. But now, thanks to Slim, that wouldn't be happening.

''Yup. Just wanted to let you know, in case you see me over there.''

''I doubt if I'll see you. I've got some business to attend to. I'll be out of town for a while.''

Slim's eyes fastened on him. "You takin' both your horses?"

"No, just him." Jack gave the gelding a pat.

"So then you'll be comin' back?"

Jack could not read the older man's expression. But for some reason he sounded eager to know the answer to that question. "I'll be back, I've got a wedding to be in. But after that, I don't know how long we'll remain in Gallatin City."

"So then you'll be takin' Josie away from us? Can't say as Hunter will be pleased to learn about that."

Jack frowned. For someone who offered so little information about himself, Slim was certainly asking lots of questions. "I don't know how Hunter will take it. But Josie will be my wife and we'll be leaving to start our own life." Jack could also be a man of few words.

"Just lemme know if you'll be wantin' a stall. Remember, I've got room to keep your stallion also." Slim moved to another stall and brought out a mule. "Gotta trim his feet. I've been puttin' it off 'cause the damn thing's so ornery," he muttered.

"Thanks for the offer for the stall." Satisfied with his grooming job, he led his gelding into the stall. Jack was thankful that Slim hadn't asked where he was going for his business, but then, the man probably knew better.

The mule brayed and kicked out at Slim as he tried to lift its front leg. Slim cursed and swore up a storm.

"I'll be off so I won't disturb your work." Jack hung up his bridle and stepped back into the street. He doubted Slim even knew he'd left.

The drizzle had changed to a light rain. Jack glanced skyward at the iron-gray clouds and wondered why it wasn't pouring. He was glad it wasn't, because the water would turn the roads to muddy quagmires. And that would make travel hard.

He grinned. Somehow, he couldn't see Hunter Douglass letting a little thing like muddy roads keep him from his trip to Bozeman. Hunter would make the trip even if it snowed, Jack guessed.

Jack planned to surprise Josie in Bozeman. He purposely hadn't told her he was going. He couldn't wait to see the pleased expression on her face. Jack imagined them having a good time seeing the city sights and spending time together. Alone.

He mounted the steps to the hotel and slipped his key in the door lock.

His room looked so impersonal, so bland. Jack was ready to build his own house. He wanted rooms that were decorated to his taste. He was becoming tired of living out of hotel rooms and the occasional night spent under the open sky.

Briefly, he thought of his family back in Kansas City. Had they received his letter yet? He thought so. They were probably resigning themselves to the fact that he was a grown man, capable of making his own choices in the world.

He might need their help to access his money held in a Kansas bank, so he couldn't alienate his parents. He couldn't build a home on hopes alone. Cold, hard cash was required. Surely the passage of time had made his parents realize they had to let go of him. They could learn to love and accept Josie as a family member. After all, he'd seen how loving and caring a family could be. Josie had taught him that.

Josie. She'd taught him that affection could and did abound in families, even in unusual families like hers. She'd shown him that females were not all domineering. She'd shown him true courage, tolerance. She was a patient person to put up with all the work that had been heaped on her. And that was why he loved her.

Loved her?

He froze. When had he started loving her? The word itself sounded so scary, so foreign, he wondered at himself. It couldn't be love he felt. There were still barriers to overcome.

There was her father. Suppose Hunter refused to let her marry? Jack would first have to talk to the man, no matter how unappealing that sounded.

❖ *18* ❖

Now this, Jack thought as he rode into Bozeman,
was more like it. The hustle and bustle of people and
animals scurrying across the wide street. Businessmen in
their suits and hats strode down the boardwalks, their
shiny watch chains swaying in rhythm. Hardly anyone
gave him a second glance, unlike Gallatin City, where
his arrival had caused quite a stir.

Wagon wheels squeaked as drivers maneuvered past
him. Horses whinnied. Children laughed and shouted. It
was easy to tell why Bozeman was the county seat. That
was another reason he'd selected ranch land closer to
Bozeman.

The only problem was where to stay. He wanted to be
in the same hotel Josie and her family would be staying
in. Trouble was, since they hadn't arrived yet, he didn't
know where that would be. But he did have some business he needed to attend to first.

Jack rode on down the street, looking for the title and

surveying office. He needed information about acquiring the land he'd selected for his ranch.

Three buildings down rose the Bozeman Title Company. Jack thought that sounded like a good place to start, and nudged his horse toward the building. He stopped his gelding in front and tied him to the hitching post. Taking a deep breath, he entered the establishment.

One hour later he emerged, smiling broadly. All had gone well. If he could come up with the money, the land was his. No one else had claimed an interest in the area he'd scouted out a week before. Soon he would go to the bank and have his funds transferred.

Across from him was the City Hotel, a grand-looking brick building right in the middle of town. It seemed like a good place to stay. The hotel was in a good location, easily seen from either end of the street. With any luck the Douglasses would choose it as well. He decided to risk getting a room there.

He was tired and mud-splattered from his long ride. The previous day's rain had made the going slow and slippery. He wanted to clean up before seeing Josie, and that meant purchasing some new clothes and getting a shave and haircut. He wanted to look his best for his fiancée.

Jack hoped the Douglasses would arrive soon. He didn't like the look of the sky. All morning dark gray clouds had swept across the sky. The temperature had dropped. So far there had been no more precipitation, either rain or snow. He hoped it wouldn't stop Josie's family. For the first time he began to doubt his plan to surprise them. Maybe he should have told her and then they could all have traveled together.

"Father, how much longer? I'm freezing." Lottie wrapped the thick wool blanket around herself and stared miserably ahead.

The sudden May cold snap was not unusual, but didn't make the best traveling weather.

"Only a little bit. We could go faster if it hadn't rained

yesterday. The mud's slowin' us down. But I promise, we'll get nice hot cups of chocolate when we arrive." Hunter guided the team of horses around a wide puddle in the road.

Josie was cold and upset too. She had thought summer was on its way. There should be no more cold snaps. The cold weather, however, wasn't what had her down.

She missed Jack. She'd wanted to say good-bye but hadn't had the opportunity. It was probably just as well. She needed this time away from him to think. She needed to think how to convince her father that her engagement didn't mean the end of the world. She also wanted to analyze her feelings toward Jack and figure out how they'd gotten so out of control.

"You're quiet, Jos," Hunter said, glancing sideways at her.

"I'm just resting." Hah. As if you could rest on an uncomfortable, jostling wagon.

"I know you weren't real keen on this little trip, but try and have fun. It's not often we do things like this. For Lottie's sake, try to enjoy yourself."

For Lottie's sake. It was always for Lottie's sake. Josie was growing tired of it. Her eyes opening wide, she just realized what she'd thought. Guilt washed over her. She should never think like that. What was coming over her? She loved her sister and would never wish her ill.

"Looky ahead, I see signs of civilization." Hunter pointed to the scattering of houses.

"We're almost there!" Lottie brightened.

They watched as the houses became closer and closer together until finally they were on the main street of Bozeman. Their wagon jostled with several others for space on the street. Numerous horses' hooves had churned the main street into a liquid brown mess.

"It's bigger than I thought." Lottie gazed all around.

Buildings crowded along the sides of the street. There were businesses, homes with picket fences separating them from their neighbors, and two churches, all in one part of the city. The side streets that jutted off were as nearly as built up as the main street.

"Let's get our room first and then warm up. There's plenty of time to see all the sights." Hunter headed toward the City Hotel looming up from its location at a main intersection.

The hotel had a beautiful, spacious lobby. The polished wood floor gleamed. Every brass fixture, even the handrail leading up the steps, glistened. A three-tiered chandelier drew Josie's eyes upward as she tried not to stare when she followed her father to the registration desk.

She half listened to his conversation with the desk clerk. Her gaze dropped down to the book, and her heart stilled when she read a name a few spaces above her father's.

J. St. Augustine.

Could it be? It had to be the same person. But how? she wanted to know. Jack had said nothing about a trip to Bozeman. What could he be doing here? Questions filled her mind.

"All righty, we're all signed in. Why don't you girls go over and order us some coffee and hot chocolate?" Hunter pointed to the adjoining restaurant. "I'll see to our bags."

"Yes, let's." Lottie grabbed Josie's hand and pulled her along. All her misery during the ride had been forgotten.

Josie's feet felt like they were dragged down by lead weights. She wanted to ask the clerk about J. St. Augustine, what room he might be in, even if it would be improper. Lottie, however, was dragging her farther and farther away from the desk.

"Let's sit here." Lottie dropped into a chair at a table against the front window. "We can watch all the people pass by."

"Good idea."

"I'd like some tea. That sounds more big-cityish than hot chocolate. Then I want a hot bath. We can't go out in the city looking so, so"—Lottie glanced down at her wrinkled skirt and crinkled her nose—"so dirty."

"Hold on a minute. We're not going to be spending money like there's no limit." Although Josie did agree a bath sounded lovely, she knew their money was not an endless supply.

A few minutes later a server brought out their hot drinks. Steam rose and swirled above the mugs.

Lottie wrapped her fingers around the cup set in front of her. "You're no fun. Remember what Father said, try to have fun for my sake. And I think a bath would be fun. Just think, this might be our only trip as a family."

"All right," Josie sighed, "we can have the bath. But we'll have to share it. What do you mean, this might be our only trip as a family?"

"With you getting married, Jack'll be around. I mean, he'll be family, but it won't be the same. I'll have to share you then. So I want us to have the best time on this trip."

"Ah, I see." Josie thought it odd how her sister referred to her marriage as having to share her, but didn't dwell on it. She turned her thoughts to Jack. If he were there, she had the perfect opportunity to appear at her best, without worrying about the wagging tongues of Gallatin City's gossips, or worrying about making any mistakes. Maybe she could even get Lottie to style her hair differently for her.

Stop it, she scolded herself. *You don't even know if it is Jack.*

She stared out the window, imagining what Jack would be doing in Bozeman. She thought about him so hard, she could have sworn he stood directly in front of the window. She blinked. His image remained in place.

"Look!" Lottie sloshed her tea over the rim of her cup as she snatched her hand up to point. "Isn't that Jack?"

Josie gripped the table. It really was Jack standing in front of her. He looked different somehow, more stylish. Belatedly she realized Lottie had motioned him inside.

"Quick, wipe your face." Lottie handed her a napkin.

"You've got a dirt smudge on your cheek."

"Why didn't you tell me sooner?" Josie rubbed her cheek harder than necessary, hoping to bring some color as well as remove the unwanted smudge.

"I didn't think about it."

Footsteps echoed on the floor. She knew Jack had entered the dining room. Her pulse quickened. She tried to look casual, but it was hard when she was burning with curiosity.

He stopped at their table and bowed. "Lottie, Josie, I'm glad I found you. May I sit down?"

"Yes, yes, of course." Josie couldn't take her eyes off him. She knew why he looked so different. He had on new clothes. He wore black pants, a white shirt, and a fancy stitched black vest with shining silver buttons.

And it looked like he also had just seen a barber. His cheeks were pink and smooth, freshly shaven. A few tendrils of wet hair curled around his ears.

She wished more than ever she'd been able to clean up before seeing him. Suppose the beautiful women of the city captured his interest? Suppose she looked so unfashionable that he wanted to break the engagement?

"This is surprising," Josie said, praying her voice didn't crack. That was an understatement, she thought.

"I had business to take care of here and I knew you had this trip planned, so I hoped we'd be in town at the same time. I wanted to surprise you." His blue eyes met hers and held them.

If Lottie hadn't spoken up, Josie doubted she could have looked away from his soulful eyes.

"Are you staying here also? That'd be good. We're gonna order a hot bath and get cleaned up before we see the city."

Josie reddened at her sister's words. She found herself imagining her and Jack sharing a bath. They'd suds each other up, warm water would slide down their naked bodies, the close quarters of the tub would lead to kissing and then to. . . . The thought was almost too scandalous to consider, even for an engaged couple, but she did. It didn't help when Jack noticed her flush and gave her a devilish grin.

"I'd be happy to escort you through the city, if your father wouldn't mind. Where is he anyway?" Jack suddenly tensed and glanced quickly around the room, relieved to find Hunter wasn't present.

"He's putting our bags in the room. He'll be here shortly."

No sooner had Josie said those words than her father strode across the polished dining room floor. He stopped in his tracks when he noticed Jack, his expression closed and unreadable.

"Well, I'll be a thorn in the side of a heifer. What're you doin' here? This trip was just supposed to be between me and my girls. You ain't stayin' here, are you?" Hunter pulled out a chair and sat down. He took a gulp of his coffee, grimacing at the bitter taste. Scowling, he looked at Jack.

"Yes, I have a room on the second floor. And I have business to attend to in town." Jack stood rigid, as if he were bracing for a fight, verbal or physical.

"That a fact?" Hunter scooted his chair closer to Josie's side and put his arm possessively on the back of it. He even attempted to tug her chair a tad closer to his own, ignoring the frown Josie gave him.

Josie sensed the tension building between the two men. She needed to intervene. "I think it's nice Jack could be here the same time we are. It'll give us all a chance to get better acquainted."

"Yeah, and Jack can escort us around while you do your business, Father," Lottie said, clearly impressed with having two men to choose from.

"Don't know about that. Seems to me the less time you girls spend with him, the better." Hunter took a swig of his beverage.

"It would be my pleasure to escort such lovely ladies." Jack's gaze slid to Josie, and he smiled at her. That is, until Hunter noticed and shot him a look that could kill.

"Father, why can't Jack escort us around the city this afternoon? We know him, an' he'll keep us safe. I mean, I know how you want to go to the jewelry stores," Lottie said, favoring her father with her beguiling baby-blue eyes.

"I don't know. I thought you wanted a necklace."

Lottie sighed. "Father, I do. But I'd rather see the sights than go looking in jewelry stores. You can take me when you've found the right store. Pleeeze."

Hunter grunted. "I guess that's better than you two roaming around by yourselves, if you'd really rather go with him than with your own father. I'll see what I can find, and then you can come help me select my cuff links."

Josie ground her teeth. Somehow, she'd hoped her father had given up on his idea to have cuff links made from his sapphires. No such luck. Nor did she seem to be having much luck with her father accepting Jack, much less an engagement. These last comments only reinforced her frustration.

"But I want to get cleaned up before we see the city. Can we go in an hour or two?" Lottie looked toward Jack.

"Now, there's an idea that makes sense. We all could use cleanin' up after our journey. Girls, go on up to the rooms. I'll stop by the desk and order us a bath. You can meet Jack at two-thirty."

Her father's dismissal made her feel like a young child, but this time Josie didn't mind. She wanted to make a good impression on Jack, and she couldn't do that wearing travel-stained clothing. There was too much female competition in Bozeman, and her situation was tenuous enough. She didn't need the extra burden of worrying about the possibility of losing Jack to a beautiful city woman.

Josie held open their room door while three Chinese workers hauled the tub and buckets of steaming water in. She marveled at their shiny black hair and the long, thin braids running the length of their backs. Bowing, they silently left the room.

"I'm first," Lottie claimed.

"All right, I'll unpack our dresses and see if I can smooth out some of the wrinkles. But don't take too long, I still need to bathe, and we don't want to keep Jack waiting."

"I'll try to hurry." Grabbing a towel and a bar of soap, Lottie climbed into the bath. "Ah, this feels good. You'll like it."

Josie smiled. She couldn't wait to soak in the warm water. She wanted to wash her hair but didn't think it would dry in time.

Listening to the water slosh, Josie opened their bags and withdrew her dress. It was the same maize calico she'd worn to the mock race, but she thought it was one of her prettier outfits.

She wrinkled her nose when she noticed the creases in the skirt. Laying the skirt on the bed, she pressed hard with her hand and tried to smooth away the crinkles.

"Don't forget to lay out my dress. I'll wear my navy blue cotton with the lace on the sleeves," Lottie said, pausing in the act of scrubbing her back.

"I won't."

"Maybe I'll meet some boys. You know, Mary Jane and I get pretty tired of the boys back home. They're soooo babyish. I mean, it's almost time I start considering who I'll marry."

"Lottie! Boys are the last thing you need to be thinking about. I thought you were interested in the latest fashions and fabric."

"I am. I mean, I do like the fashions. But boys are kinda nice too."

"Just finish your bath so I can take one." Josie shook her head and removed Lottie's dress from the bag. It had more wrinkles than Josie's. An iron would be nice, she thought.

Josie unbuttoned her dress and slipped it off. She shook the worst of the travel dust from it, making sure to aim her shakes away from the bath area.

She wondered what Jack was doing just then. Was he still sitting in the dining room, or had he gone out into the town? She hoped not. Even from just sitting at the table, Josie had seen a steady stream of beautiful women stroll by. She'd even seen a few glance Jack's way and smile. She definitely didn't want him to set his sights on another woman.

"Hey, Jos, do you think Father will ever find a new wife?"

Lottie's question yanked her thoughts off Jack. "Why do you ask that?"

"I dunno. I just thought maybe if he had a wife, he wouldn't leave us so often."

"Does that bother you?"

"Uh-huh. Well, sometimes. I mean, what if he leaves and then never comes back? Would you and Jack be enough to protect me from Aunt Portia?" Lottie's voice shook.

"Father won't leave us. He loves you, just like I do. And you know I'll never let your aunt adopt you or take you away."

These words seemed to cheer Lottie. She smiled. "Good, then I'll try not to worry. I know you'll never leave me alone."

Josie wondered at her sister's incessant talking about being left alone, but attributed it to a strange town and how that could be frightening to a young girl. "Time to get out and dry off. It's my turn to wash."

"The water's still warm," Lottie said as she rubbed herself with the thick towel.

"Good." Josie lowered herself and could feel her body relaxing. She took the bar of lemon soap and lathered her skin. The tart scent smelled good and cleansing.

Quickly, she glanced down at her naked body. She didn't think it was so bad. Jack should have no reason to look at another woman. Her breasts were full and firm. Her stomach was not rounded by inactivity. Soft, curving muscles filled out her legs, even if they were short.

Would Jack approve? she thought before she could

stop herself. She felt the heated blush creep up her throat and cheeks. What was she doing? Thoughts like that were most certainly inappropriate, even for engaged persons.

She grabbed the washcloth and scrubbed at her skin, removing the lathered soap.

"I feel much better." Josie shut her eyes and leaned her neck against the back of the tub.

"Hey! You made me hurry up. You can't take a nap in the tub if I couldn't. It's not fair. Here"—Lottie shoved a towel in Josie's hands—"dry off. We need to do our hair, and that always takes a long time."

"Yes, ma'am." Josie laughed at Lottie's tone. She liked it when they kidded and had a good time. Rising, she let the water run off her and then toweled dry.

There was one subject Josie wanted to bring up and talk to Lottie about, but something held her back. Josie longed to ask Lottie what she really thought about Josie's upcoming marriage. Outwardly, she knew Lottie was all smiles and happiness, but was that how her sister truly felt? What did Lottie think about having another man come and live in their house?

She snorted. You're being foolish, Josie told herself. Lottie had not given one clue that would indicate otherwise. Lottie was truly happy for her.

Josie reached for her camisole and petticoat. She slipped them on, messing her hair in the process. As she lifted her skirt, she heard Lottie groan.

"Josieee, you just wore that to the horse race. Jack saw that outfit not more than a few days ago. How could you bring it?"

It was plain to see that Lottie thought the mere idea to be horrendous.

"I happen to think I look pretty in this outfit. Besides, no one else in Bozeman knows I wore it recently." Josie pulled the skirt up and hooked it around her narrow waist.

"But couldn't you have brought something else?"

"Unlike you, I don't have a huge supply of dresses. I couldn't alter my mother's old dresses like you've done."

Lottie turned so Josie could do the buttons that ran the length of her back. "Still, I'm sure you could've brought another dress. Let's see, maybe we can find you a pretty bonnet or a stylish hat to match."

"I don't need a hat. You need to remember that we're not here to see how much money we can spend. Who knows, if Father finds what he needs this afternoon, maybe we'll go home tomorrow."

Lottie groaned. "No, he wouldn't make us leave. We just got here."

Josie now regretted putting the idea into Lottie's head. She didn't like the thought of them leaving so soon either. Once they'd arrived, she found she was actually excited about visiting Bozeman. There was something thrilling about the possibility of getting lost in a crowd of people, of being a nameless face without having anyone constantly observing you.

"All done." She patted Lottie on the shoulder after fastening her sister's dress. "Now you can go do your hair."

"I wish we had one of those hot irons to curl our hair with. I think I'd look pretty with tight ringlets." Lottie wrapped a strand of hair corkscrew-like around her finger and peered into the mirror.

"Well, we don't." Josie finished buttoning up her shirtwaist. She crossed to the mirror and thought she'd done a good job of smoothing out the worst of the wrinkles. The only thing left was to do something with her hair.

She wanted to just pull the front half back and tie it with a ribbon, letting the rest flow freely. But she thought that might seem to brazen. Instead, she settled on a loose French braid which she wrapped under and pinned.

Lottie glanced over. "After we see the city and what kind of styles the women are wearing, I'll try some new things with your hair."

"That would be fun." Josie smiled at her reflection. She thought she looked as nice as any of the city women, and hoped Jack thought so too.

❖ 19 ❖

"Now, YOU GIRLS be back here before supper. You can't spend all day gallivanting around," Hunter grumbled as he looked at his daughters. "Still don't know if I think this is such a good idea." His jaw jutted out stubbornly.

"I hardly think we'll be gallivanting, Father," Josie said. She was getting tired of the constant battle with her father ever since she and Jack had agreed to continue the engagement. It had strained the affable relationship she'd shared with her father.

"Huh, you're not a father and don't have my worries."

Josie bit her lip and silently counted to ten. If she did nothing else with her time in Bozeman, she was going to get her father and Jack to sit down together and make them get to know each other, if not like each other. "This is the last time I'm going to tell you, he is not a stranger, he's going to be my husband."

Hunter looked at her. For the briefest second, hurt

flickered in his bright blue eyes. "I—" He opened his mouth but then shut it—"aw, what's the use? You're as stubborn as your ma. Just watch out for Lottie this afternoon. I'll see you at dinner." He opened the hotel door and slipped out into the gray afternoon.

Josie sat in one of the lobby chairs and rubbed her forehead. She was glad Lottie hadn't been there to witness this latest go-round. Her father's mulishness was beginning to give her a headache.

Raising her glance, Josie watched her sister descend the stairs. No wonder it had taken Lottie longer to prepare. Not a hair looked out of place. Soft waves framed her face, her bangs were perfectly straight, and the bow securing the front of her hair matched her blue eyes.

"I hope it doesn't rain and ruin your pretty hairdo." Josie glanced from her sister to the gloomy weather.

"It won't. It can't. Today is our first day in the city." Lottie stopped, glancing around the lobby. She tapped her toe. "Where's Jack? Did he forget about us?"

"One thing at a time. I'm sure he'll be along."

As soon as she spoke those words, a gust of wind accompanied the opened door. Jack stepped inside and quickly shut the door. "Don't I feel lucky. I see two pretty ladies who I just know are waiting for me."

Josie clasped her hands. She knew her face was glowing from the compliment. He *did* think she looked nice. "We just came downstairs. But it looks like it's grown colder out."

"It has, do you two have wraps?" Jack's cheeks were stained red from the cold weather. He'd even put on a black sheepskin-lined jacket.

"Uh-huh, but I don't wanna wear mine. How can people see my dress if I have it covered up with a wrap?" Lottie said, pouting.

"If it's cold enough, you'll wear one. Now, run back to our rooms and fetch them, please." Josie pulled her key out of her pocket and handed it to her sister.

"Oh, all right. But I don't like it." Lottie grabbed the key and stomped off.

"May I sit next to you?" Jack walked over and pulled a chair up next to Josie. "You look very nice. I think yellow's a pretty color on you."

Heat suffused her cheeks. She should be used to him by now. But every time she looked at him, she still couldn't believe her good fortune. They were to be husband and wife. Or would be if she could figure out what to do about her father. "Thank you. You also look nice. Are those new clothes?"

"I just bought them before I saw you in the restaurant window. I have to admit, I thought I was seeing things at first when I saw you sitting at that table. But I'm glad I found you."

Was it coincidence they were in Bozeman at the same time? Or had he planned it that way? He'd said something about a surprise.

"What are you doing here?" The instant she uttered the words, she wished she could recall them. Her blunt question didn't sound at all ladylike, and here of all places, with fashionable women everywhere, she should strive to be ladylike.

Jack seemed not to notice her transgression. "I was going to tell you later. I'm here on business. Remember when I left for a few days?"

Josie reddened and nodded. How could she forget? That was when she'd told Mrs. Potter they were engaged. That day would remained etched in her mind forever.

"I thought you'd remember." He chuckled. "Anyway, what I did during that time was scout out the perfect land to start my ranch." He took a deep breath and smiled, and his eyes lightened. "Well, I found it. And I'm here to look into purchasing the property so I can start building soon."

Start to build *his* ranch? Josie's heart pumped harder. Why would Jack need to build a ranch? She already had one in Gallatin City. Her family was there and Lottie needed her to be close. His use of the singular also alarmed her. Did that mean he didn't plan to go through with the wedding?

"What's the matter? You look upset." Jack splayed his fingers on her cheek and turned her head to face him. He realized he'd said something wrong but didn't know what.

Josie stared across the lobby. "Did you mean your ranch or our ranch?"

"So that's what's bothering you. I'm sorry. I guess I'm still adjusting to this engagement business. For so long I've always dreamed of it as my ranch, I guess it's a hard habit to break." He hadn't meant to hurt her feelings but knew he had. What to do to make it up to her?

She forced her eyes to his. "I guess it is something you need to adjust to. Look, here comes Lottie." She stood up, ending the conversation.

"I've got our wraps." Lottie stopped and thrust out one for Josie.

"You won't be sorry. It's a brisk wind out there. Let me help you." Jack took Josie's wool wrap and secured it around her shoulders. He held her hair up and was amazed at how soft it felt. He longed to run his fingers through its unbound length.

He was surprised at himself. He'd been helping his sisters with their wraps for as long as he could remember. Never before had he realized how intimate the simple act could be, standing so close to Josie, breathing in her scent and feeling the heat from her body mingle with his. He could feel the stirring of desire start in his loins, making him thankful for the cold outside.

"Don't I get help?" Lottie interjected, thrusting her wrap toward Jack, making it quite obvious she wasn't happy to have to wear one. In one hand she held a cloak pin.

Jack took the items and regarded Lottie. He had never heard her sound so petulant. The Lottie he knew was bright and bubbly. He hadn't realized suggesting they wear wraps was such a big deal. "Hold up your chin, I don't want to stick you with this fancy pin."

"There, much better. Now I'll at least look decent with

this wrap on." Lottie's expression changed, and once again she was beaming up at Jack.

Josie glanced at her sister and did a double take. "Let me see that pin."

Lottie thrust her chest out. "I brought it along especially for this trip."

Jack watched as Josie's face went from disbelief to anger.

"Where did you get that pin?"

"From home."

"Lottie, where?"

"I found it. And I thought I needed something fancy for the big city."

Josie shut her eyes and took a deep breath. "Did you take that out of the box in my room?"

It was more of a statement than a question.

"Maybe. But you never use it and it'll go to waste if one of us doesn't use it." Lottie's eyes started to shine with unshed tears.

"Lottie, that was my mother's best pin. Father had that made for her. That's almost pure gold and the little diamonds are real. You have no business wearing it."

"I do too, and I'm wearing it." Lottie's lower lip stuck out and she crossed her arms. "Father always told us to share."

"Fine, wear it today, but don't you dare lose it. Or I'll never forgive you." Josie spun from her sister and headed to the front door. "What are we waiting for? The city awaits."

"Jack, will you hold my hand?" Lottie tapped him on the arm. "I don't want to get lost among all the people outside."

Jack looked down at the small gloved hand on his sleeve and glanced over at Josie. Her hands were clasped tightly behind her back. Left with no choice, he took Lottie's and started out the door.

This was not how he'd imagined the afternoon would begin. He felt like a referee in a boxing match. And he'd thought he'd left the days of bickering sisters behind him.

He found himself praying that whenever he had children, they would all be boys.

The second they stepped outside, a strong gust blasted them. Lottie squealed. Josie bowed her head and continued walking into it. The crowds that were previously on the boardwalks had dwindled as the weather changed.

Jack did have to admit he was impressed with Josie's tenacity. His sisters would have turned on their heels and gone back inside. He liked this streak in her.

Josie was not about to let a minor thing like the weather keep her from exploring Bozeman. Eagerly, she scanned the wide street. She could see several smaller side streets branching off. It was nothing at all like little, one-street Gallatin City. The only problem was Lottie's attitude. For the life of her, Josie couldn't figure out why her sister was acting so spoiled and stubborn. She'd just have to get to the bottom of it later.

"Ooooh, look up there! There's a dry goods store, let's go in. Then we can get out of this wind," Lottie exclaimed as she pulled Jack forward.

Josie felt herself soften as she looked at her sister and noticed Lottie's carefully coiffed hair blowing to pieces. Wisps of her own hair blew across her mouth. Today was not the day for being fashion-conscious.

She and Jack bumped arms as they both tried to reach for the door at the same time. Her heart tripped as she noticed the twinkle in his eye.

"Seems we both have the same idea," he said, bending his head so his breath brushed her face.

Quickly, she turned, not wanting him to see how such a little thing could get her all flustered.

"This isn't how my first day in Bozeman was supposed to be," Lottie said, trying to bring some semblance of order to her hair.

The dry goods store bustled with customers. It seemed there were more people inside than there were out on the streets. They were all probably trying to stay warm. The potbellied stove in the center of the store was ringed with people.

Josie noticed a huge section devoted to materials and clothing to her right. She'd never seen such a selection. Her sister's mouth dropped open at the sight of so many fabrics to choose from.

She glanced at Jack and noticed his expression. He didn't seemed thrilled at the prospect of spending very much time there. "Maybe we should continue our walk and come back later, without Jack," she said to Lottie.

"No, we're here now, and besides, Jack's holding my hand, keepin' me safe. It's too windy outside for me anyway." Lottie surged in the direction of all the fabrics. Her eyes rounded like muffins.

Josie followed along behind, stewing in her thoughts. She was so surprised by Lottie's actions, she didn't know what to do. If they weren't in a crowded store, Josie would take Lottie aside and explain she could not act this way.

"Lottie, why don't you and your sister go on over and look at the material. I see a glove display, I'll be over there." Jack dropped Lottie's hand and inclined his head before leaving them.

"I think Father needs some new gloves also. Go on, Lottie, I'll be over to the fabrics in a minute." Josie followed Jack across the store. At last they could have a few minutes to themselves.

"Jack, wait." She lengthened her stride and had to stop abruptly to keep herself from running into him when he suddenly stopped.

"Yes?" He reached out his arms and steadied her, but he did not let go.

"I want to apologize for Lottie. I don't know why she's acting so . . . so difficult. I hope she doesn't ruin this afternoon for you." Josie looked into his eyes and concentrated on the warmth coming from the strong hands gripping her arms. Tiny shots of heat spiraled out from his touch.

He smiled, revealing his white teeth. "I don't think she will. I have an idea. Since she's so worried about the weather, I'll suggest we take her back to the hotel and we can continue on our own. That way we'll have some time to spend by ourselves.''

"By ourselves?'' The words came out huskily. She would like nothing better than to spend time alone with him, but it worried her. Would her father get upset? Would she forget herself and do something inappropriate? Like kissing?

"You sound like you don't want to be with me.'' He let go of her arms and stepped back, putting more distance between them.

Had she? "Oh, no. That's not what I meant. I only wondered what it is you had in mind.''

"I thought we'd continue to see the city. Maybe stop somewhere for a refreshment.'' His eyes searched her face.

"Oh, of course. I feel sort of guilty leaving Lottie in our room, but she is being a pain with all her moaning about the wind.'' Josie's words were rushed. What had she been thinking when he suggested they spend time alone? She really needed to keep her thoughts on a short rein.

"To tell you the truth, I'm surprised you want to keep exploring.'' At her astonished expression, he grinned. "I should probably have guessed you wouldn't let a little thing like wind keep you inside.''

Josie didn't know whether or not to take that as a compliment. She was glad he didn't think of her as a prissy miss, but then, she *was* trying to impress him with her womanly behavior.

"I'm going to go look at the gloves. With how cold it can get here, I'm sure I could use another pair. I'll come check on you and your sister when I'm done.'' He turned and left.

She was suddenly happy. If Jack had thought of her as unladylike, then he wouldn't have planned for a way for them to be alone. And if he wanted them to be alone, that could mean only one thing: He cared for her. And if he cared for her, then he could love her. Those thoughts made her practically drift over the worn puncheon floor toward her sister.

"Jos, over here." Lottie waved her arm in the air, flagging down her sister.

"Did you find something nice?" At least Lottie was sounding more herself.

Lottie stared at her, openmouthed. "What are you smiling about? Did I miss something?"

"No, I'm just happy." Had she detected a note of gloom in her sister's voice?

"Well, I'm not happy. I'm cold, it's windy out, my hair is ruined. And I have to wear a wrap so people can't see my pretty dress with the stitching I worked so hard on, and I also have a headache. It's just not fair. I wanted my first day in Bozeman to be so nice." Lottie stared glumly at the white net fabric before her.

Ah-ha. So that's why Lottie was acting up. She didn't feel well. "Then I think we'd better take you back to the hotel so you can rest up. That way, tomorrow and the next day will be even better."

"But I don't want to waste my time in bed. There's so much to do. Look." She pointed to the netting. "I found a pretty fabric for your veil."

Josie glanced at the sheer white netting. The weave was quite fine. It really would make a nice veil. But she hardly needed to pick out veil material on her very first day in Bozeman. "Yes, it'll make a fine veil. But I'm more concerned about you. Let me take you back to our room and tuck you in. If you take a nice long nap, I'm sure your headache will be gone before suppertime."

"You'll stay while I sleep?"

"I'll make sure you're cozy, but I won't stay in the room. I'll lock the door behind me. Father will be back to his adjoining room in no time. You'll be quite fine." Odd, she thought Lottie would have wanted her to spend the time alone with Jack in the city.

"Oh, all right."

"What's all right?" Jack said as he joined them.

"I'm going to take her back to the hotel. She's not

feeling well.'' Josie glanced down at the brown-paper-wrapped package in his hands. She wondered what kind of gloves he'd selected for himself.

"We'll all go,'' Jack announced.

A half hour later Josie found herself once again in the hotel lobby with Jack. This time he faced her with a mischievous look in his eye.

"Why do you look like that?'' she asked, caught up in his boyish grin.

"Only this.'' He held out the wrapped package in his palms and extended his hand toward her.

"What?'' Confused, she looked down at the package and back up to his face. "Do you want me to hold your gloves?''

"Nope, I want you to take it.'' He thrust his hands closer.

Josie took the package and stared down at the thin twine securing the wrap. "What should I do with it?''

"Open it.'' His smile grew wider.

She eased the string from the wrap and opened it. Her breath caught in her throat as she stared down. There was no way these gloves could fit Jack's large hands. "Are— are these for me?''

He nodded. "I thought you could use a warm, sturdy pair. The last pair of gloves I saw you wear were those frilly white things when we went riding. These seemed more appropriate.''

"Th-thank you. You didn't need to.'' A gift! He'd just given her a gift. She was overwhelmed by his kindness. As she stared at the brown gloves, her happiness dampened some. They weren't a very feminine gift. Should she be upset that he hadn't given her something like a bonnet or a cameo? No, she decided, any gift from him was fine with her.

"You're welcome. But the joy on your face is all the thanks I need.'' When he saw the soft fur-lined calfskin gloves, he knew she had to have them. They would be practical and pretty, just like her.

She rubbed them against her cheek. "They're so soft.

I'm afraid to wear them. What if I ruin them?''

"You won't. Try them on.'' He felt as excited as she looked. A warm, glowing feeling suffused him. Making Josie happy gave him pleasure, he'd just discovered. Suddenly, he felt his heart expand inside his chest.

"They fit fine.'' She admired the new gloves.

"Then let's go back outside and finish exploring the town.'' Jack offered her his elbow and was again filled with warmth when she clasped her fingers around his arm. Smiling, he steered them outside.

As Josie glanced again at her present, she wondered if Jack would ever give her a betrothal ring. In order for that to happen, they'd have to have a real engagement. Would theirs ever become one?

❖ 20 ❖

Josie held tightly to Jack's arm. She didn't care if the drizzle had changed to freezing rain. Jack had just purchased her a gift, her very first from him. She couldn't keep her heart from swelling. She knew, even if Jack hadn't said so, that he must be starting to care for her. Her future with him looked very promising.

"Where would you like to go?" Jack asked, smiling down at her.

"Let's just walk." Some place private, she wanted to say. Josie suddenly didn't want to share Jack with anyone. She wanted to be alone with him.

Just as they prepared to move down the boardwalk, Hunter approached them. One look at the blissful expressions on his daughter's and Jack's face turned his mood dour. He stopped in mid-step and blocked the walk. "Where do you two think you are going? And where's Lottie?"

Josie didn't like the expression on her father's face.

Whenever he narrowed his eyes until they resembled half moons, it was a signal his temper had flared. She steeled herself to stand up to him. "Lottie's in bed with a headache. We're going to see the city."

"I promise to keep her safe," Jack said.

"I don't think I want the two of you alone together, especially after what I witnessed happenin' on my own porch. Josie, I need you to come with me." Hunter began walking toward the hotel entrance.

She felt Jack stiffen beside her. If she didn't think of something to say and fast, the situation could get out of control and she wouldn't let that happen. "Father, please don't order me about as if I were a child."

Hunter stopped and stared. His mouth worked but no words escaped.

"Josie, uh, perhaps we should go now." Jack tightened his grip and tugged her away from the hotel.

"No," she said, surprising herself and Jack. Before another hour ticked by, she needed to talk with her father. They had to settle the matter of her engagement once and for all. Jack would have to wait until the next day to see the city with her. "I think my father and I need to talk. Jack, if you don't mind, could we postpone our sight-seeing for a day?"

Both men looked like they'd been stung by a hornet. Josie took advantage of their silence and led them inside the hotel.

"Father, please, let's go to your room and talk." She removed her new gloves and gave Jack a pleading look.

"Go on, Josie. We can see each other later." Jack pocketed his hands and left the hotel. The door banged shut behind him.

"Come on, Father, let's get this over with." Josie grasped the sides of her skirt and ascended the stairs.

Once in her father's room, she tossed her wrap on the bed and turned to look at her father. "I really hate to have to say this, but I want you to understand that I'm engaged now, and you have to accept that."

Hunter dropped his large frame into the single chair

by the window and sighed. "I didn't approve any engagement. So as far as I'm concerned, there isn't one." He crossed his arms and glared at his daughter.

"Father, I'm twenty-three years old. I am a woman. I'm no longer your little girl. I have a mind of my own and am capable of making decisions on my own." She too crossed her arms and glared.

For what seemed like hours, the two stared at each other.

Finally, Josie gave in. "Is it that you don't like Jack?"

Hunter unfolded his arms and pulled on the end of his beard. "No, he's a good enough fellow."

"And?" Her father's stubbornness was really getting to her. "What is the problem, then?"

"It's that, it's that, you're my child and you don't know nothing about marriage and men."

She rolled her eyes. "I may be your daughter, but I am no longer a child. And I resent that you think I don't know about men or marriage."

Hunter leapt to his feet. "No, you don't. You don't know how heartbreakin' a marriage can be. You don't know the pain of losing a loved one."

"Yes, I do. I lost my mother when you lost your wife, so that argument won't work with me. So tell me, is the real reason you don't want me to marry is that you're afraid you won't be able to go hunt for sapphires whenever you want to?"

She'd hit the nail on the head. Her father spun away from her, tension radiating from every muscle in his body. "Josie, I don't think we should be having this conversation. I say it's over."

"No! I won't let you. We're adults and can talk like them. Will you or won't you give me your blessing on my engagement? I'd prefer to have it, but if you refuse, I might have to do something we'd both regret later."

Thick, oppressing silence hung in the room. Josie could almost choke on it.

"I don't think I told you this, but after the wedding,

Jack and I plan to live in our house," she added, hoping to sway her father.

Hunter faced her once more, his expression softening somewhat. "In our house? With us?"

"Yes."

"And Jack agreed to this?"

Josie hesitated. "Um, yes." He'd better agree now, she thought.

"If that's true, then I guess I don't see what choice I have but to let you continue with your engagement. It'd kill me to lose my daughter." He raised his arms, signaling his acceptance of his elder daughter's engagement. "As long as you plan on living in our house."

"Very well, I'll accept that for now." Josie clasped her hands tightly to keep them from shaking. She'd just won a small victory with her father, even if she did spontaneously make up the fact that she and Jack would live at her ranch. Now all she had to do was make certain Jack would go along with the latest twist to their engagement. Undoubtedly, it would be no small task.

The next day, a bright and sunny one, Josie and Jack had made plans to ride around Bozeman, taking in the sights. Her father and sister were off to the jewelry stores. As Josie was preparing to leave the room, her sister spoke up.

"Jos, are you sure you don't want to come with Father and me?" Lottie asked, adjusting her sash.

"Yes, I'm sure. Jack and I are going to ride around town."

"But, Josie, you can do that with your sister and me." Hunter didn't like the way his elder daughter smiled when she said Jack's name, even if he had reluctantly agreed to allow her to be engaged. For far too long Hunter had lived how he wanted, doing what he wanted when he wanted, and he'd grown used to it. And now all that could be ruined because some man had gotten it into his head that he wanted to marry Josie.

Since Josie'd said that she and Jack would live at the

Douglasses' ranch, well, that made the prospect of a wedding less threatening. But it was hard, knowing he'd be losing his elder daughter, the only living link to his beloved first wife. Admitting that was harder for Hunter than the thought of not being able to search for sapphires whenever he wanted to.

For the first time in many years, he regretted that he didn't have a wife to talk to, someone to help him understand his daughter. Jack's arrival had thrown Hunter's whole world topsy-turvy.

"Father, you and Lottie are going to have her necklace made. You don't need me. I'll be fine with Jack." Josie picked up the new gloves and smoothed them on her hands.

Hunter looked at the gift and scowled. All his efforts to end the engagement hadn't worked. Hell, he'd even given his daughter his permission. To his experienced eyes, and he had been married two times, it looked as though Josie and Jack intended to go through with it. Hunter felt as if a solid steel forge had settled around his neck, yoking him and limiting his influence on his elder daughter.

"I could—" Hunter began.

"Father, enough. I'm tired of arguing with you. You and Lottie have a good time this morning. I'll see you later." Josie grabbed her cloak and walked out the door.

Once in the hall, she leaned against the wall for support. Her father really was being quite obstinate. Even if he had given his reluctant permission for her to marry, he was still trying to convince her not to go through with it. She looked down at the gloves Jack had given her and she felt better, until she recalled what she'd said to get her father to agree to the engagement, that she and Jack would live at her home. How could she tell Jack? And more important, how could she get him to agree with the idea?

Ha, she thought, first she needed to convince Jack to make theirs a real engagement.

She descended the stairs deep in thought, troubled that

once again she'd done something impulsive without seeking Jack's approval. She only hoped he wouldn't totally disregard her idea.

"Thanks for having my horse brought around." Josie smiled at Jack as he handed her the gelding's reins. She felt much better just seeing the look of excitement on his face. *He must really be enjoying my company if he looks this pleased to see me,* she thought.

"My pleasure. Are you ready for a ride?" Jack's blue eyes sparkled like sapphires.

"Yes. I'm not used to such a large town, and all these buildings are making me feel cooped in." Did she look especially nice today? she wondered. Is that why he looked so pleased?

"Soon we'll be in the open country. Follow me. Once we leave the city, we can ride at a faster pace."

"I'd love that." Oops. She hadn't meant to say that out loud. But Jack hadn't seemed to have noticed. Soon she would feel the wind in her hair, the ground speeding below her. Of course, it would be better if she were on Lady instead of on one of their workhorses, but a wagon horse was better than nothing.

"Just follow me, I know exactly where we're going."

"Where are we going?" Josie glanced at the boardwalks and the pretty women strolling along. She felt a pang of jealousy when she noticed Jack staring at them. They looked so pretty, so feminine, so perfect. Could she ever look like that?

"It's a secret. I'll tell you when we get there." Jack reached up and pushed his hat farther down on his head as they neared the outskirts of the town.

"A secret?" Visions of them sitting in a secluded spot, alone and kissing, filled Josie's mind. Her cheeks flushed. She shouldn't be thinking such things as she rode past a church.

"Yep, a secret. Are you ready to let our horses stretch their legs?"

"Yes, whenever you give the signal." She tucked her

skirt more securely around her legs so she wouldn't have so much material flapping around.

Soon they reached the open countryside. Only here and there could Josie see a cabin dotting the landscape. Growing grass stretched to the hills.

"We'll let them run on this flat part. When we reach the stream, slow and head to the north." Jack leaned forward and clucked loudly. His gelding surged forward.

Josie followed. The burst of speed her mount gave her didn't compare to Lady, but it felt good to have galloping horseflesh between her legs once more.

She stretched her chin forward, letting the cool air hit her face. Her horse's hooves drummed on the grass. She laughed at the feeling of pure freedom from the back of a running horse. She hoped Jack hadn't noticed. Her racing pastime was still unknown to him.

Momentarily, it seemed, the stream was before her. Before she knew what was happening, Jack aimed his horse at the water and jumped it. Her horse followed. She was almost caught unprepared and had a saddle horn in her stomach. At the last minute she wrapped her hand over the wooden protrusion to shield her belly. Her adrenaline flowed as they slowed down on the other side.

"Sorry about that, but I couldn't resist. I hope jumping the stream didn't give you any problems." Jack grinned as he looked over at her. His cheeks were stained red from his excitement.

One look at him and her heart somersaulted. She knew herself to be the luckiest woman alive. "No, I was just surprised, that's all. I thought you said to go north."

"We are now." He turned his horse. "I guess I just gave in to impulse. We've got a little more to go. The horses should be cooled by the time we arrive."

"Arrive where?" Josie glanced around. The wide Gallatin canyon spread out before her. Nothing other than wilderness stood out to grab her attention.

"You'll see."

"How do you know about this place we're going?"

"Like I said, you'll see."

"All right, then." Since she didn't seem likely to be getting any more information out of Jack, she contented herself with looking at the scenery.

In the distance she could see the mountain ranges rising skyward. They stretched as far as she could see in a north-south direction. To her right, she glimpsed a herd of elk grazing before they spotted the riders and took off.

She knew the canyon was famous for its game. Food was never in short supply for hunters who came to the valley.

After a long, companionable silence, Jack broke the quiet.

"See this group of trees?" He pointed to a grove of hardwoods.

"Yes."

"We'll cut through them and then we'll be there."

"Where?" Curiosity gnawed at her. What were they going to see? Was there a landmark she didn't know about? Was there some historical site nearby?

Turning the full power of his smile on her, Jack said, "You'll see. I hope you like it."

"Me too."

The horses picked their way around the trees. When they opened up to another wide clearing, Jack stopped and dismounted.

"Here we are. What do you think?" He spread his arms out and made a sweeping gesture, encompassing the whole area.

Josie's brows drew together. She stared. All she saw was virgin land. Was she missing something important? "Think of what?"

"Of this." He gestured again with his arms.

"This?" The setting she saw was pretty enough, accented by mountain flowers, and the grass looked rich. In the distance she could see a river or stream snaking along. "What exactly am I supposed to be looking for?"

"This. The land. Fertile land. Rich pastures." He turned to her and held up his arms, offering her assistance. The pure joy radiating from his face was unmistakable.

Josie shut her eyes when she felt his firm hands on her waist. She leaned into his solid body, feeling quite pleased that he'd wanted to share something so important to him with her.

"Won't this area be a great place for a breeding ranch?" he asked, his lips brushing her forehead.

Pastures. Breeding ranch. The ranch he planned on building. Suddenly the impact of what she saw registered with her and her heart plummeted to her toes. How could she convince him to live at her house if he was so set on ranching this land?

She glanced up at him again and knew she guessed right. He looked exactly how her father looked when he'd found a rich vein of sapphires. Jack too had found his gems. And they weren't at her ranch in Gallatin City.

"What do you think? This is where it's all going to happen." Jack couldn't keep the enthusiasm from his voice.

"It is?" She wanted to hear him say it wasn't so. That he really wanted to marry her and live at her ranch. He *had* to want to live at her house, at least for the time being, until her father had gotten used to the thought of her marrying.

"Yes, this is the perfect spot to build our ranch. Look at it." He grasped her shoulders and spun her around, making sure she saw everything he saw.

"I am." She tried to summon a grain of excitement for him. But she found that nearly impossible when her hopes were being snuffed out and her soul felt cold.

"Have you ever seen such an ideal place to breed horses? I mean, look at the grass. Green, fertile as far as the river. Plenty of water. Plenty of wood to build a house and barn. And best of all, Bozeman is not very far away, as you've seen."

No, Bozeman wasn't far. But Gallatin City was. And Gallatin City was where she needed to be. Where they needed to live. Josie suddenly felt like weeping. Her

plans to save Lottie from Mrs. Potter and her father's
recently given permission all hinged on them actually
marrying and remaining at home. Her home. Not here,
on some ranch miles from anyone. How could Jack have
done something like this?

"What's wrong? You're so quiet. I'll bet you're just
speechless like I was the first time I came upon this
place." He pulled her snugly against his chest and
wrapped his arms over her stomach. "Yep, this is where
it's all going to happen. As a matter of fact, I've decided
to make our engagement official and thought this the perfect place to tell you."

Josie was stunned.

Jack bent his head, brushing her ears with his lips.
"Would you be my wife?"

She reached out and took his hand, needing to hold on
to something solid. Had she heard him correctly? Beneath
her ribs, her heart hammered.

"Say something. Yes or no? Do you still want to
marry me?"

She quickly found her voice. "Yes, yes, I'd love to be
your wife."

Jack pressed his lips to her cheek and held her snug
against his body. "Good, you had me worried there for
a moment."

Her hopes had come true, but not at all how she'd
envisioned they would. She felt like crying. He was right.
The area was beautiful. In fact, a part of her ached to
live there. The rich grass would nurture healthy horses.
But it couldn't be their horses. She'd just have to make
him understand that there was no need to purchase this
land. Then an even more depressing thought entered her
mind. What if he'd already purchased it?

"Hey, why so quiet?" Jack released her and spun her
to face him. Immediately the grin left his face. "What's
wrong? Don't you like your new home?"

She stared up into his eyes, wanting with every ounce
of her being to be with him but knowing she couldn't
live there. She was needed in Gallatin City.

"It's pretty, and . . . and it looks like a great place to raise horses . . ." Her eyes swept over his face, at the delight in it, and she thought she would lose her composure.

"But what?" He faltered.

"It's so far from Gallatin City. What about Lottie and my father? Are you sure you want to live here?"

Jack shut his eyes and sighed. When he opened them, he lifted a hand to her face. Gently, he stroked her cheek. "Josie, in case you forgot, you and I are engaged. To marry. When a man and woman marry, they leave to start their own life. You did know you would be leaving your home, right?"

His fingers felt so good on her skin. She wanted to think only about that and not about his words, which she knew were normally true. "I had thought we could live at our house and then Lottie wouldn't—"

He slipped his hand over her mouth. "Shh, I don't want to hear about Lottie. You're going to be my wife, and I don't want to live in the same house as your father."

She pushed his hand away. "What's wrong with my father?"

"Nothing. It's just that when we marry, it will be our life. And my dream is to start my own breeding operation. You know that. That's the reason I came out west in the first place."

"Yes, but—"

"No buts. This is our life, let's see if we can enjoy it." He pulled her closer to him, placing his hands on her lower back, bringing her hips closer to his.

Josie shut her eyes. She had no desire to argue with him now. Her world was spinning out of control and she chose to focus on the sensations Jack awoke in her. She felt the warm tingling start in her belly and travel upward. Tentatively, she put her arms around him. Her suede gloves stuck to the rough material of his jacket.

"Josie, have I ever told you how beautiful you are?" He dipped his head, capturing her lips.

She opened her mouth, touching her tongue to his. She started when he captured her lower lip and sucked on it. Her blood raced in her veins.

Wanting to feel him, she pulled off her gloves and dropped them to the ground. She wished his coat weren't separating them, she wanted to feel his heated skin on her fingers.

Jack groaned and slipped to the grass, bringing her with him. He settled her on his lap and one hand began exploring. It dove underneath the folds of her cloak, seeking her body. He rubbed her shoulders, and slowly his hand drifted downward until he brushed against the soft swell of her bosom.

The moment his hand grazed her breast, Josie gasped. She knew they shouldn't be doing this, but she couldn't stop herself. There were just too many foreign, wonderful feelings coursing through her body, enough to scatter her thoughts and make her forget about ranches and her family.

Jack broke the kiss and moved his head down, nuzzling at her neck and sucking on her sensitive earlobe, drawing it between his teeth.

Josie dropped her head backward and arched her spine. She'd no idea her ears were so sensitive. When Jack's hand moved to her bodice and started opening the buttons, her breathing quickened.

She felt his hard desire pressing into her rear. She knew what that meant. He wanted her. The knowledge gave her a giddy sense of power.

Suddenly Jack slid his hand inside her dress. Her belly rioted with sensations as he brushed her extended nipples. The muscles between her legs contracted as she lost herself in the heady feelings.

He cupped her breast and gently tugged on the nipple. She moaned at the erotic touch.

When she moaned, Jack suddenly opened his eyes and stared down at his hand teasing her nipple. He reddened and snatched his hand away.

"Oh, God, Josie, I'm so sorry. I didn't mean this to

happen. I should wait until we're wed before doing such things.''

Josie thought she should feel embarrassment, but she did not. She felt only loss. She wanted his touch. She relished the feelings his touch aroused in her body. ''You have nothing to apologize for.'' She snuggled closer into the comforting folds of his arms.

''Yes, I do. I had no business touching you the way I did. Here, let me button you up.'' He extended a hand and tried to redo her buttons. Only it proved a mistake. When his hand landed on her soft curves, his desire re-kindled.

Josie felt him growing even harder and was again filled with a sense of wonder that she could have such an effect on him. ''Here, I can do them.'' She set his hand on her lap and quickly fixed the remaining buttons.

Jack sighed. ''This will be so much better once the house is built.''

''Yes, a house would probably be preferable to the outdoors,'' Josie said, making idle chatter but unable to voice her true opinion and stress that they already had a house. Somehow, casually, she had to broach the topic.

''Are you still unconvinced about my choice for a ranch?'' Jack bent his head and whispered into her ear, stopping only to lightly nip at it.

She shivered, and not because she was cold. His body, plus the bright sunshine, heated her up. Jack seemed in a jovial mood, so she'd try now. ''About this location, have you purchased it yet?''

He pulled away from her ear. ''What?''

She snuggled deeper into his arms, hoping to distract him. ''I said, you haven't spent any money yet, have you?''

''I don't think you need to concern yourself with such things. Let's just enjoy the view.'' He nuzzled her ear again. ''And from where I am, the view is simply beautiful,'' he murmured against her neck.

No matter how tempting or how sweet his words were, she refused to let him distract her. ''It's nothing to worry about really. I just think there's no reason to spend money on land, that's all. We've already got plenty of land.''

All nuzzling halted. Jack abruptly left the comfort of her embrace. His voice hardened. ''We do? How is that?''

''Now, there's no need to sound so put out.'' She managed a laugh, hoping to lighten the situation. ''I think it would be best if we lived at my house after the wedding.''

Jack's eyes darkened, and he rose to his feet in one swift motion. ''We will be living in *our* own house. Here.'' He gestured with his arm to the surrounding land.

''No, no, you misunderstood me. I meant we'd live at my house, our house, in Gallatin City. That way you wouldn't have to buy any land or spend any money.'' She smiled what she hoped was an encouraging smile.

''Why in the hell did you think I'd want to do something like that? Did you ever think to consult me about that issue?'' He spun away from her.

Oh, dear, this wasn't at all how she intended this conversation to go. ''It's just that there's already a house. A barn, nice big pastures, and the town is close by.'' And most important, she silently added, her sister.

The venom in his words made her flinch. ''You're right, it is *your* house, and your barn, and your family. Where is *our* house supposed to be? Where are we supposed to start *our* life?''

''Ah . . .'' She floundered. She couldn't think of an argument for that one. He did have a point, but so did she, and she was the one with lives at stake here. She couldn't let Jack purchase this land.

''Well? Have you even stopped to think about what I want? You're the reason we're engaged. I agreed to continue only because I felt I needed to restore your honor, and look at the thanks I'm getting.'' He reached out and grabbed a long stalk of grass, yanking it up by the root.

She was shocked. She had an idea he'd agreed to the marriage out of honor, but to hear him actually say it, to hear him say he had no feelings for her, hurt. It couldn't hurt more if she'd sliced her hand and poured salt on the open wound. "I—I, I think it's time we left here." She spun around, hiding the tears from him, and marched to her horse.

Jack groaned. "Josie, come back here, please. I didn't mean it like that. I spoke in anger. I don't want us to leave on such bad terms."

"Leaving is precisely what I'm going to do." Through her tears she fumbled around and finally secured her toe in the stirrup. She hoisted herself into the saddle, not caring if he followed or not. All she wanted to do was to get as far away from Jack and his hurtful words. He could stay and look at his precious land for all she cared. She had half a mind to end this engagement right then. There had to be another way to save her sister, and, more important, save herself from further heartache.

Jack picked up her forgotten gloves, mounted, and followed behind Josie. He didn't want to let her out of his sight. The expression on her face when he'd said his careless words cut him to the core. He felt like kicking himself. Never had he meant to say such hard-hearted words, even if they were true initially, but they weren't anymore.

He should have known better than to speak when angry. There was no excuse for his spiteful words.

His plan had been to stay engaged only long enough for him to think of a better way to help Josie. But the more time he spent with her, the more fond of her he became. He looked forward to the time they spent together. He liked listening to her, watching her try so hard to be other than she was, but that was what endeared her to him.

Hell, he'd say he was more than fond, he was downright infatuated with her, which was why he'd made their engagement official.

He hated the thought of her in another man's arms, kissing someone else. In sum, she was what he wanted for a life mate. He loved her.

He shoved his hat on his head. Why did the woman

he'd fallen for have to be so obstinate? He hadn't meant to say the hurtful words, but Josie had a way of assuming too much. He snorted. Indeed, he hadn't come out West to live in another man's home. He wanted his own home. He'd just have to make Josie see the reason in that. Preferably before they returned to Gallatin City.

THE FOLLOWING MORNING Josie barely acknowledged Jack as she finished her breakfast. She stared down
at the curled remnants of bacon on her plate and listened
to Lottie yammering away.

"Jack, I think you should ride home with us. It'd be
fun to have another man to talk to," she said, once again
batting her eyelashes.

"My business is completed here. I don't see any harm
in accompanying you."

Jack glanced over at Josie, but she refused to return
his look. Casting her eyes downward, she fought back
the tears that threatened. How could he have been so
callous? she thought. She knew theirs wasn't a love
match, but in her heart she'd hoped he felt something for
her. Instead, he made her sound like a burden.

Even her father gave her a curious stare. "Finish up,
Josie. I've got the team out front and ready to go."

"Yes, Father," she mumbled. She wished Jack would

go away until she garnered enough nerve to tell him exactly what she thought of his comments. She didn't care if she sounded the furthest thing from a lady then. Her pride stung and she wanted it soothed.

"We're leavin' in ten minutes, Jos. So visit the convenience if you need to." Hunter rose and stretched. He patted the bulge in his shirt pocket that consisted of his brand-new cuff links.

An hour and a half later, Josie sat on the wagon seat and stared ahead, not really seeing the scenery. She was doing her best to ignore Jack's presence, but it was hard to when she kept sneaking glances at him out of the corner of her eye.

Damn him, why did he have to look so guilty? If she didn't know better, she'd swear he seemed as upset as she was.

"You seem mighty glum, Jos, and I don't think it's because of my new sapphire cuff links," Hunter said as he guided the horses down the worn trail leading back to Gallatin City.

Josie's gaze flicked to Jack, who rode alongside the wagon, before answering. She scowled at him when he attempted to smile. "You're right. I guess I'm just preoccupied."

"Yeah, I'm sure weddings take up lots of one's thinking time," Lottie said, oblivious of the mood of her sister.

If only they knew the half of it, Josie thought. Her wedding was far from her mind; in fact, she was considering her options if she ended the engagement. However, those options looked few.

Hunter grunted and stared straight ahead. "Weddin', huh? Still don't think it's such a good idea. I mean, why rush these things?"

Josie glared at her father.

"I can't wait for Josie's, then I can see what'll happen at mine when the time comes." Lottie smiled up at her father. "Mine will be here soon."

Hunter laughed at that statement. "Lottie, pumpkin,

you've got a long time before that day comes. Until then, I can be your favorite man.''

He shifted his gaze to Jack and Josie. Now, Hunter was a good enough judge of people to know when something just wasn't right, and he could sense that now with his elder daughter. He tried to keep the relief from his face. If he was lucky, the wedding wouldn't happen and then his sapphire-searching days wouldn't come to an end.

''Maybe for me, but not for Jos,'' Lottie continued. ''Now, let me see, I've got lots of sewing to do when I get home.'' She pursed her lips and stared thoughtfully ahead.

Hunter turned to Josie. ''Well, Jos, is that day near?'' He jerked his glance in Jack's direction.

Josie gripped the edge of the seat. How could her father know? She hadn't said a word about what had happened yesterday. Only she and Jack knew the engagement was true.

''You remember our talk the other night. You gave us your permission for the engagement.'' She felt the sweat slide down the collar of her dress. Why were both her father and Jack staring at her now?

''That I did. Is there somethin' else I should know?''

Josie's laugh came out more nervous-sounding than she meant it to. She quickly silenced it. ''No, nothing new to know. There's just so much to think about.''

''I see,'' Hunter said, sounding utterly unconvinced. He returned his attention to the rut-filled road ahead.

Jack joined the conversation. ''I rather liked Bozeman. What about you all?''

You would, you traitor, Josie thought, appalled at the direction of her thoughts. ''It was nice,'' she said instead.

''I had a wonderful time. After it stopped raining I had a great time. I got so excited by all the fashions I saw, I can't wait to go home and start sewing,'' Lottie said. ''I'll make the prettiest dress and be the envy of all my friends.''

"Sounds like you really enjoyed yourself, Lottie," Jack said.

"Uh-huh, although it would have been more fun if Mary Jane had been there."

"Yes, friends are nice."

Josie noticed Jack kept returning his glance to her. He looked so crestfallen each time she frowned at him that she felt bad. She felt herself softening toward him already and didn't want that to be the case. She'd forgive him when she was good and ready.

No one talked for the remainder of the trip until they reached the ferry. Hunter spoke up. "All righty, girls, let's get off the wagon and wait our turn at the ferry."

Josie watched the flatbed boat return across the Gallatin River. The current moved slowly, but the river was too deep and rocky to ford with the wagon.

After they crossed on the ferry, Gallatin City rose in sight. Jack reined his gelding to a halt. "I'll be leaving you now. I've got some papers to attend to in my hotel room. Thanks for the company. I'll be over later to check on my stallion." He tipped his hat to Josie and went down the main street.

"Looks like it's just us again. What do you say we have a nice home-cooked meal for our little family?" Hunter said, urging the team to a trot.

"Sounds good. I want to work on my fair entry. I'll put the lace I bought on my dress." Lottie ran her fingers along the wrapped packet of material.

Josie watched, and without wanting it a trace of happiness blossomed inside. The material for her veil was inside that package. A wedding veil. She really was going to get married, if she still wanted Jack. And she did. All of a sudden she couldn't wait for the date.

She sobered instantly. They'd never set a date. How could they have before? Her father had been so dead set against the prospect of a wedding. Now that had all changed. Or had it?

She and Jack had exchanged some pretty harsh words. Did she still want to spend the rest of her life with him?

She knew she'd heard remorse in his voice as she rode away yesterday, but it was agonizing to know he thought of her only as a means to an end. Where was the love that was supposed to accompany a wedding?

Her heart felt as if it were rendered in two. She loved him, and had known that for a while now. If only he had given her some hint that he might return her love. Oh, she knew he found her body appealing, his own body language had told her that. But she wanted to know what was in his heart. That was what mattered to her.

Her gaze followed him as Jack rode toward the hotel. Sighing, she knew they had to talk. She knew she needed to convince him of the benefits of living at her house. The question was how could she change his mind about his new ranch, and did she really want to?

Josie awoke just as the barest hint of day appeared. She needed nothing to wake her up. She was going to work with her mare this morning. The fair was approaching and she still had some training to do with Lady.

Quickly, she threw on her riding clothes. Today she was daring and wore trousers. She prayed no one would see her. Especially Jack.

She scurried to the barn, hoping not to be discovered. The thick fog should prevent that. She knew she was tempting fate by wearing such an outfit. That was another reason she always rode so early in the morning.

Josie rather liked the fog. She felt protected, shielded from the prying eyes of others. She wanted to prepare Lady alone, and then on race day surprise the citizens with her mare's capabilities. She knew it was risky to keep racing her mare, but it was in Josie's blood. She had to. Her only hope was that her engagement would lessen the sin of racing in Mrs. Potter's eyes. But in order for that to work, she had to make sure Jack approved of her hobby, and she wasn't quite sure how to tell him, or what his reaction might be.

"Oh, well, time to worry about that later, right, Lady?" she said to her mare.

Lady looked up at the sound of Josie's voice and nickered in greeting. Josie opened the door that housed the tack and feed. She took a saddle and bridle down from the racks and slipped them on her arms.

She draped the saddle over Lady's stall door. Entering the stall, Josie stroked Lady's soft nose and gave her a small kiss. Then she picked up each hoof, took a small metal hoof pick, and scraped out the accumulated dirt.

Satisfied all was well with her horse, Josie saddled the mare. After the bridle was buckled, Josie led the mare out into the yard.

She grabbed a handful of mane and hoisted herself up on Lady's back. A brisk walk would serve as a warmup on the way to the racetrack. Stillness surrounded her, except the soft footfalls of her mare's hooves.

A golden mist shone in the east as Josie and Lady set out for the track. The sun burned a yellow haze in the sky as it rose. Soon the fog would be gone. She needed to hurry.

They reached they track in no time. The dirt oval was empty, just like all the previous times. Josie positioned them at the start line and counted down.

On three she kicked Lady, and the mare shot forward like a runaway train. Josie felt herself becoming one with her horse. Lady's speed seemed faster than usual, until they reached the far side of the track.

Then Lady's stride faltered. She slowed, limping, favoring her right front leg.

"Whoa," Josie said, rising in her stirrups, bringing the mare to a walk. Something wasn't right.

Nothing had looked out of the ordinary when Josie had made her preride check. She had seen no recent injury or sign of illness. Josie twisted around in her saddle and scanned the track behind them. She saw no holes or anything obvious. Josie dismounted and ran her hands down the mare's legs, checking for swelling.

"Easy, girl, I'll get you home and we'll figure out what's bothering you. But first I want to go scan the track to see if there was anything on it." She made soothing sounds to her mare, who balked at moving.

After what seemed an eternity of scrutinizing the dirt oval, Josie found a few rocks. Two of them looked big enough to have caused damage to Lady's hoof. Grasping the offending rocks, Josie tossed them over the railing so no other horse would get hurt.

Picking up the right front leg, Josie bent over and cleared the dirt away, checking for signs of a puncture or bruise. Sure enough, by the soft frog that made up the center of the hoof, Josie saw a deep red indentation. A nasty bruise.

Josie set the hoof back down and rested her head on her mare's neck. She sighed. Why did this have to happen now? Only one week before the race? How could her mare heal by . . . heal by race time?

Perhaps a poultice would draw out the injured tissue and help the healing. It was worth a try. "C'mon, girl, let's go home. I need to take care of your foot."

The walk home seemed endless. With each step, Lady's head bobbed as she tried not to put weight on her injured hoof. As they reached the halfway point, Josie heard a horse approaching from behind. She turned and her heart skipped a beat. Jack! Perhaps he would have a suggestion to hasten Lady's healing.

He rode up and hopped off his horse. "What's wrong with Lady?" He glanced from Josie to her mare.

"She stepped on a stone and now has what looks like a deep bruise."

"Let me see." He knelt on the ground and lifted the hoof. Taking his index finger, he probed on the injury. Lady flinched. "It's a bad one." He set the hoof down and straightened. "Where did it happen?"

Josie met his gaze and then quickly looked away. "It, uh, happened over there." She flicked her hand back toward the fairgrounds.

Jack's eyes widened and his gaze raked her from the top of her cap to the bottom of her men's trousers, as if he were seeing her for the first time.

Josie thought she saw scorn in those eyes. She fought

to regain her composure. Her appearance didn't matter; Lady's injury did. "Can you do anything for her?"

"I think so. But where did you say it happened?"

"Um, over on the racetrack." Her heart pounded. What would he think of her? Would he rescind his offer to marry her?

Jack bent forward, narrowing the distance between them. "On the track?" He motioned with his arm behind him.

"Ah, well, yes. Yes, it did." She didn't like the scowl on his face. It didn't bode well. "Well, what about Lady? What should we do?"

Jack tore his gaze off her and studied the mare. "Hmmm, let's walk her slowly. Once we get to your barn, we'll fix her up with a poultice."

Josie shut her eyes and sighed. She wished they were home already. She hated to make Lady walk farther and risk irritating the injury to her hoof. "I'll help with the poultice."

"Good." Jack slowed his pace to keep even with hers. He kept quiet, stealing glances at her out of the corner of his eye.

Josie couldn't make out the expression on his face, but the way Jack's lips were pursed, she could tell he wasn't overjoyed. She could see he knew she'd been racing at the track, and she didn't know what to say.

Jack broke the uncomfortable silence. "Even if you don't say a word, I know what you've been doing. Racing. How come you never told me?"

She sighed. "Remember when I said I was interested in racing?" He nodded and she took that as a sign to continue. "I wasn't entirely honest. See, I'm the one who races Lady. I've been trying to get her prepared for the fair. I had hopes of us doing real well." She stopped and tried to gauge his reaction.

Jack stared at her as if she'd grown a third head. A combination of disbelief and anger flickered in his eyes. "I guess I shouldn't be surprised. After all, the signs were there. I mean, I'm glad you share my enthusiasm for racing, but my fiancée actually riding in one?" His voice held the slightest bit of sarcasm in his last sentence.

"Why not? There's nothing wrong with it." Who was he to think he could tell her what to do? She knew she was a darn good rider and Lady was one talented horse.

"I'll tell you what's wrong with it. First of all, look at you." He gestured with his hand at her body, scowling while he spoke. "You're wearing men's clothes. It's not proper for a woman to wear such things. Secondly, I doubt the race organizers would let a woman ride in the stakes races."

"So if I wore a riding dress I would be more respectable to you?" Of all the nerve, for him to tell her what she should wear or not wear.

He returned his gaze to her body, lingering on her shapely legs outlined by the trousers. Jerking his head around, he looked straight ahead. "See what I mean? The mere sight of you in those tight clothes distracts me. Think of what it would do to the other men. And I don't want strange men staring at you." Crossing his arms, he glared sideways at her.

"My clothing is not that tight. And no one is forcing you to stare at me," she said testily.

"No, no one is forcing me to stare, but it's hard not to." Once more his gaze drifted over to Josie and lingered on the curve of her rear. He clutched his reins and rolled his eyes. "See? It's hard not to stare. And besides, I still doubt the organizers would let you ride in the race."

She hadn't considered his last remark, and it rankled her to no end. She'd been busy preparing her mare and trying to keep such a low profile that she'd totally forgotten that issue. And it made her angry with herself, so she took it out on Jack instead. "My mare is as good as any of those other horses. There's no reason we should be discriminated against."

"Dammit! Josie." He slapped his palm against his thigh. "You aren't listening. It's just the rules of the game, that's all. Suppose you got hurt? I'd hate that to happen.'' His voice lowered to a husky whisper.

Her mouth opened for a retort but snapped shut. Had he just said he'd hate anything to happen to her? ''So you don't disapprove of my racing Lady?''

He groaned. ''I want to disapprove, but I can't, not when I know how much racing excites me. But we can't ignore the fact that you're a woman and that makes me wish you wouldn't do it.''

''So are you saying you care for me?''

''Dammit, yes. Yes, I am.''

Josie almost stumbled in her relief. Jack scorned her racing only because he was concerned for her well-being. Suddenly she'd wished she'd told him about her racing a lot earlier. The radiant smile blooming on her face could almost chase away the remaining vestiges of fog.

When they reached the barn, Josie ushered Lady inside. Josie drew her lower lip in between her teeth and looked at her beautiful mare.

Lady stood in the middle of her stall, holding her foot up.

Josie watched with growing fear. Her mare was lame. Very lame. What horrible timing.

''So much for our debut at this year's fair,'' she said, unable to hide the disappointment in her voice.

Jack paused. ''You were serious about entering the upcoming fair?''

''Yes, that was the plan. Let's prepare Lady's poultice.''

''Josie, I don't know what to make of you.'' Jack sighed, thrusting his hands into his pockets.

She wished he didn't look so distraught. ''What's that supposed to mean?'' Her ears and cheeks burned. She could feel him staring at her trousers. If only she'd worn a riding skirt. Then maybe he wouldn't be looking at her as as though she were an oddball.

''Nothing. Where are your horse medicines kept?'' He moved toward the tack room. ''We've got to get this mare taken care of.'' Jack shoved his hand through his hair.

"That's what I've been saying." She glared up at him. How dare he make it sound like she was the one at fault here. It hurt her.

She preceded him into the tack room and brought out two buckets filled with various bottles and curatives. "Here, we can make our own poultice with these."

Jack sorted through the selections, taking the necessary ingredients. He mixed and then slathered a generous gob of smelly substance on Lady's hoof. Next he secured the poultice in place with several strips of bandage wrapped around the hoof. "There, that should help her and ease the pain."

"Thanks for your help."

He straightened, leaned against the stall door, and asked with deceptive calm, "Is there anything else you're keeping from me? Anything else I should know?"

Why was he being so contrary? One minute he was angry with her and the next he was concerned about her. He should be supportive and she wished he wouldn't look at her with those narrowed eyes. "I never kept anything from you."

He raised his brows. "You didn't? Then why did I just find out about your racing activities today?"

He had her there. But she really hadn't kept it from him, she just hadn't gotten the chance to tell him, that's all. "I was going to."

"Humph."

Josie looked at her mare and tried to ignore the man beside her. If he had a lick of sense, he would know now wasn't the time to discuss it. Lady was injured. "I hope you don't forget Lady here. She's the one who needs us."

"Oh, I'm not forgetting her. I've been keeping an eye on her ever since I administered the poultice. And I couldn't think of a better time to have a discussion than when we have to keep an eye on her for a while anyway."

So much for her idea. "Maybe Lady needs silence."

"She doesn't. So why did you never tell me about

your racing 'hobby'?'' Jack asked, folding his arms and leaning against the stall door like a man prepared to wait until he'd heard what he wanted to hear.

Josie took one look at his steady gaze and knew she had to tell him, especially since she wanted their relationship to work. She sighed. ''I thought you might think less of me when we first met. I wanted you to think I was everything you wanted in a woman, and I didn't think you'd want your future wife racing horses.''

''You're right. I never thought I'd have to worry about my wife riding racehorses.'' Jack ran his hand down Lady's neck. ''As long as we're talking, you might as well tell me more about your racing. You know, I should've guessed when you gave me the tip about the back side of the racetrack. At the time I didn't stop to think how you could've known such a fact.''

She managed a laugh, trying to lighten the mood. ''Yeah, I was worried you would ask me about that.''

''How long have you raced Lady?''

''For two years. I think she runs real well. I planned to enter her in the fair this year, but now I can't.'' She looked at her mare, her best friend, whom she had high hopes for, then she looked at Jack and her heart swelled.

Things were going to be fine. Jack hadn't run screaming when he discovered her pastime. She knew the one issue they needed to discuss was being avoided on purpose.

''How long have you been interested in racing?'' she asked, unwilling to bring up the subject of where they would live. She didn't want to ruin the camaraderie they shared just then.

''Ever since I was a young boy. I'd love to hang around at the barns and watch the men race their horses. I could stay there all day, just watching and dreaming.'' He stopped and laughed. ''My mother hated it. I remember one time she sent our maid over to get me and bring me home. Seems she was worried about her boy looking like a ruffian.''

Josie had often wondered about his family and if she

would ever meet them. It seemed odd to be marrying Jack without being introduced to his parents. "What's your family like?"

His back stiffened. "Why do you ask?"

"Won't they want to know about the woman you're going to marry?"

Oh, they certainly would. "My family is a lot different from yours."

"Most families are different than mine."

She had a point, he admitted. "Let's just say mine are very concerned about doing the right thing and always appearing their best in front of everyone's eyes. They are very etiquette conscious." As much as he hated to admit it, he feared his mother wouldn't approve of Josie, especially if she saw her in the men's trousers she had on now.

"Etiquette conscious? Are you saying they would disapprove of me?"

The wounded expression on her face pained him. "No, I'm saying my mother might need a while to warm up to you." That was putting it nicely. One of the things that bothered him about his family was their tendency to pass judgment without giving the other person a fair chance. He knew, however, that if given enough time, his parents would come to see the good in Josie.

"That doesn't sound real encouraging," she said.

"You don't need to worry about it, I doubt you'll meet her for a long time. Unless we go to Kansas City, I don't see how you could meet her." Jack glanced at Lady, checking the security of her bandage.

"I feel sort of bad, not meeting your family."

"Believe me, it's nothing to fret about."

"If you say so." Josie's voice cracked, and she turned her head away from him.

"Hey, what's the matter? You sound upset." He turned her head toward his.

She tried to avert her eyes.

With his thumb he traced the outline of her jaw. "Why so glum? You should be happy. Lady looks like she'll be fine, and I'm here, helping you.'' Female emotions were not something he had a lot of experience with. Josie's distress tore at him.

She clasped and unclasped her hands. "It's just that— it's just that I want them to like me. I want them to—"

He didn't give her a chance to finish her sentence. He wrapped his arms around her and brought her close to him. "Shh, there's nothing to worry about. Everything will be fine." With one hand he stroked her hair and with the other he held fast to her.

"But you don't understand." Her voice was muffled against his chest.

"Shh, there's nothing to understand. Just relax, I'll hold you and keep you safe." In truth, he couldn't figure out why she seemed so distraught. He didn't think he'd said anything that upsetting. Not knowing what to do, he laid his mouth on top of hers, silencing her with a kiss.

The sound of braying mules caused Josie to jerk away, a guilty expression on her face.

❖ 22 ❖

"WHY DO YOU look so worried all of a sudden?" he asked, noting her drawn brows.

"We've got visitors. It has to be the Potters. They're the only ones with a mule team."

"Oh, the good reverend." Jack found he actually was looking forward to meeting Reverend Potter and setting up a date for their wedding.

"Or maybe his wife," Josie said reluctantly.

Jack glanced over at her and wondered why she looked so worried. He stepped out of the barn and looked. "You're right, I do see a woman."

Mrs. Potter bustled across the grass, heading toward the barn. She waved her arms. "It's about time someone showed up at this household. I've been trying to find your father and I'm having no luck."

As soon as Josie stepped into sight of Mrs. Potter, the woman inhaled and gasped. "Oh, dear Lord above. Do my eyes deceive me? Are you, Josephine, an engaged woman, wearing tr-trousers?" She practically spat out the last word.

Jack didn't like the sudden tension he felt emanating from the two women. He knew it was unorthodox for Josie to have on trousers, but to create such a harsh reaction from the reverend's wife? Jack stepped closer to Josie and took her arm. "She and I were out riding, and it made more sense. Plus it was safer for her to wear the trousers."

Mrs. Potter clutched at the handle of her umbrella. "Do you mean to say you two were together at this early hour of the morning? Alone?"

"Yes, my fiancé and I were riding," Josie said, holding herself regally erect. "What brings you over to our ranch so early in the day?"

"I came for some of Lottie's work."

Josie turned white. In a strangled voice she said, "What do you mean?"

"I mean, I'm here for the church napkins I asked my niece to embroider for me a few weeks ago." Mrs. Potter stared at them.

"Oh, I—I didn't know what you were referring to. Let's go inside and I'll fetch them for you."

Before they moved indoors, Mrs. Potter turned her stare to Jack. "You must be Josephine's intended." She narrowed her eyes and inspected him. "Although I can't say what kind of husband you will make if you allow Josephine to go out in public wearing such scandalous clothing. Makes a God-fearing woman wonder what is happening with the world today."

Jack didn't care if she was the reverend's wife or not, he didn't like the tone she used on him. She reminded him of his mother, and he knew just how to handle that kind of woman. "As I said earlier, Josie would be safer in trousers and it was foggy. The only person who saw us was you, and only then because you came to her house."

Mrs. Potter quivered with indignation. "Young man, it is never appropriate for women to be seen in anything other than a dress. You don't know how I worry what Josephine's actions will do to my niece.''

''Niece?''

''Lottie is Mrs. Potter's niece. Her sister was my father's second wife,'' Josie interjected, pausing with her hand on the doorknob.

''Oh,'' Jack said, thinking this was certainly a morning for revelations. Was there something else he would find out soon?

''Josephine, could you please get the napkins? I need to prepare for a luncheon of the Ladies Auxiliary this afternoon.'' Mrs. Potter followed and stood by the front door.

As soon as Josie disappeared inside, Mrs. Potter turned her full attention to Jack. ''My husband and I have been waiting for you to come over and set a date for your wedding. Have you selected one yet?''

Jack felt guilty for not liking Mrs. Potter, even if she was somehow related to Josie's family. The woman was simply not nice, and she was doing her best to make Jack feel uncomfortable. He decided not to give her that pleasure. ''Let's see, today is Thursday, so the date shall be a week from Saturday. That's when Josie and I would like to wed.''

''Since you are new in town, I suppose you don't yet realize that is not how weddings work. My husband has a limited number of free dates, it is best to check with him before settling on a day.'' She thumped her umbrella on the porch for emphasis. ''I shall see how next Saturday is with him.''

Blessing her with his most charming smile, he said, ''You must forgive me, but I tend to do things my own way. I'm sure there aren't that many weddings planned, so there should be no problem with Josie and me marrying on that Saturday.''

Mrs. Potter blinked at him in surprise. ''You do speak boldly. I'll be sure and let the Auxiliary know this about your character.''

Before Jack could question her, Josie returned and

handed a packet of folded linens to Mrs. Potter. "Here they are. Lottie had them finished and ready for you."

Mrs. Potter snatched them from Josie. "I'll tell my niece thank you when I see her. The Auxiliary is going over to the schoolhouse to read to the children later this afternoon." She turned and strode to her waiting wagon.

"What an unpleasant woman," Jack said.

"You don't know the half of her." Josie watched the mules pull the wagon away. "She thinks because she's Lottie's aunt that she should raise Lottie. So we've been battling it out."

"Well, you no longer need to worry about that. I'm here."

Josie nodded absently.

"Are you going to be all right? You look a little pale all of a sudden," Jack asked.

Her gaze stayed on the departing wagon. "Um, yes, I'm fine." Josie looked at him and forced a smile to her face.

Jack frowned. The tension between the two women had been palpable.

"Josie? What's wrong? You sure you're fine?"

"Yes, I mean, I'm fine. I just remembered some chores I have to do, that's all. And I know you have tasks to take care of also."

Jack hesitated. He hated to leave her when she looked so upset. His heart ached for her. But he could tell her some good news. He smiled. "I told Mrs. Potter we'd like our wedding to be next Saturday. Doesn't that make you happy?"

She smiled, her face shining like a beam of sunshine. "Did you really?"

"Yes, I did. Is that day fine with you?"

"Oh, yes. Yes, it is."

Seeing the excited expression on Josie's face pleased him. "I'm sure you have lots to do, like get your wedding gown fitted, plan a guest list, so I'll go now. Remember, I really do care for you."

He blew her a kiss as she stepped inside the house and softly shut the door.

Jack couldn't believe his own words. What had happened to his carefully guarded heart and his pledge not to get too close to her? Whether he admitted it or not, he looked forward to his marriage to Josie, even if she wasn't the meek, docile woman he'd set out to find.

Love. He stood still, pondering the word. Suddenly a huge smile stretched his lips. He felt great. In fact, he decided being in love was something he could learn to enjoy more with each passing day. And loving Josie, with all her quirky habits, was not hard at all.

Their wedding could not come soon enough for him.

"Ow!" Josie yelped as the third pin in a row stabbed her side.

"Do you think you could stand still?" Grace said while clutching her pincushion. "I can't very well help you fix your wedding dress if I can't pin it correctly."

"I can't help it. I'm so excited. My feet just don't want to stand still." Josie glanced down at the ivory-colored gown that had been her mother's wedding dress. Years ago, when Josie had last opened the cedar chest, she never dreamed she would be given an opportunity to be a bride. Now, in eight days, she would be Mrs. Jack St. Augustine.

"Well, try to be excited while standing still. We have to fix these seams."

"I'll try. I'm happy you and Lottie are helping me with the dress. It makes my wedding day that much more special." She bent her neck and watched her sister adjust the hem.

"Josieee, keep your head up. You want a crooked hem?" Lottie glared at her sister.

"Fine. What should I do?" Precise dress fitting was a pain in the behind, Josie thought. Everyone shouted orders at her.

"Stand still. With your arms at your sides, your legs straight and your head up. That way we'll be able to finish the dress sometime today.'' Grace ran her hand down the side seam, checking for gaps.

Josie let out a long sigh. "I can't be that different from ~~my mother in body shape. I don't see why we can't just~~ hem the gown." So the sides were a tad loose on her and the gown was too long, but other than that Josie did not see any problem.

Lottie and Grace exchanged frustrated glances.

"But this is your wedding. You want to look as pretty as possible, right?" Grace asked.

Vigorous head-nodding brought a poke in Josie's side.

"Stand still." Grace's exasperation was clearly getting the better of her as she spoke through gritted teeth.

"Sorry. I was only agreeing with you." *Pretty* was not how Josie wanted to look for her wedding. She wanted to look beautiful. She wanted to look so beautiful that Jack would be speechless when he laid eyes on her in the church. She didn't want him to regret his decision to wed her.

"All right, Jos, only a few more pins and then I think the hem'll be just right." Lottie scooted around on the floor, alternately pinning and eyeing her work, making sure she had the gown even.

"Thank God." This took much longer than Josie had anticipated. She wanted to get away on her mare and scout out some pretty flowers. She was going to pick her own bouquet. But at the rate this dress fitting was going, she didn't think she'd have much time for a ride.

"Josie, we really aren't taking that long. What do you think all those fashionable women we see in *Godey's Lady's Book* have to put up with? I tell you, sometimes you have to sacrifice for beauty." Grace secured her last pin and stepped back to scrutinize her work. "Slowly turn around, Josie."

Josie did as she was told. She completed one circle.

"What do you think, Lottie? Could the side seams come in a little more?"

Lottie crinkled her nose and pondered. "No, I think

they are tight enough. All we need to do now is press some of the wrinkles out.''

"You mean we're done?" Josie said.

"Until the alterations are completed. Then we're going to put it on you again for the finishing touches," Grace said.

"Let us help you out of it." Lottie stepped up and began undoing the tiny seed pearl buttons that ran the length of the gown's bodice.

"You can leave your dress here. Lottie and I will work on it in the afternoons. That way Jack won't have any chance of seeing the gown before your wedding."

Josie held her arms up while they gently pulled the dress over her head. "Thanks, Grace. That's a good idea." She watched as they laid the gown on Grace's guest bed. Goose bumps rose along her skin when she thought of her mother in the gown. She wished her mother were there to see the wedding, but then, Josie did believe her mother would be watching from heaven.

In the distance the school bell pealed, signaling the end of lunch break.

"Oh, oh. I have to go now. I can't be late or Mistress Meyer will lock the door and I'll be embarrassed." Lottie hugged her sister and flew down the steps of Grace's house.

Grace looked at Josie. "Can you stay for a little longer? Robert's not expecting me at the mercantile for another hour. I have something I want to give you."

"Yes, I can. I want to be able to see as much of you as possible. It's going to be strange to be a married woman and have a husband around the house." Josie thought of the breathtaking land Jack had found for their ranch and felt a tiny regret that they wouldn't be living there.

"I still can't believe Jack agreed to live in your house. Doesn't he want his own home?"

Josie pulled her skirt up and tucked her shirtwaist in. She was once more the regular Josie and not the ivory-clad princess. "It's just silly to spend good money on a ranch when we already have a perfectly good one.''

Guilt gnawed at her. She didn't normally lie to her friend. But she was too scared to admit she and Jack had not actually settled the matter of their living arrangements. Trouble was, she had an idea they each thought it was settled. Avoiding the issue, however, would not solve it. They must discuss it soon.

''If you say so; it sounds kind of odd to me, but I'm glad you'll still be near me.'' Grace clapped her hands. ''We'll have lots of time to spend together.''

''Wonderful. Let's go to the parlor. I'll have Mellie bring tea and we can chat.''

As Josie leaned back into the peach-colored cushions of Grace's divan, she wondered what it would be like to have a maid bring her tea. The days when her mother was still alive and the money from the gold strike flowed had long since faded into a distant memory. In a way, she felt guilty sitting while Mellie brought out the drinks.

''Josie, I have to tell you, I'm so glad all this worked out and you and Jack are going to be married.'' Grace positively beamed.

''What do you mean?''

''Well, you know. You and Jack didn't exactly have the best start, what with you announcing your engagement without the man's consent.''

''Oh, that.'' Josie reddened. She still couldn't believe she'd done that.

''But obviously you two were meant to be together. I can't imagine a better man for you, even if you didn't always keep to my advice and be ladylike.''

The two laughed.

No, Josie definitely could not see herself married to anyone other than Jack. She wondered if all prospective brides were this elated. ''You know, I think meeting Jack makes up for all those hard years I endured.''

''I know it does.'' Grace's eyes sparkled and she grinned. ''I want to give you something. I'll be right back.'' She rose and left the room.

Josie heard the floorboards squeak as Grace moved

from room to room. When Grace returned, she held a large gift-wrapped package. It was festooned with a giant bright yellow bow.

Josie stared. "What is that?"

"It's my wedding present to you." Grace held out the package.

"It's big but not heavy." Josie set it down beside her and ran her fingers along the bow. "You didn't have to get me anything."

"I wanted to. Go ahead, open it. I want to see your reaction."

First Josie untied the ribbon. She laid it aside and then tore open the package. Her breath caught. "Grace, you didn't need to do this."

Grace looked like a little child, so full of joy. "I hope you like it."

The brand-new green wool blanket was more than Josie expected. "It's so pretty." She held up a corner of the thick material to her cheek and rubbed it. "And so soft. Grace, this is too much."

"No, no. You'll need a heavy blanket to keep you warm at night while you sleep beside Jack."

The mention of them in bed together sent heat up Josie's neck. "Thank you so much. I'll cherish this forever."

With a wicked grin on her face Grace said, "Now, there'll be times when you won't need the blanket, if you know what I mean."

Josie almost dropped the gift on the floor. Grace's words stunned her. Had her friend read her thoughts? "I think I know what you mean." She looked forward to when she and Jack would unite in bed.

"Good. In case no one ever told you, the marriage act is something to revere. It is not something to endure. Think of the beautiful child you will bring into this world. Just like we're expecting in six months." Grace looked down and patted her softly rounded belly.

"I know, I can't wait to start our own family." She set her gift aside and went over to her friend. "Thanks so much, it means a lot to me." She hugged Grace and told herself she would not cry. Just because she was getting married did not mean her friendship with Grace would change.

"You mean a lot to me. You've been my best friend for a long time now. I only want your happiness." Grace wiped away a tear.

"I am happy. You wait and see. Our wedding will be the best one this town has ever seen."

Lottie ran toward the school, skidding to a stop only when she saw her aunt standing outside, hands on hips and her lips in a severe frown. Lottie'd forgotten that the Ladies Auxiliary was to read to the pupils that afternoon.

Walking sedately, Lottie approached her aunt. She hadn't been alone with her since that time at the mock race. Her aunt had scared her and Lottie'd done her best to avoid her aunt.

"Charlotte dear, young ladies do not run. They walk." Portia Potter signaled for the other Ladies Auxiliary members to go on inside the school while she remained outside with her niece.

More than anything, Lottie wanted to run back to Grace's house, but she didn't want Portia to know how much she frightened her. "Aunt Portia, I—I didn't know you were to be here."

Portia looked at Lottie's red-stained cheeks and her rapidly rising and falling chest. "I can see that. It's a good thing I was here to witness your behavior. It just goes to prove my point that if you want any chance of growing up decently, you need to come under my roof."

Lottie pressed her fingernails to her palms, trying to stay calm. "Aunt Portia, I didn't want to be late for school. So I had to hurry."

"And just where were you? All the other young ladies ate their lunches under the tree." Portia leaned down, bringing her face within inches of Lottie's.

Pulling away, Lottie said, "I—I was at Mrs. Moreland's, h-helping Josie with her wedding dress."

"Her wedding dress. Well, I guess that is an acceptable activity for you to do." Portia shook her head, letting her eyes close. "I'm afraid you don't realize how lucky your sister is. I mean, it's not every day an aged spinster finds a man willing to marry her." Her eyes snapped open. "You realize that if anything happens and the wedding does not come to pass, then I shall be forced to bring you under my roof?"

Lottie felt frozen. Her limbs could not move. It was as if she had lost all power to control her legs. "Whwhat do you mean? My sister will marry Jack, they—they love each other. Why are you saying such things?"

"Tsk, tsk, my dear girl." Portia enveloped Lottie in her ample arms, holding her niece tightly. "It is my duty, as your aunt, to see that my dear, departed sister's daughter is raised properly. Now, how can I do that if you insist on living with that father of yours and with Josephine, who does not know how to be a lady."

Lottie squirmed, finally freeing herself from her aunt's arms. Her eyes glistened with tears. "My sister does too know how to be a lady. She—she loves me, and my father loves me."

"Dear, dear." Portia withdrew a hanky and dabbed Lottie's tears. "You shouldn't worry so. I have only your best interest at heart. Surely you can see how you could become the young woman you are meant to be if you lived with me."

Lottie shook her head, denying her aunt's words.

Portia drew her lips back in what was supposed to resemble a smile. "Dear Charlotte, I will keep you safe from the evils of the world. I'll see to it that you never have to soil your upbringing by witnessing women in trousers, like your sister had on this morning."

Lottie stared across the school yard, down the street toward Grace Moreland's house. She wanted desperately to go there, to be with her sister. Lottie didn't know how she could go inside the school and sit there with her aunt staring at her, watching her every move.

"Charlotte, did you hear me?" Portia put her hand on Lottie's chin and forced her head up.

"Uh-huh. I—I have to get back inside now." She twisted her body and fled from her aunt, glad to be closing the door.

Portia remained outside and stared at the whitewashed door before her. She nodded her head in satisfaction. Yes, she was on the right track. Charlotte seemed to be realizing where she belonged.

Gravel crunched as a carriage pulled to a stop. Mrs. Garvey stepped out and walked toward Portia. Her thin body seemed in danger of being blown over by the wind. She smiled at her friend and ascended the school steps.

"I see I am not too late for the Bible reading that we're to do," Mrs. Garvey said.

"No, we are to begin shortly. I just had a nice little talk with my niece. You know how worried I am for her, what with her growing up in that household."

Mrs. Garvey nodded, waiting for Portia to continue.

"I hate to admit this, but I am afraid that her sister's engagement will give Charlotte a false idea of how courtships and betrothals work."

"Is it the suddenness of the betrothal or the claim that it was love at first sight?" Mrs. Garvey knit her pencil-thin brows.

Portia shook her head. "Both, I am afraid. It is just not natural for a young woman of quality, such as my dear, departed sister's daughter, to grow up in such an outlandish household."

Mrs. Garvey laid her hand on Portia's arm. "I know how you want to have Charlotte with you, but I honestly think that her sister has changed since the betrothal."

"Hmmm, Josephine change? I suppose it is possible. But I can only thank God that their father is home. Even though he isn't what I would call an appropriate father."

"Since Charlotte seems to be in no immediate danger of having her character sullied, why don't we wait before bringing her to live with you?" Of all the members of the Ladies Auxiliary, only Margaret Garvey had the courage to speak her mind freely to Portia.

Portia listened to the children inside the schoolhouse while her mind reviewed what Margaret had said. Slowly, she nodded. "I do believe I am making headway with Charlotte. I believe she is starting to realize she can become a young woman of quality only if she lives with me. However, I do not want to rush things and make a false move."

"I'm glad I spoke my mind."

Portia raised her lorgnette to her nose, peered at her friend, and spoke. "Yes, I do believe we should wait just a little while longer."

⬥ *23* ⬥

THE NEXT MORNING Josie stretched and jumped out of bed. She was too nervous to lie still any longer. She was getting married in one week! Yesterday's dress fitting brought home the reality of what was about to happen.

She had no trouble picturing herself being carried over the threshold as a married woman, and blushed as she pictured the wedding act.

For once Josie felt secure in her future and in her sister's future. She no longer had anything to worry about.

She selected a bright green dress, a happy color to reflect her good spirits. She secured her hair back with a matching ribbon and went to find her father.

For the late hour, the house seemed very quiet. Her sister, she knew, would still be abed. Lottie liked her sleep. But her father, he should be enjoying his cups of coffee by now.

She tiptoed to the kitchen. The pot sat on the table,

cold and empty. Josie paused. Was he still asleep? Sick in bed?

She crossed to his door and pressed her ear against the wood. No sound reached her, neither of snoring nor movement. She grasped the knob and opened it. The room was empty. Too empty.

Sucking in a breath of air, Josie entered. With her heart pounding harder in her chest, she searched the room.

Her father's heavy boots were gone. Several of his shirts were missing from their pegs. His saddlebags and canteens were gone.

She slapped her hand to her heart and sank down onto his bed, a sick feeling in the pit of her stomach. Her father had left. She knew the signs so well by now that she didn't need a letter explaining where he'd gone. Her eyes moved to the corner of his room where he always keep his gem-scouting supplies.

Gone. Like him.

Rage boiled over in her. How dare he up and leave her only days before her wedding? Things had been going so well.

"Dammit, Father! How could you?" She hit the pillows on the bed, watching in satisfaction as her fist dented the feathers, and then repeated her action.

Josie was so mad that she didn't hear her sister slip into the room.

"What's the matter, Jos?"

Josie's head snapped up. She quickly smoothed the pillow. "Father decided to leave and go search for sapphires again."

Lottie's mouth fell open. "He—he c-can't leave me. You—you're gonna get married and then I'll be all alone. Then Aunt Portia'll come and take me away!"

The truth in those words hit Josie like a fist to the gut. Lottie was now alone. She had Jack, but Lottie had no one to look out for her. Her sister stood quivering in the middle of the room.

"C'mere, Lottie. I'm here and I won't leave you." She held out her arms and tightened them around her sister.

"B-but you're gonna get married and Jack will wanna take you away from me." Lottie shook and clutched the sleeves of Josie's dress. "I—I just know it, that's what happens in a marriage."

Her sister spoke the truth. Josie felt her heart tearing in two. She couldn't leave her sister who needed her so badly. For if Josie left, Mrs. Potter would surely swoop down like a vulture and snatch Lottie away. And just as important, without her father to give her away, how was she to marry?

She was torn, torn between the man she loved and the sister she had sworn to protect. Josie wanted more than anything to be with Jack, but as she looked at her sister's tear-streaked face, she wondered if perhaps she was being selfish. Perhaps Lottie needed her more than Jack did, and that caused Josie's heart to feel like it was being shredded.

"Y-you haven't answered me," Lottie said between sobs.

No, she hadn't. For once in her life Josie felt hopeless. The reality of her world had crashed down upon her that morning. Her father's empty room had said more than words could. This was his way of telling her that he didn't want her to marry. That he didn't want his orderly world changed. And Josie resented it. She resented his treatment of her, resented his treatment of Lottie.

"W-well?"

Josie smoothed Lottie's hair. It was hard to speak when her throat was choked closed with emotion. "You won't be left alone, I promise."

"You won't abandon me also, will you?"

As much as she hated saying it, Josie did. "No, Lottie, I won't abandon you." All her hopes for a bright future vanished as if they never existed. She pictured Jack's handsome face, the man she loved but could no longer marry, and her own tears fell.

Perhaps she didn't need her father to give her away at the ceremony after all. No, she knew Reverend Potter would not marry them otherwise. His wife would see to that.

Lottie relaxed and pulled out of Josie's arms. "Good. I'm scared of being left all alone."

Josie shut her eyes as a vision of a triumphant Mrs. Potter appeared. No! She wouldn't let that happen. Aunt or not, Lottie would never go live in that depressing home. Lottie belonged here.

Their father's silent room seemed deafening. Josie wanted to be alone. She needed time to think. There had to be a way for her happiness to be included along with Lottie's security.

"When do you think Father will come home?"

"I don't know, Lottie. Soon, I hope." Within the next few days, she prayed.

"I guess we can use this time to make your wedding veil. I guess you and Jack will have to live here with me."

Josie nodded. "Yes, we can work on the veil." She decided not to tell Lottie that without their father, there would be no wedding. But working on the veil would keep her sister occupied.

Pushing herself up, Lottie stood and brushed away her tears. "I'll go put on my clothes. Then I want to go see Mary Jane and show her my necklace." Lottie pulled out the small sapphire suspended from a gold chain around her neck.

Josie smiled, marveling at her sister's amazing ability to swiftly switch her attention. The little stone matched Lottie's eyes, both sparkling bright blue. "I'll be in the barn. I need to check on Lady. Since I can't ride her in the fair, I can at least make her as comfortable as possible."

"Oh, the fair. I think my dress will win this year. I made sure I made the smallest, evenest stitches possible." With that, Lottie spun and ran out the door.

With a heavy heart, Josie stood and cast her glance once more at the deserted room. Shutting her eyes, she said a small prayer that her father would be home soon.

*   *   *

The sun had only just risen when Jack stepped into the Douglasses' barn and noticed Hunter's horse was missing. He thought it rather early for him to be gone. Perhaps he was working in one of the pastures. But Jack hadn't seen anyone. He shrugged and turned to his stallion.

The chestnut placed his head out his stall door and nickered in recognition.

"I'm glad to see you too, boy." Jack stroked the soft nose. It was almost as soft as Josie's hair. Josie. The woman to be his wife. He still had a hard time adjusting to that.

As he groomed his horse, Josie entered the barn.

"Oh. I didn't know you were here." She walked past him as if he weren't there, not even looking at him.

Jack stared after her. Something didn't seem right. When he last saw her yesterday, she had looked like the blushing bride she was going to be. Now she looked miserable, barely giving him a passing glance. "Jos?" He put down his brush and went to her.

He took her hands. "Is something wrong?"

"No." She gazed down at the dirt floor of the barn.

"Are you sure? Look at me." He released one of her hands and tilted her chin up toward him.

She squeezed her eyes shut and then slowly opened them. Her mouth opened and then closed. She struggled to form the words. "M-my father left this morning."

"Left? What do you mean, left?"

Josie took a deep breath. When she looked up at him, her eyes shone with unshed tears. "He left to go hunt sapphires. When I went to wake him, all his gear was gone. So was he."

Jack pulled her close and held her body against his. "I'm sorry. Did you know he was going to go?"

"No." She shook her head. "He just left. No note. No apology. Nothing."

"He'll be back before Saturday? For the wedding, won't he?"

She shrugged. "I don't know. I sure hope so."

Jack held her tightly. Although he was mad at Hunter for causing Josie grief, he didn't see why there should be a problem. "I'm sure everything will be fine."

"You don't understand. Everything won't be—"

Their conversation was interrupted by the horses, who began kicking at the stalls, demanding their grain.

"We'll get to you in a minute," Jack said.

He released her, stepped back, and smiled. "I hate to see you so upset. You're about to become a bride. You should be all smiles. I haven't even told you about our wedding trip."

The façade Josie had worked so hard to keep around her heart threatened to crumble. She could not think of becoming a bride with her father gone, no matter how badly she wanted it. She had responsibilities. She couldn't meet Jack's glance.

He squeezed her hands before letting them go. "Well? I thought you'd be excited to hear about our wedding trip. I planned for us to go to see the brand-new Yellowstone Park. It's filled with natural wonders. You'll love it."

Josie pressed her nails into her palms, trying to keep her heartache at bay. A honeymoon sounded wonderful. She'd never even considered they would take one. "I—I think we'd better wait a few days before we discuss honeymoons. At least until my father returns." But she was frightened that her father might not be back for a long time. He'd been against the wedding ever since he met Jack, and now his disappearance proved it.

"It can't hurt for me to make some preliminary plans."

"No. Wait!" Panic hit her. Suppose her father never returned, and if Jack planned a honeymoon, he would be doubly disappointed. "You should wait. I mean, why plan ahead?"

"Because I want it to be special." Leaning down, he planted a soft, sweet kiss on her lips.

His tenderness was almost her undoing. How could she deny her feelings for him when he was making it so hard?

How could she think of her desire when she needed to remember the needs of her sister? It just wasn't fair.

She wanted to know what it felt like to become one with him. Wanted to know how their bodies would fit together, wanted to know if she could please him. Now it looked like she would not have that chance. Unless . . .

She knew she should persuade him not to make honeymoon plans, but she couldn't voice the words. It sounded so magical, that word, honeymoon. All she could concentrate on was the feeling of his lips brushing against hers and the fire that his mere touch ignited in her belly.

"Don't you worry about a thing. I've got it all under control. I know how much work you have to do on the ranch, so I'll help out this morning." Releasing her, he stepped away.

He did not have it under control, she wanted to tell him but couldn't. "I can handle it, don't feel you need to help out." Besides, the work would do her good, get her mind off the horrible fate life had played on her.

"I insist. What can I do to help you?"

"Well, you can make sure all the horses have water and check the water barrels in the front pasture." That was her least favorite job. She hated toting the heavy bucket of water from the well to the pastures and stalls.

"I'll do it. And then if you don't mind, I'll take Zeus for a run around the racetrack. He needs a good workout."

Josie brightened. If he was taking Zeus for a run, then perhaps he'd forgotten about honeymoon plans. She could only hope so. "No, I understand. You'll have a good time riding him."

"I really had fun in Bozeman, and I'm glad you liked it. I know our home in the Gallatin valley will be everything I've dreamed about." Jack grinned at her.

"I had fun too." However, she was recalling the kiss they'd shared and the feelings he'd aroused in her. Her pain once more threatened to crack her carefully constructed façade. She did not want to cry in front of him.

Hearing him talk about their planned home in the valley only depressed her more.

All her life she'd dreamed of living in her own home, a home she shared with her husband. Now it had been given to her and cruelly taken away.

"Let's get to work. Where is the bucket you want me to use?"

"Over here." Josie opened a door and stepped into a darkened room. Bending over, she grabbed the cold handle and lifted the bucket. "Here it is."

"Great." He paused and cocked his head. "Are you sure you don't want to come with me and watch Zeus run?"

As much as she'd have loved to, she had to decline. "No, I need to stay around here. Lottie might need me."

With a heavy heart she watched Jack saddle up Zeus a while later. When he trotted away from the barn, she watched until they were out of sight. She turned, sat down on a stool, and placed her head in her hands.

If only she knew when her father would return. She deserved a husband and wanted to marry Jack with a fierceness that surprised her. She pulled out a clump of hay from a nearby bale, wadded it up, and then tossed it aside.

Fresh anger hit her. How could her father jeopardize both her and Lottie's future happiness? Was his life the only one that mattered? What about her?

A wicked thought entered her mind. If she could no longer marry Jack, wouldn't it only be right if she could at least have one time alone with him? Didn't she deserve one wonderful memory to last her a lifetime? And what better memory to have than that of them uniting together in love?

• 24 •

AN HOUR EARLIER Josie had heard Lottie leaving for her friend's house. That meant she and Jack would be alone for a while. Did she dare carry through her bold plan? Was it worth the risk just to know what it felt like to lie in his arms?

All morning Josie had mulled over her idea. She knew it was considered a sin to couple outside of marriage. However, she knew she loved Jack and did not want to miss out on what might be her only chance to become a woman.

Her palms felt sweaty as she watched Jack approach her. She loved this man with all her heart, and if life hadn't been so unfair to her, she would soon have been his wife. But without her father there could be no wedding.

She stood up. She was going to go through with it.

With her future uncertain, the only thing she wanted was him. She looked at Jack, at his face flushed from his ride, at the smile on his lush lips, and at the way he was looking at her, with affection in his eyes. And she knew what she was about to do was right. If her father never came back from sapphire hunting, she might not have this opportunity again.

Josie took a deep breath for courage before speaking. "Why don't we go inside. You'd be more comfortable in there, relaxing after your ride."

Jack cocked his head sideways, eyebrows rising. "What are you saying?"

"Nothing, it's sort of chilly and I don't want us to catch a cold. Will you please come inside? It would be pleasant." Pleasant! She could hardly call what she wanted to do pleasant—devious was more like it. But once in her life, before she withered away, she wanted to know what it felt like to be a real woman, a woman who has been thoroughly loved by a man.

"I guess so. You go on in, I'm going to scrape the mud off the bottom of my boots first."

Ten minutes later Josie sat on the edge of her bed, debating with herself. She'd made her decision, but was scared. Would Jack refuse to make love to her? Suppose she couldn't go through with it?

Nervous sweat broke out on her body when she heard the front door close. There was still time to back out if she wanted to. No. She wanted to become a woman with Jack.

"Josie? Where are you?" Jack called.

"In here." Her voice sounded distinctly uncertain. Josie cleared her throat, hoping to sound more normal. She heard his steps growing louder the closer he came. Just outside her door they stopped.

"Are you in there?" The hesitation in his voice was clear.

"Yes." Come in, she silently pleaded to him.

"Well, how long will you be?"

"Could you please come in here?"

"Now? In there? What about your sister?" He inched forward a little bit.

"She won't be back for hours." Josie put a hand to her chest and felt her heart thumping beneath her shirt-waist. She couldn't decide which emotion had the stronger grip on her, nervousness or excitement. Her hands stayed in constant motion, straightening and res-traightening her bedclothes.

After a moment of silence Jack finally stuck his head around the door frame. "You sure you want me in there?"

Nodding, she patted the bed next to her.

"Josie, I don't think you know what you're doing. If I come in there, I can't guarantee I'll be able to leave so easily." He swallowed and ran a hand through his hair.

"That's all right." God, was she nervous. Her breath came in short spurts. And frightened. Frightened that he would be turned off by her behavior and leave.

Jack entered and crossed to the bed. He knelt down in front of her, placed his hands on her knees, and looked deep into her eyes. "Jos, you're in a vulnerable state right now. You're still upset over your father's disap-pearance. Why don't you get some rest and then you'll feel better."

He was so tender with her, her heart wanted to burst. He would be gentle with her. She trusted him. Taking a deep breath, she leaned forward and ran her fingers through his tousled hair. The strands felt silky between her fingers. "I know what I'm doing."

He sighed as she caressed his head. "Jos, you don't know how hard this is on me. I desire you so badly, but I don't want to take you before our wedding."

She didn't have the heart to tell him there might not be a wedding. It might just be her, growing old all alone, watching her sister have a good time. She leaned closer and brought his head to rest on her bosom.

When Jack glanced up and realized what soft part of her he was leaning on, all his good intentions evaporated. His face was practically buried in her breasts. His blood surged. Scrambling to his feet, he sat next to her. "Jos, I—I want only what's best for you."

"This is what's best for me. For us."

His will snapped. In his mind he knew they should wait until they were man and wife, but his heart didn't want to wait until the reverend declared them married. What they were about to do was right and good.

"Oh, God, Josie, I don't know how it happened, but somehow I can't think of any other woman but you." Embracing her, he pulled her snug against him and kissed her thoroughly.

Josie returned his kiss with a fervor of her own. Never before had she felt so alive. Her pulse raced. Her whole body tingled. She knew she'd never be the same after coupling with Jack. How she wished it would be the first of many times and not the only one she might ever have.

Jack pulled away from her lips and traced kisses along her jawline to her ears. He took her sensitive lobe and sucked, blowing hot air. "Did I ever tell you how distracted I am when I'm close to you?"

"No." She wanted to hear more, needed to hear more so it could last her her entire lifetime. She plunged her fingers into his hair and held his head close to her, never wanting him to leave.

Once more he claimed her lips. His tongue danced around her mouth, flicking against her teeth, teasing her lips and tasting her sweet essence. There was no going back for him. Blood poured, engorging him, driving his desire forward.

Gently, he laid her back on the mattress. He stared down at her emerald-green eyes, at her moist, love-swollen lips. "You're beautiful," he whispered.

Panting, Josie stared up at him. She didn't understand these delicious feelings assaulting her body, but knew they would soon find release. She watched the pulse in the side of his neck beat. She reached up and lightly touched it. She smiled when he sucked in his breath.

"You're a miracle." Jack extended his hand and ran his fingertips up and down her arm, enlarging his strokes to include her side. When he slid his fingers over her breast, his expression softened as she gasped.

"Jack," she murmured, holding her arms up, beckoning him.

He laid a finger to her lips. "Shh, I'm going to unbutton your shirtwaist now and then take off my shirt." Trying not to touch her soft curves lest he be distracted, Jack slipped each button through the hole. When he finished, he opened her shirt and eased her out of it. The thin camisole she wore underneath did not hide her aroused nipples from his eyes.

Two stiff peaks thrust forward. Toward him. He kissed her and moved one hand to her breast, molding the soft mound to his hand.

Josie thought a fire had been lit underneath her, so hot did she feel when Jack touched her bosom. Her eyes flew open and she saw only Jack's eyes, darkened with desire. She wanted to make him feel as good as she did but didn't quite know how to go about doing it. So she contented herself with caressing his neck.

Quickly, he shrugged out of his shirt. Her breath caught in her throat. She'd seen him without a shirt before, but this time she was close enough to feel his chest. Laying a hand on his dark hair, she explored, reveling in the difference between the smooth skin and the rough hair. When he groaned, a feeling of power shot through her. *She* had caused him to feel that way.

"Oh, Jos, let's get out of these clothes." Before she knew what was happening, Jack had divested her of her camisole and skirt.

She had no time to feel shame being unclothed in daylight. She was too interested in looking at him. Fascinated, she watched his muscles ripple as he undressed. He was so much bigger than her in every way.

Once finished, he turned to her and she couldn't help but stare at the area she knew would soon become one with her body. Stiff and erect, he throbbed, ready to claim her. Suddenly she didn't think she could get enough air; she gasped and tried to fill her lungs.

When he caught her staring, she flushed and averted her eyes.

"Don't be embarrassed. There's nothing to be ashamed of. If it'll make you feel better, we can crawl underneath the covers." Jack stepped to the head of the bed and pulled the covers back, patting the mattress. "Come here."

Josie didn't need a second invitation. She scooted and dove underneath the covers. The bed felt cold, but soon Jack nestled against her, heating her up.

"Mmmm," Jack said, taking her lips in a deep, loving kiss.

His hands continued their exploration of her body. Free from clothes, he could stroke her satin-soft skin, feel the goose bumps that rose at his touch.

Josie arched her back, bringing herself nearer to him. "You are everything I've dreamed of."

He only smiled and looked up from where he sucked lustily on her nipple. He let go, much to her disappointment. "I want you to know there'll be some pain, but it'll pass soon."

Josie knew that. But she also knew Jack would help her overcome any fear. "I know. I'll be brave."

Pushing himself up on his elbows, Jack positioned his body over top of hers. "I'm going to enter you now. Remember, I'll stop whenever you want me to."

"I want you." Josie's body was taking over. The natural human instincts had kicked in. She would no longer fight her body's wishes.

"Josie." Her name came out a ragged whisper as Jack slowly eased himself inside her wet channel. When he reached her barrier, he stopped.

"What's wrong? Why'd you stop?" Josie broke the kiss.

"I just don't want you to regret this. It's not too late to say no." Droplets of sweat clung to his forehead.

"I'll never regret it." Summoning her courage, she met his lips in a deep kiss and thrust her pelvis upward, bringing him firmly into her body.

A flash of pain made her pause, but she soon forgot it

as she gave in to her body's needs, meeting Jack's thrusts with her own.

Soon a sharp tingly warmth came upon her like a giant wave. She could feel herself falling deeper and deeper into swells of pleasure so intense, her body shook. This was unlike anything she'd ever experienced before. No one had told her how beautiful the coupling could be.

"Josie," Jack cried as he made one final thrust, shooting his essence into her. Exhausted, he lay on top of her, body pressed intimately to body.

Josie still spun from the new heights she'd just experienced. Having Jack on top of her didn't matter. She was so happy she thought she could cry. An earthy, musky scent punctuated the air. The smell of their lovemaking. She inhaled deeply, committing it to memory.

"I didn't hurt you?" Jack asked as he brushed the tousled hair from her temples.

"Oh, no. You showed me something beautiful." Josie looked at him, at this man who was supposed to be her husband, and she felt her heart might burst from knowing things could not be that way.

"You deserve beautiful experiences. The next time, I'll take my time and show you just how beautiful lovemaking can be between a man and wife." He moved off her and lay on his side, spooning her body next to his.

The chill breeze that flitted over her skin reminded Josie that they'd thrown the covers off in the heat of passion. She was glad for the warmth from Jack's solid body. "Let's just enjoy today."

"I know I did." He nuzzled behind her ear, sending hot, breathy fans of heat.

"Me too." She needed to remember every exquisite detail about this afternoon, so she could call it up to memory whenever she wanted to.

Her intentions were almost shattered by Jack's next words.

"I'm glad the wedding is only days away. That way I won't feel so bad about making love before we said our vows."

Her body stiffened. Trying to relax, she took deep breaths, hoping not to alert Jack to anything amiss. Fat tears inched down her cheeks. "I don't want to talk right now. Can't we just lay here and enjoy the silence?"

Jack's hand paused in his stroking. "I guess so, but we can't lay here all day. Your sister could come home, or suppose your father returned?"

She hadn't thought of that. If her father did come home and found them in this position, he'd hit the roof. Or worse, grab his shotgun and chase Jack out of town, clothes or no clothes.

"I never thought of that. Well, then I guess we should dress and I'll go about my chores."

"Go about your chores?" Jack reached out and held her still. "Oh, no. That's not how this works. See, once we make love, then it changes everything. We just took our relationship to a new level. We're now committed to each other."

"We—we did? We are?"

"Of course. Now it's more important than ever that you become Mrs. Jack St. Augustine." He held her at arm's length and stared deep into her eyes. "Suppose you carry my child?"

She tried her best not to squirm or to look away. For the first time since she'd decided to lay with him, she had her regrets. What had been a selfish act for her now threatened to have the potential to be so much more. Since he'd become an intimate part of her, she longed to hold on to him even more fiercely.

She wanted him more than ever. Loved him more than ever. It wasn't supposed to be that way, and it frightened her.

"I see I've got you speechless." He pulled her closer and planted a soft kiss on her brow. "Let's get dressed."

What was she going to do? How could she continue to lead him on? She couldn't. Unable to decide, she turned around and started putting her clothes back on. She winced as she felt a slight tenderness between her legs.

"Are you sure you want to put those clothes back on?" Jack asked. "I thought a pretty dress would be befitting of a newly loved woman."

"It's what I had on before. You wouldn't want Lottie wondering why I changed, do you? My work clothes will be just fine."

He moved over to her dresses hanging from their pegs. Reaching out, he fingered the material. "I don't think she'd mind at all."

Watching him rifle through her clothes made her feel oddly happy. She'd be more than pleased to discard her work clothes in favor of a pretty dress. As a matter of fact, she could get used to him selecting her clothes. There was something intimate about him touching her clothing. Why not enjoy it this once? "You're right. Pick out a nice dress for me to wear."

"Hmmm, let's see. How about this dark green one? It makes your eyes very pretty." He pointed to a long-sleeved day dress.

Against her better judgment, her heart did a flipflop at his compliment. She felt very lucky to have Jack. "Okay. But you'll have to help me into it. I can't do all the buttons in the back myself."

His eyes twinkled mischievously. "I'd rather help you out of your clothes, but I guess it would be fun to put them on you for a change." He removed the dress and held it out. "Come over here."

In just her camisole and one petticoat, Josie stepped over to him. If only he had said he loved her as they coupled, then maybe she would try harder to find a way out of her dilemma. But he hadn't. Instead, she forced her eyes to his and almost stopped. The emotion radiating there had to be love. No other feeling could shine so from one's eyes. "Here I am."

"All right, now turn around and hold up your arms."

Josie did as he said. She gasped when he ran his hands down her sides before lowering the dress. His touch made her shiver. Before he could do any more disturbing things to her, she arranged the dress and began buttoning it.

"Hey, I thought you wanted my help." Jack stepped behind her and started slipping the buttons one by one into their holes.

Josie's eyelids slid shut. His hands on her were quite distracting. It was hard for her to formulate her words when he was practically breathing down her neck. Her pulse fluttered in anticipation of where his hands might go next. "I think I'm ready now. Thank you." She stepped out of his arm's reach.

"That was fun. I'll have to be sure and do it again. I'll let you fix your own hair. I'll go to the barn to change Lady's poultice. Come on down when you're ready." He kissed her before leaving the room.

Once Jack had left, she sat on her bed and glanced at the tiny red stain on her sheets. She reached out her hand and traced the outline. *I'm a woman now,* she thought. But did she feel any different?

Yes, absolutely. She knew the heights of pleasure a man and woman could share, knew what it felt like to be loved by one man, and now she would know the pain of losing the man she loved. A great sense of loss filled her. Not for her virginity, but for the future.

Drawing her knees up, she hugged them to her chest. Now that she had tasted the pleasures to be found between a man and woman, how could this one time be enough to last her her whole lifetime?

She ran her fingers through her hair, hoping the repetitive motion would help her think. Finally, after fixing her braid, she rose to her feet.

This one time had to be enough. How could she abandon her sister? Lottie was just a girl; she needed her older sister.

She had to tell Jack about canceling the wedding before he did something rash, like arrange the honeymoon trip to Yellowstone Park. She would think of some way to keep Mrs. Potter away from Lottie. Tugging on her boots, she rose and began what would probably be the longest walk of her life.

"Josie?" Jack said, his voice drifting out from Lady's stall.

"It's me." Josie stepped inside the stall and stood looking at Jack. Her lips pulled into a smile as she watched his gentle hands change the poultice on her mare's hoof. She really did love him. "How's her hoof doing?"

"She'll be fine. But you know you won't be able to ride her for a while." He wiped the sticky poultice off his hands with a towel and draped it over his shoulder.

"I figured as much." Had she been hasty when she'd decided they could no longer marry? After all, the ranch house near Bozeman was not even built. They couldn't live there yet. If she really loved him, which she did, couldn't they live here for the time being? That is, if her father returned home before the end of the week.

She locked her fingers together and tried to think of the best way to approach her subject. Failing to think of anything clever, she just began. "Jack, what would you think if we lived here? At my house?"

His face darkened. "Live here? I thought we already discussed that."

"I know, but what I meant was, we need to live somewhere while our house is being built. Why not here?" She smiled, releasing her tightly clasped fingers when Jack returned her smile.

"You've got a point. But we can't live here and build a house. How do you think the ranch will get built?"

"Well, we'd still need someplace to live." Suddenly she didn't seem too sure of her argument. She'd thought it a wonderful idea. She'd be able to keep an eye on Lottie, stay in her home, and be with Jack.

He moved toward her and reached for her hands. "I've already thought of that. I thought we'd live in a tent or makeshift cabin while I worked on the ranch house. That way we'd be on our land and able to complete the house that much faster."

Josie's smile faltered and finally disappeared. A fat lump seemed to grow in her throat, making breathing difficult. "I think it would be much better to live here for the time being."

He shook his head. "Nope, I've decided we'll live on our land. It will be our home."

She swallowed, forcing the lump away. "But I need to be here for Lottie and for my father."

Jack's grip tightened. "When we marry, you'll be my wife and I intend for us to live our own life. And that includes living on our land. Your father can take care of your sister."

"I still think it'd be best if we lived here for a while." She pulled her hands out of his.

"Josie, I'm sorry, but I won't live in this house and neither will you after we marry. That's final." His blue eyes challenged her.

She was on the verge of despair. He had to agree to live in her house—too much depended upon it. "No! We have to live here, at least for a while. My family needs me." Her heart thumped in her agitation.

Jack crossed his arms. "Josie, we have a hundred acres waiting for us. Anyone would want to live on their own land, and we'll be doing just that."

She knew she should remain calm, but she couldn't. With one resounding word Jack had sent all her hopes crashing down. Acting on impulse once again, she said the next words that came to her. "Then I'm sorry, I can't marry you."

❖ *25* ❖

JACK STOOD DEATHLY still. *"What?"* he bellowed so loudly that Lady squealed and jumped backward.

"You don't have to shout." Josie went over and laid shaking hands on her horse. She kept her face averted.

"Did I hear you correctly?" Jack was certain he'd heard wrong. The woman he'd just made love to and whose virginity he'd taken could not be standing there telling him that she could no longer marry him all because he wanted to live on his own land.

"Yes, yes, you did." She disappeared to the other side of her mare, hiding from his eyes. "You—you see, I'm needed here."

"Here? You're needed where your husband is, and that's not going to be here. How could you say such a thing after what we shared?"

"I told you, I'm needed here." She attempted to switch subjects, hoping to avert his attention. "Lady looks much better. I should brush her.'' She moved to leave the stall.

Jack reached out and locked his hand around her arm before she reached the door. ''Where do you think you're going?''

''To get my brushes.''

''Oh, no. Now is hardly the time to be brushing horses.'' Anger rioted inside him. All his previous fears were coming to a head. His mind lashed out at him, saying, *Fool, you shouldn't have followed your heart.*

Josie stared down at the hand clutching her. Her gaze flew up to his. ''Don't hold me so tight, it hurts.''

Immediately he loosened his hold. ''Sorry. You've given me quite an unpleasant jolt.''

''What's that supposed to mean?'' Lightning flashed from her eyes.

''You tricked me and I don't like that feeling one bit.'' Dammit, he wanted to kick himself. Turning, he slammed his fist into the wooden wall, ignoring the splinters digging into his skin.

Drawing herself up to her full height, Josie planted her hands on her hips and met his gaze. ''I did no such thing,'' she bit out. ''It's *you* who are jumping to conclusions.''

''What am I supposed to think? The only reason I agreed to make love to you was because I knew, or I should say, I thought we were going to be married. Had I known what you were planning on announcing, I would have refused your blatant offer.''

Crimson stained her cheeks and neck, contrasting with the deep green of her dress. She stepped closer, putting herself within inches of him. Her hands were balled into fists. ''I didn't see you trying to object very hard.''

He was so mad, he didn't trust himself to remain alone with her for much longer. He shoved his hands into his pockets. Just seeing her in the dress he'd picked out hurt him to the quick. He'd actually enjoyed selecting the garment for her, and he'd been looking forward to doing so for many years to come. Damn her! Why did she have to put the needs of her family before his own?

"It's hard to object when you're invited into a lady's bedroom, but then, I guess you're not much of a lady."

Her mouth opened and the blood drained from her face, leaving it chalky white. Her lips moved but no words came out for several seconds. When she finally spoke, her voice cracked. "That's not fair and you know it."

He shouldn't have said those last words, but they were already out. "I do know I wouldn't have taken your virginity if you weren't going to marry me. Tell me, when did you first decide you no longer wanted me? Before or after we made love?"

Josie's hands shook and her bottom lip trembled. "It's not that way at all. You're deliberately twisting my words. It's not that I no longer want you, it's that I can't marry you."

"Can't? And why not?"

"Because of my father, that's why."

He hated to see her looking so distraught, but he couldn't help himself. He could not shake the feeling of being used and betrayed.

"What does your father have to do with us?"

She threw up her arms. "Everything."

"No, you're wrong there. You are a grown woman, capable of making your own decisions. If you really wanted to marry me, you would." He hated himself, but he was desperate. The thought of not becoming her husband was pure misery to him. Dammit, he loved her! He even loved the way she looked after he had loved her, all rosy-cheeked and glowing.

She pointed her index finger at him. "No, you're wrong. Because of my father I can't marry. How could I leave Lottie alone? You've seen how my father likes to take off and hunt for sapphires whenever the mood strikes him. Who would take care of Lottie? Mrs. Potter would take her away in the blink of an eye."

That made a little bit more sense to him. But, still . . . "So this isn't about your father but your sister?"

She sighed and turned toward her mare, her shoulders slumped, giving her the appearance of someone who was resigned to her fate. ''Yes. I have to think of her. She needs me.''

Think of her? What about him? Who would think of him? he wanted to know. ''What about yourself? When is it time to think of Josie's needs?''

Her voice trembled and she refused to meet his gaze. ''I don't know. I don't know.''

He had to get out of there before he said any more words he would regret. He might as well leave Gallatin City. If she no longer wanted him, then what was the use of him staying? He had a breeding ranch to start, with or without her. ''When and if you ever decide to consider your needs, and mine, let me know. Until then, I'll be gone.''

Misty eyes regarded him, but she said nothing.

Jack exited the stall. As he shut the door, he paused. ''By the way, you might want to wipe that look off your face. You look like a woman who's been made love to and enjoyed it.''

Forcing his legs to carry him out of the barn and away from Josie, Jack stared at his gelding. His ticket away from her. He couldn't stand in that stall and look at her one minute longer. His pain was too fresh.

His heart cried out for him to stay, to comfort her, to listen to her and understand. His mind, his rational mind, however, refused to allow him to linger. She'd used him. She had used his body and crushed his heart. And it hurt him, it cut him to the core knowing she no longer desired him.

Grabbing the reins, he swung onto the gelding and kicked him into a gallop. He'd pictured them working together, side by side, with children playing nearby, but now he knew that was just a dream. A shattered dream.

His heart felt as if it were being ripped in two. Half of it was left with Josie and the other half, the empty half, was with him.

Cursing, he swiped at the moisture in the corner of his eyes, refusing to admit what it really was.

For a long time Josie stood still, listening to the sound of Jack riding farther and farther away. When she was certain he was gone, she gave in to her grief. Silent sobs racked her whole body. She wrapped her arms around Lady's neck and held the warm body close, seeking comfort in another living being.

When her tears had dried up, she latched on to Jack's parting words. Did she really look like she'd slept with him? Was it possible? Suppose someone came and noticed it?

If she focused on his words, then she might not have time to mourn him. But she knew he'd be back. His stallion was still in the pasture. Whether or not he spoke to her was another matter.

She left the stall and went to the tack room to retrieve her brushes, to groom Lady as she'd been meaning to ever since she and Jack had argued. If she kept her hands busy, then her mind wouldn't be able to dwell on thoughts of Jack, or so she hoped.

She ran her hands along the bristles, freeing the dust in the brush. Starting on Lady's neck, she carefully brushed her coat until the gray hairs gleamed. But her thoughts kept returning to Jack.

She recalled with painful clarity the hateful words they'd exchanged. She wanted to cry again when she remembered him calling her anything but a lady. That hurt more than she'd thought. She had been trying so hard to please him, to make him see that she was the perfect woman for him. But she'd ruined everything.

She did acknowledge that today she hadn't acted like a lady. Ladies didn't request men, even if they loved them, to make love to them. She was a churchgoing citizen, she knew what was right and what things weren't done. Perhaps her forward behavior had helped scare off Jack.

It didn't matter, she tried to convince herself. He was

no longer her concern. She'd made her bed and now she would lie in it.

Then why did her heart hurt so much? Why did she feel like half a person without Jack? Because she loved him. Loved him with all her being.

Hoofbeats broke her train of thought. She wanted to run out and look up the lane. Could it be Jack coming to apologize? She held her breath in anticipation.

She wouldn't give him the satisfaction of seeing her look so lovelorn. She would just wait there, inside the barn, and Jack would have to come to her.

She tried to relax as she heard the horse stop and foot-steps follow. Take deep breaths, she told herself.

"Josie? You in there?"

Her heart plummeted. Slim's voice was the last one she wanted to hear. What was he doing here anyway?

Swallowing her disappointment, she replied. "Yes. I'm just taking care of Lady."

Slim stopped as he came near her. "What's the matter? You look so glum? Didja get up on the wrong side of the bed this mornin'?"

Her spine stiffened and her chin thrust upward. Could Slim tell what she and Jack had done? "What do you mean by that?"

He leaned against the stall wall and shoved his fingers into his front pockets. "Nuthin'. You just look so weepy, that's all."

Josie wiped at her face. "I—I canceled my wedding."

He pushed away from the wall and strolled over to peer inside Lady's stall. Resting his wrists on the door, he glanced back at her, ignoring her comment about the wedding. "What happened to her hoof? I see you got it all wrapped up."

"She has a nasty bruise. Jack and I put a poultice on it to speed the healing."

"I'da done the same."

"Unfortunately I won't be able to ride her for a while."

Slim's bushy brows rose. "I guess that kinda eliminates you from any racin'."

"Yes, you're right there."

"Since I know you're safe, I'll be on my way. Just wanted to check up on you."

"What? Wait a minute. How did you know to come check up on us?" Her spine went rigid.

"Hunter told me he'd be gone for a little bit. So I knew what I had to do." He spat a wad of tobacco.

Angry red dots danced before Josie's eyes. If what Slim said was true, then her father must have told him he was leaving. As the full impact of the words hit her, she grabbed the sides of her dress. "I see. Well, thanks for coming over, but I must get to the chores."

Slim patted her on the back. "Glad to be of help."

Learning her father had told Slim his plans to go sapphire searching but not his own daughters infuriated her. She wanted to be alone. But Slim was not taking the hint. He stood there, looking like he might launch into a long-winded story at any moment.

Action was called for.

Grabbing a rake, she began scraping it along the barn aisle, raising more dust than necessary. "I've really got a lot of work to do. No time to stand around."

"Oh, I guess I should be leavin'."

"That's right. Good day to you, Slim." Deliberately she turned her back on him and raked so hard, she dug trenches in the dirt. After she raked her pile to the end of the aisle, she turned her head and noted he had finally left.

Alone once more, she collapsed to the dirt floor and drew her knees up to her chin. She wrapped her arms around her legs and rocked herself.

She felt betrayed by all men—her father, Slim, and especially Jack. Jack because he didn't love her enough to do what she asked. He didn't love her enough to live on her father's ranch, even for a little while. Realizing that hurt, hurt like a knife to her heart.

She leaned against the side of the barn, not caring that

the wood dug into her neck. In fact, she welcomed the pain. It took her mind off her bleak situation.

She was now back to where she'd started, no husband for her to love. And no husband for Josie meant an insecure future for Lottie. She had to do something. She couldn't sit there and wallow in her misery. But for the life of her, she couldn't think what to do.

Two nights later, Jack sat in his hotel room, nursing a bottle of whiskey. Desperate black thoughts crowded his brain.

His life had been going so perfectly. Now, with a few words from Josie, his plans had fallen into a crumbling heap at his feet. Sighing, his gaze moved over toward the slip of green ribbon he'd taken out of her hair a few days before.

He propped his heels on the window ledge, staring out at the rising mountains. Instead of mountains, he saw Josie's face. He could not get her image out of his mind.

He wanted to throw back his head and wail out his anguish. He wanted to shriek in misery until he could feel no more. Without Josie he felt as if his life had come to an end. He knew he'd hit rock bottom.

He hadn't realized how much pleasure she'd brought to his life until he had been denied her. The sound of her laughter brought warmth to his soul. Her caring knew no end, and her body, it had been pure heaven to have her in his arms.

Someone banged on his door.

"Jack?" the hotel clerk, Natty, said from the other side of the door. "You in there? You missed supper. Everything all right?"

Jack merely swung his glance in that direction. With mild detachment he watched as the wooden panels bulged in and out with each strike of the clerk's fist. It reminded him of the constrictions of his heart.

Jack heard the floorboards squeak as Natty walked away.

Raising the half-empty bottle to his lips, he let the comforting liquid travel down his throat. The more he drank, the fuzzier his vision became, but the clearer Josie's image became, so beautiful and full of love.

The whiskey bottle slipped through his fingers, landing in his lap, sloshing alcohol on his thighs. As he watched the wetness spread, he came to a realization. Sitting alone in his room wasn't going to solve his problem. He had to do something if he wanted his chosen woman for his wife.

"Stop feeling sorry for yourself and do something about it, St. Augustine," he grumbled to himself.

He leapt to his feet so fast, dizziness overtook him. Clutching the windowsill for support, Jack set the whiskey bottle on the ledge. If he wanted Josie, he had to find her and tell her he loved her. He knew life was too precious to spend it regretting the choices not made.

He weaved over to his jacket and snatched it up. Several minutes passed before he was able to get his arms in the sleeves. Sweating and feeling nauseated, he sat on the edge of the bed. His head spun and throbbed. *Maybe I'll just lie here for a moment, until I feel better,* he thought.

The soft mattress enveloped him and his eyelids slid shut. Within seconds he was fast asleep.

Jack didn't stir again until the sun blazed into his room. Stretching, he opened his eyes and then shut them quickly, trying to hide from the brightness.

His mouth felt like cotton and his head ached. All he wanted was a huge drink of water and to crawl back under the covers until the glaring sun was long gone from the sky.

As much as he wanted to fall asleep again, something kept sleep at bay. His muddled brain refused to function. He squinted at the window and saw the drained whiskey bottle. Groaning, his head fell back to the bed.

Just before his head hit the mattress he caught a glimpse of Josie's ribbon.

The fog in his brain lifted. Josie.

He had a decision to make. He could either lose her forever or move in with Hunter for a short time. The choice was his.

❖ *26* ❖

THE COLD, UNFORGIVING muddy bottom of the Missouri River sucked and pulled at Hunter's boots. His feet ached from the chill penetrating the leather. Straightening his back, he massaged the sore muscles and made his way to the shore.

He ignored the sunlight reflecting off the surface in bright flashes. He'd been fooled too many times by the deceptive winking, thinking he saw a beautiful sapphire when he knew better. He'd even strayed farther away from the gravelly banks into the frigid waters, hoping to find more gems.

Sinking down onto his sleeping roll, he tugged off his boots and damp pants. Taking a towel, he rubbed the chill away. But he wasn't able to rub the chill away from the place where he hurt most. His heart.

He leaned back and stared up at the cloudless blue sky. "Oh, Jos, I've been a selfish old man." Saying the words made him feel somewhat better, but he knew what he'd done was inexcusable.

He had no right to keep his elder daughter from living her own life. He had no right to expect her to stay complacently at home while he ran out and had adventure after adventure. He had no right to deny her the love of a good man.

Pain stabbed at his heart as he remembered his two wives. He'd been lucky to know their love, even if the Lord had taken them from him. He couldn't deny the joy they had brought to his life. And his two beautiful daughters, well, he wouldn't trade them for anything.

He jumped up, startling his horse. His hand landed on the uneven lump in his vest pocket. The one sapphire he'd found earlier. His fingers closed over the rough gem, and he contemplated throwing it back into the water's bed, but decided not to. Instead, he would give it to Josie as her wedding gift along with his sincere blessing for a long life filled with love.

Like a man possessed, he tugged on clean pants, yanked on dry boots, and shoved his items into the saddlebags.

It was time he went home. Time to worry about his daughters instead of searching for sapphires. Time to be there for Lottie and to let Josie live her own life. The time had come for him to be a real father to his girls.

Josie's heart ached. She tossed her broom aside and collapsed onto the porch steps, gulping in air. As much as she tried to ignore it, she could not rid her mind of Jack completely.

Ever since she and Jack had argued, she'd tried to keep herself busy. She couldn't remember a time when their house looked so neat and clean.

She'd carefully polished what few pieces of silver they had. She'd aired and beaten the dust out of all their rugs and even washed all the bedclothes.

Josie had no sooner shut her eyes, when she heard what sounded like several wagons pulling up in front of the house. She raised her head and her heart iced when she saw Mrs. Potter and several ladies from the Auxiliary.

Their presence could bode no good.

Nor could the number of trunks that were in the bed of Mrs. Potter's wagon.

Josie leapt to her feet. Her blood ran cold. My God! Mrs. Potter had come for Lottie! Her worst fears were now coming to life before her very eyes.

Shaking off her stupor, she ran inside the house and pulled the string latch inside, effectively locking the door. She ignored Mrs. Potter's summons for her.

Six women crowded on her porch, their heels sounding like a barrage of hammers. "Josephine! I know you're in there. Unlatch this door at once. I've come for my niece."

Josie shook from her head to her toes. Where was her sister? Had Mrs. Potter already snatched her and had her locked in her home? She swallowed back her fear. Now was not the time to let her thoughts run out of control. "My sister is not going anywhere."

"Josephine. I can no longer allow my niece to grow up in such a household. It is not natural. When I heard you canceled your wedding, I knew we had to act at once. That is the final act of unorthodox behavior that I can tolerate. Now, let me in so I can gather up Lottie's belongings."

Josie could see the wood vibrating from each rap of Mrs. Potter's umbrella on the door. "Lottie belongs with her father and with me," she said, surprised at how strong her voice sounded. None of the terror she felt was evident.

"That is an outrage. My niece cannot stay one moment longer in this house. If Slim hadn't told me about the wedding cancellation and that your father has left once again, I hate to think what would happen to my niece's morals. For the sake of my dear, departed sister, I must take Charlotte into my custody."

"There is nothing wrong with how Father and I have

raised Lottie. Go away. I won't open this door for you.''
Josie was so afraid, she thought she might throw up. She
braced herself against the door, as if her own body could
stop the threat to her family.

"I will get my niece one way or another. Don't you
doubt me. I will pray to the good Lord to pardon your
sin of refusing my requests. I'm going now to prepare a
room for my niece." She thumped her umbrella with
each step she took as she left.

Josie slumped against the door and slowly slid to the
floor, not caring that her dress scrunched up behind her.
The pretty yellow dress she'd selected in vain, in case
Jack came back to declare his love for her.

She sat there, enveloped in misery, until she heard hesitant
steps. Her eyes flew open. Standing in the hallway
was Lottie. She stood there with huge, shimmering eyes.
She clutched a half-finished dress to her chest.

"J-Josie. Th-that was my aunt, w-wasn't it?"

Josie wiped the water from her eyes and stared at her
sister. She had no idea Lottie had been in the house this
whole time. How awful for her sister to have heard the
confrontation with her aunt. "What all did you hear?"

"E-everything." Lottie threw down the dress and
raced into Josie's arms. "I don't want to go live with
her. She can't make me. Please don't let her take me.
Please," she cried.

"Shh." Josie rocked her sister back and forth. "Don't
worry. There's no way your aunt Portia can take you
away. Father and I will protect you." *At the expense of
my own happiness,* she silently added.

"What about Jack? Won't he protect me? Aunt Portia
was lying when she said you had canceled your wedding,
right?"

Pain laced Josie's heart, squeezing it. Josie had to tell
Lottie the truth. No more lies. "No, she wasn't making
that up. Jack and I decided it would be best if we didn't
marry."

"But you can't! I was looking forward to my new
brother and Jack'll keep Aunt Portia away from me."

Josie sighed. She was suddenly tired of being the big sister, always looking out for Lottie. She wanted someone to take care of her for once. "I'm afraid without Father, I can't marry. Reverend Potter wouldn't let the ceremony take place."

"Oh." After several moments of silence, Lottie spoke up. "But Jack's horse is still here. I saw him out in the pasture. So why can't you just wait till Father returns and then get married?"

She'd thought of that, indeed had planned on it. Then Josie recalled the harsh words exchanged between herself and Jack. They'd both said hateful things, words that would be hard to rescind. Lottie couldn't know this. Josie had ruined her chance with Jack and must face the fact that he probably didn't want to marry her at all now. "Some things just aren't meant to work out, that's all, honey."

Water-filled baby-blue eyes regarded her. Lottie's lashes were wet and clumped together. "But if you really want something, you can have it, that's what Father always told me."

Her words made it all sound so simple, when Josie knew it really wasn't. "Let's just worry about keeping you safe and then we can worry about Jack later."

"But the fair starts tomorrow. How do I know Aunt Portia won't snatch me away from the grounds?"

"She won't, even Portia Potter wouldn't do anything like that." Josie only hoped her words would prove to be true.

Saturday, Fair Day, turned out to be a beautiful, sunny day. Not a cloud marred the sapphire-blue sky. Josie realized her word choice and sighed. Because of sapphires, she was not going to get married. Shutting her eyes, she forced those maudlin thoughts away.

Today was the biggest day of the whole year, and she wouldn't let herself mope, even if her love life was destroyed and she couldn't ride her mare in the races.

She had work to do. She had to keep an eye on her

sister, plus she needed to hold her head up high. She couldn't let the townsfolk know the cancellation of her wedding made her feel dead inside.

It was also time to confront Jack.

She knew Jack would be over by the racetrack, preparing Zeus. Affianced or not, she would go over and wish him well. Besides, she ached to see him again and hoped he would grace her with one of his smiles. She'd just taken one step, when she heard her name called.

"Josieee! Guess what?"

The blond curls bouncing up and down could be none other than her sister's. Josie stopped and then waited for her. "What is it?" She'd left Lottie in the embroidery tent, safe in her knowledge that Mrs. Potter wouldn't try anything at the fair. Mrs. Potter would be busy in the Ladies Auxiliary tent, supervising the baked goods sale.

"You just have to come over to the embroidery area. I gotta show you something." Lottie grasped her hand and started pulling her sister in the opposite direction of the track.

Before she could answer her sister, a calliope blaring music passed. A string of laughing children followed the brightly painted wagon and instrument.

"Right now?" If she didn't get to the prep area soon, she wouldn't have a chance to wish Jack well.

"Yes, now. C'mon, why're you being so stubborn?" Lottie pulled harder. "I want you to see this and be with me."

Josie sighed. "Oh, fine. Since you seem to need me so badly." What else was new?

"Good." Lottie dodged the people who were strewn about the fairgrounds. "Don't you just love all these people here? It sort of makes our little town seem like a big city for once."

"It is crowded." Josie looked around at what seemed like a sea of colorful heads. Hats and scarves of every color festooned the fairgoers' heads. Women, children, and men strolled about, soaking up the warm sunshine and the exciting atmosphere.

Vendors stood around colorfully painted carts, their voices filling the air as they hawked their wares. A few clowns entertained groups of children, and a small acrobatic troupe performed under the shade of a tree.

"C'mon, stop dragging your feet. I've something to show you," Lottie urged.

"I'm coming. Don't pull my arm out of the socket." Josie's lips drew back as she realized they were going farther and farther away from the racetrack.

"We're almost there." Lottie pushed past the women viewing the stitching entries. "Here it is." Lottie's face beamed.

Josie stopped in front of the table and stared at the blue ribbon decorating Lottie's sampler entry. She smiled and laughed. "You won! I knew you could do it. You do such beautiful work." She hugged her sister. "I'm really proud of you."

"Are you? That means as much to me as winning does. I just wish Father were here to see this."

"He will. He'll see your blue ribbon." Josie hoped she was correct.

"Now, it would be really neat if my dress won its category. I'll go find Mary Jane and show her." Lottie's voice suddenly quivered. "Do you think I'll be all right?"

Indecision tore at her. Josie needed to stay near Lottie, but she also wanted to talk to Jack. If he would speak to her. "I'd rather you come and watch the races with me." If she hurried, she might be able to make it to the prep area before Jack mounted and began his warmup.

"But I want Mary Jane to see—can I go find her?"

"All right. You'll be fine, don't worry about your aunt, she wouldn't dare try anything today. But come right back to this tent. After the first race, I'll be back to find you."

Hurrying was next to impossible. Josie made her way through the crowd, but still found the going slow. By the time she reached the track, she could see horses being ridden.

Darn, she was too late. She'd try to elbow her way to the rail and yell good luck to Jack.

The people gathered around the track didn't take too kindly to her pushing them aside. At last she managed to squeeze into a tiny spot and could rest her hands on the rail.

Her gaze sought a shiny, tall chestnut. A few minutes later her diligence was rewarded. "Jack," she said, waving to catch his attention.

He paused and then brought his horse closer to the rail, all the while looking at her uncertainly.

She ignored his expression and smiled. "I wanted to wish you luck. I tried to make it over earlier, but I couldn't."

"You did?"

Was that hope she saw flickering in the backs of his eyes? "Yes. Have a good ride. I'll be cheering you on."

He smiled, but it didn't reach his eyes. "Thanks. I need to keep him moving." He clucked and Zeus moved forward.

She longed to reach out and touch him, but knew it would be impossible. She watched him ride away and knew she'd made a big mistake in telling him she couldn't marry him.

As the horses moved into formation at the starting line, the crowd around her swelled. She was flush against the rails. For a second she worried that she might be pushed through to the track side.

A sudden stillness hung in the air. Anticipation for the start of the first race gripped the crowd, silencing them.

The six horses waited nervously. The official extended his arm, pistol raised skyward.

"On your marks, get ready, get set . . ." Bang! The wisp of smoke from the pistol was lost as the mass of horseflesh exploded forward.

Josie gripped the rail as the ground below her feet trembled. In a rush, the horses were past, moving as one.

Around the track they thundered. Soon she could see

Zeus surge forward. Jack had the lead! Josie yelled for him to go faster.

The noise surrounding her was deafening. Everyone shouted for their favorites. Before she knew it, the horses rounded the final bend and headed for the finish line.

Zeus still led the pack. His long legs ate up the ground like a starved giant. She held her breath. One horse was closing in on Zeus.

She let out a rush of air as Jack and Zeus crossed the finish line. They'd won this heat. She considered his win a victory for her also. If she couldn't ride Lady, then she could ride with Jack in spirit.

"Damn! Bet on the wrong horse, I did," a man next to her ground out.

Josie heard his lament and didn't feel sorry for him.

As the onlookers started to disperse, she felt someone standing very close to her.

"It seems like I picked the right horse for my money this year," Hunter said.

❖ 27 ❖

Josie's hand flew to her heart. "Father! What're you doing here?"

He looked down at the toe of his boot twisting a hole into the dirt, and blushed. "Coming to my senses."

"Coming to your senses?" She was glad of the rail in front of her for support. She hadn't seen her father look so contrite in a long time.

"Yep. It's high time I did too." He took her hand. "Come over here, let's sit down on one of these chairs." Hunter led them over to a few empty chairs that only minutes before had been occupied by race viewers.

Her heart pounded so hard, she thought her father must be able to hear it. What did he mean by coming to his senses? Could he have accepted her marriage? No, he couldn't. Not now, not after what she'd done . . .

"Jos, have a seat."

She complied as her father propelled her onto the wooden seat. "Where have you been? Do you know how

worried we were when we found out you'd disappeared?''

He grimaced and looked away. "I've been out
thinkin'."

"Thinking?" Josie was too tense to relax. She perched
on the hard edge of the chair.

Hunter ran his fingers through his beard several times
before speaking. "Josie, I've been a fool. Will you ever
forgive your father?"

As much as she wanted to remain angry at him, she
couldn't. The more she looked at his weary face, the
more her heart went out to her father. "Of course I can
forgive you. But where have you been?"

"I was out huntin' for sapphires. But I just couldn't.
See"—he turned to his daughter, eyes pleading with her
to understand—"it's like this. When I realized how serious you and Jack were about your weddin' after we
returned from Bozeman, I got scared. Like a fool, I was
worried more about my own welfare instead of my
daughters'. So like a man on the run, I up and left."

"But why? Why did you did you leave? You told
Slim, but not your own daughters.'' She was trying hard
to understand.

Hunter shut his eyes and sighed. "Like I said, because
I was a fool. Here I was, worried about my sapphire-
huntin' days coming to an end, when I should have been
more worried over my elder daughter's happiness and
more concerned with Lottie and that meddlesome aunt of
hers."

The impact of her father's words, words she had
longed to hear, were overshadowed by the memory of
her impulsive ones to Jack. Would he still want her as
his wife?

"Jos, say something. Say you forgive me. I promise
to stay at our ranch and raise Lottie properly, after I tell
Portia to stay out of our lives for good. I no longer want
to rely on you for everything. It's time you lived your
own life. You need a house to call your own. It's not
right for you an' Jack to have to live in my house."

"Oh, Father. You don't know how relieved this makes me. Just yesterday Mrs. Potter came over threatening to take Lottie after she heard about your absence and about the canceled wedding."

Hunter's gaze locked on hers. "What canceled weddin'?"

"I—I told Jack I couldn't marry him, not when I had Lottie and you to worry about. Seems like Mrs. Potter took that as her signal to move in." At the fierce glint in her father's eyes, she continued. "Don't worry, I kept Lottie safe."

"I feel real bad about you cancellin' your weddin'. Try to patch things up between you and Jack. He really is a good man, you deserve his love. And most of all, try to forgive me." His face softened with love.

She felt water gathering in the corners of her eyes. She refused to cry with all these people around, even if they were happy tears. "Father, I forgive you. You don't know what your words mean to me." So she did the best thing that she knew to do. She wrapped her arms around her father and squeezed him.

"Jos, careful, you could squeeze the air out of an old man." Hunter chuckled, feeling all was well with his world. He'd done the right thing in confronting his fears. What kind of father was he anyway? Gallivanting off to find sapphires. All that would change now. He had Lottie and a ranch to think. And maybe soon, a grandson.

Noticing several curious stares coming their direction, Josie pulled away and straightened up. She needed to find Jack and straighten things out with him. If it wasn't too late.

"Father, Lottie's sampler won the first prize. Why don't you go into the tent and look at it? I know she'll be thrilled to see you, and you'll probably be able to talk to Mrs. Potter."

"Tryin' to get rid of me already?"

"No, but Lottie needs to know you've returned." Josie stood up and smoothed out her skirts. "Will you come and watch the final race with me later this afternoon? Jack's in it.''

"Sure will. I'm off to find Lottie. And that no-good busybody, Portia.''

Hunter stepped inside the Ladies Auxiliary tent. Immediately he found the person he sought. "Portia, I'd like a word with you.''

Portia's eyes widened, and she set down the tray of corn muffins she'd lifted out of a basket. "Hunter, what are you doing here?''

"I need to speak to you in private. Care to step outside with me?'' He wanted to call her every name in the book, but knew that impulse needed to be held in check. Instead, he settled on glaring at her.

Squaring her shoulders and thrusting her chin out, Portia stepped from the tent. "Well, Hunter, I have only a few minutes to spare. I have work to do and a room to prepare.''

Hunter's nostrils flared. "What I have to say won't take but a minute. It's about that room you're preparin'. I know you're tryin' to take my daughter an' I'm here to tell you to keep your nose outta other people's business.''

Portia's mouth dropped open. She gasped for breath. "I am only doing my duty.''

"Hogwash. Lottie is my daughter and I aim to see she stays in her own home. With me. I think she's turnin' out to be one fine young lady. Josie and I have done right by her.'' Hunter did his best to keep his temper reined in. But the smug look on Portia's face was almost his undoing.

"I regret the day my sister fell in love with you, but I cannot change that now. You are no father to Charlotte if you are off hunting for gemstones.'' Portia closed the space between them, trying to use her bulk to intimidate Hunter.

It didn't work.

"Portia Potter, you may be the reverend's wife, but

that doesn't make you the judge of other people. What you are is an interferin' busybody.'' Hunter ignored her gasp of indignation. ''If I ever hear one more word about you tryin' to take my daughter from me, you'll regret it. Lottie will be stayin' with me, do you get that?''

Portia's face turned an unbecoming shade of red. She reached for her fan and rapidly cooled her face. ''I don't believe anyone has ever addressed me like that before.''

''That so? So you understand you're to leave my daughter alone? I never want to hear talk of you tryin' to take her away from me. Or else I won't let you see Lottie again.''

''I understand,'' she croaked.

She looked like she was fit to be tied, Hunter thought, unable to keep the grin from his face. ''Glad we had this little talk, I shoulda done it a long time ago. Now, I'm off to see my daughter.'' Hunter pivoted and didn't look back at Portia.

Now, where would Jack be? Josie thought. She had to find him to share her good news with him. She set off in the direction of the track, her feet practically floating over the ground.

After acknowledging his victory, Jack quickly moved out of the winner's circle and dismounted. One look at Zeus told him the horse was still breathing heavily. Jack didn't want the animal to become ill. Taking the saddle off, he grabbed a towel and walked his horse while wiping the sweat from him.

He should've been happier with his first win of the day, but he wasn't. He'd wanted to share it with Josie, but he'd seen her only briefly before the race. That was hardly the most appropriate situation for a heart-to-heart talk. And not having her to share his victory with made it much less important.

Jack didn't want to lose her. If her family meant so much to her, he'd decided he would rather live in the same house as her father than not have Josie as his wife.

Once he realized how deeply he loved Josie, he knew he wouldn't give her up without a fight.

"Good race, boy," Slim said, stopping right in front of Jack. "I see you'll be up against my horse in the final run,"

"That's right. They'll be six of us. Best of luck. I need to keep my horse moving." Jack sidestepped Slim and grinned. He hoped he was as spry as Slim when he was his age.

The voices died down as Jack led Zeus farther along the back side of the track. He preferred it that way. The noisy crowds reminded him too much of Kansas City and all he'd left behind.

Zeus stopped, pricked his ears forward, and craned his neck around.

"What do you hear, boy?" Jack turned also. He stood still, watching Josie approach. His heart swelled as he looked at her. She was so beautiful and proud.

"Jack? Do you mind if we talk?"

Her voice sounded so uncertain, it pained him. Even though he wanted to talk to her, he didn't want to make it too easy. After all, she *had* rejected him. "We can talk, but I need to keep walking Zeus. He needs to be in fine shape for the final race."

"I understand." She fell into step beside him. "I saw your race. You looked great. It kind of made up for me not being able to ride."

Jack looked sideways at her. "I'm sorry you couldn't enter Lady." This was stupid. He didn't want to discuss horses. He wanted to talk about their relationship, but found it harder to do once she was next to him. He felt awkward and uncertain.

"Me too. Um, listen, I, ah, have something to tell you." Her fingers wove together and her eyes stared straight ahead at the distant tree line.

Jack's body tensed. What more did she want to tell him? The tone of her voice alerted him to something. Was she going to tell him to get out of town? Leave her barn? "What do you want to say?"

"Where to begin? See, sometimes, I can be, oh, impulsive and say things before thinking." She glanced at him, attempting a smile.

"I'll say you can be impulsive." He'd never forget returning to Gallatin City and learning he was engaged to her.

"Well, now things have changed. I know I told you earlier that I couldn't marry you. But now I've found out that I can. What do you say?"

He was stunned. He stopped in his tracks. "What do I say?"

"Yes, um, did you still want to carry on with the wedding?"

Her question took him by surprise. "Hold on a minute. What suddenly made you change your mind? And how do I know you won't do it again?"

"Things are different now."

"How so?"

"Remember when I said my father had left? Well, he's back and we had an honest, long talk. He wants to stay at home and be with Lottie and end all threats from Mrs. Potter. He wants me to be happy." Her voice cracked on the last sentence.

Her family. The one obstacle in their path had now been cleared. But did she really want to marry him? This was important to Jack, since she'd recently stung his pride. "What do you want?" He resumed walking.

"To marry you."

"Why?" He knew he was being cruel, that he should be taking it easy on her. But he had to be certain of her reasons for wanting to marry him. He wanted a wife who loved him. He did not want to go into a marriage for convenience's sake. Nor did he want a marriage that resembled a business agreement, like his parents' did.

She looked up at him, brows drawn together, eyes flashing. "Why?"

"Yes."

She snorted. "You know why, because, because I care for you, that's why."

He was disappointed. He had hoped to hear more. "You care for me? How?"

Exasperated now, she wrung her hands. "I—I like you."

"Like me?"

"Oh, fine. This is hardly the place to discuss this, what with all these people around. But if you must know, I love you. Is that what you wanted to hear? Are you happy now?"

She'd said the words he wanted to hear, but they hardly seemed very convincing. "Yes, I'm happy. But you didn't have to shout them. Look, those people are staring." Jack pointed to the crowd of men at a temporary gaming table set up under a stand of aspens.

Josie reddened and averted her eyes from the curious men. "You made me yell."

A wicked grin crossed his face. "Let's give them something to really stare at." Before she could move, he swept her into his arms and placed his lips on hers. His blood jolted at the feel of her soft skin. He hadn't tasted her since they made love. He wanted her, and he couldn't believe how happy he was with her once more in his arms.

Her eyes flew open the same time his did. She jerked her head back, avoiding his plundering lips. "What're you doing? There are people everywhere!"

Breathing harder than he should be, Jack stared down at her, at her clear green eyes, her rosy cheeks, and her wet lips. "I was just making sure you still wanted to marry me." He let her go and resumed walking Zeus as if nothing odd had happened.

"Yes, I do. Please do not make any more displays like that. We're going to be the talk of the town. Just keep your lips to yourself." Red-faced, she made a show of straightening her hair.

"I will if you promise me one thing."

"Anything. Oh, God, look. Mrs. Potter saw you do that. See?" Josie pointed. "She has her hands on her hips. I wonder if my father has talked to her yet."

"Forget her. I need to tell you that I agree with your suggestion of living at your house until ours is built. Does that make you happy?"

Josie beamed. "Do you mean it?"

"Yes. I'd rather be with you, wherever that is. I love you too much to risk losing you over where we'll live. But I do have one request."

Her brows rose. "What is it?"

"I want to move up our wedding date. I find I can't wait any longer to make you my bride."

"But what about Lottie? I have to make sure she and Father will be fine."

"That's very noble of you, but I think you've been neglecting something."

Josie looked at him quizzically. "Like what?"

"You've been neglecting *your* needs. When was the last time you stopped and did something for you? You have as much right to happiness as Lottie." He should know because that was why he came out West in the first place. He knew he couldn't find the happiness he wanted in Kansas City. Josie seemed to be having a hard time accepting that happiness was her due too.

"I don't put my sister's needs before my own."

"Yes, you do. You even put your father's before your own. It's time for Josie's needs to be first for once." He reached out and held her hand.

"I don't do that."

"Yes, you do. But don't let it worry you. I used to do it too. I used to always ignore what I wanted in favor of what my parents requested. It's a hard lesson to learn, but believe me, you'll be happier." He hated to see her looking so upset, but he needed to say that. "Hey, stop worrying, let's just concentrate on our wedding. Let's move it up from Saturday to Wednesday."

"Why?"

"Because I don't want to chance another thing going wrong and putting a halt to our wedding. We've decided to marry, and let's do it."

"Fine with me." Josie watched as Mrs. Potter

squeezed her frame through a break in the track rail. The woman's skirts swished as she stalked down her prey.

Before either Josie or Mrs. Potter could open their mouths, Jack thrust Zeus's reins into Josie's hands and with outstretched arms walked up to the reverend's wife.

"Mrs. Potter, just the person we were looking for." Smiling broadly, he pumped her hands in a greeting that was a little too enthusiastic.

Slack-jawed, Mrs. Potter stared at Jack, her expression going from anger to disbelief.

Jack rushed onward. "You see, Josie and I really want to get married as soon as possible. Do you think it would be possible for my fiancé and I to move up our wedding date?"

"I thought it was canceled, but I can see I was wrong." Stepping closer, Mrs. Potter glanced at them. "I hardly think I should let my dear husband wed you people. After the words your father assaulted me with, Josephine, I've a mind to ban him from the church. Imagine threatening never to let me come over and see my dear niece again."

Josie wanted to shout in joy. Her father had given Mrs. Potter a talk she wouldn't long forget. "I'm sure Father knows what's best for Lottie."

Mrs. Potter quivered and fluttered her fan in front of her face. "Yes, well. Getting back to the wedding, is there a reason for moving up the ceremony?"

"No reason other than love and the desire to start our lives as man and wife." Jack moved back to Josie's side and put his arm around her shoulder.

Josie wished he would stop smiling so broadly, it seemed so . . . so inappropriate. But one look at the woman and Josie knew Mrs. Potter was enthralled by Jack's charm. Hunter's words, whatever they were, had momentarily left her mind. "Should we speak to your husband?"

"What?" Mrs. Potter had to drag her gaze away from Jack to look at Josie. "Oh, no. I know my dear husband's schedule. I know the good Lord would want to see such people as yourselves united in that most revered of states, marriage.''

"Has he got anything this Wednesday?''

"Hmmm, I believe he could marry you Wednesday afternoon. That doesn't give us much time. I'll have to be sure I make all my visitation rounds before then. I know no one will want to be left out of the wedding of the year, especially since it was already canceled once." Mrs. Potter sighed and then picked up her skirts. "I must be off. I must spread the news."

"Thanks so much for your help," Jack said, bowing slightly.

Before leaving, Mrs. Potter narrowed her eyes and glared at Jack. "And, young man, we do not need any more of those . . . those . . . public displays of affection, like that kiss." She shook her finger and was off.

"Wow, you handled her well." Josie was amazed they'd managed to escape a full-blown lecture from Mrs. Potter.

"It's called diffusing the situation, my dear. And I would say it worked quite well. I'll just stop by their house in a day or two and double-check the time." Retrieving Zeus's reins, he wove his fingers in between Josie's and held tight.

Warm spirals ran up her arms. She loved to be touching him; even innocent hand-holding pleased her. "You certainly diffused that situation. I have a lot to do in the next few days. I hope I can get it all done."

"Jos, there's not that much to do. The most important part will be the actual ceremony, all the rest pales by comparison."

"That's a typical male thing to say. Of course there's lots to do. It's a wedding. My wedding."

"Your wedding?" He teased.

"Yours too. I want it to be just right. I guess this means more to a woman than to a man." Sometimes, no matter how understanding men seemed to be, Josie knew men and women operated on different levels. Weddings were one of those things that separated them.

"You've got almost four full days. Plenty of time."
He squeezed her hand. "Come on, let's put Zeus up and
get something to eat. Those smells from the food tent are
driving me crazy."

Four hours later, as the sun lowered in the sky, the
throngs of fairgoers filled the grandstands and the area
surrounding the track. The final horse race was to be held
in a few minutes. The prize money was high, two hundred dollars. The atmosphere crackled with anticipation.

Bets were rapidly being placed. Coins jingled. Cur-
rency changed hands as the men studied the list of final-
ists. Which horse would bring them more money?

From her vantage point in the grandstand, Josie
watched all this with keen interest. She longed to be
down with the bet makers to see how many people were
laying money on Zeus. She just knew in her heart that
Jack and Zeus would win.

"Do ya think Jack'll win?" Lottie asked.

"I hope so."

"Sure he will. I know it 'cause he won his other race.
But Mary Jane says he's gonna lose, 'cause her father
will win."

"Well, let's just watch."

"Girls, looks like the horses are moving into formation. It's about to start," Hunter said, leaning around Lottie so he could face Josie.

Happiness filled Josie. She was sitting with her family,
watching her soon-to-be husband in a horse race. What
more could she ask for? "Look, they're moving to the
starting line."

Down on the track, six horses walked or pranced toward the starting line. Each rider concentrated on his
horse, trying to ignore the others. Fair-committee members gathered near the start, pressing a shiny long-
barreled pistol into the official's white-gloved hand.

Josie leaned forward in her seat, straining to catch
Jack's eye. She thought he looked nervous, and she could

tell Zeus was ready to go. The horse pawed the ground and tossed his head.

Silently, Josie counted down with the official. When the pistol fired, she almost jumped to her feet.

Six horses bolted forward as if they were all connected. Neck and neck they remained as they thundered down the straightaway.

Shouts echoed in her ears as everyone around Josie cheered their favorites. Josie's eyes didn't stray from Jack's red horse. She felt as if she were riding with him.

The pack neared the first turn. Still no horse had broken into the lead. All of a sudden one horse stumbled. Zeus!

Horrified, Josie leapt to her feet as she watched Zeus falter.

In less than one second's time, her heart almost stopped as she witnessed Zeus regain his footing and move forward.

But the pack had already left him behind.

"Oh, no," she wailed, sitting down again. What had happened? She no longer wanted to watch, but had to. She felt so sorry for Jack and his horse.

Numbly, she registered that someone was tugging on her sleeve. "Jos, look! Zeus is gaining speed!" Lottie couldn't contain her excitement. "He's not gonna let them beat him."

She blinked her eyes. Lottie was right. She could see Zeus's long, ground-covering strides carry him closer to the rear horses as they thundered down the backstretch. Josie leapt to her feet as the crowd rose as one.

"That's my boy!" Hunter yelled as Jack overtook a second horse. Three still remained in front of them.

The crowd hung on tenterhooks. The four fastest horses were surging toward the last curve. Slim glanced backward and noticed Jack gaining on him. He took out his whip and started smacking his horse's rump.

It didn't work. Using his mighty legs, Zeus pulled ahead. The finish line was in sight.

Josie held her breath.

Only a bit more to go. Leaning forward, Jack loosened his reins and gave Zeus his head. That was all it took. The tall chestnut inched forward.

The white line rose ahead. With one last burst of speed, Zeus crossed the finish line with only a body's length to spare.

The crowd went wild. Josie gulped in air and jumped up and down.

"Hurray! I knew he could do it," Lottie yelled, trying to make her voice stand out above the din.

Josie offered a silent prayer of thanks. She was glad Jack won, but hoped Zeus wasn't hurt from his stumble.

"Yee-haw!" Hunter shouted. "I just made a bundle."

Instantly Josie wondered how much her father had bet.

Congratulations were offered all around. Not only for Jack's winning run, but also for her rapidly approaching wedding date. It seemed Mrs. Potter had wasted no time in spreading the news that the wedding was back on.

A few minutes later, an exhausted Zeus and Jack walked to the winner's circle. The official presented them with a long blue ribbon and the winner's purse.

Jack smiled as he held the bag up high for all to see.

Josie, Hunter, and Lottie pushed their way down to the track. The crowds parted for them. Josie desperately wanted to be at Jack's side when he collected his prizes.

Jack turned to her, and what could be described only as a look of love wreathed his face. He thrust the purse at her. "Here, this is for our ranch. It's only fitting Zeus's winnings should help us build our future home."

Sparks of happiness shot through every nerve in her body. Josie didn't think she'd known such elation before.

❖ 28 ❖

"LOTTIE, YOU KNOW after Jack and I build our house we won't be living here any longer," Josie said the day before her wedding. She wanted to make sure her sister understood.

Lottie looked up from her sewing and smiled. She grinned until all her teeth showed. "I know. I'll be sorry to see you go when your home is done, but Father'll be here, so I'm no longer scared. He's promised to stay here with me. He says I'm more important than any sapphires."

"Yes, you are. I won't be on the other side of the world. Get a message to me if you need me or just want to see me."

It suddenly hit Josie that she was leaving the life she knew behind. From now on she would be a married woman and soon would have children of her own. It was an awesome and frightening thought.

"Are you gonna miss me?" Lottie asked, pausing between stitches.

"Of course I will."

"Me too, but you aren't going anywhere for a while."

"That's true." Josie had no idea how long it would take to get her and Jack's house built. Once the house was finished, they could start work on the barn and corrals. "I'm going to go pick the rest of my bouquet." Josie stood up and took the front steps two at a time.

Along the path to the barn were several lupines, golden asters, and black-eyed Susans. Josie planned to pick ones that were just beginning to open. She wanted them to be at their fullest tomorrow.

As she walked along, her expression turned thoughtful. She wondered what her life would be like as Jack's wife. Would they start their family immediately? Would their firstborn be a boy or girl? Most important, what would it be like to sleep next to Jack every single night?

She wrapped her arms around herself, full of wonder for her life to come. She headed to the back of their house, to the flower garden.

Stopping, she kneeled down and scrutinized the blooms. There were several reddish lupines that were just starting to open. She also saw a few yellow and multicolored ones that looked perfect. She took her clippers out of her pocket and measured the stems, making sure all would be the same length, and then she cut the flowers. As she laid them aside she heard her father's voice.

"Josie, there you are. I need to check something." Hunter hurried over.

He looked younger, more carefree. Perhaps staying at home and ranching agreed with him, Josie thought. "I'm just gathering my bouquet. What do you think?" She held the flowers up for his appraisal.

"They'll look fine. I need to ask you a favor. Shut your eyes and hold out your left hand."

"What?" His strange request caught her off guard.

Hunter grinned. "Shut your eyes and hold out your hand. And no peeking."

"All right." Josie squeezed her eyes shut even though she was tempted to open them when she felt her father slip what felt like a ring over her fourth finger.

"Hmmm, looks pretty good. Keep those eyes shut."

Could it be her wedding ring he was trying on her? She longed to open her eyes and check. Were her father and Jack in on this together? That thought sent a tingle through her insides. "Can't I just peek?"

"Nope. I'm all done." Hunter pulled the ring off her finger and placed it in his pocket before Josie opened her eyes.

"Was that my wedding band?"

Hunter shrugged his shoulders, feigning uncertainty. The glint in his blue eyes gave away what he refused to say out loud. "You'll just have to wait and see."

"Father!" Josie laughed, reaching for her father's hand, trying to see what he'd just hidden.

"Now, Josie. You'll see whatever it is soon enough. I'm off to get ice to make you a batch of my special ice cream for the wedding celebration."

The sun shone down on a cloudless Wednesday afternoon. Josie sat in the warm beams as she stared out Grace's window. Since Grace lived close to the church, it was decided Josie would dress at her house. In less than an hour she would be a married woman.

"Why're you just sitting there?" Lottie cried, wringing her hands. "Why aren't you gettin' dressed?"

"I was waiting for help. I thought I'd wait until you and Grace were dressed." It was a lame excuse. She was so nervous, she could hardly move, much less put on a wedding gown.

"At least you could've put on the proper undergarments. Here." Lottie thrust them at her. "Put these on and then we'll help you."

Josie looked at the corset, the lace petticoat, and the fine camisole. They seemed so delicate, it was almost a shame to wear them, she thought. But nevertheless, she shed her old undergarments and put on the new ones.

"All right, we're ready. Let's get our bride dressed."
Grace came over, the gown draped from her arms.

"Now, stand still till we tell you to move," Lottie
admonished. Her quick hands worked the satin down Josie's body.

After much fussing, the gown was declared done.
Every last tiny button was secured, the veil placed on her
head.

"Want to look at yourself?" Grace led her over to a
cheval mirror in the corner.

When Josie glanced at her reflection, she sucked in her
breath. Was that beautiful woman in the glass really her?
Were those shining green eyes staring at her really hers?
She looked better than she'd dreamed. She just knew
Jack would approve.

"Oh, Josie, you look so pretty. I'm jealous." Lottie
squealed and ran over to fuss with the gown's hem.

"You do look beautiful. I always knew you'd make a
beautiful bride." Grace sniffled and wiped at her eyes.

Josie cried too. She could not believe her good fortune.

In the distance, they heard the church bells pealing.

"I guess it's time we go. You've got a groom to
meet." Grace clutched her handkerchief and steered Josie
to the front door and the waiting carriage.

Josie stopped when she saw the carriage. "A carriage?
But the church isn't far away."

"We can't have our bride walking, can we? Your
gown will get all dusty. Now, be careful and get in."
Grace signaled for her husband to help Josie.

"You really look good, Josie," Robert said as he
helped her into the carriage.

"Thank you."

Josie looked straight ahead at the church. The number
of horses and wagons surprised her. She didn't think so
many people would be attending her wedding. A tiny
tremor of fear ran down her spine, of so many people
watching her every movement.

As she was stepping down from the carriage, she noticed another carriage enter the other side of town. They

seemed to be moving awfully fast, but she dismissed it as she heard the piano music swell from within the church.

The time had come. Soon she would be Mrs. St. Augustine.

Hunter joined them at the church landing. "Are you ready, Josie? We walk down the aisle after Grace."

Too nervous to speak, she only nodded her head. She wrapped her fingers around her father's offered elbow and held on to his solid strength.

She watched as first Lottie and then Grace glided down the aisle. The church was packed. She wondered where all the people had come from. Soon everyone rose and turned to watch her.

"Here we go," Hunter said, excitement tingeing his words.

"I—I'm scared," she whispered, gripping his elbow tighter.

"I'm here for you, and so is Jack. Look, there he is."

Josie pulled her eyes off the hordes of people and looked at Jack. He was standing tall and silent, waiting for her by Reverend Potter, a smile on his face.

Just looking at him made her heart speed up. He was so handsome in his dark pants and jacket. The gold vest underneath his jacket brought out the gold highlights in his hair.

He was to be her husband. The man she would spend the rest of her life with. How could she have been so fortunate?

She could hear the murmurs of appreciation as she and her father walked down the aisle. She never knew the church aisle was so long. In the front she could see Mrs. Potter, a hanky at the ready in her hand.

Before she knew it, her father released his grip on her hand and she was standing at Jack's side. Her whole body was atremble with nerves.

She met his eyes and knew that all would be fine.

"You look beautiful," he whispered before Reverend Potter could start the ceremony.

Reverend Potter held out his arms to Josie and Jack. In his loud, clear voice he addressed the church. "Dearly beloved, members of this congregation, we have gathered today to witness the joining in God's name one of our own, Miss Josephine Douglass."

Josie was thankful for the veil that covered her. She could feel every eye in the church looking at her, and she knew tears crowded at the corners of her eyes.

"Marriage is the divine state, sanctioned by the Lord, and it brings me no greater pleasure than to unite these two as man and wife. A moment of silence so we may pray for the couple's happiness." Reverend Potter bowed his head and placed his palms together.

Josie heard a door open in the back of the church but paid it no mind. She was too busy concentrating on breathing to worry about any latecomers. She drew from Jack's strength as he stood beside her, so close that she felt his body heat.

"Amen."

Reverend Potter gave the assembled guests one last glance and then cleared his throat, bringing his Bible close to his face. "And so—"

"Stop!" A loud, high-pitched voice cut through the reverend's words.

Josie grabbed at Jack's hand for support. What could be happening? The same moment she clasped Jack's hand, she felt him stiffen. His whole body went ramrod straight.

"This wedding cannot continue. It is a sham," the woman's voice said.

Ripples of unease spread throughout the church.

"What is the meaning of this?" Reverend Potter boomed, not liking his ceremony interrupted.

A tall, elegantly attired woman strode down the church aisle. In her wake was an impeccably dressed, distinguished-looking man and a petite young version of herself.

The tall woman turned her scathing gaze to Josie. "As I said, this wedding cannot continue. My son, Jackson, is engaged to marry another."

❖ *29* ❖

Shock. Disbelief. Shame. All of these hit Josie at
the same time. She let go of Jack's hand and could only
stare at him. Before she could ask Jack what was the
meaning of this, the reverend cut her off.

"If what you say is true, then I will not continue this
wedding." The reverend's face was a deep red.

"It is true." The tall woman turned around and beck-
oned to the other. "Come forth, Gloria dear."

Holding her head high, Gloria walked up beside the
tall woman. The tall woman thrust Gloria before her, pro-
claiming, "She is to be Jackson's bride."

The church went wild with accusations. Talk broke out
among everyone. The guests speculated over who would
be wed today.

Josie staggered backward until her legs hit the railing.
"Jack! Why? Why did you do this me?" Her words
came out a strangled cry, a plea for understanding.

Josie looked from Jack's white face, to the smug features of his mother, to Gloria. Wildly, she sought out her father. He looked furious.

"Jackson, I am so ashamed of you. How could you go and attempt such a stunt?" His mother and father surrounded him, separating him from Josie. They barely gave her the slightest look of concern.

Mortified, humiliated beyond all measure, not caring if her tears were visible for all the world to see, Josie grabbed the hand Grace offered her and started to leave the church.

Until Jack's voice stopped her.

"Josie, wait! Please don't go. Listen to me first." His anguished face sought hers, begging for her.

She paused, torn between getting out of the church and wanting to hear what he could possibly have to say. She looked down and saw her beautiful bouquet dropped to the floor in her shock, crushed, the pollen scattered. Its beauty was gone, just like her hopes for a bright future. Gone. Vanished.

Why, oh, why, hadn't he told her he was already engaged?

Furious red haze obliterated Jack's vision. His body shook with rage. How in the hell could his parents be here, and on this day of all days? If he hadn't heard the anxious voices in the church, he'd think he was hallucinating. But he wasn't. Before his very eyes, before his beloved Josie and her father, his parents had announced that he was to marry Gloria.

"What are you doing here?" He stared at his mother. "And it had better be a damned good explanation."

"Tsk, tsk, tsk, Jackson, how many times do I have to tell you, our family does not use profanity, especially in the house of God." Her pinched nostrils gave away her inner feelings, even if she did try to sound pleasant. "Now, come along with us."

Jack raised one foot to follow his parents, more out of habit than anything, and then stopped. He looked at Josie's beautiful face contorted with pain, to Hunter's livid one. No doubt the man wanted to slug him right now, then his gaze shifted to his mother's impervious one to Gloria's neutral face.

He remembered his words to Josie at the fair. That they needed to live their own lives as they wanted. He stood firm. He wasn't going anywhere until he was a married man. Married to Josie. It was time he stopped running away from his past. Time to stand up for what he wanted.

"Mother, Father, I'm not leaving here with you. I'm going to marry the woman I love, and that is Josie."

The sound of several indrawn breaths filled his ears. His mother stiffened and sought her husband's eyes. "Beauregard, did you hear our son?"

"Excuse me, perhaps you would like to use my private chamber to continue this discussion?" Reverend Potter asked, blotting sweat beads off his forehead.

"Yes, Susanna. I'm sure he will apologize for his inappropriate public behavior. Let's adjourn to the reverend's quarters," Beauregard St. Augustine said.

"Come, Jackson, let us finish this in private," Susanna said.

Jack grimaced. He hated how he sounded in front of his parents. Somehow they always made him revert to less desirable behavior. "Yes, let's." The loudness of his words startled even Jack.

Jack and his family moved to the reverend's room at the side of the church. Josie stood clutching Grace's hand, while a stunned congregation watched in rabid fascination.

Sensing impending doom, Reverend Potter clapped his hands. "Everyone, please. Why don't we take a short break and assemble in another hour. We cannot have such goings-on in God's house."

The door clicked closed behind Jack. He drew a deep, steadying breath and began. "Mother, Father, I love you, but you need to realize I'm living the life I want to right now. I'm in love with Josie and intend to make her my wife. I'm sorry you had to bring Gloria out here with you in a wasted trip."

Susanna turned her immaculately coiffed head to him.

"Dear boy, when the days kept passing and we did not hear a word from you, I could only assume the worst."

Jack's eyebrows rose. "I'm safe and sound, as you can see."

"Safe, yes"—she sniffed—"but not sound. Why else would you be contemplating marriage to some backwater girl?" She shut her eyes and shuddered.

Jack's muscles tightened. He was tempted to leave. In a crisp, tight, controlled voice he said, "I refuse to let you insult Josie. You know nothing about her, therefore you cannot judge her."

His mother blinked several times in surprise. "Jackson, I am your mother. I forbid you to ever use that tone of voice with me. Remember that."

"Josie. What kind of name is that? I don't believe it is a proper name." Beauregard stared at his clasped hands before regarding his son.

"Josie is short for Josephine." Jack kept his reply short on purpose. In the foul mood he was in, he did not trust himself to say much more. "Mother, how old am I?"

"Why, you are twenty-six. Past the time when you should have an heir."

Jack's fingers flexed and closed into fists. "That's right. I'm twenty-six years old. Do you know what that makes me?"

His mother looked bored with him already. "My son?"

"Yes, but it makes me a man. A man who is capable of making his own choices, like choosing my wife."

"But you already have a woman to wed. Gloria. And because we are such thoughtful parents, we invited her to come with us. For the wedding. Your wedding." Susanna pierced Jack with her icy blue gaze.

"I had a wedding planned. In case it slipped your notice, I was right in the middle of it."

"Aren't you lucky we showed up when we did. If we had been any later, I shudder to think about the consequences." Susanna gave a little shake.

Jack sighed. He loved his parents, he really did, but times like these tested his love. Trying once more, this time in a soft voice, he began, "You haven't heard a word I said."

"Jackson, please. We want only what's best for you," his father said.

Frustration built up inside of Jack. His parents were not making this any easier. He grunted. Had he actually thought they would accept his decision without a fuss?

"Of course we hear you. You cannot help it if you are misguided. That's why we are here. You should be thanking us. We are rescuing you from this uncivilized territory." His mother gave him a ghost of a smile.

The words whistled through Jack's teeth. "I am not misguided, nor am I in an uncivilized place."

"Son, I don't believe I have ever heard you address your mother in such tones. Please cease it at once."

"I'm sorry if you don't like my tone, but the words have to be spoken." Jack felt as if he were trying to penetrate a thick stone wall. His parents were no more interested in listening to him now than they were when he still lived at home. "Didn't you receive my telegram?"

"No, we did not."

His mother fussed with the material of her satin skirt. "Words, words. The only words I want to hear are 'I do,' and those should be spoken to Gloria, who is on the other side of this room."

"I will say 'I do,' but not to Gloria."

"Oh, come, come. Surely you don't mean to wed that girl. I can understand how your loneliness could cause you to take such a drastic step. But, really." His father reached for his pipe.

Jack wanted to shout out his frustration. "Josie is a fine, honest woman. Do not put her down in front of me again."

"Jackson, calm down," his mother snapped, motioning with her eyes to Gloria, who waited patiently by the door. "How could you even entertain the notion of wedding that woman? I mean, you knew we had Gloria picked out long ago. Her parents have probably already prepared the announcement for the papers.''

"Too bad. You should have consulted with me first.''

"Do not be ungrateful. Look at all we did for you. We gave you an excellent education. Although why you insist on being near horses is beyond me. Your sisters never acted so obstinately.'' Susanna's sharp gaze never left her son's face.

Jack merely shrugged. ''I guess I'm different.'' He was tired of arguing. It got him nowhere.

"I'll say you're different. I cannot figure out where we went wrong. Beauregard, see if you can speak some sense to the boy.''

"Like your mother says, parents know what is best for their children.'' Beauregard stared at Jack, challenging him to contradict him.

Jack gripped the edge of the wooden seat which he sat on so hard, he was afraid he might crack it. ''Your children are now adults.''

"Your marriage to Gloria will unite two excellent families. Something we've waited for for a long time. You couldn't ask for a better match,'' Beauregard said.

Jack looked at Gloria's tightly pulled back hair, her soft doe eyes, her docile expression revealing no will of her own, and he knew that even if he didn't love Josie, he could never have that type of woman at his side.

Jack knew his father followed him as he moved to leave the room, but he didn't care. He cared only about seeking Josie and comforting her. When he felt a hand close around his arm, he stopped. ''Take your hands off me,'' he ground out.

The elder St. Augustine complied. ''Jackson, you cannot run away from your family. We are here now and you must listen to us, please. We know what's best for you.''

Stopping, Jack swung around. He and his father were the same height and had the same blue eyes, but there the similarity stopped. "Father, if you knew what was best for me, you would leave me alone."

"How can I leave my only son alone? I want you to have a good life and know you can if you come back home and marry Gloria. You are causing your mother anguish." Jack's father turned and walked back toward his wife.

His mother feel anguish? The woman was hard as nails. Josie was the one he was worried about. The look on her face when his mother stopped the wedding was enough to cause him physical pain. He had to go to her. Now.

❖ *30* ❖

JACK HADN'T EXPECTED to find an ally in Gloria.

"Jackson?" she whispered, glancing right and left, making sure his parents couldn't overhear her conversation.

He paused and looked at her. "Yes?"

She glanced down. "I—I'm sorry to bother you, but I know how horrible you must have felt when we ruined your wedding." She gulped and looked up at him.

Jack's brows drew together. "Then why did you?"

"You know your parents. Once they get an idea into their heads, there is no dislodging it."

He had to grin. She was right. He did feel sort of sorry for her, having to be dragged clear out to Montana Territory for a wedding that would never take place. "Look, I'm sorry they brought you here, but you must understand I cannot marry you."

She blinked and a tiny smile curved her thin lips. "That is all right. I understand, you see, I—I have someone else I'm in love with." She stared down at her clasped hands.

Jack couldn't believe his ears. "Did you just say you don't want to marry me?"

Gloria shook her head. "I—I love another. I really didn't have any choice about my coming on this journey. My parents and yours wanted the wedding so badly, they would not listen to reason. They dismissed my protests, so here I am."

Jack smiled at her. "Guess what, Gloria? You can marry him. We can both marry the people we love." Jack opened the door and peered into the church.

Gloria stepped forward and gave him a timid smile. "I'm really not all that upset over making the trip out here. I was able to see parts of the country I never dreamed I'd see. I'll treasure the sights for as long as I live."

"See, there was some good to your travels."

Behind him, Jack heard his parents sighing in resignation. He looked around the partially empty church and went straight to Josie.

Hunter glared at him. "What do you have to say for yourself? Hurting my daughter like that?"

"Relax, everything is fine. I'd just like to talk to Josie alone, in the reverend's room."

He took her hand and led her across the nave. His parents exited the room, giving their son his privacy.

"Josie. Please don't look so hurt, it's all a big misunderstanding. I was never engaged to Gloria."

She sniffed. "Are you telling me the truth?"

He cupped her face in his palms. "Yes, I am. I love you and want only you as my wife."

Her lips quivered as she slowly smiled. Her heart had been right. Jack did want her. She held out her arms and Jack wrapped them around his body.

Josie pressed against his solid form, reassuring herself he was indeed here.

"Oh, Josie, my sweet Josie. I'm so sorry." Jack buried his face in her hair and his body shook.

Strange muffled sounds came from him. Josie wanted to look at him, but dared not to. She thought he was crying, and that touched her so much that she thought her heart would burst.

They remained locked in an hug, until Jack pulled back and looked her in the eyes. "Josie, I want to tell you something."

Josie looked into his deep blue eyes and saw love reflected there. She also saw a hint of moisture in his thick lashes. "What? What do you want to tell me?"

He placed both hands on her cheeks and looked straight into her eyes. "I love you. I've known that for a long time. If I can't have you for my wife, I'd rather live to be an old toothless bachelor."

"You really love me that much?"

"Let me show you." Jack leaned forward, captured her lips with his, and kissed her deeply. He held her close, drinking of her sweet essence, tasting the dried salty tears by her lips.

After a long time Josie dropped her head to his chest and sucked in air. "I think I could be persuaded if you kiss me like that every day."

The wedding would go on. Whether or not his parents chose to stay wouldn't stop him from marrying the woman he loved with all his being. Jack's voice held no doubt. "Good, then think about our wedding, which will continue as soon as I get my fill of holding you."

"I believe you."

"But first, this." Jack locked the door and turned to face her, grinning. He walked toward her, a devilish twinkle in his eyes.

"What are you doing?" Tremors ran up her back at the mere thought of what he might be thinking.

"Nothing. Just going to hug my wife."

She blushed. "I'm not your wife yet."

"Almost."

He stopped right in front of her, running his hands up her arms. His eyelids dipped shut as he moved in to claim her lips.

Josie surrendered to his kiss, taking as much as she gave. When she gasped for air, her mind intruded once again. Would his parents ever accept her? She had to get an answer. "Jack?"

"Um?" He nuzzled her neck.

She pushed him away with her hand. "I want to talk to you."

"Now? We're busy."

"Yes, now."

He took a step backward and sighed. "Can we at least sit down?" He motioned to the two chairs in the reverend's room.

"Yes, we can sit."

He led her over, sat down, and pulled her into his lap. "All right, what do you want to say?"

Josie groaned, more out of frustration. How on earth was she to have a sensible conversation sitting in his lap? When she could feel his body respond below hers? And in the church, in the reverend's own room no less? "What about your parents? Will they hate me forever, since I stole their son?"

Jack's hands tightened around her waist. He looked at her possessively. "You did not steal me, only my heart. And yes, they're a little sore, but we talked and they reluctantly agreed that I should make my own choices. And that is to marry you and live in Montana."

Josie's heart soared. She thought if she weren't being held by Jack that she just might fly up into the clouds. "You don't know how happy those words make me."

He smiled. "Yes, I do. I can see it in your eyes."

Boldly, Josie reached for him and pressed her lips to his. She was his, mind, body, and soul.

Jack groaned deep in his throat and fell backward in the seat, bringing Josie with him. "God, Josie. I love you. I've waited my whole life to find a woman like you, and I'm never going to let you go."

His words were an elixir to her soul. Her body responded, urging them closer and closer. "I love you," she whispered.

Jack held a finger to her lips, tracing their slicked outline. "Good, let's tell the reverend to finish our ceremony. I can't wait to place this on your finger."

"Place what on my finger?" Josie asked, leaning into his side.

Jack slipped his hand in his pocket. Reaching in, he withdrew a small package. "Here, I know it's a little early, but I can't wait any longer to see your expression."

Josie took the package and stared at it.

"Open it." Jack sounded like a little child, barely able to contain his excitement.

"I am." She unwrapped it and stared at the round object. Her mouth dropped open and she forgot to breathe. "Oh, Jack. I—I don't believe it." She stared at a ring. Her wedding ring. A beautiful perfect blue sapphire set in a silver band.

"Your expression is thanks enough." He kissed her lips.

"Where did you find such a ring?"

"Believe it or not, your father gave me the stone and I quickly had it set."

Josie held the ring up to the light, watching the colored patterns wink. "My father wanted you to have this?" It was unbelievable. Her father, who'd left to hunt sapphires just so Josie wouldn't marry, had given one of his precious gems to Jack.

"Yup, he said it would mean a lot to you, and I can see we made the right choice. But you can't wear it yet. I just wanted to see your reaction." Jack reached over and plucked the ring from her hand. "It will match your necklace."

"Hey!" She wasn't ready to relinquish the ring just yet.

"You have to wait for your wedding, madam."

Exactly one hour later, Josie and Jack stood in the church sanctuary, facing each other. Josie couldn't keep the smile from her face. This time the hordes of people were absent. Everyone had tired of waiting for the festivities to start and had left.

"Do you Josephine Douglass take this man as your lawfully wedded husband?" Reverend Potter said.

"I do."

Reverend Potter turned to the sparsely populated church, arms encompassing the couple. "May I present Mr. and Mrs. Jack St. Augustine. You may now kiss the bride."

Jack raised Josie's veil and brushed her tears away with his thumb. "I love you with all my heart."

"Kiss me," she urged.

Slowly, lingering, Jack kept his lips to hers, drinking of her nectar until Reverend Potter cleared his throat several times.

For Josie the long years of waiting for a husband had paid off. She would never be happier than she was right now with Jack. Their future looked like a shining ray of sunshine, beckoning them forth.

Love wrapped around them like a blanket as Jack and Josie walked down the aisle as man and wife. Forever.

Our Town
...where love is always right around the corner!

●●●●●●●●●●●●●●●●●●●●●●●●●●●●●

__*Harbor Lights* by Linda Kreisel~~ 0-515-11899-0~~/$5.99

__*Humble Pie* by Deborah Lawrence 0-515-11900-8/$5.99

__*Candy Kiss* by Ginny Aiken 0-515-11941-5/$5.99

__*Cedar Creek* by Willa Hix 0-515-11958-X/$5.99

__*Sugar and Spice* by DeWanna Pace 0-515-11970-9/$5.99

__*Cross Roads* by Carol Card Otten 0-515-11985-7/$5.99

__*Blue Ribbon* by Jessie Gray 0-515-12003-0/$5.99

__*The Lighthouse* by Linda Eberhardt 0-515-12020-0/$5.99

__*The Hat Box* by Deborah Lawrence 0-515-12033-2/$5.99

__*Country Comforts* by Virginia Lee 0-515-12064-2/$5.99

●●●●●●●●●●●●●●●●●●●●●●●●●●●●●

Payable in U.S. funds. No cash accepted. Postage & handling: $1.75 for one book, 75¢ for each additional. Maximum postage $5.50. Prices, postage and handling charges may change without notice. Visa, Amex, MasterCard call 1-800-788-6262, ext. 1, or fax 1-201-933-2316; refer to ad # 637b

Or, check above books   Bill my: ☐ Visa ☐ MasterCard ☐ Amex _____ (expires)
and send this order form to:
The Berkley Publishing Group   Card#_____

P.O. Box 12289, Dept. B   Daytime Phone #_____ ($10 minimum)

Newark, NJ 07101-5289   Signature_____

Please allow 4-6 weeks for delivery.   **Or enclosed is my:** ☐ check ☐ money order
Foreign and Canadian delivery 8-12 weeks.

Ship to:

Name_____	Book Total	$_____
Address_____	Applicable Sales Tax (NY, NJ, PA, CA, GST Can.)	$_____
City_____	Postage & Handling	$_____
State/ZIP_____	Total Amount Due	$_____

Bill to: Name_____

Address_____   City_____

State/ZIP_____

FREE

Romance

(a $4.50 value)

Send in the Coupon Below

To get your FREE historical romance and start saving, fill out the coupon below and mail it today. As soon as we receive it we'll send you your FREE Book along with your first month's selections.
